# PAYBACK

# OTHER TITLES BY ELIZABETH ROSE QUINN

*Follow Me*

# PRAISE FOR ELIZABETH ROSE QUINN

"In the glittering world of influencers, perfection is the currency and authenticity is just another hashtag. But behind the curated feeds and polished captions lies a chaotic battleground where every post is a skirmish in the war for relevance. *Follow Me* is a wickedly funny, heart-wrenching tale that peels back the Instagram filter to reveal the messy reality of modern motherhood. With biting humor and searing insight, Elizabeth Rose Quinn holds a mirror up to society that simultaneously deifies and condemns mothers. It's a splashy beach-read thriller that's low-key a treatise on how capitalism and influencer culture have co-opted women's agency and identity in the pursuit of an unattainable ideal. This novel is a must-read for anyone who is a mother or has lost someone to the all-consuming vortex of modern mommyhood."

—Adele Lim, screenwriter of *Crazy Rich Asians* and director of *Joy Ride*

"*Follow Me* is a hilarious takedown of mommy influencers and the mighty rule of algorithms. How far will someone go to stay at the top of your FYP? Elizabeth Rose Quinn's masterful mix of humor and sarcasm makes this *the* book to read about #momlife. Especially if you secretly hate Insta-mommies. A must-read . . . I found myself sucked in and couldn't wait to find out what happened."

—Amina Akhtar, critically acclaimed author of *Almost Surely Dead*

"Whip smart, cacklingly funny, surprisingly gutting, and wholly original—*Follow Me* embodies the very essence of contemporary motherhood, its messy rage and questing hope set against the backdrop of its fraught pursuit of unattainable perfection. I frankly can't believe what Quinn has pulled off here. Comedic horror? Earnest satire? Anti–domestic thriller? Whatever it is, give me more and keep it coming."

—Julia Whelan, international bestselling author of *My Oxford Year* and *Thank You for Listening*

# PAYBACK

A THRILLER

ELIZABETH ROSE QUINN

This is a work of fiction. Names, characters, organizations, places, events, and incidents are either products of the author's imagination or are used fictitiously. Otherwise, any resemblance to actual persons, living or dead, is purely coincidental.



Published by Thomas & Mercer, Seattle
www.apub.com



EU product safety contact:
Amazon Media EU S. à r.l.
38, avenue John F. Kennedy, L-1855 Luxembourg
amazonpublishing-gpsr@amazon.com

ISBN-13: 9781662524820 (paperback)
ISBN-13: 9781662524837 (digital)

Cover design and illustration by Logan Matthews
Cover image: © Claudio Divizia, © DavisZane / Shutterstock

Printed in the United States of America

*For my little family of four.*
*You are my light.*

# PROLOGUE

## Steven Bard: Then and Now

Steven Bard had been a creepy child.

This was not hindsight. Even at the time, he knew it. His parents knew it. Everyone knew it. Ironically, or maybe not, Steven himself was the least bothered by his Level 10 creeper vibes, with his parents being a close second. He felt no compulsion to change or adjust his behavior. By two years old, he'd insisted everyone call him only by his surname, and by four years old, Bard's prickly attitude had unnerved the vast majority of adults and more or less repelled other children. He was not there to please or be pleased. Every school counselor and therapist thought they could "crack him," and as a result, he'd taken all manner of diagnostic test. He was screened for ADD, ADHD, giftedness, autism, and oppositional defiant disorder. When those all proved fruitless, he was even assessed for the dark triad of sociopathy/psychopathy/narcissism. No dice. Bard was an enigma whose personality never fit any of those tidy DSM-5 boxes. So adults threw up their hands, kids gave him a wide berth, and Bard was allowed to continue his flow of life unperturbed.

Bard's most common memory of childhood was separateness. Not loneliness, which implied a desire for closeness—but instead, a contented solitude. Bard had no interest in friends, no interest in school, no interests, period, really. It was difficult for him to even fathom extending himself in any way, because any forecasted/alleged reward for the initial effort looked like more effort. His parents loved him; he loved his parents. He enjoyed his pet cat, who seemed to move through the world with the same calm disinterest he had. Bard was complete.

Then one day, in the fourth grade, his class went on a field trip to a small local theater. It had been advertised as an afternoon of fairy tales. Most of the students dressed up as princesses, knights, dragons, and the like. Bard arrived as himself, content within, initially bemused and then quickly bored of this anomaly from the normal schedule.

Single file, they entered the theater at stage level, the class line contracting and expanding like an accordion as the teacher guided them forward, hissing about manners. They sat in the first and second rows of metal folding chairs that scraped against the sloped cement floor. The theater was small, and once the stage lights turned on, the temperature jumped ten degrees.

Then the play began. Stagehands dressed in mismatched black clothing pulled back the visibly frayed curtains.

A little sign that read *The Maiden Without Hands* was lowered from the rafters.

Bard's interest was piqued.

He felt his peers exchange worried looks.

A haggard miller sat center stage, his clothes nothing but rags. He was desperately trying to separate wheat from chaff using a large woven disk, through which he shook the grains.

"Not enough! Not enough! How will we make it through winter!" the miller cried out.

A devil came onstage from the wings—no comical red-painted face or pitchfork. He was handsome. Debonair, even. The only clue was a long red tail, which he carefully tucked under his cloak as he approached the mill. The devil asked the miller if he could purchase whatever was behind the mill, and offered a huge sum.

The miller was not taken in just yet. "I will need to see the gold first."

The devil gave a dramatic bow, comically tucking his tail once again as it popped out from his cloak. "Of course. A sage request." With a flourish, the devil pulled a silk bag from his breast pocket. "I will give you all I have." The devil turned the bag over, and coins tumbled out. The gold caught the stage lights and glittered brilliantly against the miller's rags.

The miller, stunned by the gold falling through his fingers, agreed without even looking at what lay beyond his view. "Yes, yes. Whatever is behind the mill is yours, my friend."

The little girls next to Bard let out an audible whimper, for what the audience could see was that the miller's daughter had entered from the wing seconds before and was now behind the mill.

The devil removed his cloak, and in so doing revealed a red silk vest, his forked tail, and his true identity. The miller scrambled away, but it was too late; his face fell in horror when he saw his daughter come around to join them center stage.

"No, no. Not my daughter!" the miller pleaded from his knees, clutching at the devil's cloak.

The devil didn't even respond to the miller, and instead spoke directly to the daughter. "Hello, child. You are my bride now. And you will join me in hell."

The miller was distraught, and saw no way out of the bargain. He threw himself on the stage floor, screaming. He was a terrible actor, wrestling equally terrible dialogue, and Bard struggled to hold back a laugh.

Meanwhile, the girls in Bard's class had started weeping.

"Where is Snow White?" one of them urgently whispered as another hid her face behind a pink cape she had worn for the occasion.

The devil reached out to take the daughter, but he shouted in pain when he touched her skin.

"I am pure, and you cannot take me!" the daughter yelled, defiant.

While there were small sighs of relief from the classmates on either side of Bard, he sat simmering in anticipation. He knew the devil would get his due.

The devil accused the miller of trickery. "You told a lie and took my gold! But I will not be cheated."

The miller offered all the gold back, but the devil wouldn't hear it.

"I demand something as precious as a wife. I demand you cut off your daughter's hands."

The miller shrieked, "There must be another way!"

"I can take her hands, or I take you and she will starve when winter comes." A fake tree was shaken by an unseen stagehand to signify rising winds, and a pile of dried leaves was clumsily thrown onto the stage from the rafters.

Bard saw his two teachers' rising alarm as they stuttered over what to do next, their eyes telegraphing *Do we leave? Do we stay? Do we do the unthinkable and cause a scene?*

Finally, the devil produced an axe from under his cloak, and the miller, trapped by his own greed, chopped off his daughter's hands in one swing. Two rubber hands, covered in fake blood, dropped to the floor, mere inches from the children's faces, directly at eye level. The maiden fainted away, two bloody stumps poking out of her home-sewn burlap sleeves.

This was met with a chorus of screams from the children. The teachers stood up and started to urgently usher the students into the aisles. This was not a quiet exit, and they were not the only ones.

"Up! Up, up, up! Let's go! Everyone to the lobby!" one teacher frantically called·out, trying to regain authority over the moment.

One small boy said through white lips, "I'm gonna be sick!"

Another child was nearly catatonic, blocking the row of kids behind him from freedom. They climbed around him as he stood unblinking, teachers desperately trying to get his attention.

All the while, Bard sat in his seat, enraptured.

Something inside him had lit up. A tiny ember of a feeling was brewing, and he was afraid to move, afraid any jostling would startle this feeling away. His brain felt like it was sizzling with thoughts, unformed ideas zapping behind his eyes. His body was rigid, but he sensed every hair on his neck standing on end, the skin on his arms puckered from goose bumps.

Eventually, a teacher came and physically pulled him to his feet. "We need to get on the bus," she said sternly.

As the class shuffled through the lobby, Bard saw his other teacher yelling at the director. "What the hell was that? You said fairy tales!"

Up close, Bard saw that the director's mustache had been filled in with pencil and his shoes were deeply creased under the carefully glossed leather.

The director was unmoved, his arms folded. "That *is* a fairy tale. A real one. Read a book."

"That"—the teacher pointed angrily toward the stage door—"is not in a book."

"Grimm's? Ever heard of it? Don't blame me for the dulling of the American mind!" he said smugly.

"We will be demanding a refund!" the teacher warned, turning toward the door and taking Bard with her.

When they returned to their classroom, with many of the more sensitive kids still weeping and others in a state of shocked silence, the teacher knew it was time for damage control.

"I'm sorry the play was so upsetting. Would anyone like to talk about how they feel?"

A blond-ringlet nightmare named Carol shrieked, "That was not Cinderella! I thought it was going to be Cinderella!"

"I did, too," the teacher said, bonding with her solemnly.

A little boy with a voice wheezy from constant allergies said, "My dad is the pastor at our church, and he is not going to like that I saw the devil."

The teacher took a deep breath. "Technically, that was just an actor playing a character. But I understand why you are upset."

"I liked it," Bard said clearly.

Every eye in that room turned toward him in uniform shock. For a second, Bard didn't know why he'd said it. He never spoke in class. And he certainly didn't need them to know he'd liked it. But something inside him had pushed the words out, and in the group's aghast reaction, he immediately saw his reward. Their attention was his little plaything, like his cat when she caught a cockroach and flipped it on its back, batting it around for hours in her own game of invertebrate air hockey.

The teacher stammered, "W-what did you like about it, Steven?" He heard the apprehension in her voice, and it made his stomach turn warm and cozy.

"I liked that the devil couldn't be tricked. I liked how he used his power."

He let an icy grin bloom slowly across his face and strategically refused to blink.

He saw his teacher lean away from him.

He watched even the bravest bullies shrink into their oversize '80s T-shirts, their Saint Bernard on the Big Dog tees big no more.

He felt sheer delight when he saw the tears on Carol's pinched face. And a bolt of certainty hit him: He would be chasing this feeling for the rest of his life.

Bard was sent home with a note from his teacher and a recommendation for therapy.

Bard's parents were as distant from him as he was from the world. He felt loved and cared for, but a lot of their daily life moved to the rhythm of a détente. It was easy and predictable. Bard's parents seemed to trust him to handle life, and as such, he did. Quite well. This letter home was no exception.

"We saw a play for the field trip today," Bard informed them over dinner.

"Oh?" his father said.

"Oh?" his mother said, their voices overlapping like a door chime. They had signed the permission slip without reading it, so this was the first they were hearing of a play.

"Yes. The other children were quite upset."

Another chime of "Oh?"

"I liked it. I would like to read more about it."

Bard marched to his public library the next day, and after combing through the sparkly pink monstrosities, he found what felt like a biblical text. A large, heavy, and very well-worn edition of *Grimm's Fairy Tales*. Pencil illustrations in the margins leaned in over the words. The paper was soft with wear, taking on an almost velvet feel.

The stories themselves were magnificent.

Page after page of death, gore, and terror.

Villains of every fantastical shade, with every manner of devious motivation. All of them entrancing. Most of all, though, Bard finally saw himself. The villains were outsiders who didn't crave to be anything else. They didn't want to be the wholesome miller or the anointed king. They were happy being themselves. Just like Bard. Freaky weirdos unite while the Carols of the world contorted themselves to belong.

Bard would lie in bed at night and replay *The Maiden Without Hands* in his mind, the shaking branches outside his window reminding him of the branches on the stage. He loved how the devil had seen the whole world and twitched this and that to make the people perform for him. Bard loved how, once they were in his web, there was only an illusion of escape, an excruciatingly delicious prolonging until the inevitable.

---

As Bard grew up, he was lucky in that he was objectively handsome, tall, slim, and physically strong. He even had a dimple he could flash at will. With thick blond hair and dark-brown eyes similar to those of a popular matinee idol, people were drawn to him, accommodating, and desirous of his attentions. That is, until an expectation of emotional reciprocity emerged on their part. So predictable! So tiresome! What they never understood was, Bard did not want intimacy. He wanted to dominate and decimate others. His only true struggle was how to re-create this one-sided dynamic in his daily life without repercussion. He wanted to be up close when he wielded his power, to look in the eyes of the people he was controlling, to see their distress when he walked into a room. He wanted to smell fear. That required prolonged proximity, and as such, he had learned to hone his manipulation skills in both directions—to draw others in and to make them run away on command.

From the beginning, Bard felt that men were boring to bully, because at some point it always became a fistfight. Bard won some and lost others. The violence didn't bother him—either to receive or inflict. But it all felt so one-dimensional that it bored him before the fun even started. If he heard "Come at me, bro" in a crowded bar one more time, he was going to make said bro eat a pint glass.

Girls, however, were another story. Bard perfected a stunning ricochet personality switch by the time he was fifteen. Using his good looks, he reeled girls in, dated them, courted them, and then, when he felt their every defense drop to the ground, he flipped the dynamic on its head. He would be the darling, charming, doting boyfriend, and then, in private, he would twist all his energy into an implied threat. The deep observations he'd made in the positive (complimenting the exact flint of gold in their eyes, for example) would be weaponized when they were alone (admonishing them for enjoying compliments and accusing them of vanity). When his girlfriend *du jour* inevitably told her besties about his new dark side, he savored that she was uniformly disbelieved. Then, to add delicious insult to wonderful injury, he would reach out to those same friends in a soul-affirming manipulation.

Employing his most perfect pout, he would say, "Hey, have you heard from (girl of the month)? I'm really worried about her. I felt like we were moving too fast, so I asked to take a step back. Now she seems to be really struggling."

Without fail, the dim-witted friends would rush to gossip, siding with him. "We are so glad you called. We are also so worried about her. She is saying the craziest stuff about you."

He would let a lone tear run down his face. "I just don't want her to be alone right now. But I am so glad that you are seeing things clearly, since she can't."

They would sigh. He would sigh. Sometimes they would hold hands. And inside, he was fizzing with joy.

As he grew up, so did his less-than-ethical needs. Bard pushed every limit he could find. One favorite pastime was engaging in some small-scale stalking to unnerve his girlfriends long after the relationship was over. Stealing their clothes. Copying house keys. Removing cherished items from their rooms. Whatever fun he could think of. Then he would contact a trusted friend or a stupid parent. He would ask to meet for tea (even more beta than coffee). He would arrive early. He would wear a cardigan. His tone would be softer than a whisper. "Thank you so much for coming. (Girl from six months ago) says she saw me outside her house, but I was not there. I swear. Maybe check in on her. See if she needs some therapy to figure out why she's so fixated on me. But don't tell her this came from me. We all need space to heal." They would, in turn, gush that he was so thoughtful, and they absolutely believed him. (More hand-holding. More sighing. More fizzing.)

However, this easy joy was slowly becoming more difficult to come by. Firstly, in this digital age, it was getting harder and harder for Bard to cover his tracks, since everyone carried a personal recording device in their cell phone, with text messages easily produced like evidence. Secondly, women were more demanding in relationships, so the window of manipulation to set the stage for his eventual dominance was too short before she got clingy. He cursed feminism and its expectations of equality. Lastly, and most inconveniently, women were more likely to be believed now when they complained about a man's bad behavior. Even Bard's previous hobby of following a woman on her walk home just a little too closely, watching her pace quicken and her eyes flick over her shoulder again and again, no longer scratched the itch without a disproportionate risk. All she had to do was go into a store and say she was being followed, and some slack-jawed male with a white knight complex would come after him and Bard was back to his previous issue of a tedious physical altercation with yet another meathead looking to prove his self-worth. ("Come at me, bro!")

So, all of a sudden, Bard was twenty-five and, for the first time since childhood, without an appropriate space to express his particular array of needs. Bard really disliked people who scared kids or hurt animals. Talk about a power imbalance. No fun in that at all. Bard wanted a peer to toy with at his leisure, not a bug to crush. Factoring in all this, he wondered if the professional sphere would be a better place for him to embody his more authentic self, instead of his well-trodden emotional sphere.

When he graduated from college, Bard—due to his intelligence and people skills—was accepted to and moved up the ranks of any job he applied to. First, a waiter in a bastion of fine dining, then low-level finance, and finally a stint in corporate-world marketing suckage. In each environment, Bard was in search of something beyond a paycheck, seeking out the professional villains he hoped to mold himself after. Unfortunately, he found each field surprisingly lacking. Chefs, subprime-mortgage hawkers, titans of pitiful industries all proved dead ends. Politicians were wretched opportunists thirsty for power (fun!), but they had to pretend too much to sell their lies to the masses (bleh), so that wasn't for him. Surgeons who held a beating heart were enticing! However, threat of malpractice seemed like it would stifle Bard's more creative instincts. He actually enjoyed nature, so destroying the earth via an oil company wasn't going to work.

Then, three days after his twenty-seventh birthday, inspiration came to Bard from the US Constitution, of all places. *You shall be tried by a jury of your peers*, the envelope said in preprinted script, with a watermarked Thomas Jefferson smiling from behind the words.

It was a jury duty summons.

At 8:00 a.m. on the appointed day, Bard sat in a large municipal courtroom, where every wall panel of faux wood peeled at the edges and 40 percent of the fluorescents emitted a high-pitched buzzing noise. The scent of burnt instant coffee and Lysol was so thick that it clung to his teeth in a thick film. Once the selection process had started, the lawyers read out a list of juror ID's, and half the people around him were immediately dismissed. Bard remained, and then was the first questioned.

A public defense attorney with bags under his eyes and a cheap stained tie asked in a rote voice, "Do you have any firsthand experience with the criminal justice system?"

"No," Bard answered.

"Do you have any secondhand experience with the criminal justice system?"

"No."

"Do you think you will be able to be unbiased towards someone who has broken the law?"

Bard was confused. "Isn't that what we're here to find out? If they broke the law?"

Bard's deviation from the standard yes/no answer startled the public defender out of his stupor, and the bags under his eyes wobbled as he searched for a reply that never came.

Finally, the judge leaned forward with a condescension that oozed across the room. "The defendant is currently an inmate for previous charges and is now on trial for additional charges. Will you be biased?"

It was a ridiculous question. How could Bard *already* know if he would be biased? That was, by definition, unknowable. An ethical debate better suited for a philosophy midterm than a courtroom. Nonetheless, Bard knew the "right" answer. Giving the pleasing, expected response came easily to him; he'd done it for decades with no concern for messy moral considerations. Why deal with the discomfort of people's unmet expectations when he could simply satisfy them with a soothing lie?

"Oh, I see. Yes. I can be unbiased."

And *voilà.* He was selected as a juror.

Bard sat in the second row of the juror box for what turned out to be a quick trial.

Unlike everyone else, who'd entered the court from the lobby, the defendant/inmate was escorted in from a metal door that had a lock the size of a brick.

Each morning, the judge would take his seat and then say dramatically, "Bailiff, open the crypt."

The bailiff would then open the door, and Bard could see rows of holding cells. An inmate in prison garb shackled ankle to wrist was escorted in and then cuffed to the defense table.

The inmate had been *allegedly* seen passing drugs, but mixed in with those drugs was *allegedly* a message that some people *allegedly* believed were communications from his gang, whom he was barred from speaking to.

Court machinations were equally dry and convoluted. So much random Latin and endless bizarre procedures to cover up that there wasn't much there. A stack of hearsay. A lot of chirping from a prosecutor, who took her shoes off under the table and put them back on when questioning hapless witnesses. A depressing exposure of a public defense that was flimsier than a cocktail umbrella in a hurricane.

Then the correctional officer came to the stand. The final witness.

His chest swelled. His stiff uniform dug into his neck, leaving a red mark on the freshly shaved skin. The heavy utility belt creaked under the weight of his service gun, and his cartoonishly large flashlight hung down almost to his knee. His boots made heavy clomping sounds every time he shifted his feet, which was often. It should have been comical, but instead it was the definition of *gravitas*. Bard was mesmerized.

The prosecutor tucked her feet back into her shoes and then stood before the court. "Sir, how long have you been a correctional officer?"

"I have been a correctional officer for twenty-two years, miss."

The prosecutor giggled. "I haven't been called 'miss' in a long time."

"Well, that's a shame," the CO said. "You should call me as a witness more often."

"Maybe I will," she replied, coming dangerously close to flirting. "Could you share your observations of the defendant's personality based on your expertise on inmate psychology?"

The defense objected. "The correctional officer is not a psychologist."

The judge allowed it. "You can get him on cross-examination, Mr. Turner."

But Mr. Turner got nothing on cross. He got less than nothing. The correctional officer was a boulder clad in dark khaki who rubbed shoulders with the people society had locked away, and no freebie legal rep was going to turn his head.

The lawyer was trying to make a long-winded point about the safety of the prison facility when the correctional officer interrupted him. "Have you ever been in the yard?" he asked. "Have you ever sat in a cell? Have you seen one inch of a prison beyond the cushy interview room? No. So don't tell me what a prison is like. I am there eighty hours a week, son."

The public defender got so upset he said to the judge, "Permission to treat him as a hostile witness?"

The CO calmly said, "Son, I get the sense you're trying to rattle my cage, and that's gonna be hard to do."

The public defender (stupidly) took the bait. "And why's that?"

"Because I'm a professional cage rattler," the CO replied with an asymmetrical grin that exposed too much of his gums.

The entire courtroom—even the stoic court reporter—laughed. The defense attorney desperately looked around the room and realized, in that moment, that he had lost the case. Even the defendant threw up his cuffed hands like he was throwing in an invisible towel. Meanwhile, the CO leaned back in the witness box like a satisfied man who had just finished a big meal and was ready for a nap. More than that, while everyone else looked anywhere else, the CO made near-constant eye contact with the defendant. He had no fear of this alleged violent criminal. The CO wanted to see up close when the defendant felt his life taken away.

At long last, Bard saw the power dynamic he had been looking for every single day since he'd left that fairy-tale theater production. All these people were a part of the performance—the lawyers, the judge, the bailiff—but somehow the correctional officer was the only one who embodied the strategic force he craved. The CO was that bewitching character, with his red tail tucked under his coat.

Bard felt the devil in the wings of the courtroom, just outside of his view, and his destiny laid out ahead of him. He would apply to be a correctional officer.

Six months was all it took to complete the training. Six measly months to hold people's lives in his hands. An American scandal, if anyone cared enough to look, which they didn't. And on the day he turned in his final forms, Bard was offered (and immediately accepted) a position at a state penitentiary in Nowheresville, USA.

His first day working in a state prison, Bard realized how right that prosecutor had been—there was a deep psychology to this work. The power dynamic was paramount, and the inmates were testing, testing, testing all the time, looking for a weak spot, of which there were many, either administratively or in the form of persuadable/unscrupulous guards. It was also a numbers game, with staff being the minority compared with the prisoner population. To maintain the hierarchy, the guards mostly used brute force and a not-insignificant amount of humiliation. While effective, those weren't Bard's preferred tools. He preferred means with more panache.

Bard enjoyed planting gossip to pit gangs against each other and, after destroying their opponent, watching their members slowly turn on their own to find the nonexistent rat in their ranks. He liked using any inmate transfer as a reason to start rumors of snitching. But the threat of a true riot was too high to do anything more than that, unfortunately. Bard wanted to be entertained, but he didn't have a death wish.

For ten years, this was enough. But as his second decade inside started, Bard felt the familiar craving for more. His curiosity whispered relentlessly in his ear. His desire burned at the edges of his thoughts. This control felt good, but what would more feel like? He needed to go further. He had to. Or he would lose his mind.

In an effort to satiate this ever-increasing appetite, Bard let his desire run him all the way to the end of the line exactly once. He stabbed an inmate to death. Bard had planned it well, with a confiscated shiv and a blind spot in the camera that allowed him to watch as the man died. Bard had expected a release, a peak of joy. But it didn't come. The man merely died, and then he was dead and it was all over. Bard felt like he had bought a new toy and then immediately broken it, left with nothing but useless pieces and boredom. He learned in that moment that what he loved the most was extended cruelty. He loved watching someone wrestle with their own fear over and over, like they were trapped in a tide of powerful waves that mercilessly knocked them to their knees.

Much like his life prior to this career, Bard was immediately revered by and then subsequently disliked by his colleagues. He listened while people talked about poker nights and barbecues he hadn't been invited to. Because no one would vouch for him, Bard was passed over for the more prestigious promotions, despite often being the most qualified. He did not get upset.

Bard trusted the winds of destiny and waited.

He waited for sixteen years.

Then Bard heard whisper of a special appointment—a prison so separate it even had its own name: Pay to Stay.

One day, while in the staff room waiting for his turn at the microwave, two of his most obnoxious coworkers came in mid-conversation.

"Don't let them fool you. Pay to Stay is harder work," one officer said. "Fewer shifts, which seemed good until I read the fine print. Shifts are long as hell."

"No kidding," the other one chirped as he refilled his stainless steel mug with communal coffee. "Whole weeks on call, sleeping in the office on-site. Plus, there's community service every day. Sounds like a pain in the ass."

So far, Bard wasn't hearing anything to put him off the job.

The first officer spoke up again. "I asked around, and my cousin knew a guy who filled in there once. Turns out, you always have to be on your best behavior because the inmates were 'special.' What the hell is a 'special' inmate? Hannibal Lecter?"

At this, they both guffawed too loud for such a tired joke, then left. Bard went to his office and began to research the posting. He read about how Pay to Stay was an auxiliary system of prisons where if the high-powered lawyer could swing it and the inmate had the money

($200 per day, to be exact), the inmate paid to go to jail only on the weekends, then returned to their regular lives Monday through Friday.

Bard applied, and due to the dearth of competition, he got the gig.

The Los Angeles County branch of Pay to Stay was located on the northwest corner of a nondescript city block on the outskirts of downtown LA. The only things that made it seem out of place with the rest of the struggling industrial neighborhood were the eighteen-foot-tall chain-link fences, and twenty-four-hour floodlights. The entire block was police property containing four factory-style buildings dedicated to various levels of municipal-vehicle repair. Police cruisers getting fenders replaced after ramming a car chase to its close. A morgue van with a pesky check engine light. Prisoner-transport buses whose chains had rusted. All were brought here for servicing. Cops, correctional officers, even some rogue coroners milled around, dropping off and picking up these mechanical extensions of themselves. Those four buildings had their own entrance to and from the street on the south side of the block.

Tucked away in all this was Pay to Stay, the inmate-arrival driveway on that same northwest corner unseen by the rest of the block. When the inmates did leave for their community service duties, they were loaded into a van that stayed parked on the south side courtyard and then driven through the main police municipal gate on the south side of the block. Even with a dozen officers coming and going at all hours, few had ever bothered with the van that sometimes left on the weekends, or the nondescript building on the back side of the property. Half of them hadn't even noticed it was there. Protect and serve, but do not observe. This was fine, though. Bard didn't desire the attention.

Once he'd transferred to Pay to Stay, it took Bard a full calendar year to understand the psychology of this particular ecosystem. Control was inherent to prison, but Bard's training officer made it clear that control had its limits here. On his first day, two inmates were using scissors without getting proper authorization first. Bard stood up, his hand on his baton, ready to confiscate the scissors and write them up, but his superior held him back.

"Don't treat this like max. They'll call their lawyer so fast it'll make your head spin. Before the day is out, you'll be on two weeks' unpaid disciplinary leave."

Bard was incredulous. "Put on leave for doing my job?"

"Oh yeah. More than once, some councilman has called to ream me out because one of them snitched." The training officer misread Bard's face and slapped him on the shoulder. "Don't get discouraged, son. You'll find the rhythm."

But Bard wasn't discouraged in the slightest. Instead, he felt a shiver of pure excitement. This was the chess match he had been looking for.

When the inmates went to bed, he locked the scissors up for the rest of the month, but inferred to both prisoners that the other was to blame for the confiscation. Their tight friendship completely broke down in front of Bard's eyes over forty-eight hours, fracturing an alliance that had made them feel safe. Delicious.

Nevertheless, the more subtle dynamics of the place eluded him for a time. How was he supposed to do his job? How could he satisfy his cravings, both professional and personal? The power he held was simultaneously his greatest strength and suddenly the ultimate hurdle.

Utter control, but an illusion of choice.

Total dominance, via a delicate touch.

Bard needed a precise lever of manipulation. A scalpel instead of a hammer. He waited. He watched. He clocked in and out. And then one day, as a group of inmates started bickering, Bard understood. He remembered every word of the conversation.

A haughty film agent who had been caught up in a drug sting stood, arms crossed. "You don't understand; my client has a premiere this weekend with Zoë Kravitz."

"You're missing work?" sneered a (relatively) famous ethics professor who had a penchant for shoplifting.

"It's a premiere. A celebration of the arts," the agent corrected her.

"Right. So you're missing a boozy little party where you can advance your career? Everything is about money for you, I guess," the professor snapped. "I'm missing the best weekend of the year to see whale calves make their migration along the west coast of Mexico. My study will be set back eighteen months without that data. This paper could change the direction of conservation. What are you changing the conversation on? Nepo babies?"

"Firstly, how dare you. Zoë is an undeniable talent. Secondly, I've been working with my client Shayla Saint since she was singing in outlet malls as Cheyenne Tuttle. I made that star. Me. My eye, my taste. You just count whales in Cancún."

"Cancún is on the east coast of Mexico, you philistine!" the professor shrieked.

Listening to this exchange and the weeks of fighting that followed, Bard almost doubled over in laughter. He finally understood. Inmates in max normally tried to flex, prove they were the hardest, the most ruthless. They wanted everyone to know they had already done time and were willing to do more if you messed with them. Pay to Stay inmates were the polar opposite! What these inmates were primarily paying for was proof that they *weren't* criminals. They were *different*. They were *special*. Every penny they spent to be here—liquidating 401ks, taking out loans, going into major credit card debt—it was all a financial investment in a collective fantasy that they were *actually very good people* who had been *ensnared* by the *very unfair* justice system. As if the justice system had ever been fair to anyone. As if—and this was the part that really got Bard the most—these privileged little twits were somehow the *most* aggrieved victims of the system. Marie Antoinette had a better handle on the experience of the common man! Let them eat cake, and let them bring that gluten-free ethically sourced livable-wage cake into their posh prison.

In order to rule Pay to Stay like the devil in the theater wings, Bard needed to destroy this narrative they cherished. But he needed to do it slowly, deliberately. No sudden moves to draw attention.

Bard decided to wait until every inmate who predated him was released. That took a year. Then, as each new inmate started, Bard set his plan in motion. Finally, after three years of gently cajoling each puzzle piece into place, it was at last all going to come to fruition this week. December 27. Day one of an extended stay for the inmates.

Bard grinned, savoring the beginning of what had taken years of planning. He felt a heady mix of pride and power, and he knew that feeling would only grow with every passing minute for the next five days. The buzz in his fingertips. The lift in the balls of his feet. His acute awareness of his cotton uniform against his skin. Every inch of him was yelling *I'm alive! I'm alive! I'm alive!*

Not long now until the 5:00 p.m. inmate-arrival time.

The haunting fairy tale of his own making was about to be played out for his pleasure.

"Once upon a time," Bard said to himself, loving the way his whisper whipped around the empty cells, a ghostly game of telephone.

Destiny was calling him forward at last to have his moment in the spotlight. He was the devil, and the director, and the unseen hand shaking the fake tree.

Bard was the theater itself.

But Bard had forgotten the most crucial message from *The Maiden Without Hands*: Destiny cannot be controlled.

# DAY 1

## DECEMBER 27

# CHAPTER 1

## Cami Garcia: Cleansing

Cami might have been the newest addition to Pay to Stay, having arrived in mid-November, but she was no stranger to the arbitrary workings of the justice system. Since her arrest eighteen months ago, Cami's world had taken on the shelf life of a banana. A thing of beauty and joy that was also constantly molding in front of her eyes until, within a matter of seconds, it became mushy trash. Every four to six weeks, she would trudge down to the courthouse perched on one of downtown LA's surprising hills, go through the metal detectors, take the elevator with a sweaty scrum of other anxious people, then check in with the bailiff in Department 104 on the tenth floor. Various officers of the court would confer with her lawyer, do whatever clerical check-in was allegedly urgent—bits of paper shuffled this way or that, calendars checked, dates adjusted—and then Cami would leave.

Or she *hoped* she would leave.

Because once Cami entered that building, she never actually knew if this time she would be taken into custody, disappeared into the holding cells without notice. She had seen it happen. She had seen people enter, their lives waiting for them, a hot coffee stashed at their seat for the walk back to the office, and then fate turned another way. Coffee abandoned. The judge liked to say, "Fresh meat," to the bailiff, who would then forcibly escort the defendant into custody—which was nicknamed "the crypt." It was precisely this combination of administrative tedium and the very real threat of danger that made every second unsettling. Like if every game of the Hokey Pokey ended with someone getting an ankle monitor and an orange jumpsuit. Pin the tail on the cell door. *Simon says: Three hots and a cot!*

At her very first court appearance, Cami had shown up early, an electrified ball of unchecked apprehension. She was dressed in a business suit that made her look about fifteen years older than her twenty-three years, and her hair was back in a low bun. She wore no makeup. She had sensible flat shoes from Goodwill, recognizing that the extremes of her stiletto heels or Nike Cortez sneakers were not going to match the vibe. She had based this ensemble on a lesser character in a Ryan Murphy show. She waited, jittering, in the hallway for her slick lawyer, Adam Mansfield, to show up. Adam was a new associate at his firm and eager to make a name. Cami wished his ambition meant he spent more time on her case, but instead it seemed like his focus was more on self-promotion and flirting with court staff. He also liked to tell her stories in which he had done something brilliant to get his client out of jail time.

At their first meeting, he had preened, "There's this one judge, Judge Riordan—his son is an addict, so he's been on the other side of the bench. That's why he's so lenient with first-time offenders."

"Is he my judge?" Cami had asked hopefully.

Adam had been irritated by this question. "No. He's in Orange County. And retired."

His stories were as relentless as they were irrelevant to Cami. But in order to keep Adam's attention on her case, she knew she had to smile through each and every unrelated anecdote, even as she felt her life disappearing under her feet like sand.

On that first court date, Adam strolled in late, as per usual, and walked right past her, then did a double take. "Oh my God, Cami. What the hell are you wearing?"

Cami looked down at her pinstripes and demure blouse. "I thought I should look professional?"

He sighed and said, in a tone of pure exasperation, "Oh, no, sweetie. Our defense is, you were not involved in the gambling and had no idea."

Cami pleaded, "I didn't!"

Adam's phone pinged, and he kept right on texting as he responded, "Yes, that—exactly. So you need to look . . . more dumb." And without a second glance, he walked into the courtroom, leaving Cami to hustle after him.

Cami whispered urgently, "This is like if going to the DMV meant there was a fifty-fifty chance you would get your registration renewed, but they would also take off your toe."

Her lawyer looked surprised. "Wow, that's true! And funny! I never thought of it like that before." He scowled a bit. "But don't say that kind of smart stuff in front of opposing counsel. Remember, your saving grace is that you aren't that bright. Besides, today will just be setting the calendar for our next hearing—totally routine."

Cami tried to keep her voice from breaking. "Nothing about this is routine for me!"

Even if she wanted to be annoyed at his dismissive attitude, Adam had accurately predicted the court proceedings for the day. They stood in front of the judge for less than five minutes, with everyone arranging the next court appearance as if they were trying to coordinate a birthday brunch. And so began the next year and a half of her life. She would arrive downtown, barely functional from the cortisol running through her body like off-brand steroids sold in the parking lot of a GNC. Her court appearance would pass like a rote roll call, and she would be released back into freedom, drunk on possibilities—fresh banana energy! Then she would spend the next three weeks watching her options slowly shrink, the sweet stench of the inevitable rising until she was returning to court once again.

During a call to prep her defense for a trial that seemed to never be coming, Cami did the unthinkable when she asked, "How can I make this stop?"

Her lawyer was mid–latte sip. "What are you talking about?"

"It's been a year and a half of court appearances. There is still no trial date set. I can't keep doing this—continuance after continuance. I can't keep having my life restored and then yanked away. How can we make it stop?"

Adam thought for a moment. "You can plead no contest." He saw Cami's blank stare and continued, "No contest is like Guilty-Lite. Diet Guilty. It's 'we all know I did it, but don't make me say I did it.' You basically take responsibility but without all the long-term ramifications of having a guilty plea on your record."

Cami considered this for exactly five seconds and then declared, "Great. Good. I want to do that."

"No contest doesn't make this go away," Adam said, his clarifying tone tiptoeing toward condescension. "You get that, right? We have a strong case for your innocence. If you plead out now, you *will* serve jail time."

What he did not know, though, was that Cami had come to this conversation prepared. "If I plead no contest, can I go to Pay to Stay?"

Adam's shock was satisfying as he stammered, "W-where did you hear about that?"

Cami knew the real answer—copious research fueled by flat whites—wouldn't work, so instead she made a confused face with a thick layer of pout. "I can't remember. Probably TikTok?"

He believed her.

It took another six weeks of court proceedings—and meeting with the district attorney, which would provide nightmare fuel for the next decade—but at long last, Cami's Court Era was over and her Incarceration Era was due to begin. Her own moment of #WomenInMaleDominatedFields.

When Cami arrived at Pay to Stay for her first weekend in mid-November, she had followed her GPS to the appointed address, the blocks getting more and more industrial the closer she got. She saw the eighteen-foot fences and spotlights before she saw anything else, and a weight dropped in her stomach so dramatically it was like she was being pulled back down to the center of the earth, belly button–first. Pay to Stay was unremarkable from the outside. A single-story cinder block building with high rectangular windows. She pulled her car into a driveway, and a man in head-to-toe khaki opened the padlocked gate.

Cami had decided to meet everything with her best protection: her sunny attitude. "Hi!" she said after she got out of her car, extending a hand.

"My name is Bard," the man said, looking at her hand like it was a cursed curio. "I feel strongly that inmates and staff do not touch. There is no reason for it."

Cami could see how someone else saying this—setting a protective physical boundary that worked both ways—would be reassuring. But that sentiment coming from this man, with his disarming good looks and a grin just shy of wolfish, did not exude assurance. Instead, it made him feel alien and unpredictable to her.

Cami was used to eyes being on her. She had been beautiful her whole life, with long dark hair that was effortlessly shiny, a perfect triangle of a nose that came straight down from strong eyebrows, and a pout most women paid an injector for. She'd never had an awkward phase, had never needed braces. Cami wasn't vain; she knew beauty was a total crapshoot—a moving target across centuries that had happened to align for her in this time, in this body, but would have failed to garner admiration in the waif ideal of the 1990s, or the pale gooseneck of the eighteenth century. For this moment, she happened to be at the feminine peak, and therefore men's attention was a dial she could gauge up or down depending on how it would serve her. The shellac of unthreatening girliness was her social armor of choice, which had never failed her.

Until now.

From the second she saw him, Cami knew Bard was different.

She could feel immediately that he did not want her in any traditional sense that she could maneuver, but his eyes were full of hunger nonetheless. Then it struck Cami: He wasn't objectifying her; he was looking for a suitable target, and she had to show him she wasn't one. A hard target, she remembered, was something that was difficult to attack, but with a big payoff for the effort. A soft target was something easily attacked but with fewer spoils. She wanted to be neither. She wanted to be so uninteresting that her very presence bored him.

Bard led her forward. "Thank you for coming early."

Cami smiled. "Of course! Happy to!" As if she had any choice. Bard had specifically requested that she arrive at 4:00 p.m. instead of the usual 5:00 p.m.

Bard opened the double front doors. "First weekends go more smoothly if you know the routine before the rest of the inmates arrive. So, those are the front doors. We only use those at the start and the end of the weekend. Directly across are the back doors." He pointed to an identical set of doors on the opposite side of the building. "Those lead to the small courtyard on the south side of the building. When we do community service, we leave via those doors to our dedicated transport van, which is parked back there."

Cami nodded, more big smiles. *Disarm disarm disarm,* she kept thinking.

Bard continued his tour, turning her to the left and walking down the hallway. "Here is the kitchen, and the bathroom is next to that. Not very sanitary, but perhaps easier for plumbing. Last door on that side is a closet where we keep the janitorial items. Other side of the hallway is my office. Past my office is a small mechanical room—electrical fuse box, generator, HVAC. The east side of the building has one fire door at the end of the hall. The fire door is never used, as it is electronically tied to the alarm system in the other four buildings on the block. Opening the fire door will alert any and all officers on-site."

Cami smiled and nodded. "Kitchen, bathroom, closet. Those are the only doors I need to know about."

He nodded, smiling as well. "Very good." He turned back down the hallway with Cami trotting behind. "The west end of the building is the rec room. That's where the cells are."

Bard opened the double doors to the rec room, with a little bit of flair that betrayed how much he was enjoying this one-on-one time.

Cami smiled more. *Smile smile smile.*

Bard walked into the center of the room. There were three cells on either side and two at the end. Bard walked her to a cell on the right. "This is you."

Cami stood in front of the square for a second, then realized that Bard wanted her to step inside.

*Smile smile smile.*

Cami stepped in and did a turn, as if she were looking at a possible coworking space and plotting where to plug in her laptop. Then a heavy, loud clang slammed behind her, making her jump.

She spun around in panic and saw Bard, standing outside her bars. He had slid them closed, and was holding them shut, his heavy steel-toed boot blocking the glide frame.

His face was still, but there was a gleam of pure pleasure in his eye.

Cami faltered for a second, the fear tight in her throat, and then she smiled and laughed. She laughed at herself, laughed at her own silly little reaction.

*Disarm disarm disarm.*

Clocking her lack of fear, Bard's gleam dimmed, and then he slid the bars back open. "I think it's important for inmates to see what it's like in the cell before lights out."

Cami nodded more, smiled more; her cheeks hurt like hell. "Of course. So smart."

She knew, in that moment, that the biggest problem she would have at Pay to Stay was going to be wrangling Bard's attention in the direction she wanted it to go. Namely, away from her.

After that first meeting, the subsequent weekends were uneventful. Cami clocked in. She smiled. She clocked out. She was used to this rhythm from court—her life restored and then slowly dissolving. *Same banana, different tree,* she told herself. And now it was December 27, the beginning of a double stretch of days when, instead of lounging on the couch eating the last of the sugar cookies and snacking on leftovers while watching holiday movies ("Come on, Kate Winslet, Jack Black is right there!"), she would go to that cinder block square, where time was snatched away along with all her festive cheer.

She tried to see the sunny side—five days of time served, with each day counting for double per state guidelines meant this one period of time would equal ten days more off her sentence than a regular month. Cami was normally excellent at finding an upside to everything. She had even spun her weekends at PTS as Self-Care! Dedicated hours to do her most elaborate skin-care routines! (Not that she needed them at twenty-four years old.) Her restful break from the hustle and bustle of the city! (Not that being unemployed was really so taxing on her daily life.) Of course she would have rather this been at a spa or a winery, or if she was really being greedy, at least it could be voluntary. But she was making do with what she had.

All that said, it wasn't as if she loved her high-rise apartment in West Hollywood.

After her arrest, when her whole life had seemed to fall apart, her boyfriend, Thaddeus, found the apartment for her, paid for the lease and all other monthly expenses, including her considerable Pay to Stay fees. It was his way of apologizing for getting her mixed up in his mess. He also got her clothes, jewelry, spa packages, flowers—it went on and on. He showered her with gifts she did not want, gifts that telegraphed he did not know her at all. He said it was the least he could do, considering this was entirely his fault. Really, if she wanted to be picky, the least he could do was fess up to the cops that it was all him, but somehow, magically, that wild idea had never occurred to Thad. The concept of interpersonal accountability was just too outside-the-box for his (self-proclaimed) galaxy brain.

Pea-size intellect aside, Thaddeus really did appreciate her so much. And that was nice. Cami just wished he appreciated her in a way that didn't control her life to such an extent.

The apartment style was coined *AirSpace*, which was sleek-speak for *What If You Lived in an Apple Store?* Every surface was either slate gray or shiny white lacquer. The AC never ever shut off. Floors were always cold to the touch. What she struggled with most, though, were the windows—all floor to ceiling, none of them opening. The building was one block below Sunset Boulevard, tucked away just east of La Cienaga, where the Hollywood hills rose up sharply from the city. Her unit faced north, which meant that unless she was pressed up against the glass, she saw no sky. Just a wall of hillside that, by some optical illusion, felt like it was inching closer to her each day. She could almost enjoy the view during the day, the city lights fading away into the rugged landscape. At night, however, the hills became pitch black, looming over her like a tsunami about to crash through the plate glass.

Cami tried to decorate it when she'd moved in. She bought a squishy oversize peach velvet couch with a chaise made for napping, and a shaggy rug in a wild swirl of colors that smushed between her toes. She painted an accent wall by the front door a butter yellow. She hung floral curtains so that when the day was done, she could slide them closed and seal herself away from the eyes of the neighboring buildings and the claustrophobic hillside. After hanging up a few family photos, Cami took a long bath in the soaking tub and thought perhaps it would all be okay. It really was so kind of Thad to pay for all this. And, really, what was to be gained from him telling the truth and serving the time?

As soon as Thad opened the front door after she had decorated, stinking of blueberry-bubblegum vape, he scowled. "Cami. I thought we agreed that I needed a space to just chill. All this is not *chill*," he said, gesturing to her furniture.

"But I thought only *I* lived here," Cami said quietly.

"You do, you do." He was immediately contrite, in that way that let her know he wasn't going to change his point, only his approach. "But I'm just so sensitive to my environment, and since I pay for it, I think it's only fair if I get a say, too—right, babe?"

Cami nodded and waited for whatever came next. Because something always came next with him. Contrition with a core of coercion was his specialty.

The next weekend, while she was at Pay to Stay, Thad employed Drake's (supposed) interior designer to "recalibrate the space." Thad explained the goal was to make the style "so Champagne Papi." They replaced her peach velvet couch with several "artistic" (i.e., *uncomfortable*) armchairs in nubby white fabric that felt like knuckles in her back. ("Babe, this bouclé is so chill," Thad gushed.) He had gray window shades put up instead of the floral curtains she liked. ("This color is called Pigeon Wing.") He had the building replace her soaking tub with a steam shower. ("We love steam showers. Don't we, babe? Only kids like a bath.") He even threw away her fridge magnets. ("Clutter!") It was later revealed that this designer had never worked for Drake but had merely been inside his house to help water his plants while Drake was away on tour. But by then the damage was done and Cami felt like she was living in an ice-cube tray.

Cami tried to keep the sadness from her voice. "Everything is square. Everything is white. Everything is sterile."

"Everything is *AirSpace*," Thad said, doing a bizarre magic show flourish with his hands.

"A perfect place for a murderer to hack a victim to pieces and hose the evidence away. All I need is a drain in the floor. Did Drake have that?"

Thad was legitimately hurt. "Don't talk about Drake like that, babe. Don't disrespect Drizzy."

By no means did Cami like going to Pay to Stay, but she'd found her silver lining: If her home didn't feel like her home, then she wouldn't miss it when she was in jail.

This silver lining had dulled to an old nickel when Cami woke up on the 27th, though. She fast-forwarded in her mind to what she would do when she got home on New Year's Eve. This was a visualization technique suggested to her by a therapist who had turned out to be a text-bot. AI source aside, visualizing in great detail that she would be free once again did help her mental health. She could see it now: She would drive back home in her sleek little SUV (also paid for by Thad, also disliked by her), park in her designated spot in the underground garage, and take the elevator up to the fifth floor. She would walk in her door and immediately dump the contents of her duffel bag into the washing machine (setting: sanitize). Then Cami would pick out which shower bomb to use during her customary scorching shower. This week, she decided on a holiday bath bomb pressed into the shape of a snowflake with an industrial level of peppermint scent to refresh every one of her senses and, with any luck, revive some festive cheer. Then she would scrub her skin raw with her brown sugar–exfoliating paste from head to toe, channeling Kevin McCallister, who famously washed inside his belly button during his solo Christmas in the Chicago suburbs. At the end, she would wrap her hair in a preheated towel and wear a fuzzy pajama set with tiny Christmas lights printed all over it and queue up as many movies featuring New Year's Eve as she could remember.

This was her physical and emotional cleansing ritual, her attempt to wash the incarceration away like it was a contaminant before it infected her home.

Just then, Cami heard the front door open and her mom's voice call out, "Cami?"

"Hi, Mama. I'm in bed."

Cami's mother, Lourdes, had the forceful energy of an NFL lineman in the package of a four-foot-eleven Filipina woman. She entered the room, pulling the shades up. "It's noon! Are you sick? Why are you still in bed?"

"I'm just tired, Mama. Rotten Banana Day."

Her mother frowned. "Oh, Cami. I wish you would call your cousin. She could help."

"Mom, Gabrielle is just a regular cop."

"A cop who caught that psycho mommy killer."

"She lives four hundred miles away. What do you think she could do? Call off the whole LAPD and the district attorney?"

"Gabrielle might have some connections, that's all I'm saying. She was on the news many times, you know. The family is very proud."

"Sure, Mama. Maybe."

They had had this exact exchange a million times since Cami's arrest, and Cami knew that once her mom just got it out, they could move on with their tasks. Lourdes looked the same today as she did every day. At some point in the '90s, Lourdes had found a uniform she liked and never looked back: light-wash Levi's, a short-sleeved button-down in any and all colors and patterns, heavy white sneakers she swore felt like clouds. This endlessly repeated outfit template had been so embarrassing when Cami was younger and all the other moms were in skintight yoga sets. However, style had circled back around, and now Lourdes was often confused for the hippest creative director in Silver Lake. Once, while getting hideously expensive coffees together (macadamia nut–lavender pour-overs), two men got in a bidding war for Lourdes's button-down of the day. Even as their bids soared into the triple digits, Lourdes refused them both, naturally.

When they left the squabbling men behind, Lourdes muttered, "I can't wait to be unfashionable again. This is exhausting."

Cami didn't need help packing, and her mother knew Cami didn't need help packing, but she loved that her mom came anyway. Lourdes started folding all her clothes into tiny little squares, and stacked things in such a perfect geometry that Cami was able to bring so much more for the weekend than if she packed herself. More crucially, though, her mom also brought stacks of Tupperware so Cami could eat food that smelled like home. No mass-produced, microwaved microplastic meals here. Every container Lourdes packed was a hug and a tether reminding Cami that people loved her. Every bite said *You'll be back soon, and we will be waiting.*

Cami lay back down and stared out the window.

"Camilla, what are you thinking about? Are you visualizing your return? Your cleaning ritual?"

"Cleansing," she corrected gently, then sighed. "Yes, Mama, I am. If that's my ritual to come home, what is the opposite of a ritual?"

"What does that mean, 'opposite of a ritual'? Are you on drugs?" Lourdes reached over and pulled Cami's eyelids open for a better look at her daughter's pupils. She let out a harrumph when she saw two normally dilated black circles looking back at her.

"I just mean if my ritual to *return* is so important, then what is *this*?" she said, pointing to the tiny piles of folded clothes, and her travel humidifier, and her dedicated jail slippers.

Cami's mother dug into her oversize tote that she used as a purse. "I have just the thing!" She pulled out three sudoku books, a crossword puzzle book, and then finally found what she was looking for and handed the thick paperback to Cami.

Cami laughed. "You carry around a pocket dictionary?"

Her mom snorted. "Of course not. It's a pocket combination dictionary and thesaurus. Very handy for my crosswords."

Twelve years ago, Cami's mother had been in a terrible car accident, where her car had flipped twice and she had never driven again. Instead, she took the bus across the vast Los Angeles basin, and on the bus she passed the time with her puzzle books.

"You want to know the opposite of *ritual*? That can tell you," Lourdes said, pointing to the weathered paperback.

Cami flipped through the pages in the thesaurus and then read:

*RITUAL—Antonyms: unhallowed, desacralized, deconsecrated.*

These words felt deeply depressing, so Cami kept reading, looking for something else.

*Temporal, earthly, profane . . .*

Profane!

*Profane* was the word.

Every Rotten Banana Day was a profane desecration of her life.

Then the next word on the list caught her attention: *mundane.*

She flipped back to the dictionary portion of the book and looked up the exact definition.

*Mundane, adjective: dull, of this earthly world rather than a heavenly or spiritual one.*

Yes, that described prison to a tee, but with a thick layer of physical and emotional threat. *How does one combat the mundane?* Cami wondered. Should she become mundane too? Try to camouflage herself in a cloak of boring? That felt too close to surrender. Besides, she had been trying that the last weeks at PTS, but she still felt Bard sniffing around for an entry point to exert punishment. He probably thought he was hiding it well, but Cami could see the truth. She saw his handsomeness as a mask that concealed his cruelty. She was adept at using her looks to control people, and she recognized that he was using the same tricks. She knew her end goal: self-protection. She couldn't quite see what his goal was beyond abusing others, and that was terrifying. Cami was going be stuck with him in close quarters for quite some time—and to survive, she needed a plan.

Then Cami had an idea: If becoming mundane wasn't going to work, perhaps another extreme position could. A shock-and-awe performance of herself, *as* herself, to create confusion. Pepper him with so many targets he can't focus. A lion in a ring distracted by the chair and the whip and the whistle, therefore attacking nothing. Cami felt energized now that she had a flicker of hope of how she could keep Bard's attention from seizing upon her as his favorite target.

Cami felt her mother's eyes on her, narrowing, trying to bore her way into her daughter's brain. So she quickly asked, "Do you want to go get our nails done?"

"But, sweetie, there is so much more to pack!"

"I know, Mama, I know. After? Please?"

Lourdes held Cami's face and smoothed her hair back. "My Camilla, never with the right priorities."

Cami wanted to yell that that wasn't true, that she had the exact priorities she needed to survive, but it was easier to just nod and leave her mother to the packing.

Cami picked out a vintage velour tracksuit in a sweet lavender color. It was an aughts throwback, with the slinky soft material hugging her body and a tiny slip of midriff peeking out from under the hoodie.

She put her long hair up in giant Velcro rollers until it held a high bump of volume, even as the dark waves cascaded around her shoulders. She dug into her bathroom cabinet and found a body spray that she'd kept because it reminded her of trips to the mall when she was in junior high. In short, Cami searched for everything that felt like the most exaggerated expression of High Femme in every metric.

A few hours later, Cami sat next to her mother as the nail tech finished her fresh set. Each nail was bejeweled, making her hands twinkle at the slightest movement.

She no longer felt like a rotten bit of fruit destined for the garbage can. Colors burst from every part of her body. An outfit that her boyfriend would dislike. A shower of sparkles every time the sun touched her fingertips. A waft of cherry scent around her.

Lourdes had gotten a sensible pale pink on her nails, but she gasped when she saw Cami's hands. "My girl, you look like a beautiful gem."

"I feel like a gem, Mama. Gorgeous and strong." Then Cami said to herself, "Let that mundane asshole try to desecrate this. I'll break him into a million pieces."

# CHAPTER 2

## Steven Bard: A Plan Comes to Fruition

Like clockwork, the cars lined up outside the PTS driveway entrance at 5:00 p.m. Bard opened the heavy padlock and unlaced the chain from the fencing. Over here, there was no guard shack where he could continuously watch the gate, as this access point was so rarely used, but Bard liked the feeling that this was his own personal fortress. His key to the lock the only key between the world and them. He slid the eighteen-foot-high gate to the side, and the five cars entered the side parking lot designated for the inmates. Sister Bridget, the sixth inmate, entered on foot; she took the bus here each weekend. Bard returned to his usual spot by the door and watched from the main entrance as the five cars turned off their engines, their drivers grave faced as they got out. These six women, if not for their own bad choices, wouldn't have shared an elevator together, let alone lived side by side every week. No cheerful greetings between them, and in some cases, barely even an acknowledgment of each other. Bard noted that—besides the newbie, Cami—no one could tell five of these inmates had been incarcerated together for over a year. Big *I'm not here to make friends* energy, with an extra helping of holiday grumpiness.

"Happy holidays!" Bard said as he flashed his best movie-star smile.

No one responded.

Pay to Stay wasn't cheap, but the perks were real—first and foremost, the schedule, but it went well beyond that. The inmates got to bring in their own food. They wore their own clothes. They were allowed to bring in as many personal effects as they could carry; in the case of one inmate, Janet, that haul included an emotional support iguana named Nacho.

Bard observed them with keen interest today, excited for what was to come. He felt a twinge of frustration over the fact that none of the women met his eye as they unpacked their cars. He wanted to yell, "Just you wait!"

Janet wrenched the back of her aging Volvo station wagon open, propping the broken door up with a two-by-four she kept at the ready. The smell of french fries wafted out from under the hood, due to the engine running on used canola oil she got from burger stands around town. She was an aged spinster at seventy-two years old, whose number one hobby seemed to be grasping at her long-gone youth. Her hair—tight gray curls—sprung out of her faux-religious head wrap, which of course matched her seemingly endless swaths of layered linen. She was clearly going for New Age yogi, but the effect made her look like a bit-player pauper from medieval Chaucer. A variety of cotton tote bags emblazoned with faded logos (local PBS affiliates, defunct grocery co-ops, losing Green Party candidates from past elections) loaded up onto her shoulders, until the pièce de résistance: her cherished iguana, Nacho, in his oversize terrarium.

A large orange sticker on the terrarium read *Emotional Support Lizard*. Janet had had them custom printed on the advice of her lawyer.

Janet struggled toward the building and huffed across the threshold. Nacho hissed at Bard.

The sharp beep of a car alarm turned Bard's attention to Ayse's top-of-the-mid-tier sedan. An expensive suitcase that effortlessly wheeled every which way was tucked tightly next to her body as she put her keys into an equally expensive purse. Ayse's face didn't flinch a single iota as she turned toward her weekly incarceration. Bard respected that, even if he didn't want the other inmates taking the hint. LEGO bricks had softer edges than this woman.

Bard said, "Nice to see you, Ayse." He extended the two syllables—*Aye-shhhhhha*—in the way he knew peeved her, and today was no exception. The frown was small but unmistakable. The tiny lines on her forehead and around her mouth aged her beyond her forty-three years, but not by much. Ayse went right back to texting as she crossed into the shade of Pay to Stay, as if she were merely showing up for a voluntary appointment or picking up some papers from her accountant. The essence of *unbothered.*

At the end of the row of cars, Didi whisked her foot with increasing frustration under the bumper of her flashy SUV, failing to activate the hands-free trunk closure. From her arms hung heavy bags of overpriced groceries, and her hands held two pop-up carts stuffed with crafting supplies. After her fifth attempt to swipe her foot under, a weathered hand reached up to press the door-close button.

Didi turned to see Sister Bridget smiling benevolently.

"Thank you, Sister," she said with genuine relief. "Nice that someone offers to help!" Didi snipped in the direction of Ayse's quickly distancing footsteps.

"Repentance by deeds, my dear," Sister Bridget replied.

They were a study of contrast in every measure. Sister Bridget traveled light. A single backpack was all she carried, old and stained and, Bard assumed, from a charity shop. Bridget's habit was varying shades of gray that matched the wisps of salt-and-pepper hair visible at her temples and her silver eyebrows, which seemed to get more unruly every week. Meanwhile, Didi was in her uniform of teetering high heels, impossibly tight black jeans with a sprayed-on pleather sheen, and a blouse she wore only in patterns that varied from Loud to Louder to Loudest. Today was Loudest: a recognizable motif of Italian silk with printed lions chewing on jewels. *Garish* would have been the word, except that would more accurately describe her actual jewelry. Her blond hair fell to her waist, but the telltale edges of split ends midway down her back betrayed the truth: massive amounts of extensions. Bard also noticed that Didi's skin had a new taut sheen, and he could tell that her Botox had been refreshed during the week. Oddly, the perfectly smooth forehead aged Didi just as much as Ayse's wrinkles aged her.

Sister Bridget put her hand on one of Didi's carts. "May I pull this in for you?"

"Oh, yes, please, thank you."

"More than usual," Sister Bridget noted without an ounce of judgment.

"I offered to do a vision board for the Masquerade Ball centerpieces for the hospital fundraiser. My husband is on the board of the hospital. Did you know that?"

"You seem to mention it every week, dear," Sister Bridget said, smiling as she trailed after Didi, a puff of glitter in the air every time the cart bumped on a pebble.

Maureen was on her phone, frantically trying to get as much information out as possible as she slammed the door on her sensible yet aging Prius in the ubiquitous light blue. "Did you get my last email? Yes, that one, with the seven attachments. Okay, you need to print the donors' list for Trisha today so she can start the seating chart, which I will approve by EOD January second. Why a seating chart? Remember the golden rule of campaign finance: Just because they are on the *same side* doesn't mean they want to sit *side by side*. No, that wasn't a silly question." Maureen was trying to straighten the skirt of her cheap suit, but it was no use. She had better luck tucking her mousy bob behind her tiny ears, the severe bangs hardly moving at all. Maureen continued, her can-do attitude one beret toss away from Mary Tyler Moore: "You may be just an intern today, but you are a smart, capable young woman, and I know your dad is proud of you. That's why he features you so heavily in his campaign mailings, especially since you took out the nose ring." Maureen's suitcase-briefcase combination, with every tidy zip and clip sorted for maximum efficiency, was her rolling campaign headquarters for whatever candidate she was shepherding toward office this month.

Meanwhile, Cami bumped her door shut with her hip, her entire body a vision of skin-hugging velour in a muted lavender that complemented her tan. Cami's entire life was in a duffel bag the size of a Fiat, emblazoned with a pop star's lime green logo that Bard did not recognize. Cami seemed to be bringing a summer camp vibe to Pay to Stay, which Bard deeply disliked, but he reminded himself that she was new. He would crush her soon enough. Just like he had crushed all the others. She waved cheerfully to Bard as she passed him, her acrylic nails jingling with jewels and her long hair a cloud of frothy tropical scents.

"You remember where to go?" Bard asked her.

Cami nodded and smiled meekly.

He liked that. He liked meek.

With his six regular inmates inside, this was normally when Bard would shut and lock the door for the weekend. Instead, he stood there checking his watch. Waiting. Not long now. At last, amid the civilian cars, a correctional van arrived, the windows barred, a metal partition between the shackled passenger bench and the front seat that came complete with rifle rack.

Bard walked out to greet the van. Here was the injection of reality he desired, something to set every woman inside on edge.

The front passenger side door opened slow and lazy. Gary heaved his weight out of the van and did his best to resituate his belt across his middle. All this discomfort could be relieved by getting a new uniform that actually fit, but Gary was always in the midst of a crash diet that he swore would restore him to a weight he hadn't been in fifteen years.

"Bard," Gary said, tipping his invisible hat. "You're really doing me a solid."

Bard spread his arms wide. "I love to be a team player."

Gary snorted before he saw that Bard was serious, then tried to cover the noise with a vague sneeze. He was not successful. Moving on, Gary jerked his head toward the back seat. "This won't be any trouble. I appreciate you taking him for the week. Otherwise, I was going to have to drive the seven hours to his next stop today, and my wife would have had my ass."

Gary and Bard walked to the back of the van, and Gary unlocked the bolted doors. He dramatically swung the rear open and announced loudly, "Inmate 4-3-1-1-3-0. Last name: Washington. First name: Russell."

Bard looked into the dark van and saw a single inmate shackled around the wrists and ankles, a long chain going through each set of cuffs and then secured with a padlock to a bolted hook on the floor between his feet. The white jumpsuit was clean, with snaps down the front, and Bard noticed there was even a slight press to the front of the pants.

Bard was taken aback. "Why is he wearing white?"

Gary replied, "They wear white in Texas."

Bard thought for a second. "Well, inmate, in California you wear blue. I might have some extras inside from another transport."

Russell Washington nodded his head.

Bard took the paperwork Gary was holding out and repeated back to him, "Inmate 4-3-1-1-3-0 transport from state custody into Pay to Stay custody, complete."

Gary stepped into the van and opened the padlock at the floor, un-looped the chain, and then secured it back again to the leg shackles. This gave the chain a little extra slack, and Russell Washington slowly rose into a hunched position as he exited the van.

"I'm Correctional Officer Bard. I will be in charge of you until the next leg of your transport arrives on December thirty-first at nine a.m."

Russell nodded, squinting even though the sun had nearly set and clouds were gathering. Bard realized the back of the van must have been almost pitch black, making even this muted light an adjustment.

"How old are you, Washington?"

"Twenty-five."

Gary stepped forward. "He's six years in on an eight-year bid."

Russell had the glazed exhaustion Bard recognized from someone who had been inside for many years. Nevertheless, the inmate had recently shaved and his hair was neat. His fingernails were short and tidy. There was an air of personal care that Bard hadn't expected from someone who had been incarcerated for his entire adult life so far.

"If you aren't a problem for me, I won't be a problem for you. Understood?"

"Yes, sir," Russell said, his voice hoarse from dehydration. But even as he said it, his eyes lifted upward. The palm trees that lined the block around Pay to Stay were blowing in a cool breeze that smelled like the ocean. A flock of wild parrots chattered, flitting back and forth between the fronds. For an instant, Bard saw the world through Russell's eyes.

"Let's go, inmate," Bard said, tugging Russell back toward the interior sphere, where he was in total control.

"Adios, Bard!" Gary replied, already back in the van and once again tipping his invisible hat.

Bard had to fix his face because he could feel a shit-eating grin about to bloom. He led the inmate through the heavy entrance doors that had been propped open, walked the four feet past the empty check-in desk, then turned down the central hallway that ran the length of the building.

Bard halted Russell by merely lifting his hand as a sign to stop, then pointed. "Left down the hallway, we have the kitchen, with a bathroom next door. You do not need to know about or use any other doors besides those two. Understood?"

Russell nodded.

Bard turned his charge to the right. There was a set of closed double doors, and when Russell saw them, he stopped in his tracks so quickly that Bard almost walked into his back.

"What are you doing?" Bard snapped.

"The doors are closed," Russell responded.

It took Bard a second to realize what Russell meant, and then his mind Rolodexed back to the more secure units he had worked in—Russell saw closed doors and assumed they were locked. Bard had to bite back a chuckle.

"I'm the only one here, inmate. Those doors stay unlocked."

Russell whipped his head around with a look of utter shock, and for a second Bard regretted telling him that. But he quickly seized the upper hand again by nudging Russell forward. Russell reluctantly pushed the doors open himself, leading the duo into the cells.

The cell unit—or "the rec room," as Pay to Stay called it—was a clash of opposites. The center was an open area with four metal tables and three metal chairs per table, all bolted to the floor. On either side of the room were three cells each, with two cells at the end. However, instead of the now-standard solid doors with narrow wired windows to look out of, these were old-school cells, with open bars for doors, a steel sink and toilet in the corner, and beds bolted to the walls. Each bolt had rust, and the bars were chipping paint something awful. Every sink was on its own drip time, and one toilet on the end randomly flushed even though the cell was empty. The center of the ceiling was raised higher than the tops of the cells and ringed by narrow windows, allowing natural light in without giving the inmates a view of the outside world. The two cells on the end, however, did have windows, and that was why Bard kept them empty.

In contrast to this bare-bones setup was the absolute mountain of personal crap the regular inmates of Pay to Stay brought with them. Bard could truly never reconcile how they packed so much in such tidy suitcases. Every week, each cell became a tiny diorama of their outside life. A penal dollhouse spun open on its hinges, revealing the unique person in their prescribed square.

On the right, farthest back, Gen Z Cami tilted a mirror with a wavy soft peach frame against the wall and tucked a white faux-fur rug under her bed. A small specialty lamp shaped like a rainbow's arc was aimed at the ceiling, giving the impression of direct sunlight. Everything was a shade of peach, pink, white, or cream. A snake plant was next to her bed on a collapsible side table made of clear plastic infused with glitter.

Next door, Ayse didn't bother with her floor, as she had five different pairs of shoes she assigned to various parts of the facility—shoes she wore when she arrived, work boots for outside, sneakers for inside the facility, heavy rubber clogs for the bathroom, and leather slippers for inside her cell—all lined up neatly on a door mat. From out of her suitcase, she screwed together several stainless steel poles until she had reconstructed her rolling rack, then hung up all her clothes on maroon velvet hangers. Her most personal item was a giant stack of books, all in Turkish, save for the Turkish-English dictionary (half credit), which she arranged on a shelf a previous inmate had had installed and Bard couldn't get off the wall. He had tried. Twice.

Closest to the front, on the right, was Maureen. She struggled with being offline every weekend and so instead turned her cell into her own mobile election headquarters. She fanned out early editions of every major newspaper in the country, taped up a map of every congressional district in the county, and had a stack of heavy binders full of election briefs for every ballot being cast in the country that weekend. Four calendars for every FEC-filing deadline and binders organized by projected runoffs. When Maureen had first come to PTS, she was running state campaigns with a lot of national attention. Governors who were plotting to run for POTUS level. Now she was lucky to get a city council candidate to take her on as mid-level staff. Her bizarre choice was a full-size cardboard cutout of Pete Buttigieg, which she had to gently reconstruct using PVC pipe connectors that ran along his back like a Home Depot spine. When writing speeches, she often would pace in front of 2D Mayor Pete to rehearse. There were even a few election cycles during which Maureen taped the face of her current candidate or opponent on the cutout in order to stay focused on work.

Across from those three were the other three inmates. Sister Bridget, always with the vow of poverty, arrived as the lightest, with a single crucifix and a pillow she needed for her sciatica. Even her linens had been thrifted, including a quilt someone's grandma had spent hours on only to be donated by an ungrateful relative.

Didi laid heavy brown paper down on the floor first, securing it to the edges with a heavy washi tape in a cheerful design, which she'd cut using a tiny bird ring she wore on her finger. Once that was settled, she could unwrap whatever elaborate project she had packed up for the weekend. Today, she opened an eight-tier Caboodle that was closer in size to a paramedic kit to reveal piles and piles of sequins in every shade of iridescence. She never shut up about her husband being on the hospital's board and that she had given up her career as an OR scrub nurse to effectively party-plan for him (after stealing him from his first wife). Bard saw Didi was clicking a small remote toward an open linen sack. Out of the linen rose a fully automated artificial Christmas tree. It was pre-lit, pre-baubled, and seven feet tall. Didi did a girlish hop when she saw that it just barely touched the ceiling without being squished.

"Merry, merry!" Didi said as she twirled in its light. Bard looked forward to confiscating it tomorrow.

But even with a full Christmas tree and Mayor Pete watching his every move, it actually was Janet who pushed Bard over the edge. Her large area rug was on the floor; its design was a rainbow-colored chakra chart on a life-size person in lotus pose. Once the rug was down, out came the seven sound bowls, each one aligned with a different rug chakra. Janet would brag/trap anyone who would listen that her bowls were hand-crafted crystal singing bowls that rang at a perfect pitch of 440 hertz. And last, her iguana Nacho was set in his terrarium. During one long weekend, the inmates had voted which was more annoying—the crystal bowls' humming or the iguana's scratching. It had been a dead tie for eight rounds.

Bard watched as Russell took in this scene, the regular inmates too busy unpacking to pay any attention. Bard kicked the door all the way open, the metal slamming hard into the cinder block wall. The six inmates jumped, with even screams from Didi and Cami mixed in; Sister Bridget made the sign of the cross.

Then they saw Russell.

Bard had a rush of pleasure as he watched their eyes widen in terror at this six-three tatted wall of a man shuffle into their space. He slowly led Russell across the room to the empty cell on the back right, every step a jingle of chains. Once inside the cell, Bard dramatically pulled the door closed. Well aware of the expectations, Russell slowly turned toward Bard and reached his hands through the bars so Bard could unlock his handcuffs. The atmosphere was so rich with their fear that Bard felt like it was a slice of sonic chocolate cake.

"Lay down on the floor with your hands behind your head and your ankles at my feet," Bard said to his new charge.

Russell complied in silence, and Bard reached inside his cell to unlock his leg shackles. He could have lifted the shackles out, but instead chose to drag them across the bars so the rattling sound filled the space. "Stay put, inmate." Bard crossed the room and pressed the *Cell 5* button on the wall mount to manually lock Washington's cell. The lock clunked hard into place, and the women jumped a bit.

Bard knew every one of them was praying this inmate's van was just getting gas or having a spare tire put on before the stranger went on his merry way. He was excited to extinguish that hope. His first domino falling.

Bard took his customary seat in the middle of the rec room, his file box labeled *Welcome* already there, waiting. In a tone so chipper it could double as an ice pick, Bard said, "All right, everyone, let's gather!"

The six regular inmates left their cells and sat at the adjacent tables. Janet, Didi, and Ayse didn't take their eyes off Russell, though. Even from Maureen and Sister Bridget, the tension was high. A clowder of hissing feral cats would have been friendlier. Russell, to his credit, stared right back.

Bard smiled, his golden ratio face beaming. "I hope you all had a wonderful holiday with your loved ones. Today marks the beginning of that dead week between Christmas and New Year's Eve. Not even normies know what day it is, so why not kill the time in PTS." Bard laughed at this little quip, even if he got only weak smiles from his charges. "Ladies, let's show our houseguest how it's done. Janet Fox."

Janet walked over to Bard and handed him her check for the weekend's fees and placed her cell phone in the box next to him.

"Didi Sorel."

Didi came forward and did the same as Janet, but with the addition of taking a small plastic cup from the box.

"Didi, how about you go do that now," Bard said. Didi headed toward the bathroom in the hallway, but Bard stopped her. "Let's use the cell next to our new guest. Don't want any confusion like last month." He smiled once more, deliberately flashing his dimple. "Everyone, eyes on me while Didi gives her urine sample."

Didi's face was gray, but she nodded, her eyes hardened with shame as she walked to the back of the room.

The roll call went on until everyone had handed over their funds and their cells. At the end, Didi added her sample to the box, too, sealed in a plastic bag with official *biohazard* tape across the top. She took her seat and refused to meet anyone's eyes.

"Please join me for a little tour." Bard stood and then walked backward so the women would follow him like he was a guide at the Louvre. "This way, this way," he said, waving them forward, as if there were anywhere else to go. He made an unnecessary serpentine path through the chairs and then ended with the group in front of Russell's cell.

"This is Russell Washington, inmate 4-3-1-1-3-0. He is being transported from one max facility to another, and in order for the schedules to line up, he will be staying here for the next five days."

Bard clocked more furtive glances between Didi and Janet, bored disinterest from Ayse, studious attention from Maureen, and a benedictory salute from Bridget. Cami was looking at her nails, distracted. He continued, "You are not to talk to him. You are not to share food with him. You are not to engage with him in any way. Do you understand?"

"Yes," Maureen said quickly and clearly, almost as if she were speaking on behalf of the whole group.

The entire exchange, happening within two feet of Russell, without Russell saying a word, felt off-putting, like the freak show tours of old. Look but don't touch. Judge but also fear. Bard loved it. "Besides Washington here, the rest of the weekend will be the same. Who wants to guess the community service assignment this week?"

Ayse had had enough. "You can't be serious."

Bard gave her a wink. "Come on. Let's try. Everyone say one guess."

Maureen put on her best can-do attitude. "Freeway cleanup."

Janet winced. "Oh no. Being that close to the freeway was so bad for my asthma."

Ayse muttered, "Being out of shape is not asthma."

Didi coughed back a laugh, but it was too late—Janet had heard it. As retaliation, she said, "I hope we clean up the county hospital parking lot. That was so fun seeing all the staff coming and going."

Didi went three shades whiter. "We aren't doing that, are we? *Are we?*" Her panic rose with every syllable. "I used to work at that hospital! My husband is on the board!"

"Your husband is on the board?" Ayse snarked. "Oh my gosh! I totally forgot since the last time you mentioned it five minutes ago."

Bard ignored their never-ending spat and cheerfully moved on. "So, that's two guesses for the hospital parking lot and one guess for freeway cleanup. Anyone else?"

Cami clasped her hands. "Oh, are we going to cuddle shelter animals?"

Sister Bridget smiled at Cami's enthusiasm. "That's a nice idea. Very Saint Francis of Assisi."

Bard shook his head as if they were contestants who'd bid too high on a patio set. "Oh, all such great ideas. But no. For community service this week, you have morgue duty tomorrow. Yay!"

The group let out an audible groan at this. Cami even said, "Ew," quietly.

Bard went on, an intentionally grating pep in his delivery, "It's the holidays. A lot of murders. A lot of suicides. A lot of murder-suicides. You know how it is. They need us!"

This was not true. He had specifically requested morgue duty because he hoped it would be extra depressing.

"What about the other days?" Cami asked. "Then can we hold kittens?"

Janet rolled her eyes so hard it was a miracle they didn't pop out of her head.

"The other days we will be staying close to home. Building maintenance," Bard answered.

Maureen frowned. "It's supposed to pour with rain this week. We're working outside?"

Bard shrugged. "Work has to get done. I knew these wouldn't be your favorite assignments, so I have a surprise for you. Follow me!" Bard led them back to his original spot and lifted a different box out from under the table. "New work vests for the occasion!"

Bard pulled one vest off the folded pile. The orange panels were stiff, and the reflectors were so new they almost glowed. Bard shook the vest out so they could get a good look. In huge letters across the back, it read INMATE COMMUNITY PAYBACK.

"What the hell is that?" Didi asked, her voice going up several octaves. "Last week it just said *Community Payback*. Why does it say *Inmate* now? Why?"

Ayse stepped forward as well. "That's unnecessary."

Bard looked at the vest as if he were just seeing it. He frowned and shrugged. "Well, it is accurate, though."

Maureen had a calm conciliatory tone. "I think what we are trying to say is, it's humiliating. Was this added because of a court order? Or a higher-up in the system requiring it?"

Bard bit the inside of his lip to keep from smiling. He had special-ordered the vests himself. Had even paid out of his own pocket for an extra third row of text. "You know, that's a good question. I'll sort it out in January. But for now, we will wear the vests. Your safety is paramount." He gave them a wink. "All right, twenty minutes to lights out."

In short order, the inmates were back in their cells, and the rain that had been threatening all day finally broke. Every window took an absolute lashing.

Bard sat quietly in the middle of the rec room as the inmates did their final move-in activity of the day. Each woman unfurled something large to clip to her bars for privacy. Didi had a Pottery Barn beach blanket, which had started as a little satchel with a pocket. She unbuttoned the edges and, from the pocket, pulled out four large binder clips, which she used to secure the blanket to the bars across the top. Sister Bridget had a plain white bedsheet. Janet used a large cotton tapestry with a Buddhist mandala on it, with little ties on one edge that perfectly lined up with the bars. ("A sign," she had announced the first time she used it.)

Maureen and Ayse were the most practical, both using opaque shower curtains with their pre-applied fasteners that looped as easily around the bars as they would a shower rod.

Cami appeared to have decided on a large wall hanging that was a highly detailed print of a forest. Dense trees, moss, a whisper of a brook in the middle ground, and tiny woodland creatures peeking out from various nooks. Once it was all affixed with (matching) green binder clips, Cami looked to the group, seeming thrilled with her new addition to the repertoire.

"I thought this would be nice. For everyone," she said, smiling from ear to ear.

"It's very sweet, Cami," Maureen replied genuinely.

Bard surprised everyone when he said, "Washington, come with me. Everyone else, I'll be back for final checks."

Every inmate shared a look of worry as Bard pressed the large manual button on the wall and Russell's lock disengaged.

Russell stepped out slowly and reluctantly. He crossed the room toward Bard and, as he did so, took a long look at each woman staring back at him.

Bard led Russell back to his office like they were old pals. Bard pointed for Russell to take a seat and felt that familiar rush of fun when this giant man immediately did what Bard wanted. He knew how this conversation was going to go. He had been planning it for weeks. He was ready to dominate this violent offender in a great spectacle, and use that domination as a signal for the women that the stage had shifted.

"First off, here is this." Bard reached into a metal cabinet behind him and pulled out a pair of blue sweatpants and a matching top, each with the yellow letters *DOC* on them. "You can stay in your whites for now, but by tomorrow morning, you need to change."

Russell nodded and took the clothes.

Bard said, with the casual vibe of just two guys hanging out, "So, Washington, I wanted to check in. Are you going to be a problem this week?"

Russell said immediately, "Me? No. But you do have a problem."

Bard was so eager to live his planned fantasy that he almost plowed ahead with his speech before he registered what Washington had said. "My expectations are simple. Wait"—his brain had caught up—"Wh-what are you talking about?" Washington's hesitancy wasn't a put-on, and Bard suddenly saw that the man's shoulders were tense and there was a flush to his cheeks that hadn't been there before. Bard had misread this as just another inmate acting hard in a new environment. Now he wasn't sure. He pushed on. "Washington, tell me what you mean."

"I mean—I . . ." Russell stammered, his eyes shifting, but Bard held his gaze firm on Russell's face, willing him to look up.

Bard could see that Washington was weighing his options. To run against prison's most sacred rule, *don't snitch*, was difficult even in a placement as temporary as this. Especially since, in prison, information had a habit of following people, and there was no guarantee that a whispered tip here wouldn't bite Russell later on.

After a minute of silence, Washington pointed toward the cells. "Someone in that room isn't right."

Bard laughed—really, really laughed—the relief hitting him like a spring breeze. "That room? That gaggle of geese? Ha! That's amazing. You've been inside too long, seeing shivs in your oatmeal."

But Washington didn't stutter. "No, I've been inside just long enough to know when someone is off."

Bard pushed back. "You're gonna have to give me more than that."

"You ever been in a prison riot?" Washington said. "Not a little drama popping off by the commissary—I mean a real riot, where multiple blocks are down?"

"Yes. Once," Bard replied. The memory still made him uncomfortable.

Washington said, "You remember the day before? That feeling in the air like someone had pushed something too far? And you can tell that once one person snaps, everyone is gonna snap? I feel that here." He stared dead into Bard's eyes. "Those women are fucking crazy. A lit match in a dry forest."

Bard wasn't enjoying this. "All right, all right. That's enough. Enjoy your freedom here, and just lay low."

Washington shook his head. "I'll stay in my cell, thanks. I don't want any part of what's about to happen." Without waiting for permission, Washington stood up and left the room. Bard didn't catch up to him until he was nearly back in his cell.

Bard walked down the center of the rec room, and he felt the women's eyes on him more than ever before. As he passed their cells and said, "Check," with the inmate in front of him answering "Check," there was an energy here he had never once felt. His senses were heightened, and he struggled to not whip his head over his shoulder at every noise. He had to force himself to make his customary eye contact, even as every cell in his body told him to barricade himself in his office and call for backup.

Finally, Bard got to Washington's cell. "Check."

Washington looked back, eyes sure. "Check."

Bard yelled, "Lights out in one minute."

Bard returned to his office. He placed the box of cell phones into the safe and added his own phone to the stack. He liked staying totally focused at work, and besides, he had no one to call. He took out Didi's urine sample and tossed it into the garbage. No need to test it. Bard heard the familiar clunk of the lights in the cells, rec room, hallway, and ancillary rooms all switch to darkness, as they were on a timer. The only overhead light in the whole building that remained on was above his desk, but he even turned that off, preferring the warmth of his desk lamp only.

The CO's office was a far cry from the mini homes of the inmate cells. There was a large metal desk with four drawers on either side that rattled when opened, and an uncomfortable chair behind it. There was a semi-ancient desktop computer, where he filled out the requisite paperwork. To his right was a small table with a printer and the internet router, its row of little green lights blinking to indicate whatever purpose they served. Above the table, mounted to the wall, was his four-quadrant surveillance screen of the rec room, the hallway, the kitchen, and the courtyard on the south side of the building. On the opposite side of the room was a metal cabinet with extra inmate uniforms and office supplies.

To the left of the desk was a door to his tiny private bathroom. A toilet, sink, and a small shower with a curtain that always clung to his legs. It wasn't fancy, but it was very clean, its surfaces always gleaming.

Behind his desk was another smaller door, and as Bard stepped through it, he wondered if the inmates even knew what was back there. It was slightly narrower than a standard door; he could understand if they assumed it was just a closet. Through that door was Bard's sanctuary—the correctional officer's designated sleeping quarters. If someone were dropped into this room, they would think it belonged to a Midwestern grandma. For starters, when Bard had officially taken over this post, he spent a week putting up wood paneling to cover the cinder block walls. This, along with the single high window, gave the feeling of being in a suburban basement as opposed to inside a prison. He had one of those rugs braided from old scraps and wound into a giant multicolored spiral. The full bed had come in a package the size of a shoe box, and then expanded over twenty-four hours after being opened. It would have to be cut up to be removed. He had even added a headboard upholstered in dark plaid with a thick layer of batting underneath. This was extra ideal because the service panel between the head of the bed and the adjacent mechanical room let in too much sound when the power grid surged or (more often) failed, and the cushioned headboard muffled the noise greatly. Bard also had a nightstand and a set of shelves for his few personal effects (if one considered deodorant and a travel alarm clock personal).

On top of all this was his seasonal décor, which he rotated religiously. As it was Christmastime, Bard had holly garland tacked along the ceiling with blinking lights. He had a kitschy nothing-but-tinsel tree, with a tree skirt fluffed out to look like snow. Bard stirred his cinnamon potpourri to release its scent and complete the ambience. He deeply enjoyed marking the holidays when his professional life existed in a space outside of time, where years were stretched into elastic eons designed to break a man. The rhythm of the outside world was reassuring, and was one of the few ways he felt in sync with the wider public.

The only sign that this room was part of Pay to Stay were the two file cabinets, three drawers high, along the opposite wall. It wasn't the most restful to sleep among the paperwork, but it was necessary to have the files in here, as secure as possible from the inmates during the day. He had another small desk lamp on top of the cabinets—the kind with a wide circle base and a neck that had three hinges before the standard metal cone around the bulb. He turned it on with a flick, tilting the neck at just the right angle that the warm glow lit the entirety of the small room. The beam of light hit the tinsel tree in the corner, the reflection glittering across the ceiling like stars. Bard opened the file drawers, pulling the complete paperwork on all present inmates. Then he walked back to the front office, shutting the bedroom door behind him with a satisfying click.

He sat down at his desk with the stack of six manila folders, thick with papers. From one of them, a thumb drive tumbled out. Bard tucked it into his pocket absentmindedly, thinking he really needed to take it home. Then he reached down into another locked drawer, drew out six sheets of Correctional Department stationery, and slid them into the printer.

His heart utterly bursting with joyous sadism, he began typing.

Six identical as-yet-unsigned letters.

One for each of his regular inmates.

After printing them, he added a handwritten sticky note.

He folded the letters and slid each one into its own envelope.

He turned off the desk lamp. Total darkness now, except for the thin beam of light under the closed door from his bedside lamp.

Bard exited the office, pulling the office door closed behind him.

Then Bard walked quietly down the hallway and back into the rec room.

He could hear Sister Bridget snoring. He could hear Janet doing some meditation she would claim was from a shaman but he was sure really came from a meme featuring a golden retriever. Ayse's and Maureen's cells were silent. Cami had her sound machine on, a looped recording of a babbling brook emanating from behind her woodland tapestry. He could see a faint glow from Didi's cell, which he assumed was from her Christmas tree. He questioned whether he had waited long enough; some of them could still be awake. This worry made Bard feel a fissure of emotion—a heightening of senses he struggled to identify. He shook his head to refocus on the plan he had spent so long setting into motion. It didn't matter if they were still awake. They would find these letters whenever they found them, and that was when the real fun would begin.

He slid a letter through each set of cell bars. Not so far that it would be visible from their beds, but tucked between their privacy screens and the bars.

A morning paper. Special delivery.

Washington was sitting on his cot, looking out the window at the rain coming down. He looked up from his bed as Bard passed by. Bard smiled at him, but Washington did not smile back.

Bard walked the length of the building from the rec room, all the way to the end of the hall, where the emergency fire door was. At the top of the door were two metal panels—one on the door itself and the other on the bulked-up doorframe. Both metal panels needed to be grounded into the alarm system so the current could run uninterrupted from the frame through the door. If the door was ever opened, the panels would separate, the current would be broken, and the alarm would sound.

Or at least, that was how it used to be.

Several months ago, there had been a maintenance crew on-site during the week when no inmates were present. They had been painting the cinder block hallway a new variation of institutional green, and the crew was trying to tempt a breeze by opening every door in the building.

"Jeez, not a lot of windows in this building," the maintenance man had noted.

"Yeah, windows that open are kind of frowned upon in a jail," Bard had joked.

"Oh, right. Well, then, I guess I can use the fire door."

Bard had watched with interest as the man unhooked the wires from the panels on the fire door and, after a quick bleat from the alarm, twisted the wires together into a secure knot, silencing the noise. "This keeps the current going so the alarm won't trip when we open the door," the maintenance man had said, noticing Bard's keen attention. "I'll reconnect the plates before we leave."

Bard had replied, "You should leave the door open for now. So the fumes can clear. I'll refasten the wires when it's all dry."

But Bard had deliberately never refastened them.

Instead, he had added a sign that said OPENING THIS DOOR IS A VIOLATION OF FIRE CODE 28.34. OPENING THIS NOT DURING AN EMERGENCY WILL RESULT IN IMMEDIATE CONSEQUENCES. He had many signs like that around PTS—quoting fake codes or citing rules that didn't exist—and enjoyed watching the inmates as they contorted themselves to adhere to them.

Tonight, Bard pressed the wide bar—a low thunk resonated—and opened the fire door. No alarm sounded. No key needed. Nothing. Just a rush of cool air. He stepped out, careful to move the large rock into place in case the door swung shut. Not that it would. Not that there was any lock waiting to latch him out. This was his little personal portal to the outside world.

He unfolded a metal chair he kept there and sat under the small overhang, watching the rain. It was coming down in great sheets illuminated by the floodlights. The palm trees were shaking from the constant pelting, and every once in a while the leaves would reach out in a synchronized movement, pushed by a wind too high up for Bard to feel on his face.

This week at PTS was Bard's Christmas gift to himself. He had a lot he wanted to accomplish, and that was part of why he had approved the state inmate to be incarcerated there for the week. Washington was here to remind Bard's whiny charges of what *real* prison does to people. Washington was here to remind them that the stakes were so very high, and they better perform.

Bard had hardly been a saint as he waited to get this plan sorted out. He loved loosening the reins until the women relaxed and then giving a sharp yank, reminding them of the bits in their mouths and the rider controlling their every movement. For example, there was the time he'd hired a crew to remove every personal item of theirs while the inmates were on community service detail and then made them pick their belongings out of the dumpster. Or when he'd manually shut off the AC for one of the hottest weekends of the year, claiming a malfunction, while his office was as cool as ice. All that would pale in comparison.

Bard smiled. And then he felt the mental fissure again. He sat with the feeling, turning it over in his mind, trying to get a good look at it, trying to identify it. It took several minutes of sitting quietly, taking an inventory of his mind, to finally name the unfamiliar emotion.

Fear.

Bard was afraid.

He thought about what Washington had said, about one of those women being dangerous. About one of them being pushed too far.

As the rain came down harder and harder outside, Bard heard the leaks starting behind him, echoing down the hallway. While he knew this building wouldn't pass any inspection, every *drip drop* made his head turn, looking for footsteps. His heart was racing as he admonished himself for taking the bait so easily.

What did Washington know? He had just gotten here. Bard knew these women inside and out. Even Cami the newbie had all the depth of a Kleenex—he would crack her by the end of the week. There was nothing to be afraid of, he reminded himself.

And yet his shoulders stayed high and his hands were balled into tense fists. Even when he eased his fingers out straight, within seconds, he realized they had returned to their position of defensive readiness.

Bard looked out toward the various parking areas and driveways he could see from his vantage point. Rainwater poured out from every storm drain, and the streets were flooded several inches. Los Angeles was a city built for dreams, but it was not built for drainage. He sat outside for over an hour, watching the storm gather to its full strength. Suddenly, there was a flicker as all the lights on the campus dimmed up and down, until going out. The heavy thud of the power grid failing. The darkness was inky, both in its depth and its wetness. Bard vaguely wondered what this power outage meant for his inmates, but he didn't chase the thought too far. It rubbed elbows with the fear he was trying not to indulge.

The wind shifted, and the rain started to blow toward him. The leaks behind him were getting worse, the water starting to run toward the interior. Plus, the dark was playing tricks on him. First he thought he heard footsteps; then he imagined the chain-link fence had disappeared until the light hit the metal again, illuminating the endless loops going up, up, up. He would make Russell pay for getting in his head. This was unacceptable.

Bard stood, stepped back through the door, and gently closed it. As if by magic, there was a heavy clunk, and the power turned back on. Bard sighed, feeling relief from the fear that had been trying to cling to his mood like ivy. The bright square of light from his open office door beckoned him to bed.

Bard entered his office and sat down in his desk chair. The shadow he cast onto the desk from his bedside lamp in his sleeping quarters made him look tall and ominous, soothing his rattled nerves even more. He thought he had closed that door, but he was happy it was open now, giving just the right amount of light.

Bard reached for his ancient iPod and a pair of very large, very expensive noise-canceling headphones from his desk drawer. Christmas yesterday had been like any other day. He had been at home, alone, preparing for the workweek ahead. But still, he liked the festive energy, and had special playlists for each season. Bard turned on the headphones, and the familiar whoosh of dead air greeted his ears. He scrolled through his music and found his Boxing Day mix in less than a second. The first track was his favorite: "What Are You Doing New Years Eve?" A jazz standard that had been recorded dozens of times. He had once spent an entire day listening to them all, creating a March Madness–type bracket system to rank each one. In the end, this rendition by Karen Carpenter reigned supreme.

The strings swelled up in a dreamy haze, and the tinkling of chimes were like musical snowflakes dotting the soundscape. A saxophone turned in the melody, sexier than perhaps anticipated. Then Karen Carpenter's voice came forth—strong and clear. This Christmas album had been released after she died, and Bard had always felt some deep haunting in her singing. As if she knew no one would hear this song until she was gone. He was certain her death was why her brother had cut the first verse, in which Karen would have asked the listener if she would be among those missing the New Year's Eve celebration. Nevertheless, Bard felt like he could hear her sing it, feel the words hanging loose in those chimes like a séance. He leaned back and closed his eyes. The fear was finally receding like an unwelcome memory.

This week was his.

He was effervescent with malice.

It had all come to this.

Then, through his eyelids, he sensed a blocking of light. Then he felt it.

His eyes opened to see nothing but orange.

An orange inmate work vest. It was over his eyes, over his face. Bard clawed at the fabric, but it was being pulled tight, held by two strong hands at the back of his head. And underneath the vest was lined with something that made his hands slip. He suddenly realized with horror it was Saran Wrap that was stretched across his nose and mouth. Bard tried to stand up, but the fabric was pulled down toward the floor, and he couldn't get his feet under him. The plastic clung to his mouth and nose. He couldn't find a breath.

He kicked and kicked, making the desk chair jerk back and forth.

*No no no no. No. I have so much to do.*

Bard tried once more to get his feet under him, but his heels merely scuffed the cement floor. His nails scraped along the desk. He pulled at the vest, but his fingers couldn't get traction. The plastic suctioned to his mouth, pulling in farther and farther, the pressure on his tongue claustrophobic. He could see as his feeble attempt to exhale inflated the words INMATE COMMUNITY PAYBACK a few more times.

He gasped, and gasped, and gasped.

Karen sang, and sang, and sang.

What will he be doing New Year's Eve.

Bard would be doing nothing.

Bard was dead.

# DAY 2

DECEMBER 28

# CHAPTER 3

## Cami Garcia: The Discovery

Cami woke up to the sound of frantic whispers. The quiet chatter had first snaked its way into her dreams like a wine stain soaking a tablecloth, seeping toward her by the second, until her eyes finally opened. It took her a second to realize she was, in fact, awake and the whispers were quite real.

Cami slowly got out of bed and unclipped her woodland scene from her bars. As she did so, she discovered a white envelope on the floor of her cell. She picked it up and then looked around, confused. Cami saw the whisper brigade: Didi, Sister Bridget, Maureen, Ayse, and Janet, all awake and pressed up against the bars of their cells. More importantly, Cami noticed everyone else was holding a similar envelope.

"What's this?" she asked no one and everyone.

"A bunch of bullshit," Ayse said with an edge in her voice. "It's not even signed."

Didi pressed her face into the bars and, in sheer desperation, asked, "You think it's really bullshit? You do? Please tell me."

Maureen was soothing. "Don't panic, Didi. There's a lot that would need to happen before these letters can become real."

Cami opened her letter: It was an official recommendation from Bard for her to be transferred out of Pay to Stay and into a state penitentiary, effective immediately. Three years. Hard time.

Cami's stomach dropped through the floor. Her hands shook when she saw a Post-it note at the top of her letter. In Bard's handwriting, it read *Impress me this week, or I file for your immediate transfer.*

Cami's eyes flew around the room, and she quickly surmised by the five grave faces staring back at her that everyone had gotten the same letter. "He can't do this. Can he do this?"

Sister Bridget was resigned to the point of grim, her mouth a thin line and her eyes closed. "I think he can. Seems our repentance was not enough." She made the sign of the cross.

Ayse was furious. "Says Bard! And I'm sorry, but he is not any moral authority I respect. The second I get out of this cell, I am calling my lawyer."

Maureen nodded. "I think that's a good plan. We all need to stay cool, talk to our legal counsel, and then we will know what's what. No need to panic over hypotheticals."

"This doesn't feel very hypothetical. It's on letterhead," Janet said, then added, "Typical cop." She said the last word like it was an insult, which, to her, it was.

While the rest of the inmates continued their speculation, Cami sat back down on her bed. The waves of stress seemed to crash over her again and again, her vision blurring. A hot rush of sweaty anxiety made her pajamas stick to her skin, followed by a flooding of nausea so strong she tipped her head toward the stainless steel toilet in the corner. Luckily, her oil diffuser (lemon verbena) was there, too, and as she breathed it in, her nausea passed.

She watched as Janet gently lifted Nacho out of his habitat and into her lap. Janet stroked his cool scales, and he lifted his head in appreciation. Cami wished she had an iguana for emotional support. Molly the Snake Plant was not going to do it today.

Janet was coming close to hyperventilating. "I can't go to prison! I have a dependent!"

"The lizard?" Didi asked incredulously. "I can't go to prison—I have actual kids."

"Stepkids," Ayse corrected her. "And last week we all heard when you forgot their names."

Janet took some more deep breaths, but they only sped up her unraveling. "Normally, I begin my morning by setting a spiritual intention. My Buddhist Thought for the Day calendar featuring a little cartoon panda. But I forgot to pack it this week!" She was nearly screaming by the end, as if this was a Level 10 emergency.

Ayse's tone bordered on cruel. "Can't you find a spiritual thought from within?"

"Not now! Not when I'm feeling like this!" Janet replied.

Sister Bridget offered, "I have some devotionals I could lend you."

Janet snapped, "And clutter my spiritual practice with patriarchal Christo-fascism? Ha. No thanks." And with that, she went back to petting Nacho like he was a genie's lamp.

Suddenly, there was a loud banging. Ayse had taken one of her heaviest shoes (a solid rubber clog reserved for the communal prison areas) and was hitting it against the bars. "Bard! Bard, where are you!"

Maureen hissed, "What are you doing? Are you trying to make things worse?"

Ayse held her watch out through the bars showing the time. "He wants to mess with us? Leave us these little letters? Fine. But he is fifteen minutes late to open our cells for the day." She resumed banging. "Bard! Where are you!"

Ayse was right. Cells were supposed to be opened at 7:00 a.m. on the dot, and it was 7:15.

Ayse gave her bars another unholy bang, and then something remarkable happened. The bars shifted a full inch to the left, making a terrible screech in the rusted glide track.

No one moved. No one spoke.

"Well, that's new," Ayse whispered.

Janet stood up and walked to her own bars, Nacho perched on her shoulder. With the gentlest touch, she pushed on the handle.

Her bars also slid open.

Didi said, in a hushed tone tight with panic, "Did you hear the locks open? I never heard the locks open this morning."

"What's different about today?" Ayse asked.

Cami slid her bars open with a single finger and said, "I heard the power go out a lot—it kept interrupting my sound machine. These locks are, like, electric or whatever, right?"

Janet reached back into Nacho's terrarium and flicked his sunlamp switch. Nothing. "Yeah, seems like the power is out—and that disengages our locks."

Sister Bridget bravely stepped out of her cell. "Doesn't seem like the most secure system."

Maureen also stepped carefully into the open rec area, as if she expected a booby trap to swallow her up, and said, "Maybe it's for earthquakes?"

There was a small rustle from the end of the room, and all six women's heads swung in speedy unison. Russell was lying in his bed, his eyes open. He hadn't said a word. He showed no sign of getting up or joining the conversation. Even so, his stillness seemed to unnerve the other women on the floor. Cami wondered what they expected him to do. Join their hysteria? Sing a jingle?

Her teeth itched with the emotional tension, but she pushed out a hopeful smile. "We need to talk to Bard. Show him what's going on with our cells."

"Cami's right. Let's go, as a group," Maureen said, pushing her shoulders back, ready to handle the situation.

Janet grimaced. "Seriously, Maureen? You want to listen to Malibu Skipper?"

Ayse said, "Well, we can't stay here."

The six women started toward the hallway when Cami turned around. "Russell? Do you want to come?"

Didi's jaw dropped. "I'm sorry, are you inviting this *criminal* to join us?"

Cami made her naturally big Bambi eyes even bigger. "Of course."

For the first time, Russell looked up. His mouth was open slightly, and he took a second to respond. “No.” Then quickly, he added, “No thank you.”

“You sure?” Cami asked.

“I don’t need to look for trouble,” he said.

Cami gave a sweet shrug. “Okay. We’ll let you know what Bard says.”

Russell nodded. “Okay. I’ll be here.” A small smile purposefully tipped the joke.

Cami laughed, and Janet rounded on her, incredulous. “This is insane. Let’s go.” Janet looked to the group for backup and saw Ayse laughing, too.

“What? It was funny,” Ayse said in her signature haughty tone, looking down her nose.

They opened the double doors, and when confronted with the long dark hallway awaiting them, Maureen grabbed the flashlight that lived by the cell lock panel.

Didi whispered, “Sister Bridget should take the lead. Jesus being on her side and whatnot.”

Sister Bridget said, “I don’t know if God is in here.”

Maureen, ever practical, said, “I think we start with Bard’s office.”

Ayse was just behind her shoulder. “Yeah. Doubt he’s whipping up brunch in the kitchen.”

The six women moved forward in an awkward huddle like they were in a haunted house at a county fair.

They got to the closed office door.

Janet pushed Didi forward. “You knock.”

Didi backed up into the middle of the group. “What? Why me?”

“You’re nonthreatening,” Janet said.

Didi took yet another step back. “Why not Sister Mary Meek over there?”

Maureen stepped forward. “I’ll knock. Can’t be worse than the time I told a state senator his sex tape was online.”

“Which senator?” Cami asked, shocked.

"Not the one you think," Maureen said as she rapped her knuckles on the door.

They waited, barely breathing.

Didi exchanged a tense look with Maureen; then Cami felt a shove in her shoulder as Ayse pushed through to the front of the group.

"Oh, this is ridiculous." Ayse banged on the door hard. "Bard? Bard, are you in there? The power is out. Also, these letters—"

Maureen cut her off, her voice just as loud. "We think the power is why our cells are open." Then she whispered to the group, "Let's slow-play the letters."

Ayse rolled her eyes. "Fine. But he needs to come out of his office already. We have to report for morgue duty in fifty minutes." Ayse banged on the door again. "Bard? Bard, we're coming in."

She pushed the door all the way open, and they entered with the grace of an avalanche, with Cami crushed in the middle. She was turned around by the momentum, before coming face-to-face with Sister Bridget, who gasped, "Oh, dear God."

Didi let out a scream of shock.

Ayse's body went rigid.

Maureen's hand reached out and found Cami's. Cami's entire attention was on her hand. Why was Maureen holding her hand? Why was everyone being so weird? Then Janet turned her around by the shoulder, and Cami finally saw what they all could see.

Bard. In his desk chair. Illuminated by the flashlight beam. The orange safety vest wrapped tightly around his head. Front and center, across a face that clearly had no breath, were the words INMATE COMMUNITY PAYBACK.

Ayse's voice was low. "The irony. Jesus Christ."

Sister Bridget knelt down and started muttering a prayer that Cami could only assume was some version of last rites.

Didi was a flood of tears immediately. "What happened? *How* did this happen?"

Ayse was matter-of-fact. "He was murdered."

The words charged the room like an electric shock. The hairs on Cami's arms stood up and a chill went down her spine.

Cami whispered so very quietly, so very hopefully, "Maybe he wasn't murdered."

Even before the words left her mouth, she felt herself tip from a point of optimism to the point of insanity. Her mind seemed to writhe at the reality it was simultaneously trying to confront and trying to deny in equal measure. But was reality any less surreal? Cami looked around—Sister Bridget on her knees, Didi weeping, Maureen with her hands in her hair, Ayse's eyes calculating around the room, Janet and that googly-eyed iguana on her shoulder. A Dalí painting by way of Olivia Benson on an acid trip.

Maureen gently corrected Cami. "He was murdered." She pointed. "The vest was secured behind his head by someone else. And . . ." She leaned closer and then winced. "Oh God."

"What? Spit it out!" Janet said.

"There's Saran Wrap underneath," Maureen said, pointing to the visible plastic suctioned to his chin and neck.

Cami put her hand over her mouth in shock; her palm was cold and clammy.

Didi was shaking now, and the tears continued. "But who could have done this?"

Without a second's thought, Janet said the unthinkable: "One of us."

"What? Why?" Didi's voice jumped three octaves, as it always did when she was stressed.

Janet held up her transfer letter. "For starters, we all have motive. Typed up in black and white."

Cami looked down at her own hand, which was holding her transfer letter, which now suddenly felt dangerous. Motive? Why was she saying that? Did she actually believe it? Why was she so calm? Where were these answers coming from?

She heard her lawyer's voice: *Your defense is that you are dumb. Play that.* It had worked once.

Ayse slowly walked to the back side of the desk, her arms behind her back like she was getting close to a priceless work of art near a fastidious docent. Maureen angled the flashlight for her, working the tiniest spotlight on the smallest stage. Ayse plucked a pen from his desk and used it to open the top drawer. "Bard's service gun is still there." Her eyes came up to meet the group. Her gaze was level and her hands were steady. "I want to check the magazine."

Cami looked around. "What magazine?"

Maureen whispered gently, "The gun magazine."

Cami said, "Oh," on a sharp intake of breath.

Ayse's voice remained calm. "Does anyone object to me touching the gun?"

Maureen answered her as if they were the only two people in the room. "I think you have to. To be sure."

Ayse reached down and picked up the gun. She held it at 90 degrees so it was parallel with the floor as her right thumb pressed a small button toward the side of the trigger. The magazine popped out into her expectant left hand. The sound of the ejection made Didi jump. Then Ayse set the gun on one side of the desk and placed the magazine on the opposite side. She raised her hands like a dealer ending their shift at a casino.

No. Not a dealer. Like a magician. Cami was watching a magic trick, where the pure spectacle of the uninteresting was part and parcel of the trick. Two rings that linked and unlinked. Spinning the box with the assistant's legs poking out before being sawed in half. A gun full of bullets.

Ayse gently lifted the magazine up high so everyone could see it. Maureen dutifully followed with the beam of light. Cami waited for the trick, for the reveal, a bouquet of silk flowers among the barrel or a dove behind the firing pin. She shook her head to come back to her senses. There was no trick here.

Ayse pointed to the two lines of six holes each and counted. A brass bullet was visible in each one. "This gun hasn't been fired," she said, finishing her presentation. "I am going to put it back in the desk drawer." She reloaded the gun and placed it back where she had found it.

Once the gun was put away, Cami leaned forward. "Maybe the safe is open and we could get our phones. That would be good."

Janet shot her a look. "Your need for an upside is nearly pathological."

Cami stepped around Bard's body slowly and rushed the last two steps to get to the perceived security at Ayse's side. She bent down to the safe in the corner and pulled on the door. When it didn't budge, Cami let out a tiny whimper. The outside world had never seemed so close and yet so far.

"What do we do?" Sister Bridget asked from the back of the pack, off her knees and done with prayer.

Didi was wringing her hands so hard the skin was a mottled red and white. "I think we use the desk phone and call 9-1-1. Or check with the officers here at the maintenance station. Let the cops figure it out."

Maureen put her arm around Didi in a show of solidarity. "Didi is right. The sooner we report this, the better. I have some police contacts from my union work—I could call them directly. They know me."

Then a new voice came from the doorway. "That's a bad idea." Russell had finally joined them. From the doorway, he continued, "If you call the cops, you will all go to state prison."

Maureen wasn't here to be pushed off her plan, though. "That's not true." She turned back to the group, ever the campaigner. "That is not true."

Cami noticed Russell's voice wasn't harsh or condescending. He was kind, quiet, measured as he spoke. "You're all on suspended sentences, yeah? Meaning you get to stay here in this nice prison as long as you don't get arrested again?"

This was true. Cami had pored over her paperwork when she was offered Pay to Stay as an option. Her lawyer had reviewed every stipulation and had sternly said over and over, "If you are found in violation of anything in this offer, you are done. Done. I won't be able to help you."

Russell continued, "No one is wasting taxpayer dollars on finding out which of you did it. They will just say it was all of you and wash their hands of it."

There was a long silence, the only sound a faint drip of the rain outside echoing off the cinder block walls. Cami looked at each of their faces and knew they were remembering their own paperwork. Remembering their own stringent terms and conditions.

At five eleven, Ayse was the tallest among them, and she pulled herself to her full height when she spoke now. "Russell is right."

Sister Bridget looked solemn. "Okay. He's right. What does that mean for us? What do we do?"

Ayse said, "One of us is a killer." She paused, letting the words hang in the air like a burning zeppelin. "We have to solve the murder ourselves."

"Before New Year's Eve," Cami added, her hope finally waning.

Ayse nodded. "And . . . the clock is already ticking."

Another potent silence draped over the group. A weighted blanket of dread.

Janet said, without looking at anyone, a naked gleam of hunger in her eyes, "If we find out who the killer is, we can use them to get the rest of us out of this mess."

Cami felt as if she were seeing Janet clearly for the very first time. Behind the namaste key chain, hidden among the sound bowls, there was a relentless desire for self-preservation wrapped in razor wire, and Janet didn't care who it cut.

Cami knew what she herself had done to get into Pay to Stay, the devil's bargain she had signed up for: trapped with Thad until her sentence was done, living in an apartment that felt like just another state of surveillance, all to protect what she had worked so hard to build. Cami now wondered who Janet had offered as sacrifice to save herself from hard time.

She wondered what any of them had done. What cruel wreckage had they each left in their wake in order to stay safely in these privileged walls?

Cami made eye contact with Russell and realized, in that instant, he was wondering the same thing.

# CHAPTER 4

## Ayse Demiri: Act Natural

It had been maybe three minutes since they had found Bard's dead body, but Ayse struggled to remember a time when she wasn't in this office. It had been months. Or seconds. Ayse stood behind Bard and watched the other five women slowly melt down as her own brain went into a state of mild disassociation. A detached observatory mindset took over—all visual, no audio. Details aplenty, emotions lacking.

Janet stood, dumbfounded, with her ridiculous iguana. Cami chewed on a glittery fingernail like a child. Didi's face was streaked with big tears. Sister Bridget had her hands crossed on her heart. Maureen's balled fists were on her hips as if she were looking for a task. Meanwhile, Russell the inmate stood in the hallway—removed from the rest but centered perfectly in Ayse's line of sight.

It was a bizarre tableau that reminded Ayse of something, but she couldn't place it. A Renaissance painting? A still from a cop show? A final climax in one of the forgotten noir movies her dad fell asleep to almost every afternoon? Maybe none of the above. Her mind wanted to chase the association down, but Ayse forced herself to refocus. Identifying this moment as "similar to that one episode of *Homicide: Life on the Street*" wasn't going to actually help her.

In her momentary daze, Ayse wondered why everyone was continuing to panic, then realized the enduring novelty of a dead body was keeping the hysteria quite fresh. She physically shook off her mental fog and cracked her knuckles to center herself back in the present moment.

With an authority she did not feel, she cleared her throat and said, "Let's look around. Maybe the killer left a clue."

Did she really just say that? Was this *Scooby-Doo*?

But before her self-doubt could kick in, Ayse did notice something odd: a door, behind her, smaller than the standard height and slightly ajar. "Hey, what's in here?"

The rest of the group looked back at her, shrugging.

"Should we all go in together?" she asked.

Didi piped up from the back. "I'm good here."

Ayse clenched her teeth. Would it be helpful to let her simmering dislike of Didi boil over right now? No. But would it feel good? Extremely good, yes.

Maureen came forward, leaning away from Bard's contorted body like he could reanimate any second, and stood next to Ayse. "Let's open it."

Ayse pushed the door open using her elbow, in some vague nod to protecting her fingerprints or something. (Then wincing at the realization that she had just touched every crevice of a gun. Oh well. Too late now.)

The room inside was nearly as dark as the outer office, save a slip of a window across from them with a heavy shade that allowed in slivers of gray morning light at its edges. As Ayse's and Maureen's eyes adjusted, they saw the bed—still made up—but they couldn't make out much else. Maureen stepped forward, and her foot made an unrecognizable sound against something on the floor. *Sweep, crunch. Sweep, crunch.*

"Oh God, crunching! Are there piles of bones?" Didi shrieked.

Ayse snapped, "You think a gentle *shhh* is the sound a pile of bones makes?"

"How would I know? I'm not a criminal!" Didi said.

"All evidence to the contrary," Ayse muttered.

Janet said, remembering, "Aren't you a nurse?!"

Didi crossed her arms. "I am a cardio OR scrub nurse. I don't work ortho with the jocks."

"Okay, but seriously, what is under our feet?" Maureen whispered to Ayse.

Ayse pointed to the window. "If I pull the shade, there might be enough light to see."

She gingerly stepped across the room, a disconcerting swish with every step, and then she felt something hard ram into her leg.

"More bones?" Cami asked, her nail still between her teeth.

Ayse couldn't tell if Cami was joking, so she answered her straight. "No, just the corner of the bed." She took two more careful steps forward, fumbled until she found the cord for the window shade. With one swift pull, the shade went up, and the room was flush with indirect sunlight.

The bed had several decorative Christmas pillows, and a handmade crocheted blanket that had pilled up over a decade of washes. There was a rug, and vintage lamps, and kitschy Christmas decor.

The sight was so unexpected that Ayse had to laugh. "What in the 1970s Macy's catalog is this?"

*"Silent night, freak show night,"* Janet sang.

"I guess this was where he slept?" Ayse said back to the rest of the group still in the office. "But the bed is made, so seems like he was killed before he went to sleep."

Beside the bed, there were two file cabinets, with three drawers each. All the drawers had been fully pulled open, empty, their contents shredded all over the floor. The ribbons of paper went wall to wall and almost two inches high.

"Guess this was the swishing sound," Ayse said.

"So no bones?" Didi asked again.

Maureen said soothingly, "No bones."

Didi let out a sigh. "Well, that's a relief."

Ayse cocked her head and, in a tone drier than a WASP martini, said, "Yeah, all our problems are gone now." Ayse pushed the paper aside with her toe, making a small pathway back toward Maureen, who was kneeling at one of the drawers, sliding her hand across it like it was a tired horse. "Looking for something?" Ayse asked her.

"What? No," Maureen said absently. "I don't know. I don't know what I'm doing."

Ayse looked back into the office and saw that Janet was dangerously close to touching Bard, her hand stuffed into her pocket like a child with a secret. "Janet, try not to touch the body."

Janet was defensive. "I wasn't! Ugh." She craned her neck around the corner to see closer. "What the hell is all this?"

Maureen looked at the six empty drawers and hung her head. "This is us. These are our files."

Sure enough, Ayse saw their names labeled on each drawer.

"Great! Just what we needed! More motive," Janet snapped.

A heavy CLUNK sounded, and the power surged back on. The fake tree in the corner blinked to life, and the office lamp made the reflections from the tinsel glitter. The sudden flood of everything turning on, beeping, blinking, and charging made each woman jump.

Janet sang out, *"Joy to the world! We are trapped in a murder!"*

Didi shrieked, "Janet, can you please stop singing? I really don't want every Christmas carol ruined!"

"Oh look, video surveillance," Sister Bridget blithely observed.

Ayse and Maureen both ran back to the outer office to see. Each of the four quadrants on the (now on) screen displayed *No Video Feed Available* over a square of blackness.

Maureen sighed. "I guess this has to be rebooted or something to get the cameras back online?"

"Maybe we can review the footage from last night?" Ayse asked. "There has to be a hard drive or something." She started looking around the screen for a cord to follow.

Cami asked, "You think the hard drive would be a black plastic square? Maybe the size of a small book?"

Ayse nodded. "Sounds about right."

Cami said in a quiet voice, "I don't think we are going to get much from it, then." She pointed to a drive of some kind whose wires ran up into the TV screen, but the drive itself was submerged in day-old coffee.

Russell sighed. "We're all in the cut now."

"The cut?" Sister Bridget asked.

Russell replied, "Security blind spots. Every prison has them, even when all the cameras are up."

Janet pulled the dripping hard drive from the coffee mug. "We have no cameras and no footage. The cut, indeed."

Ayse closed her eyes and tried to find a rational thought amid the Anxiety McFlurry that was her brain. "Let's start with the basics. All this shredding would take a long, long time to do. All night, maybe."

"So maybe Bard did the shredding?" Cami said.

Sister Bridget put her arm around Cami. "Oh, dear child, I doubt that."

Janet's bad mood was intensifying. "Can you stop saying hopeful stuff, Cami? It's really beginning to bug me."

Maureen wasn't having it, though, and said, in the tone of a stern babysitter, "Janet, that is not helpful."

Janet crossed her arms. "Well, neither is Cami."

"I think she's quite helpful, actually. Because an optimistic attitude will be necessary if we are going to work together," Maureen replied with more benevolence than Ayse felt was humanly possible.

Janet scoffed, but in that way only a defeated person can.

Russell cleared his throat almost as if to ask permission to speak, and when everyone turned to look at him, he nodded to Ayse. "She makes a good point."

Ayse pointed to herself. "I'm Ayse."

Russell smiled at the introduction. "Russell."

Janet sniffed. "We know," she said, which earned her another admonishing eye roll from Maureen.

Russell went on: "The power going on and off all night was a fluke. If someone from outside here had killed Bard, I don't think they would have waited around with a dead body to shred all those files. They would have left as soon as they could undetected."

Ayse looked closely at the body again. "Plus, there are only two key passes for the outside doors, and they are both there on Bard's utility belt. I doubt he died, reanimated, let the killer out, and then came back to restage the crime scene."

Didi's face was in her hands. "So we really have to accept that one of us killed him."

Russell nodded, but he didn't seem to get any pleasure out of it. "Makes the most sense. They could shred the paper when the power was on and sneak back into their cell when it was off. Only takes a few seconds to run back to that side of the building."

Ayse had returned to the sleeping quarters and was swirling the shredded paper with her foot. "Does all this shredding mean it was premeditated, or spur of the moment?"

"Why does that matter?" Cami asked.

Ayse shrugged. "I don't know. Could help identify the killer. Which of us has the ability to plan ahead? Who has impulse-control issues?"

"Why are you looking at me when you say 'impulse-control issues'?" Janet snapped impulsively.

"I wasn't!"

Janet put her hands on her ample hips. "You were! That's ageism! I'm the oldest person here, and now I have impulse issues?"

Didi shook her head. "No one said that! No one is saying that. We have to be a team. We have to really trust each other!"

Ayse pursed her lips. "Since when are you Miss Sisterhood? Every other comment out of your mouth is that you're better than me."

"That's not true!" Didi replied a little too fast.

Ayse laughed. "You literally *just* did it two minutes ago!"

Cami winced a little. "She's right, Didi. You did."

Janet's eyes were narrowed at Didi. "Why are you working so hard to be friends now? What are you hiding?"

Didi's eyes widened. "Hiding? I'm not hiding anything! You know me—you all know me. And you know I could never do that." She pointed to the corpse in the desk chair.

Ayse wasn't buying it. "Do we know that? Do we actually know you? Come to think of it, I don't know the first thing about you."

This pissed Didi off. "You know what—you're right. I'm not trying to convince *you* of anything, Ayse. You are an actual criminal. We all know it. *I'm* just a victim of circumstances."

Janet laughed. "Aw, Didi. Nice to see your denial isn't disturbed by *the prison you spend half your time in.*" She comically waved her arms in every direction, pointing to the thick cinder block walls around them.

Ayse was getting really heated, mentally and physically. The stress of it all had boiled up and over, and now she had a suitable target. "If you're such a victim, Didi, then why are you lying to everyone you know? Your friends think you're at a sleep study at UCLA, right? That's why you're gone every weekend? Yeah, I heard you lying to them when we cleaned the hospital parking lot. Then you, Ms. Innocent USA, went and—correct me if I'm wrong—hid in the bushes? Right? I might be a criminal, but I'm not a liar."

The flush on Didi's face had migrated from her shirt collar to her hairline. "Nice intimidation. Did you learn that from your friends in the Russian Mob? Yeah. I know about that."

Maureen stepped between Ayse and Didi. "Stop. Stop it, both of you. We don't have time for this. We have one shared goal, and every minute has to go towards achieving that."

"So what do we do?" Cami asked.

Maureen said, "We buy as much time as we can by acting normal."

Ayse willed her pulse to slow a bit, then said, "Yes. And 'normal' in this case means we head out as scheduled for the day's community service at the morgue."

Maureen nodded along. "Exactly. If we don't show up there, people will start asking questions we aren't ready to answer."

"How do you guys leave the facility for that, exactly?" Russell asked from the hallway.

Sister Bridget said, "We leave by the back doors and take the van. I drive. Everyone else sits in back, and they let us out the back gate when—" She gasped, suddenly realizing.

There was a tense pause.

"When what?" Russell asked.

Ayse answered, "When Bard scans his badge at the gate and the guard opens it from the observation deck."

Cami looked sick. "Oh God . . . how are we going to do that?"

"Could one of us dress up like Bard?" Didi wondered.

Maureen bit her lip. "It would leave us one person short in the van, though, if anyone was looking. A missing inmate would raise questions."

Didi pointed at Russell and said, in a tone that was a little too close to a command, "He can do it."

Russell took a big step back. "No. No no no. I'm really sorry y'all are in the shit, but I am not risking being tagged as an escapee. I stay here."

Didi crossed her arms and huffed. "Well, that's selfish."

Sister Bridget was on Russell's side, though. "We are supposed to leave the premises; he is supposed to stay on the premises. That's what's normal."

Ayse grimaced. "We need to bring Bard into the van with us. I normally sit behind him—maybe I can hold his arm out the window with the badge?"

Cami looked grossed out. "How do we get a dead man to hold a badge? Tape?"

Maureen scrunched up her face, problem solving. "Tape might be too visible. Didi, did you bring any hot-glue guns?"

Didi didn't seem to believe what they were discussing. Her mouth was so wide Ayse wondered if she had unhinged her jaw, and her voice was back to Peak-Panic Octave. "I'm sorry—Ayse's brilliant suggestion is we *Weekend at Bernie's* it? And you're all going along with this?"

"What's *Weekend at Bernie's*?" Cami asked Russell quietly.

Russell shrugged.

Sister Bridget looked closely at the body. "Could we cut a hole in the back of his coat—and, Ayse, you could put your arm through the sleeve; then you hold the badge."

Ayse nodded. "Yeah, his shoulders are broad enough, and the rain will make it hard to see. Especially if you pull the van right up close."

Sister Bridget gave a little salute. Mission accepted.

Didi's jaw was on the floor, and the tears had started again. "Is this seriously happening? We're going to puppet a dead man so we can go to a morgue so we can solve a murder? Is this a Mad Libs from hell?"

Maureen turned to Didi and held her shoulders, staring into her eyes. "Didi. Think about it. What else can we do? Play the tape to the end. We have to investigate on our own, right?"

Didi nodded, dazed, her tears stopping.

Maureen continued, her tone calm, "And for that, we need time, right?"

Didi nodded again. But now she was making eye contact with Maureen, her breath slowing.

Maureen smiled. "And that means we are off to the morgue, right?"

Didi took a deep breath. "Yes."

"Okay," Maureen said reassuringly.

Janet flicked Bard's finger, which didn't move. "Well, I've got—actually, I'm not sure if it's good news or if it's bad news."

"Weird news?" Cami offered.

Janet smiled at her, the tension from earlier forgotten. "Yeah. Weird news. This guy is stiff as a board."

"Rigor mortis," Didi explained in a quiet tone. "Nurse, remember?" she added through a sad little smile.

"When's he gonna loosen up?" Ayse asked.

Didi stuttered but her voice was clear, "Rigor mortis completely sets in about 7 hours after death."

Ayse said, "That tracks, if he was killed last night."

Sister Bridget looked at her watch. "Midnight, at the latest."

"It will start to fade in about twelve hours," Didi continued.

Janet flicked another rigid finger. "On the one hand, awkward to carry Officer Stiffy. On the other hand, a desk chair is a lot like a car seat, and it may help him look normal in the van."

Cami asked genuinely, "Define 'normal . . .'"

"Upright," Janet said matter-of-factly.

Maureen closed her eyes and put her arm around Didi, bracing her. "At some point, we have to take the vest off his face."

Everyone in the room recoiled.

"Not it," Cami said quietly.

And that started a cascade of "Not it!" from everyone else.

Ayse was mid-*Not* when everyone else had finished. "Ah, fine. I'm gonna open the top drawer again. I saw scissors."

She opened the drawer, and the gun sat there, among the office supplies, like it was just the world's most lethal stapler. For a wild millisecond, Ayse had the urge to pick it up, relishing the power it would afford her in the powerless scenario. She yearned for the comfort it would give her. But she knew that comfort would dissipate in seconds when every peer in this room became an open adversary. She took the scissors out and started to angle the bottom blade under the vest at the back center of his head.

"Wait," Russell said. "If there are prints or something, they'll be back there. Maybe cut on the side."

A good point was a good point, and Ayse instead cut along the ear line until the vest slowly slipped off and onto the floor.

Bard's contorted face was a mask of death, his swollen tongue jutting out of his mouth, skin mottled in an unholy shade of mauve. But his eyes were the most disturbing. His dark-brown eyes that had made him look like a movie star in life were now ringed with neon-red blood. Black pupils in orbs of crimson.

Ayse instinctively looked to Didi, who said, "Petechial hemorrhaging. A sign of—" Her voice caught for a moment. Then: "A sign of asphyxiation."

Ayse picked Bard's sunglasses off his desk and awkwardly slid them onto his face. "Guess Bard is wearing shades today." The frames rested at a tilted angle on his nose, making him look like a child playing dress-up. "Good enough."

Maureen said, "Has to be." She checked her watch. "We need to get going, or we'll be late."

As everyone went back to their quarters to get ready for the day, Maureen called out, "Everyone, remember to wear natural fibers for the morgue today."

Cami looked to Ayse. "Why?"

Ayse didn't have the heart to tell her just yet. "You'll see."

Fifteen minutes later, everyone was dressed, Sister Bridget in her never-changing habit and Maureen in a DNC T-shirt and sweats.

Didi exited her cell in jeans and a silk blouse. Off Maureen's questioning look, she responded defensively, "What? Cotton and silk!"

Ayse kept her eyes to herself. She couldn't really talk, as her own clothes were from a store literally called Quiet Luxury.

Janet exited her cell in one of her seemingly endless linen sets that she liked to mix and match. A-line in every direction, dyed to every shade of earth tone, plus purple, always fitting like a little tent with rough wooden buttons. Ayse had come to think of them as the hippie septuagenarian equivalents of Garanimals.

Noting that she was the last one ready, Janet cast about for someone else to take the group's attention. There was one obvious answer. "While we're at the morgue, what are we going to do with—" She jerked her head back toward Russell.

"He has a name," Cami shot back.

Janet crossed her arms. "I know he has a name."

Russell put his hands up. "Like I said, I'm not looking for trouble. While y'all are out, I'll stay in my cell."

"We can manually close his cell from the panel in the corner of the room," Maureen said with some hesitancy.

Cami was surprisingly huffy, her brows furrowed and her mouth pouty. "Why does he have to be in his cell, though? You'll stay in Pay to Stay, right? You aren't going to go anywhere?"

Ayse sighed. "Russell, you seem on the level, but right now we need to reduce variables. You being loose while we are out feels like a variable."

Cami revved up to defend him again, but Russell stopped her. "To be honest, my worry is someone comes by, and me being out of my cell looks suspect as hell." He turned to Cami. "I feel safer in my cell. I promise."

Janet wasn't done. "How do we make sure he stays in there, though? What if the power goes out again?"

Didi was at the ready. "I have something." She went into her cell and, after rummaging around her craft center, returned to the group with several half-inch wide zip ties.

Ayse was surprised. "You travel with flex-cuffs?"

Didi, irritated: "These are not flex-cuffs."

Ayse retorted, "Okay, they are extremely flex-cuff *coded.* Happy?"

Janet turned the zip ties over in her hands. "Didi, where were you on January sixth?"

Didi snatched the zip ties back. "See? This is why I don't help you."

Maureen stepped in the middle. "Guys, please. We really need to get going. Didi, thank you. I think this will be very helpful *for everyone's peace of mind*," she added in the tone of a not-angry-just-disappointed mommy that shut the bickering down.

As a show of cooperation, it was Russell who took the zip ties from Didi and walked toward his cell. Cami and Sister Bridget walked on either side of him as if to guard him from the judgment of others.

Russell tried to lighten the mood a little. "So, community service, huh?"

Cami frowned. "Yeah. Kind of a way to even the scales of only going to jail on the weekends. Highway cleanup, beach cleanup, road-kill cleanup. You get the picture. If it's gross, we do it."

Russell looked around. "Seems like a good trade, though." He smiled.

Sister Bridget said, "I'll lock you in when you're ready."

Russell went into his cell, and Cami slid the bars closed. She added the zip ties at the top and bottom.

Cami gave Russell a nod, and then Sister Bridget flipped the switch on the large panel on the wall labeled *Cell 5*. A heavy thunk resounded as the lock on Russell's cell latched.

The group gathered at the door of the rec room, about to leave, when Cami said, "Wait!"

She ran back to her cell as Didi called out, "We don't have time for this!"

Cami ran back out a second later and handed a small iPod to Russell. "We can't have our phones, but we can have these."

Russell started scrolling through the music. "Thank you."

Cami, flushing from her good deed, rejoined everyone in Bard's office.

Ayse took charge once again, pulling Bard's key card pass off his belt. "The red light over the back door is on, so that alarm is engaged. We'll use Bard's pass to let Sister Bridget out first so she can get the van. Once she's pulled up, we will come out with Bard."

Everyone nodded in unison like this was a football huddle and they had just chosen the winning play.

Didi slid Bard's coat on over one of his arms but not the other. Next she cut a hole in the back seam of the jacket for Ayse's arm.

Then the real work began.

Didi squared up behind the office chair. "All right, let's wheel him to the van."

Maureen let out a heavy sigh. "The chair won't fit through the doorframe. I remember when it arrived and Bard had to take the arms off to get it into the office."

Ayse nodded. "We have to carry him."

Didi: "Gross."

She and Janet both put their hands under Bard's knees, Ayse and Maureen tucked their hands under Bard's arms. In unison, they lifted the stiff body into the air and tipped it back so Cami could hold his head.

Maureen's face was pale. "Oh God, I heard fluid."

Janet said through clenched teeth, "If this man pees on me in death, I will lose my mind."

Didi said, "His bowels have already loosened in death."

Cami let out a childish, "Ewwwww."

Janet said, "You don't get to say *ew*. I'm the one touching his pants."

Ayse was looking ahead. "Okay, he seems narrow enough that if we get him through this office door, we should be in good shape."

The five women shuffled awkwardly around the desk, and Sister Bridget held the door open.

As they moved forward, Janet said, "Okay, lower half is through the door."

Ayse looked at the doorframe. "Maureen, we might need to tip him a bit to the side; otherwise we might catch."

"Oh good. Cadaver Jenga," Janet snarked.

They shuffled along the hallway and then got to the back door. Sister Bridget swiped the key card, and the red light changed to green, showing the alarm was disengaged. She opened the door, and Cami followed her, Bard's head still resting in her hands. The back door started to swing closed, and Janet shifted her position so the door would bash into Bard's ribs instead of her hand.

"What?" she said in response to their looks. "He's not gonna feel it."

Didi snorted. "Yeah, let's not desecrate the body by bonking his shoulder."

They all looked at Bard, frozen in a W shape, sunglasses hanging off his nose, bloodshot eyes staring out at them. Didi had a point: It was too late to play the "human dignity" card.

Just then, Sister Bridget pulled up in the van. She hopped out and opened the front passenger side door as the other women tipped Bard upright and slid him into the seat. The effect was bizarre, like a Barbie sitting in a chair for another brand doll. The angles all off, the knees too straight, the feet not touching the floor of the car, arms hovering over armrests.

Sister Bridget got back in the driver's seat and leaned over the body—which made everyone recoil a bit. After pulling his seat belt across him, she clicked his buckle into place. "Devil's in the details."

In this same spirit, Cami straightened his sunglasses and closed the passenger door.

Ayse took her seat behind Bard and slid her arm into the hole in the back of the jacket. Ayse had expected her skin to crawl being so close to him. Instead, she felt nothing but calm. The motionless meat that was his arm registered in her own body as an object incapable of harm. Bard's death was a blessing, and Ayse almost leaned in closer, her proximity to his corpse a balm to her worried mind. His threats toward her and her frail father were dead, just like him.

Sister Bridget drove to the gate, and Ayse waved the badge. If anyone anywhere would have looked closely, there was no way this would pass muster, but as per usual, the guard at the gate barely flicked a glance, instead glued to a football game on his iPad.

No one in the van spoke. No one moved. No one blinked. Sister Bridget slowly steered the white passenger van out of the lot.

"And we're off," Ayse said, "on an undead adventure."

Sister Bridget said, "Everyone say a prayer to Saint Joseph of Arimathea."

"Why him?" Didi asked from the third row of the van.

"He's the patron saint of grave robbers," Sister Bridget replied.

# CHAPTER 5

## Ayse Demiri: The Morgue

Halfway between Pay to Stay and the morgue, Sister Bridget pulled the van under one of Los Angeles's many freeway overpasses. Everyone looked around to make sure the coast was clear. With a sure-footedness fueled entirely by fear, the women were able to slide Bard out of his front seat.

Didi said quietly, "Pivot!" Then she looked at everyone else to see if they got the joke. "Remember on *Friends* when they move Ross's couch? 'Pivot'?"

Ayse had to try very hard not to bite Didi's head off. "Hey, Central Perk. Can we focus on the corpse we're currently holding in broad daylight?"

They pivoted and then maneuvered Bard into the rear cargo area, laying him down on his back, his arms and legs still frozen in office-chair angles from rigor mortis.

Cami said, "He looks like when my turtle died."

Ayse choked back a laugh. "Well, let's hope he smells better."

Cami shook her head. "He does not."

Ayse pulled a tarp over Bard and closed the door.

At first there was a flush of victory and some happy chatter, as they had successfully executed so much of their plan with nary a hiccup, but as they got closer to their destination, the women settled down again.

Finally, in the quiet, Maureen said, “I think we need a plan of action.”

Janet was confused. “What does that mean?” she said with derision.

Maureen replied, “Well, I guess I’m wondering if we can make this morgue shift work for us? You know—help us with our investigation.”

Janet snorted. “Oh, yeah, for sure. Let’s bring Bard in with us. Put him on the table. Open him up. Have a poke around. *What* are you talking about?”

Maureen was incredulous. “What are *you* talking about? I mean, like, are there supplies that we could maybe, you know, borrow? Gloves, smocks, those little booties.”

Janet backtracked. “Okay, that’s actually a good idea.”

“But we can’t ask for the stuff outright,” Maureen continued. “We have to play it cool. We can’t let Dr. Leclair suspect.”

Dr. Leclair was the morgue tech they worked under while completing their community service. While most of the other personnel were professional to the point of being aloof, Leclair seemed to enjoy having the inmates in his workspace. He had the energy of an awkward homeschool kid getting to join the local junior high field trip.

Ayse thought for a minute. “We need a distraction. Which one of us does he like the most?”

There was a beat while everyone came to the same answer, and Didi knew it. “Ugh, no! Why me?”

Dr. Leclair had a personality that could only be described as unctuous, and that unctuousness was uniformly directed at one person: Didi.

“He respects you,” Maureen cajoled her. “You have that whole Hippocratic oath thing in common.”

“So? Lots of people have that!”

Ayse added, “He used to work at the same hospital as you.”

Didi still pushed back. “Yeah, but I was on the operating floor while he was in the tombs of the basement!” When neither of these reasons gained traction, she pleaded, “Come on, I don’t want to talk to Dr. Leclair.”

Sister Bridget turned her head from the front seat. "Which do you want less: To talk to the morgue tech or to go to prison?"

Didi pouted like a child. "You owe me. You all owe me."

Sister Bridget pulled the van into the morgue parking lot, which looked exactly like any typical warehouse from the outside, with a loading dock complete with a shipping-and-receiving area. She parked the van in their regular spot at the end of the row of black-paneled coroner vans, this time opting to back in so Bard's trunk space was against the wall.

The group entered the morgue through the staff doors per usual. In some ways working at the morgue was the least stressful of their community service assignments. Everyone here was either a professional accustomed to crimes, or dead. This was a stark contrast from being stared at while doing community service in the public eye. Nevertheless, tensions were high. Ayse felt a physical pain across her chest with every breath, but she focused on keeping her face still. Her mind spun, looking for any aspect of this that was good, and mercifully it came in the form of a distracted guard, unknown to all of them, sitting at the check-in desk.

"Names and reason for visit," the guard said without an ounce of interest.

Ayse was ready, and repeated the phrase she had heard Bard say so many times. "We are here for our morgue shift on Level 1. Paperwork has already been filed with the city."

The guard looked at the six inmates in their orange safety vests. "Where is your CO?"

Ayse clocked the burst blood vessels on the guard's nose and the way his skin sagged around his face with telltale bloat, and she knew the answer that would satisfy him. "He's hungover as hell, sleeping it off in the van."

The guard nodded slowly. "I wish that could be me right now." From under his desk, he produced a large bottle of Pedialyte and took a deep swig. Apparently, the 28th of December meant the regular staff were on vacation, and that worked to the inmates' advantage. "All right, Level 1 is expecting you, yeah?"

Didi sighed. "Unfortunately." This earned her a jab in the ribs from Janet's elbow.

The guard buzzed them in, and the heavy metal double doors opened automatically. The women entered, took two lefts, then a right down identical fluorescent hallways, passing the freezer and the isolation units for what Leclair ungenerously called "the stinkers." At the end of the hallway was another set of double doors with *L-1* painted in bright yellow.

As soon as they entered the windowless room, every single one of them took a big deep inhale through their nose. Except for Cami, because this was her first trip to the morgue. Her previous weekends had been dedicated to roadkill cleanup and city park–litter collection. Cami had barely crossed the threshold when the odor knocked her back several feet.

"Oh my God, what IS that?" she shrieked.

Of course it smelled terrible, but everyone tensed at her outburst—they needed to lie as low as possible. Ayse dropped her voice so only Cami could hear her. "Yes, it smells horrendous, but there's no avoiding it. See how we are all taking deep breaths?"

Cami looked around. It was true. Each of the other women were breathing long dramatic breaths through their nose—in out, in out—as they gloved up and put on multiple hair covers.

Ayse continued, "The sooner your nose adjusts to the smell, the sooner your brain will stop registering it as—"

"A toxic hellscape we should flee from?" Cami cut in, her face green.

Ayse smiled. "Basically, yeah."

Cami was dutifully matching Ayse's breath. "Do you ever get used to it?"

Everyone answered in unison: "No."

Cami let out another "Ewwwww."

Ayse handed Cami several hair covers. "Put these on quick, unless you want the smell to get into your hair, too."

Cami was putting it together now. "And the natural fibers?"

Didi answered this time. "They hold the smell less than synthetic fibers. R.I.P. my tech fleece running set. It never recovered."

Two full walls were the stainless steel refrigeration crypts, stacked three high and nine across. A hoist loomed over them like a metal tree limb. This hoist was for moving bodies from storage to the work surface, and it was currently, mercifully, empty.

As they were snorting the stink in and out, the swinging doors opened and Dr. Leclair entered, pushing a gurney with a fresh corpse zipped up in a body bag. They called him Dr. LeClown behind his back because the man was quite literally a clown in his off hours, as evidenced by the startling number of framed photos he had of himself in his full clown regalia that he had hung around the exam room.

"Happy holidays, inmates!" Dr. Leclair said as he wheeled the body toward the center of the room. A ding chimed from the counter. "Oh, yay, my balls are sanitized," he enthused, snapping off his rubber gloves.

Leclair crossed over to another workstation. There was a three-quart container with a sous vide heating element clipped to the side, which made the water within come to a rolling boil. Leclair removed the heating element and then, with tongs, scooped up two metal balls about the size of tangerines out of the water. "New juggling balls for Christmas. My gift to myself."

He dropped the balls into a waiting ice bath.

Ayse wondered who this performance was for and why he had clearly timed it for their arrival. But she didn't care. He was in a good mood, and that was great for them.

Leclair pulled the metal balls out of the ice bath and started doing an elaborate routine of rolling them up and down his arms, around his wrists, and twirling them in his fingers.

Maureen gave Didi a pointed nudge forward, and Didi choked out, "Cool juggling."

Leclair gave her a smile that exposed every tooth in his head, even his molars, "It's not just juggling; it's *contact* juggling. Extremely different."

Didi nodded. "Oh, really? Wow." She was ready to stop, but a sharp look from Ayse made her keep talking. With difficulty, she managed to ask, "How so?"

Leclair was already repeating his routine, as clearly he had burned through his limited repertoire within the first fifteen seconds. "Well, I have to remain in contact with the objects at all times. It's also called *contact manipulation*. Sounds kind of . . . sexy, don't you think?"

Cami had to cough to cover up her laugh.

Janet asked, "When do you throw them?"

Leclair immediately ceased rolling the balls and stared at her. "Toss-juggling is for peasants. This is art, okay? I'm not a dog catching a Frisbee—I'm an artist."

Didi saw her opening. "Yeah, Janet. Can't you see how different this is?"

Leclair seemed to like that a lot, and saw an opening of his own, moving closer to Didi. "You know, Didi, if you want, I could teach you some basic moves."

Didi recoiled from his touch, but to her credit, she said, "I don't want to do anything in here by the . . ." She pointed to the cadaver behind them. "But maybe in the hallway?"

Leclair smiled. "Absolutely!"

As Didi led him out of the room, she gave her group a meaningful glance: *This is your chance.*

The second the doors closed, the five remaining women fanned out, opening every cupboard and drawer.

Maureen said quietly, "Remember, we need anything that could help us investigate what happened."

Cami held up some bagged sets of bodysuits and crime scene booties. "Maybe these to wear while we are in the office?"

Ayse nodded. "Definitely. Grab six."

"Seven," Cami corrected her. "One for Russell."

Ayse gave her a small smile. "Of course."

"Who has the biggest boobs?" Cami asked matter-of-factly.

Janet shot her a look. "What? Why?"

Cami pointed at the space below. "The bigger the boobs, the easier to hide stuff under them."

Ayse asked, "How do you know that?"

"Shoplifting," Cami said, shrugging. She looked from her own chest to Ayse's. "You have the biggest."

Ayse gave a thumbs-up in fake victory. "Winner, winner, chicken dinner. I'll zip up my jacket—cram stuff in there." Cami stuffed the vacuum-sealed packages down Ayse's front. Ayse gave them a little pat. "Okay, they'll stay. What else can we get?"

Sister Bridget had taken on the role of lookout and was peering through the window in the door. "You better hurry. Didi has dropped LeClown's balls several times, and he is getting upset."

Janet grabbed handfuls of swabs and evidence bags, stuffing them down her jacket.

Maureen was kneeling at a rolling kit and looking through drawer after drawer. Finally, she exclaimed, "Yes! Fingerprint stuff."

But before she could grab them, the doors swung back open, narrowly missing Sister Bridget's nose.

Leclair was tense and cradling his balls. "No, no, it's fine, Didi. These are just really expensive."

Luckily, he was too focused on buffing the metal orbs with a special cloth to notice that every other woman in the room had frozen like a raccoon caught in the garbage can.

Sister Bridget stepped forward to block his view of Maureen. "Dr. Leclair, I was praying about you this week."

"What? Why?" Leclair said, his face telegraphing his dislike of the idea.

Sister Bridget continued, at her most pious, "I was reflecting on how it feels to work in the morgue with you. God told me we are here to be the last voice for the dead."

Leclair, who at first seemed poised to recoil from her spirituality, suddenly softened. "That is exactly how I feel, Sister. People think just because my patients are already dead that I'm not a real doctor. But in some ways, I am even *more* of a doctor, specifically because I *can't* help them. I mean—I can't heal them, I can't kill them again. And because I have nothing to *do*"—he made exaggerated air quotes—"that's actually a good thing. My ego is totally removed from the care. Unlike some dumb brain surgeon, who is just ego ego ego all day."

Sister Bridget made the sign of the cross. "Absolutely. I myself have heard many deathbed confessions. What am I doing besides listening? Nothing, really. And yet these are powerful moments before meeting God." Ayse caught Sister Bridget's eye over Leclair's shoulder, and Ayse made a motion that said *Move him that way.* Sister Bridget gave a covert nod. "I'm curious—this gentleman over here . . ." Sister Bridget crossed over to the body on the exam table, with Leclair trailing behind her. "I wonder, did he have last rites?"

"Let's open him up!" Leclair said with relish, pulling the zipper down on the body bag, releasing a fresh stench into the air that made Cami woozy, forcing her to grip the nearest table.

Janet used the cover to grab gunshot-residue swabs, also stuffing those down Ayse's coat with Cami faux-casually standing in front of them, her hand still futilely trying to block the smell from her nose.

With Leclair, Sister Bridget examined the body, leaning closely over the man's forehead. "I don't see any smudge on his head. You know, I carry some with me at all times." She reached into her pocket and pulled out a tiny vial of sacred oil. "Oh Lord, let me anoint this man in Your name so the penitent can join you in heaven."

Just as her oiled thumb was about to touch the dead man's head, Leclair grabbed her wrist. "Firstly, I'm pagan. Secondly, that's against the law."

Sister put her hands up in mock surrender. "I will just pray for him, then."

With almost everyone's attention diverted, a movement caught Ayse's eye—Didi taking three drugs tests from a shelf and putting them in her pockets.

Maureen had joined them over the cadaver now, to keep Leclair's focus there and not on the scurrying women in his periphery. She pulled on the man's toe tag and grimaced. "BE FAST." Off Leclair's blank look, Maureen continued, "The signs of a stroke. *Balance, eyes, face, arms, speech, time*? No? Could save a life. Could have saved this man's life." She gave the toe tag a little flick.

Leclair clearly did not like that Maureen knew something he didn't, and huffed to his full height. "This man died roller-blading off the Santa Monica Pier. His stroke is part of his medical *history*; it is *not* his cause of death." At this, Leclair dramatically zipped the body bag back up.

The shared look between the six inmates conveyed a silent agreement: They had gotten as many supplies as they could, so it was time to move on. Ayse was all ready to get the mops out when Cami strolled over to the wall where there was a framed photo of Leclair on a movie set. In the picture, he was flanked by a man in a headset and a script rolled up in his hand. On the other side was a C-list actor whose one claim to fame was a sitcom from the '80s that had been entirely overshadowed by his #MeToo allegations and Twitter racism. Cami made her eyes go wide.

"Oh, wowwwwww, did you consult on a movie? What was that like?"

Ayse was a little confused. Cami was impressed by that pile of hair plugs? This was Los Angeles, after all. Ayse's dog groomer had more famous faces on her wall than that. So did her dry cleaner. Even her plumber had signed headshots in his little plumber van! A veritable who's who right next to the drain snake!

Leclair's chest puffed up. "Oh yeah. Big film. Huge budget."

Cami got within an inch of the photo, squinting to read the script title. "What movie was it? Can you tell me? Or is it a secret?"

Leclair smirked. "It was . . ." He paused for effect. "*Laceration Station.*"

Cami's eyes went wider. "No way! 1 or 2?"

"The first one. They couldn't meet my quote for part 2, and I am highly sought after. But that's why the quality went way down in the sequel. Gotta leave the money on the screen."

"Oh yes, one hundred percent. What did they ask you?"

Ayse watched in awe—she could feel Cami was in control of the conversation, but she didn't know where she was going with all this flattery. Meanwhile, Leclair waxed on and on. About how much the script had gotten wrong. How the writers had really needed him. He quoted a Reddit thread about the film. It was excruciatingly boring, and yet Cami was breathless.

Or was she *performing* breathlessness . . . ?

Because what woman isn't adept at this performance? At the faux-rapt attention. At the perfect feminine expression of little gasps, a well-timed "wow" and, the pièce de résistance, a demure giggle. She was an open-ocean fisherman reeling in a marlin using only feminine wiles. Ayse saw the other women were aware, too. They receded into the back of the room—stock-still, silent, not even exchanging glances.

Finally, Cami unveiled her point. "I had to cover my eyes during the barbershop murder."

He smirked once more. "Too gruesome for you?"

"After I saw it, I had to move my floating couch against a wall! I kept worrying someone would come up behind me! Can it really happen like that? Someone can smother you from behind, but you stay seated? Does the murderer have to be strong?"

"Oh, no. See, if the vic—*vic* is short for *victim*—is sitting, they can't get their feet under them to fight the attacker. Meanwhile, all the attacker has to do is sit, and their body weight does the work. Would only take a few minutes, the attacker is protected, and the vic has almost no chance."

"So someone small—like a woman—could kill a man?"

"Oh, sure."

"Like any of us?"

Leclair looked around, assessing each of them. "One hundred percent. No question."

The phone rang, and Leclair went to answer it.

Maureen was amazed. "What was that?"

Cami looked like she was coming out of a daze. "What was what?"

Ayse said, "All that information—that was incredible."

Then a dawning realization crossed Cami's face. "Oh, wait! That's how Bard died! I totally forgot! Do you think what Leclair said was helpful?"

Ayse felt the world right itself on its axis—this was the airhead they knew. Regardless, Cami had gotten solid information about the mechanism for murder, and from an expert source. Intention wasn't necessary when the results were so good.

At that moment, Leclair came back into the room, and Cami turned to him, all smiles. "So, which room are we mopping today?"

Leclair answered, "Room 4, down the hall on the left. Use double concentration of the cleaning fluid. We had a decomp come in—the smell is hideous. And, Didi, call me if you want another lesson." He whirled his metal balls back into his lab coat pocket and then wheeled his roller-blading victim into cold storage, closing the door behind him.

The blast of freezing air hit Ayse with a new thought. "Guys. When we get back to Pay to Stay . . . we need to put Bard in the freezer."

Janet sighed. "Oh good, more time with Cadaver Ken."

# CHAPTER 6

## Cami Garcia: A Plan in Motion

As they left the morgue, Cami took her spot in the last row of the van and leaned her forehead against the window. She still felt queasy from the smell, which seemed to have taken up permanent residence in her nose, and the cold glass pressed to her face gave her something else to focus on as Sister Bridget gently pulled out of the parking lot and back onto city streets.

Regardless of what the work detail of the day consisted of, the van rides to and from Pay to Stay always felt surreal as Cami watched from behind sealed windows as life outside in the wider world continued uninterrupted. It was especially uncanny today. Despite the tension within the van, and Bard bonking around in the back like poorly secured luggage, the hot spotlight of public attention was not on them in the slightest. People were enjoying the winter sun before the next storm hit tonight. They were riding bikes. They were carrying groceries. They were texting while leaning against a storefront. Normally, that felt almost insulting—as if the distress of being incarcerated was being dismissed by everyone they passed on the street—but today the anonymity was security.

*Rattle away, Bard. No one can hear you.*

The six women returned to Pay to Stay just as they had left. They restored Bard to the front seat under the same overpass. Ayse puppeted her arm through Bard's coat as the lifeless body, not a single guard taking a second look.

Cami was surprised to realize how little she felt for Bard being dead. In fact, her most honest reaction was relief. Even as they quickly carried him back inside—legs and arms stiff—she felt relief. Even as they pushed him into the walk-in freezer in the industrial kitchen, she felt relief. Even as she walked past Bard's empty office, where he had been brutally killed less than twenty-four hours ago, Cami again felt relief. It was a massage for her soul to know he wasn't sitting behind his desk, plotting like a giant spider. A quick U-turn in her thinking reminded her that Bard wasn't just gone, transferred to a new post far, far away. In fact, in many extremely obvious ways, Bard was a much bigger problem for her now. Nevertheless, the choice was either dealing with Bard the living person or dealing with Bard the murder victim, and she would choose the murder victim 100 percent of the time. No question. Murders end. Bullies were forever.

Cami entered the rec room and saw Russell sitting on his bed, eyes closed, still listening to her iPod. His knees were pulled up and his long arms were draped around his shins. A sliver of sunlight splashed across his face from the high window. He had a slight smile she hadn't seen, and his shoulders had relaxed from the tense height she was used to. He must have had the music blasting, because he didn't open his eyes when she used the control panel on the wall to manually unlock his cell door.

After she snipped the zip tie with some of Didi's craft scissors, Cami knocked on his bars, and he finally broke his focus.

"Oh, hey, you're back," he said. He took the earbuds out of his ears and delicately wound the cord into a small loop, twisting the ends into a soft knot to keep it tethered together. He held the iPod out to return it, but only met Cami's crossed arms.

"You keep it," she said.

Russell's response was almost put out. "No. I can't. Thank you."

"Why not?"

"They won't let me transport personal effects prison to prison. It'll get confiscated."

"So you have to give everything you own away every time you transfer?" Cami was scandalized.

"Yup."

Cami thought for a second then. "Okay, keep it for the days you're here, and I'll mail it to you once you get to your next location."

"You want to stay in touch with me?" Russell's brow was raised high in charmed disbelief.

"Of course. Why wouldn't I?"

He gestured to his blue DOC-issued shirt and pants as if to say *Did you forget who I am?*

In response, Cami gestured to the jail surrounding them as if to say *Did you forget where we are?*

Russell laughed. "Fair point."

Cami pointed to the iPod. "Besides, with that thing you're actually smiling now. Hopefully, that makes the other inmates relax one percent."

Janet had entered during this exchange and called out, "Not me. I have my eye on you, Washington."

Russell gave a salute. "I expect nothing less, Janet." Then Russell sniffed the air. "Oh my God. What is that smell?"

Cami frowned. "Me. Everyone is gonna try to shower the morgue off."

"Good idea," he said.

Cami picked up her shower caddy from her cell, complete with scrubs, creams, and conditioners. "Hey, Russell, feel free to borrow any products while you're here. No offense, but your skin is in dire need of hydration."

"Says the person who smells like literal death?" he snarked.

"Rude. True. See you in the kitchen for dinner? Twenty minutes?"

Russell nodded. "It's a date." Then his face fell in shock. "I mean—um, I don't know why I said that. It's not a date."

Cami laughed loudly. The juxtaposition of this alleged hardened criminal who was scared to say the word *date* cracked her up. She composed herself. "It's all good. See you there."

After a scalding-hot shower, and scrubbing the top five layers of her skin off with a terra-cotta paddle (cleansing ritual on-the-go!), Cami entered the kitchen absolutely starving. Russell came in a second behind her. Ayse, Janet, and Sister Bridget were already seated, eating their packed food from home. No one had been interested in lunch while smelling like decomp, and so dinner was eaten in ravenous silence.

Ayse was tucking in to a platter of lamb meatballs in a rich-looking tomato sauce.

Sister Bridget, pecking away at a sad casserole of indeterminant ingredients, sniffed the air. "Oh, wow, Ayse. Those look gorgeous."

Ayse smiled in a way that was uncharacteristic. "Thank you. My dad and I make them together."

Janet scowled. "I can't imagine eating meat. Barbaric."

Didi, who was sucking down a gray smoothie, added, "It's also terrible for the environment."

Ayse didn't miss a beat. "Well, that almond-milk smoothie you drink is one of the biggest water drains on the agricultural system. And, Janet, your soy patty is ninety percent chemicals. So you can both go choke." She ended this threat with a very big grin that pinged with DGAF energy.

Russell looked unnerved, but Cami waved them away. "They're always like this," she whispered.

Russell sheepishly grabbed his prison-supplied meal from the industrial fridge.

As per usual, Cami's mom had packed her more food than she could ever eat. She unpacked stacks and stacks of Tupperware containers. As she selected which combination was ideal for today, she noticed Russell unpacking his brown bag. He had an egg that had been hard boiled so long it had taken on a gray tinge. She saw something she hoped was oatmeal but could also have been putty to repair subway tile. There was a small square roll with not enough peanut butter to reach all the edges. Worse than any of this, though, was the shame on his face.

Cami didn't want to make a big thing of it, but she couldn't stand this; she slid silverware and a napkin toward Russell. Without eye contact, she opened several containers and divvied them up, with half going in front of him as well. After it was all done, she saw genuine excitement in his expression. She whispered, "Those two go together."

Russell took a bite of the first dish, careful to add a bit of spicy vinegar to his spoon per Cami's direction, and closed his eyes as the intense flavor hit him. "Holy hell, Cami. What is that?"

"Lechon—pork with crispy skin. And that vinegar is packed with bird's eye chilis. It's my mom's specialty, requested for every family holiday."

"It's incredible."

Cami smiled, loving his appreciation for her mother's skill. "I'm glad you like it, because there's five more Tupperwares where that came from."

Russell mock-braced himself for impact. "My body is ready." He ate a few more bites hungrily, and finally said, nearly breathless, "I can't explain it, but this tastes like my grandma's house on Christmas."

Cami shrugged. "I can't explain it, either. But here." She pushed the entire Tupperware of lechon in front of him. "It's yours. Merry Christmas."

Janet had watched all this, and when she couldn't help herself any longer, she blurted out, "We aren't supposed to share food with him."

Ayse rolled her eyes. "Oh, give it a rest, Janet."

Janet was huffy. "I'm just saying."

Ayse retorted, "And how are you gonna report her to Bard? Ouija board?"

Before the argument could begin in earnest, Maureen walked in, rolling a whiteboard. Didi let out a mock scream and pointed. "Oh no. The OfficeMaxxinista is here."

Maureen gave her a warm smile and a little Vanna White wave.

Sister Bridget coughed in surprise. "Where did you find that?"

"It was in Bard's office. I don't think my drawing is to scale, but this is the crime scene." She turned the board so they could see the front. It was, in fact, an impressively detailed aerial view of Bard's office, sleeping quarters, and private bathroom. She had used colored tape to divide the room into smaller portions. Maureen couldn't help admiring her handiwork. "I think having a plan for the morgue went really well—"

Didi interjected, still irritated, "You're welcome, everyone!"

Maureen replied with genuine gratitude, "Yes, thank you, Didi. That was a huge help, and crucial to our success. So I want to keep up that focus as we turn our attention towards the investigation here."

Ayse couldn't help herself. "Are you running for mayor of this murder?"

Cami bit back a laugh.

Maureen was undeterred. "Look at the facts: We have a Popsicle for a CO and a ticking clock. We need to be strategic. I have seen great candidates with solid policies lose because they didn't have a plan, they didn't spend their resources well. I am not going to prison because some of you have executive function issues."

Janet huffed. "Once again, I feel like you're looking at me."

Maureen said, "Not at all. What I *am* saying is, we each have strengths and I want to make sure we're using them to ensure the best outcome for all of us." This little pep talk was met with silence. "So, who has a strength?" More silence. Maureen struggled to shellac her exasperation in a sheen of enthusiasm. "Don't all shout them at once."

Didi raised her hand slightly. "So this one summer, before I met my husband, who is on the board—"

Everyone yelled, "We know!"

She continued, "I was working nights at the hospital, and the TV in the nurses' lounge was stuck on a single channel. Between Memorial Day and Labor Day, I watched maybe seven hundred hours of *Forensic Files*.

Lemme tell you, a case is made by what's bagged and tagged. I think I could inventory the evidence—I know what to look for and how to bag it."

Maureen's smile was huge. "Didi, yes! Excellent."

Didi's confidence sank down again. "But I am not the most organized person. Once stuff was *bagged,* I would need help with the *tag.*"

Maureen said, "If I can track voters who love the Affordable Care Act but hate Obamacare, I can keep track of little baggies."

Crickets from the crowd.

"Get it? Because those are the same thing? No one? Okay, fine." Maureen turned back to her whiteboard, a little embarrassed. "I've already broken the room down into smaller sections for ease of investigation. We can make a search grid. We can create a chart. We got this. Fantastic. What else can we do?"

Ayse said, "Just in case anyone is checking on us, I think it's important that we keep up appearances. We should do the outside maintenance tomorrow as scheduled. I'm cool under pressure, so I can spend the day acting normal while police come and go from the rest of the area."

Janet nodded. "I can help with that. Besides, Nacho is going to need some outside time in the sun. Otherwise, his scales start molting."

Cami wondered what was the best way to play her card, and decided on stealth. "Russell had a great idea."

Maureen tried to hide the surprise in her voice, but it slipped out. "Oh?"

Cami could feel Russell's posture stiffen, but she pushed on. "We have all those shredded files, yeah? The killer must have been trying to hide something in their own file and tried to divert attention by shredding everything."

Janet wasn't impressed. "Waiting to hear something we didn't already know."

"Russell noticed that the file *folders* weren't shredded, and they still had the staples."

Ayse was trying to follow. "What do the staples mean?"

Cami said, "Russell thought if paper is still stuck in the staples, we can use it to help sort the pages. Not everyone's paperwork is the same—different-color paper, some photos, maybe even some sheets from a legal pad. Isn't that what you said?"

Russell was too stunned to respond, a spoonful of lechon halfway to his mouth completely forgotten midair.

Cami gave everyone a giant smile. "I mean, maybe we can't find every paper perfectly, but we just need to find whatever the killer was trying to hide. And Russell's plan gives us a place to start."

Maureen was impressed. "Absolutely. You two go work on that."

Sister Bridget added, "My eyes are too old for files, and I don't have the knack for organization. I'll help Ayse and Janet outside."

As Maureen wrote everyone's name along the edge of the whiteboard and their respective jobs, Cami grabbed the food she and Russell had been eating and led a still-stunned Russell back to her cell.

"You finish eating," Cami said. "I'll bring the files in here."

It took three trips with the tall garbage can to get all the shredded ribbons of paper from Bard's office back to Cami's cell.

She laid the file folders themselves open on her bed and, using tweezers from her beauty kit, slowly loosened each staple in each folder, then delicately separated the papers caught within the points and the crown. Cami then methodically taped each tiny scrap down to the folder using clear tape. It almost looked like a botanist's collection from a day's work, except instead of butterfly wings or fungi specimen in a microscope slide, it was various levels of paper and photos and yellow legal pad notes.

Cami then studied the folders themselves, pointing. "Janet's and Didi's both have coffee stains on the edges of the folders. I wonder if the pages inside have coffee on them, too." She held out the stained manila folders for him to examine.

Russell wasn't looking at the paper, though. He was looking right at Cami. "Why did you do that?"

"Do what?"

"Why did you say this staple thing was my idea? It wasn't. It was yours."

Cami shrugged. "I want them to like you."

Russell was not thrown off in the slightest, and his eyes didn't move from her face, "Don't get me wrong, I like that answer—but that's not the truth."

Cami felt a little heat at the back of her neck, and she doubled down on examining the folders, hoping he would move on to another topic.

Russell paused and then said quietly, in the soft tone he had used before when they found the body, "Why don't you want anyone to know you're smart?"

Cami's breath caught in her chest. Her mind raced through a series of moments—the lawyer telling her to lean in to her apparent lack of knowledge, her mother not understanding her priorities just two days prior, and then back even further to her grandfather's funeral. How each of those moments had made her keenly, painfully aware of the chasm between her real self and everyone else.

Cami had a rush of clarity that this conversation with Russell was an invitation to be honest for once, with no repercussions. Like telling a priest or a therapist. He wasn't sworn to secrecy, but he also didn't have any connection to her real life, making this the perfect test for what had only been an idea for so long. If she declined this moment to share, she would regret it. So, for the first time, she told the story that had rattled around her head every single day for decades.

"When I was seven years old, my grandfather died. We had a big, big funeral; the entire family was there. Even two of his brothers flew in from the Philippines. The service had felt endless, so afterwards me and my cousins were all wound up—just rambunctious as hell. I was running forward while looking back over my shoulder when I ran directly into a table of cut fruit and puffed rice all meant to top the halo-halo. The entire bowl smashed into my new shirt, fruit all in my hair. Totally disgusting. So I go find my mom. She was so stressed by grief that once she saw me, she was ready to unleash a tirade. She hadn't even started talking yet, and I was already wincing. Then, all of a sudden, my grandmother, my Lola, said to her, 'You can't be upset. Cami is just how she is. Head always in the clouds.' Then my auntie yelled out, 'She's a ditz, Mama.'

"I can still remember my Lola's face so clearly—she was shocked by the word, and then suddenly she started laughing. She laughed until tears squeezed from her eyes. And then my auntie started laughing. And an uncle. And soon even my mom was laughing. It was like a magic trick. The funeral shifted from silent sadness to a joyful celebration. I mimed running into everything in the room. Every time I collided with a side table, or the piano, or even my auntie's legs, everyone laughed and laughed. I was the ditz. The little clown. The silly girl who was never looking the right way."

"And the role stuck," Russell said.

It wasn't a question.

Cami nodded. "I've been the family ditz ever since. As the years passed, anything counter to that narrative was dismissed. When I got good grades, they said it was a fluke or the teacher was grading me easy. Any smart observation I made was attributed to someone else. While my cousins became teachers, or engineers, or even a famous police detective, I meandered along. It was so weird—the more I flailed through life, the more they loved me. Like I was fulfilling a prophecy or something. For them, my inability to achieve confirmed their intelligence. To push back on this idea was to insult them, hurt them." Cami sighed. "At some point I gave in. I started to dress the part, act the part, shed any and all qualities that did not meet the role of the Family Ditz."

Russell nodded in recognition. "Nice to meet you, Ditz. I'm the Bad Kid." He tried to toss off the words, but there was an edge of devastation he couldn't soften.

Cami felt her heart break as soon as he said it. "When was the first time someone called you that?"

Russell thought for a minute, the man in front of her melting back into a little boy. "Second grade. Once that teacher said it—'you're a bad kid'—they passed it along to the third-grade teacher. And the third-grade teacher told the fourth-grade teacher. On and on. They had me pegged as a problem before I even stepped through the door. Watched every second, called out for the smallest mistake. Never mattered if I wasn't the only one or if it wasn't even me. At a certain point, I thought if I'm already being punished for 'being bad,' I might as well be bad." He shrugged. "It made sense at the time."

Cami asked a question so bold she didn't even know where it had come from, but she had to know. "Did you believe them? Did you believe what they said about you?"

Russell didn't respond right away; then he said thoughtfully, "For a while, yeah. I mean, every adult said it, so it had to be true, right? By the time I realized I wasn't actually bad, it was too late." He gestured to his prison uniform. "What about you?"

Cami nodded. "Same. Now it feels like a sweater that's on too tight. Or like I'm waking up after sleeping in a weird position. I can't stay here, but I don't know how to change without my life being turned upside down. Does that make sense?"

Russell smiled. "Yes. Perfect sense."

During this whole exchange, they had continued sorting the slips of paper into sections by color. They hadn't needed to say it aloud, the task had just started naturally, their hands working in a familiar tandem.

Cami picked up a shred, but instead of the eleven-inch slip she was used to, a short, mottled bit of green came out.

Cami looked closer. "Does this look like money?"

Russel took the shred and felt it in between his fingers. "Definitely."

Cami's memory snapped back, "Wait. Wait wait wait." She opened Janet's file and saw, taped to the card stock, a tiny shred of a bill taped in the row. Her eyes lit up and met Russell's.

They started sorting with quiet focus until they found five strips. They lined them up to complete a $20 bill with the words *ASK JANET ABOUT MARCELLO* written on it in red Sharpie.

Cami gently taped the bill together, then said with authority, "Find anything with a coffee stain."

Russell nodded and began sorting, handing Cami anything with the recognizable brown hue.

Cami took what he handed her and then separated them again into piles of paper that was pure white, off white, and then most notably yellow legal pad.

After nearly fifteen minutes, Cami had a tight bundle of the legal pad shreds, Bard's handwriting chopped to bits but easily identifiable.

The other five inmates had finished with dinner, and were milling about the rec room and their cells.

Cami asked the group, "Where's Janet?"

Janet popped her head out from behind her mandala curtain, "I'm here."

Cami held out the twenty-dollar bill and saw a mix of recognition and dread on Janet's face. Then she passed the bill to Maureen, who in turn passed it along to Ayse. Sister Bridget and Didi caught a peek as well. None of them looked happy.

Janet stood, arms crossed. Instead of denying it, she had clearly decided to go on the offensive. "What? Spit it out. What do you think?"

Maureen was even, her face soft with care, "I think that's the whole thing—we don't know what to think."

Ayse's jaw was set, ready for an argument. "Can we skip the eight rounds of denial or deflection or whatever the hell yuppies are calling it now, and just spit it out?"

Didi chimed in, "Yeah, this isn't a gym membership you're trying to get out of."

Janet's mouth was set in a tight line. "Why does it even matter what I say? I could just lie. You won't know. Marcello is my boyfriend." Ayse's eyebrows went up at that. "Marcello is my lawyer. Marcello is my—my—my . . ." Janet searched for another role a man could play in her life, but nothing came.

"Wow. Boyfriend and lawyer, and you're tapped out of lies?" Ayse snarked.

Cami held up the bundle of shredded yellow legal pad like it was the worst bouquet of flowers ever selected. "We have Bard's notes from your file, and we are going to assemble them. So if you lie, we will know sooner or later."

Janet huffed. "And here comes Cami, of all people, with a loyalty test. Real nice."

Cami was stung. "What's that supposed to mean?"

Janet pointed at Russell. "Just saying, you really know how to pick 'em. Maureen knows."

Maureen was gentle but firm. "Please, Janet. Stop. We don't have time for dramatics. If you want us to rule you out, for us to know that you didn't have an extra level of motive, you need to tell us the truth."

Janet's mouth became an even sterner line. "Well that's the problem. This story is going to make you definitely think I did it."

"We can decide that for ourselves," Maureen continued in her kind tone.

There was a long beat as Janet seemed to be weighing her options. Finally, she sighed in defeat. "Marcello was my neighbor. I moved to Highland Park on the east side. It was the only place I could afford a house. And in my new neighborhood, everyone hated me on sight. They thought I was a gentrifier—can you believe that?"

Everyone muttered some version of "Yes," "Absolutely," or "One hundred percent."

Janet's frustration surged. "It wasn't like I personally foreclosed on the little *abuela*! But suddenly I was the mean white lady who had ruined the neighborhood. They called me *Brote*, because I was the *Outbreak* monkey. They said first it was me, and next it was going to be angular gray condos with orange accents, and then finally an Erewhon. What's the problem with that? Erewhon is an extremely nice grocery store!"

"Aren't their smoothies like forty dollars?" Didi asked.

Ayse rolled her eyes. "Didi! You were literally just drinking one of their smoothies!"

Didi waved Ayse away and said, without an ounce of shame, "Yeah, but I bought it in Beverly Grove. That's flagship, baby."

Maureen cut across them, prodding, "Janet, please continue."

Janet closed her eyes, recalling the memory. "So in an effort to save the neighborhood, I burned some stores down. Anything that my neighbors complained about, or didn't like, or had pushed out a mom-and-pop, I torched it."

Cami had a flicker of recognition. "I remember reading about this! You didn't just burn stores—didn't you also lock raccoons in a restaurant?"

Janet nodded. "And ran hoses through HVACs. And smeared patios with manure."

Ayse was shocked. "Why?"

Janet cried, "So my neighbors would like me, okay! You may be shocked to hear this, but I've never had a lot of close friends. I even got kicked out of a cult once." (No one was shocked.) "And I wanted to be a part of this community. I wanted to help protect what they said I was going to ruin."

Cami remembered too much of the story to buy the spin outright. "But the neighborhood *hated* you. There was a crowdfunded reward for your arrest!"

Janet nodded, ashamed. "It all backfired. So many angry people called in that the DA had to set up a dedicated tip line. There was a waitlist of aggrieved victims who wanted to testify against me."

Maureen was trying to put the pieces together. "But that would all be in your arrest file. What are all these notes by Bard? Who is Marcello?"

Janet's shame was palpable now, and big tears streaked down her cheeks. "Once they caught me, I was going to go to prison for a long time. I was scared out of my mind. The DA demanded something really good to justify me going to Pay to Stay. Well, not *something*; they wanted some*one*. So I offered up my neighbor. He was into all kinds of off-the-books deals, but mostly illegal animal trade. Black market stuff, high end. I told the DA when he was home, when I saw suspicious trucks or cars on the block. They arrested him, and I got to come here."

Maureen was still looking at the twenty-dollar bill. "And this money?"

Janet pursed her lips. She did not want to go on, but she knew she had no choice. "My tip about Marcello was listed as anonymous. The neighborhood was furious when he was arrested. So I stepped in. I organized a fundraiser to help pay for a good lawyer. I got fifteen piñatas and booked food trucks. We set up misters for the elderly. A *musica norteña* band played. People stayed out all night, enjoying themselves. Everyone told me it was the best block party they had ever been to, that it felt like old times. It was incredible." She smiled at the memory in spite of herself.

Ayse gasped. "You got him arrested, and then you used his arrest to make the neighborhood love you?"

Janet nodded.

Maureen's eyes were closed in frustration. "You asked me how to set up a tax-free account. Is that what it was for?"

"I told you!" Janet protested.

Maureen shook her head. "No you didn't. You said it was for legal aid."

"Ugh, yes, legal aid for the man who I happened to trade for my own freedom. Are you happy now? Happy I said it?"

Ayse took the bill from Maureen and turned it over in her hand. "Let me guess: Bard found out you were throwing the fundraiser and he showed up."

Janet nodded. Her defensive attitude was obliterated and replaced with desperation. "I still don't know how he knew. I was so careful."

Ayse took a deep breath. "Tell us what happened at the block party." Her voice was full of an emotion she had never shown in these walls before: compassion.

Janet nodded, then bit her lip so hard Cami expected blood to run down her chin. Finally, Janet whispered, "Bard threatened to put this twenty-dollar bill in the collection pot. He told me he controlled my whole life. Not just when I was inside these walls. Not just for the duration of my sentence. He told me he was going to be everywhere forever. I would never escape him. He told me I belonged to him. He even wrote a little note on my transfer letter." She pulled the note from her pocket and showed it to the group. It read *I own you.*

Cami said, "So you did have more motive than the rest of us. It's true. Did anyone else get a Post-it on their transfer?" She looked around at the group, expecting nods of agreement. Instead, no one met her eyes. It was as if they were all five hundred miles away in their own minds. Cami pushed again. "These notes could be a clue about motive. This seems important to hash out, no?"

But Ayse said, "It's lights out in an hour. We should all get ready for bed."

No one spoke much after Janet's revelation. The other five women were lost in their brooding thoughts, and Cami wished she could beam inside and see what was preoccupying all of them in this sudden coordinated silence. What had become clear was that Janet did have one hell of a motive, and instead of everyone else pressing her for as much information as possible, they had let it be. Cami could not understand why they were all happy to abandon their one and only lead. This disconnect made her feel an overwhelming loneliness, like she was a ghost and any attempt to communicate with them was met with silence as they walked right through her.

Cami returned from the bathroom, her toiletry bag tucked under her arm. Everyone else was in bed already, or at least tucked away in their cells behind their curtains. Cami passed her own cell and went to

Russell's, driven by her emotional isolation, which was starting to feel like a chill she couldn't shake.

"Hey, Russell?" Cami asked. He looked up. "Would you mind sleeping in my cell tonight? I could help you drag your mattress in. There's enough space on the floor, and my rug is really squishy."

Russell looked at her, confused. "You want me to sleep in your cell?" His voice was thc dcfinition of *incredulous*.

Cami shrugged. "Is that so weird?"

He chuckled. "Um, yes. Extremely weird."

Her feelings were hurt. "Never mind."

Russell sat up. "Hey, I'm sorry."

She turned to go. "Forget I said anything."

"No, please don't go. Cami, come on." He almost put his hand on her arm, but he pulled it back, something close to regret on his face. But regret for what, exactly, she didn't know. "I guess it just feels weird to be trusted from the jump. I'm the bad kid, remember?"

Cami scuffed her slipper on the linoleum floor. "Yeah, well, this ditz doesn't like to be laughed at."

Russell's face dropped. "I'm sorry. I didn't mean it like that." He stood up. "Let me grab my stuff."

A few minutes later Russell was settled in on his mattress, on Cami's floor, with his outstretched hand petting the furry white carpet underneath him. "I feel like I'm sleeping with a yeti," he joked.

Cami smiled and turned on her forest sounds. "Good night, Russell."

"Good night, Cami."

Right on schedule, the lights all over the building went out for the night.

# DAY 3

DECEMBER 29

# CHAPTER 7

## Cami Garcia: The Nightmare Continues

Cami's sleep was restless, her dreams tugging her in and out of consciousness, with neither stage feeling anything close to rest. This wasn't new. Cami was one of the unlucky ones who both dreamed every night of her life and always remembered her dreams down to the smallest detail. She yearned for a night of time travel—where she woke up with no memory of the passing hours. For a while, to try to understand why her mind was so busy even when unconscious, she had studied dreams. She learned about REM sleep. She learned about what dreams had meant at different times, in different cultures. She was able to identify the waking dreams that her cousin had unhelpfully called "when the devil is sitting on your chest." Her knowledge was encyclopedic, but it never achieved her goal: a quiet night.

Making dire matters worse, since childhood until now, Cami would estimate that well more than half her dreams were nightmares. They were all so vivid, and often violent, that friends and family had all at some point pleaded with her to not report them to the group in the morning. She just had to hold them in, all on her own, wondering why her own interior world was so dangerous.

In an effort to quell these endless nightmares, Cami had learned a technique called *lucid dreaming*. When a dream started to take a turn toward terror, Cami would try to do something concrete like read a sign or look at her watch. Normally, the logical part of her brain would struggle as the numbers slid off the watch face, or the letters were backward. This was enough of a clue to her unconscious mind that she was in a dream and she was in control of what happened next, saving her from walking into the murder cabin or going up the rapidly thinning ladder to nowhere.

It was no use tonight, though. Her dreams were unformed and stressful, with no clear edge between waking and sleeping. She was lost in a dark room with no exit but also no direction. She couldn't see a watch or find a pen to write her name. Her only choice was to sit down and try to will herself awake. Instead, the floor turned to sand and she slid deeper into nowhere.

When she finally woke up, late and groggy, Russell's bed was empty, his sheets and blankets folded neatly on top of his mattress, which he had rolled up tightly into a compact coil. Before she could even wonder where he was, Russell walked back into the rec room, freshly showered.

"Having a bathroom all to myself is heaven," Russell said, and Cami was happy to see he had taken her up on her shower caddy offer. He placed it precisely back where she had left it, not a loofah out of place. "Ready for breakfast?" he asked with a fresh pep in his step.

Cami wanted to share in his positive mood, but breakfast was just as strange as bedtime the night before, and Cami couldn't stand it. She was prepared for the usual sniping from the viper pit. Instead, what she found was so much worse. They were all being extremely nice! What the hell? She didn't necessarily miss the snarky remarks that Ayse, Didi, and Janet seemed compelled to hurl at each other, but this uniform politeness set her teeth on edge.

"Nice that no one was murdered in their bed!" Janet chirped.

"I don't think that's funny," Maureen said as she rinsed her dishes in the sink, but the smile twitching the corners of her mouth said otherwise. Janet tossed a retaliatory pinch of Sugar in the Raw in Maureen's direction, but Maureen playfully ducked out into the hallway.

Ayse shrugged and said, "Pretty sure Bard's murder was a one-off. And a public service, if you ask me."

Didi raised her matcha. "Hear, hear." They clinked coffee mugs.

Russell and Sister Bridget took a seat at the same time. He gave her a warm smile. "Good morning."

"Good morning, Russell," she said as she tucked into a tiny lemon-flavored yogurt.

"No grace?" he asked. Sister Bridget looked up, confused, so Russell repeated himself, in the same jovial tone but with added clarification, "No grace before breakfast?"

Sister Bridget's eyes twinkled with mischief. "Sometimes I just say it in my head while I sit down."

Janet put her hands up. "Uh-oh. We have a renegade nun on our hands."

The group shared a laugh that was genuine and wholly unexpected. Whatever had cracked open for the other inmates last night had re-formed into a camaraderie that was unlike anything Cami had seen in the previous weeks. Going along with this was so very tempting, but she couldn't make herself. She saw this happy mood as a sign that everyone's guard was down, so she casually asked, "I feel like things have been different since last night. What were you all thinking about?"

Janet gave a comical pout. "I don't call Sister Bridget a Christofascist one time and now we're best friends? My ethical dogma is stronger than that."

Didi put a hooked finger to her lips like she was Sherlock Holmes with his signature pipe. "Very suspicious, Janet. Where is your Lefty moral outrage?"

Janet checked her nonexistent pockets. "Oh no! I left it at the antifa clubhouse!"

Didi's eyebrows went up. "You mean the cardboard box behind Trader Joe's?"

Both Janet and Didi started cracking up at this.

Ayse gave Cami a friendly nudge. "Cami, great job with the twenty-dollar bill, but let's not start seeing conspiracies everywhere we look."

Cami opened her mouth to protest; this wasn't a conspiracy—it was a fact that one of them was a murderer! But before she could, Maureen walked into the kitchen wearing head-to-toe protective gear for collecting evidence. "Good morning, fellow inmates!" As she did a fake bow, her hairnet fell off, and this started another peal of laughter.

Ayse pointed. "Tracy Flick, your hairnet fell."

At this, Ayse, Didi, Janet, Sister Bridget, and Maureen all fell out laughing. Even Russell was chuckling along. And Cami felt absolutely certifiably detached from reality. What was this bizarro world where suddenly everyone was besties? In the previous weekends Cami had spent here, these women had barely looked at each other and were vicious when forced into even the most banal interactions, like passing in the hallway or breathing the same air. Suddenly it was an episode of a sitcom where everyone was quirky cute, with funky backstories and kicky inside jokes.

Ayse (Ayse!) had shoe booties on her hands and was making them talk like puppets. "Stop in the name of *CSI: Muppets*!"

Everyone else laughed uncontrollably, taking turns putting on the hairnet.

Cami pressed, "I just feel like something has shifted and we should talk about it." But only Maureen heard her.

Maureen put her hand on Cami's arm and said quietly, "This is good, Cami. We need to be on the same side to get through this. Don't question it." With that, Maureen stood up, the picture of efficiency, and said to the group, "All right, everyone! Off to our stations for the day!"

Cami felt a hot rush of embarrassment that was all too familiar. How many times had she had a good idea, only to be rudely dismissed by others? How often had she seen a situation accurately, only to be told to stop making a fuss? She knew she was right, but in order to push her point, she would be forced to throw off the role of the unserious girl that had offered her so much cover for so long. She was disappointed to realize she was too scared to go through with it, clinging to the protection it offered her. So instead, she smiled her big glossy-lipped smile and chirpily cleared away breakfast, while inside she absolutely seethed.

*Something is off.*

At the door to the kitchen, Russell asked, with an unexpected amount of enthusiasm, "Ready for more paper?"

Cami topped off their coffees and said, "Ain't nothing to it but to do it."

When Cami reentered her cell, though, Russell was giving her that look again.

"What?" she asked, all smiles and bashful lashes.

"What did you want to say back there?" he asked. "I saw that shadow over your eyes."

Cami playfully swatted at him and turned her attention toward the paper. It was hard to meet his gaze. Cami was used to men staring at her, and their greed to flatten her into an object for their desire allowed her to detach from them entirely. But recently she had experienced two new extremes. First, Bard's gaze had made every cell of her being want to run for safety. And now, Russell's attentions made her feel deeply seen on an emotional level, which was, in fact, worse by a factor of fifty. She regretted telling him about her role as the family ditz. If this was what life would be like after shedding that persona completely? No thank you. Count her out. That was intolerable. She'd rather stay on her side of the chasm, alone and separate.

But it was too late here and now, so at long last, Cami answered him. "Something feels so different to me after Janet's story. Everyone is being bizarre. These women were at each other's throats last week, and now they're doing bootie puppets?"

Russell nodded. "Yeah, I felt that change."

"Thank you! But they all gaslight me, like, 'Oh, no, we've all always been fine, you're crazy.' I don't get it!" Cami turned on him. "And you!"

He pointed at himself, smiling in a disarming way. "Who, me?"

"Yes! Why were you laughing back there?"

"I know that you've only been here in Pay to Stay, but in real prison, you gotta match the energy of the room. You gotta go along like a drop of water in the river."

"So your idea is to blend in with a murderer?"

Russell nodded. "Yeah, that's kind of the whole deal with prison. You think I'm locked up with people who had too many parking tickets?"

"Oh. Yeah," Cami said in a small voice.

"For what it's worth, I think you're right—something is going on. But instead of coming at it directly, let people relax. Let them forget what's at stake. See what you see when their guard is down a bit." Cami scoffed at this, but Russell pressed. "Listen to me, Cami. I'm serious. One of those women is a killer. Don't make yourself their adversary. Don't stand tall, because that's the blade of grass that gets cut."

She felt the weight of his words in her stomach. "Okay. So we play this calm. We play this controlled."

"Not only that, but I think we don't tell anyone anything we find in these pages until we have something concrete. No conjecture. Conjecture causes chaos, and chaos is one step closer to violence."

Cami took this in. She could see the logic.

Russell looked genuinely concerned. "This seems like the safest way to—"

"To find the killer?"

"To make it out of here alive," Russell replied, gently correcting.

Cami felt uncomfortable at the thought. "You don't think someone else could get killed, do you?"

He shrugged. "You wanna die to find out?"

In an unspoken agreement, they turned back to the task at hand. After a few minutes, Russell held up a ribbon of paper. "Hm. No writing on this one. Looks more like an image."

Cami looked. "Yeah, and the paper is glossy. Must be a photo?" She noticed a color bar at the bottom. "Maybe this could help—it's from the printer when it's running out of ink."

"Wow, printers have come a long way since I was outside."

Cami scoffed. "They really haven't." Then, looking: "Wait, this is from another photo?"

Russell held up another strip. "This one, too. The colors are totally different."

They slowly gathered all the shreds of images into a pile. "Picture is worth a thousand words, am I right?" Cami said.

Russell laughed. "If it saves us from this pile of confetti, I'll up it to two thousand."

Cami started by laying each shred flat on the ground of her cell. But no discernible pattern emerged. Cami bit the inside of her lip. "Let's assume each photo is five inches by seven inches. If each strip is a quarter-inch wide, that means we have twenty, maybe twenty-two vertical strips per photo. Feels frustrating but doable."

Russell pulled edges of photos that had both part of an image but also part of the blank margin on them. "When you do a puzzle, you begin at the corners, so we should do the same, yeah?"

Cami plucked from the array on the floor seven more slips that looked like edges of an image. "Okay, the photo would most likely be printed at the top of the page, so the extra-long blank portion on the bottom makes this the left side of a photo. Same thing with right side, just reversed."

Russell surveyed their progress. "Eight edges means four photos." He examined the four left sides and four right sides, looking for matches. "Here, these two both have similar colors."

With the sides of the photo set, he looked through the shreds on the floor for the same color pattern. Within three minutes, they had assembled a picture of Didi in her cell looking through her art supplies.

Cami squinted at it for a long time. "I don't get why this would be important enough to have in her file."

Russell had just finished assembling a photo of someone putting money in a parking meter in front of a nice little faux Spanish mission–style building. "Yeah. This is just someone parking."

Cami looked closer. "Could that be Ayse in the hat? But I don't recognize the car, or the older man she is with."

They kept working, and Cami watched as her own face was reconstructed via shreds of paper. Russell looked at it. "This is you walking out of a credit union."

She used every ounce of energy she had to remain calm. "Huh. That's so weird."

He stared at the picture. "Why would Bard care if you went there?"

She shook her head. "I don't even belong to that credit union. I just needed a roll of quarters for laundry, and it was on my way home." The lie came so quickly that it made Cami feel nauseous. To cover, she took another sip of her coffee but saw her cup was empty. "I'm going to grab more coffee. Do you want some?"

Russell handed her his mug. "Yes, please, and thank you."

"Cream? Sugar?"

"Both, please. Lots. Like an alarming amount."

Cami laughed. "Absolutely."

Russell smiled. "In real prison, we call that a *Cadillac*."

"And I needed to know that because . . . ?"

He smiled a little sadly. "If this investigating all goes south, I gotta prepare you for real time, Garcia."

Cami nodded. "Right. Let's hope it doesn't come to that." She added a little laugh for cover, and he seemed to buy it.

As Cami turned away, she let the full weight of what she had just seen wash over her. It had to be random that Bard had photographed her coming out of that credit union. She assured herself there was no way he had known what she did. Or had he?

It was strange how it had all happened. It was so dreamlike that, more often than not, Cami herself forgot about the money all together. About a year into Thad's weekly poker ring, a game had been going for over seven hours and shown no signs of slowing, so Cami was at the ATM, getting additional change for the house. She had also swung by to pick up a catering platter from a restaurant in DTLA, and had tacked onto the order several sandwiches for the front desk at the hotel where the game was being held. Thad promoted the games and found the players, while Cami handled all the logistics for hosting. Normally, she booked rental homes, but this week the house she had already paid for had had a burst pipe in the kitchen. They refunded her credit card (which Thad had gotten her) and she was able to book a hotel suite for two nights and even upgrade it by using points. It was all pretty standard.

As she chatted with the grateful front desk staff, the manager offered her a refund for the second night. "We aren't going to book it because we have someone staying there on Thursday. If you can be out by four p.m., then the cleaning staff will have time to reset the room."

"Oh, wow, thank you so much," Cami said.

"I can refund you in cash. Or do you want it back on the card?"

Without even thinking about it, Cami replied, "Cash is great, thank you."

She signed what was required and entered the elevator, bound for the suite. The $800 she had just been refunded was in her pocket. What she was supposed to do was hand the money directly over to Thad. It was his money, after all. He paid her credit card every month. But he didn't know. He would get progressively more drunk as the night went on, and when the game broke up (most likely around 10:00 a.m. the next morning) he would Uber home—also on her account, which he also paid for without ever looking at the bill.

Suddenly, an entire periphery of opportunity was visible to her.

For the next three years, Cami bought items for the weekly game nights, then returned them. She overbooked, and later adjusted. She offered extra deposits, to be returned directly to her. Thad fancied himself "an artistic mind," and part of this (besides his terrible taste in music) was he couldn't read a receipt if his life depended on it. He couldn't even calculate tips correctly! Cami was the logistical point person for everything, and yet Thad got all the joy, all the credit. Her frustration at being taken for granted grew from an ember to an inferno.

Cami felt the intelligent part of herself waking up, and it needed to be satiated. Before too long, she was skimming the take. Not a lot. Just enough to make her feel secure. So much of her act to be a ditz had required her to be passive, allow her life to be determined by the choices of others. To make decisions, to be direct, to change course from Thad's plans, was an unfathomable counter to her performed softness. It gave away the game. So instead, she built up her bank account, and every dollar she took from that sniveling control freak Thad made her feel a sense of strength she had missed, or perhaps never had.

Her pile of money quickly amassed to $70,000. She joined a credit union and deposited all the money into the account. Thad "didn't understand" credit unions, so that lessened the chance of him asking any questions. Not that he would have even noticed.

Month after month, she added to her take. $70,000. $80,000. $125,000.

It was glorious.

She promised herself she would stay with Thad until she hit $200,000. Then she upped the Exit Amount to $250,000. Then she would leave Thad and all his coercion behind. And most importantly, she would at long last shed this act of being silly. She would finally live out loud as the smart, capable person she had always been.

That was the plan, anyway. Instead, $2,000 shy of her exit, Thad's game had been raided.

And there was Cami's name on everything. The credit cards. The reservations. The bank statements. (Not her credit union, though.)

The DA pushed her to flip on the players. "Ms. Garcia, while your game was illegal, we are willing to make a deal. You confirm that these players were at your poker events, you walk free."

But Cami feigned stupidity. It had worked so far.

Sensing the dead end, the DA pushed her to flip on Thad. That was truly tempting. But when she played that scenario through, she knew it wouldn't work out for her long-term. Thad was such a whiny brat that he would fight the case all the way to the end, including an extended trial with as many appeals as his rich doormat parents would fund to assuage their guilt for raising such a twerp. Cami couldn't risk a trial, because that would mean law enforcement going over the books with a fine-tooth comb, and that would put her in their sights. She needed this to end quickly. Her nest egg was her way out of this life, and she had to keep it safe from prying legal eyes. That meant keeping control of the case even while playing dumb. So she took the only deal offered to her—the deal she'd effectively made them offer her.

Thad was foolish enough to believe she did it for him. For him! The man who used her and forced her to be his shield from consequences. The man who only liked her when she mirrored him back to him, an interior world of her own not required. But she stayed in his good graces because she couldn't afford Pay to Stay on her own without depleting her secret cash stash to pennies. And anyone becoming aware of that money was a whole new kind of trouble. She and Thad would both be screwed, and she would have nothing to fall back on.

Cami's jail sentence was more than Pay to Stay. And it was more than staying with Thad. Her jail sentence was her own play-acting of idiocy. She had to keep it up until her variety show of physical incarcerations—plural—were over.

And it was because of all this that the photo of her coming out of the credit union was so alarming. Maybe it was just random surveillance.

*But what if it wasn't? What if Bard knew?*

There was no way to know now.

After refilling both their mugs, Cami entered the hallway and heard Didi and Maureen talking in Bard's office. Cami thought about what Russell had said, about staying low-key, but she felt like so much was happening just outside of her periphery that she needed to take this opportunity to hear them unguarded.

The office door was open, but the whiteboard was wedged in such a way that it blocked the door from opening any farther—and more importantly, concealed Cami in the hallway entirely.

Didi's voice rang out with a note of genuine distress, "Maureen, I shouldn't have said I could gather evidence. What do I know about anything?"

Maureen was soothing. "No, Didi, you got this. I believe in you. You were a nurse. Treat this like the operating rooms you used to scrub into."

Didi seemed calmed by this suggestion. "Okay, treat this like an OR. I'm just tracking sponges, gauze, cc's of epi—but it's actually hair fibers and scuff marks." She took a few deep breaths. "I think I'm just on edge because of Russell. I wish he wasn't here."

"I know. Me too," Maureen said sadly.

Cami's breath caught. And then rage started to simmer just beneath her skin.

Maureen continued, "I actually have something I should share with the group, but I don't know how." There was a tense pause before she finally said, in a hushed tone, "I got Russell's arrest record."

Didi was genuinely shocked. "What? How?"

"I have a second phone," Maureen said with a little twinge of guilt.

Didi let out a nearly guttural gasp. "A second phone?"

"I always have it. I couldn't be out of touch with work every weekend, so I would turn in my regular phone to Bard but without my SIM card. Then, using my backup phone, I would check poll numbers, answer emails, whatever. Same deal this weekend. When Washington showed up, I emailed a contact to ask what he did. They sent me this."

Cami couldn't see, but putting together what she could hear from the hallway, she assumed Maureen was showing Didi her phone and whatever information she had gotten on Russell. Didi's response all but confirmed her assumptions.

Didi said, just above a hiss, "I knew it, Maureen. I knew he was violent. You can see it in his eyes. Always darting around, looking for a victim."

"I didn't want to believe it, but I had to know. For all of our safety."

"Should we tell Cami?" Didi asked. "I don't want anything to happen to her."

"Not yet. The right time will come."

There was another pause; then Didi asked the harder question: "Do you think he killed Bard?"

"It makes sense when you think about it," Maureen said calmly. "He's the only thing that's different this weekend. Seems more likely than one of us randomly snapping."

Didi whispered urgently, "Maybe Bard was his CO somewhere else and Russell held a grudge."

Maureen whispered back, "You think?"

Didi was keyed up now, chasing down her theory. "Remember that little nighttime talk they had in private? What was that about? Seems weird, if they just met."

"That's a great point."

Cami's hands shook. Energy coursed through her muscles. She had to warn Russell that they were turning on him as soon as possible, so he could be ready for whatever accusations were going to come his way. She got back to her cell and saw him hunched over the little side table, his back to her. "Russell, hey—" she began. But when she saw his face, eyes wild and color drained, she immediately forgot. "What?"

He turned his body to the side so she could see what he had been working on.

On the table he had a completed crime scene photo. The photo was different from the others. It was much larger, at almost double the size, taking up the entire 8.5 x 11 paper. There was also better definition, a scaling ruler along the sides, and *LAPD* watermarked across the bottom.

The photo was of a face wrapped in gauze, bloodied and bruised. The eyes were nothing but empty sockets. Bottomless pits of darkness. It was unclear whether the person in the photo was alive or just near death.

Cami whispered, acid in her throat, "Whose file is that from?"

Russell whispered back, "I don't know."

# CHAPTER 8

## Ayse Demiri: Outside Time

After getting the rakes and shovels out in a fit of industriousness, Ayse, Sister Bridget, and Janet didn't actually start working immediately. Instead, Ayse sat on the low retaining wall between Sister Bridget and Janet, who also had Nacho in her lap. Although the wind blew high up in the palm trees, it left the three women unruffled. The ever-present flock of parrots twittered hither and yon.

Ayse had lived her whole life in the Los Angeles Basin. She knew it was an easy city to misunderstand. Its vastness, mixed with the fact that so much city life happened in private spaces (backyard barbecues, movie nights at guild theaters, industry events), meant it could feel alienating as a visitor but like a series of cozy villages to a resident. Even on an aesthetic level, the city existed in extremes. The manufactured kitsch of Hollywood Boulevard, studio back lots housing spaceships on fake oceans, and plastic surgery faces plumped to a supernatural sheen in the grocery store line were all unremarkable here. A total buy-in from everyone on the land of make believe. Yet natural beauty also thrived in this sprawling city, wild and free. The screaming magenta of bougainvillea that draped over entire buildings. The scent of night-blooming jasmine cradling tranquil canyon trails, where packs of coyotes roamed freely. April was Ayse's favorite time of year, when every warm breeze sent down a shower of purple jacarandas petals, while in the distance she could see the snow-capped mountains. As she sat here, in this industrial square of punishment, all she had to do was look up and she could imagine she was free.

Ayse felt strongly that Los Angeles was the most American city. A place for immigrants and citizens alike to reinvent themselves. A place that cherished ease, encouraged strange dreams, and welcomed everyone who was too weird for their place of birth. Michelin star–quality meals were in strip malls next to dry cleaners. Dreamers made a living by giving massages to dogs. Organic juice brewed in moonlight was gulped by the gallon. A man even wandered the streets of West Hollywood dressed as Jesus and no one batted an eye. Not everyone could handle the density of New York, or the winters in Chicago, or Seattle's endless rain. Meanwhile, everyone could find their place in LA. Even the tropical birds. How different were these green parrots—who, by all accounts, could no longer thrive in their original habitat of Mexico—from the hopeful starlets from dusty flyover states who flung themselves into the City of Angels by the busload? Each and every one of them—bird and babe—were desperate to soar above their beginnings, and Los Angeles offered them a home. Just like it had offered Ayse and her father a home when they arrived from Turkey all those years ago.

All around them was the *drip drip drip* of rainwater running through the gutters toward the storm drains, eventually emptying into the Pacific. In the near distance, they could hear the vehicle-repair shop clanging away. The rain was due to return before the end of the afternoon, and the three of them leaned against the wall and let the brief moment of sun warm their faces. Eyes closed.

"Remember that week on the internet when everyone learned the word *apricity*?" Janet asked.

"Get off TikTok, Janet," Ayse said.

Janet sighed. "Guess it was a youth thing."

"Janet, you're seventy-two."

"Youth is in the heart, Ayse."

"Then I'll be sure to ask Cami about it."

Last week this would have been a sparring match. Today it was a gentle game of conversational ping-pong.

Ayse winced a little at how she had dismissed Cami earlier at breakfast. While the girl wasn't bright, she didn't deserve the brush-off Ayse had given her. But Ayse wanted to have a very particular conversation with Janet in private, and Cami had inadvertently been getting too close to the topic at hand. Besides, Cami had been smiling along within seconds, so maybe she hadn't even clocked Ayse's snarky comment. The idea of Cami's obliviousness protecting her soothed Ayse's worries.

Sister Bridget took in a deep breath and then said, "All right, should we begin?"

Janet rocked to her feet. "I guess."

Ayse said, "The maintenance schedule in the shed said weeding, sprinkler checks, and power washing the building. We're allegedly painting the exterior tomorrow if it doesn't rain."

Sister Bridget looked to the clouds gathering on the horizon. "Seems unlikely, but we can pray."

"Do you mind if I work at the end of the building?" Janet asked. "There's a nice patch of sun, and I can tie Nacho to the fence."

Ayse saw her opening. "Of course. You carry Nacho, I'll carry the rake down." As Ayse and Janet walked out of Sister Bridget's earshot, Ayse said, "Janet, I wanted to know more about Bard coming to your fundraiser."

Janet's stride broke a little bit, but she put up a good show. "What do you want to know?"

By this point, they had turned the corner, and Ayse leaned the rake next to Pay to Stay's fire door as Janet tethered Nacho to the fence. Ayse decided to come right at it. "What did he ask you to do?"

Janet looked at Ayse, her face telegraphing how caught she felt. "How did you know he asked me to do something?"

"Because he did the same thing to me."

Janet's exhale was one of pure relief, and her shoulders softened into round mounds. "I thought I was the only one."

Ayse shook her head. She felt a tenderness toward Janet, so unexpected and genuine that it was like an emotional possession.

Janet absentmindedly stroked Nacho from nose to tail as she spoke. "He told me to spy on Didi for him. He told me to get close to her, to find out whatever I could about her life, any secrets she had, anything she cared about that he could use to pressure her."

Ayse nodded in recognition. "He said the same thing to me."

"About Didi?"

"No. My job was to find out what Cami was hiding."

"Did you do it?"

Ayse wished she had a good answer. She wanted so badly to spin a tale that she'd told Bard to go to hell and she wasn't going to snitch. But that would be a lie. "Not yet. And apparently I was too late. Or at least, that's what his Post-it to me said on my transfer letter."

Janet asked, "Were you going to do it, though?" It wasn't a recrimination. It was hope for empathy.

"Yeah. I was. Because it wasn't about me." Ayse took a deep breath, willing herself to jump into the topic she had kept private for a decade. "My dad is a real estate agent. Nothing flashy. Real small-time. Just some little commercial buildings around West Hollywood. One day, a long time ago, he was brokering an extended lease on a building. Everyone involved seemed a little shady, but he was used to that. He had been sorting through this paperwork for weeks—it took over the whole dining room table. There were all these weird stipulations by the applicant of an updated HVAC and new internet ports when both things were already new. The projected cost seemed ridiculous to him—they even had preferred contractors with no opening for outside bids—but the owner was all for the lease. At one point my dad thought he had messed it up because on a few forms, the owner and the applicant had switched addresses. Then it all clicked. This was a sham lease to launder money. All these improvements would be overpriced, never actually get done, but the money would exchange from one shell company to another all the same. Basic stuff. Easy way to clean a lump sum of cash up top and then clean a couple thousand dollars per month in perpetuity."

Janet couldn't seem to help a sly smile. "So you *do* work with the Russian Mob. I thought that was just Didi being racist."

Ayse laughed. "A stopped watch is right twice a day, and a prejudiced rich lady sometimes correctly spots a criminal. The initial deal went off without a hitch after my dad gently corrected their forms. The Mob was grateful, and he got a nice kickback for the help and his discretion. After that, my father did more and more leases for them over the years, and after a time, he took ownership of some of the buildings at their behest. All fronted by them, of course. All mixed into a swirl of shell companies. He was a tiny public face behind which they carried on protected. He was a prop in a game of three-card monte."

Janet's face scrunched up. "All this makes sense, except for the end result. Why are you the one in jail?"

Ayse took a deep breath, willing herself to hold back any emotion that could come with this familiar story. "Ten years ago my dad had a major stroke. It was terrifying. For three days, I didn't know if he would ever wake up. When he did, he needed to relearn so much. How to walk, how to talk. But the physical fallout was only the first half of the crisis. It became quickly apparent that the stroke had affected his memory. It's called vascular dementia. These days, he is permanently living in the past. Sometimes he's back in Turkey and I'm his big sister. Sometimes he asks me how my SATs went. He lost so much English that I had to brush up on my Turkish just to communicate with him. *Iyi olacaksın, Baba,* I would say to him again and again when he was in the hospital. *You will be okay, Dad,*" Ayse added, translating her halted Turkish. "It felt like in an instant he slipped away into some other dimension where he is both the oldest person on the earth and a child I have to care for. The long-term care costs seemed to spring up into a mountain overnight. In order to get him what he needs, I had to keep the business moving like normal—I had to keep our income."

"Did the Mob know about your dad's stroke?"

Ayse shook her head. "Nope. They think I'm just an intermediary. Another level of buffer between them and my dad to protect their interests. Really it's the exact opposite. I'm protecting his interests."

Janet's eyes were wide. "So you're simultaneously working *for* the Mob and lying *to* the Mob. You have balls of steel. Were they exposed by your arrest? Did they panic?"

"Ironically, it wasn't the money laundering that got me here. I was showing one of our legit properties and got dinged for not having a real estate license."

Janet let out an actual guffaw. "You gotta be kidding me. The cops didn't find out about all the Mob stuff?"

Ayse shrugged. "They thought something was up but couldn't justify a warrant beyond me, so they accepted the little fish they had on the hook. And I was all too happy to be caught if it kept my dad safe."

Janet was clearly impressed. "Self-sacrifice was not what I expected from you, Ayse. I'm sorry for selling you short."

Ayse was surprised at how much the apology meant to her. "Thank you, Janet. Don't tell the others, though. I have a reputation to uphold. Heartless bitch, reporting for duty."

Janet laughed a little, then asked the inevitable: "So where does Bard fit into this?"

Ayse's eyes darkened. "I drive my dad all the way to San Clemente to see a stroke specialist. I tell him it's Istanbul and the Pacific is the Sea of Marmara." Ayse smiled at the memory: her father, sun on his face as they drove, singing along to the playlist Ayse made of songs from his youth, the only music he recognized now.

"Why San Clemente?" Janet asked.

"I didn't want the Russians finding out about my dad's condition, so I needed his treatment to be outside of their reach. Meanwhile, the Probation Department says I can go exactly one county away from Los Angeles without needing permission from the court. San Clemente is the last city in Orange County—as far as I can get."

"Makes sense."

"The doctor's office is in a strip mall built to look like a Spanish mission. There's a little trolley that runs to and from the pier in the summer. Stops right beneath the exam-room windows. I couldn't believe my luck. My father grew up by one of the vintage tramways in Istanbul. When we drive there, he thinks he's going home. He thinks I'm his older sister. He asks if we can stop at Istiklal Street for ice cream, and wonders why they took the flags down off the lampposts. For a minute there, I thought I had it, you know? We had made it through the worst of his stroke. I had smoothed out things with the Russians. I had even found a doctor with a trolley outside. Just had to keep jumping through the hoops and spinning the plates while walking the tight rope through the ring of fire during the hurricane. But then it all fell apart."

"Bard," Janet said knowingly.

Ayse's stomach dropped any time she thought about it, and today was no exception. "One day we were in the waiting room, when the front door to the office opened and Bard entered. He sat down next to my dad. I had a second of wild hope that maybe it was all a coincidence. But then Bard started talking. I froze. Completely and utterly froze. It was a nightmare. The precision with which Bard got incriminating detail after incriminating detail out of my addled father." Tears welled at the corners of Ayse's eyes, and she turned away so Janet couldn't see.

"He had enough to get your dad arrested."

Ayse whispered hoarsely, "Yes." She found her voice again and tried to go on with more strength, but still her words quavered. "My dad needs around-the-clock care. He needs physical therapy, occupational therapy, constant monitoring. If his meds are late even ten minutes, the entire routine falls apart. Sometimes he gets lost in our little two-bedroom apartment. If he went to prison, he would die."

Janet let out a deep sigh. "Jesus, Ayse. That sounds terrifying. You must be worried all the time. I am so sorry."

Ayse had the instinct to shrug, to brush it all off, to revert to her factory settings of Unbothered. Instead, she felt so comforted by Janet's words. The tears she had held inside for years were finally released. "I'm realizing I've never said all of this aloud to anyone," she said, her voice quavering the tiniest bit. "Ever. I've just been carrying it."

"I see now why, when you heard my story, you knew what Bard was up to."

Immediately, Ayse's tears of relief burned hot with anger. "He had me pinned—dangling my father's life over my head like the sword of Damocles. I'm glad Bard is dead. I felt joy when I saw his twisted face. My only regret is I wish I had done it."

Janet took Ayse by the shoulders and said, "Me too."

They had a quiet moment where a world of distress was finally released out of their chests and into the common air between them. There was nothing that needed to be said. They knew the ins and outs of this manipulation game of Bard's, and they both smiled, knowing they would never have to play it again. Then Janet said, "Ayse, listen to me. We are going to get out of this."

Ayse let out a small snort of air. "Please tell me how, because it is looking dire as hell from my point of view."

"I'm working on a plan. I'll make it happen."

Ayse just smiled, loving the vision of her life where she got to return to her dad. After a few minutes, she gave a small laugh, sniffling. "We should probably rake some stuff, I guess."

Janet looked around. "I suppose. These ficus are struggling so badly. Does anyone water them?"

"Oh no. I think that's supposed to be us."

Janet and Ayse started cracking up.

Just then, Sister Bridget popped her head around the corner. "I seem to have gotten my rake stuck in the storm drain again, and I can't quite bend over to get it."

"I'll come help you, Sister," Ayse said with kindness.

It was clear the fair Sister needed more help than just the stuck rake, so Ayse stayed with her. As they worked together, circling around the retaining wall, clearing weeds, and gathering debris, the building's look did start to improve. Not by a large margin, but enough that they felt like they had achieved their goal. Ayse relished digging trenches around faulty forgotten sprinkler systems with a targeted anger that had been bubbling like a puddle of ingested lava since the day Bard had entered the doctor's office.

"You missed the last drop. That's 20K you owe us," Bard had whispered to her father, Kerem, that day in the doctor's office.

Bard's voice made Ayse's head whip around so fast she felt her eyeballs rattle in her skull. And then the panic hit her, making every muscle in her body tense, frozen in horror.

*It can't be him.*

But it was.

Kerem, who had been sitting peacefully, humming a song only he knew, was immediately agitated. "What? Who are you?"

As his eyes seared into Ayse's, Bard said quietly into the old man's ear, "You know who I am, Kerem."

Kerem, frantic for answers, asked, "Sergei?"

Ayse's stomach dropped below the crust of the earth. Her arms weighed a thousand pounds. Her voice had been snatched by the trolley rumbling below the windows.

*How did he know to come here? On this day?*

Bard nodded slowly. "Yes, Kerem. Where is the last payment? We have been doing the same thing for how long now?"

Kerem's lip quivered. "Years, Sergei. Years and years I've been loyal. Dependable. Please, this is just a misunderstanding. I will sort it out."

Ayse's mouth was as dry as the Santa Ana winds blowing outside. She was desperate to speak, to intervene. But instead, her father kept talking. Every word an implication.

Kerem fumbled for a phone he no longer carried. "I will call. You know you can count on me. Your father and I have had an agreement. He can trust me."

Bard needed a bit more still. "What about your daughter?"

"Ayse?" Kerem's voice was shaking.

"Yes, Ayse. Can she help?"

Kerem's fear was at its peak, his every trembling word wrecking Ayse's heart, "No, no, she is young, still in high school. She doesn't know anything. She won't have anything to do with this. Not ever."

Bard's voice softened. "When does she graduate high school?"

"Next spring."

Ayse's stomach turned again and again. Her father was in another time, outlining a starting point dating back decades. Every word he spoke gave over timelines, and names, and arrangements.

Bard leaned closer still, his voice nearly a hiss. "I could call the police. I know enough now. I will say Kerem has been laundering money, in effect funding crime all through the city by his complicity, and deserves to be punished."

This last part may have terrified Kerem, but Ayse understood the message wasn't for him. It was for her. At long last, Bard knew her deepest vulnerability and was ready to exploit it.

Ayse had arrived to Pay to Stay after Bard's ambush at the doctor's office, her fury burning hot and fresh every time she thought of his smug face whispering in her father's ear.

Ayse had entered Bard's office without knocking and closed the door behind her. She swallowed hard, willing her rage to go down with it, to lay dormant for just a few minutes until this meeting was over. The other women were busy nesting in their cages, but even so, Ayse wanted privacy. Bard was sitting casually behind his desk; he was even twirling a goddamn pencil.

He smiled his movie-star smile, that obnoxious dimple even making an appearance. "Ayse. To what do I owe the pleasure?"

Ayse sat down. "What do you want?"

She had thought through this meeting one hundred times and knew that being direct was the only way to handle it. It was too late for flattery, and Ayse knew herself well enough to know she wouldn't be able to keep up a facade of groveling for more than three seconds.

Bard put his pencil down. Ayse noticed it was perfectly sharp, and for a second she wanted to grab it and drive the tip right into his eye. But she resisted. Barely.

"What makes you think I want something?" he asked coyly.

Ayse needed to stay calm. "I doubt you came to San Clemente to enjoy the pier. You have more than enough to put my father in prison. But you didn't. I assume because you have another aim."

Bard did a cutesy golf clap. "Well done, Ayse. I must say, you have really been a joy to watch. On paper you are merely the license-less real estate agent. But immediately I knew there was more to this. Your eyes—always watching, always taking everything in. No movement wasted or word unexamined. A true economy of energy. I found you quite intriguing. Then I discover your entire real estate business has quite the . . ." He searched for a word. "*Stench* about it. Russian Mob implied in every nook and cranny."

Ayse crossed her arms. "The district attorney said the same thing, and yet nothing was provable."

Bard nodded. "Yes." He golf clapped again. "So I asked the bigger question: Where had your father gone? And so I set out to look for him."

Ayse's breath caught, but she tried to keep her face still.

Bard gave a comical grimace. "His health. Suddenly, it made sense to me that the dutiful daughter would do anything to protect him. It's quite moving when you think about it."

Ayse threw her one Hail Mary. "You saw him. No charges are going to be brought based on the word of someone with advanced dementia."

Bard's answer was all too ready. "I did some research. Apparently, for people in your father's mental state, consistency and routine are key for their health and safety. Do you want to subject him to multiple interrogations? That sounds like it would be extremely distressing for him. And who knows what else would come to light once the cops started looking in the right places, asking the right questions. This little pay-to-stay arrangement for you would definitely be off the table. And if you go down for hard time, what happens to him?"

Ayse knew he was right, so she circled back to her original point and her original posture. "You drop the dime, my dad dies alone in an anonymous care home within six months. That's what's at stake. I get that. So what do you want?"

Bard shook his head. "Such a head for business, but always ruining my fun. Never letting me play with my food. You are right, though: I do want something." He slid a file across the desk. "New inmate starts next week. She reminds me of you."

Ayse reluctantly took the folder and opened it. She saw the mug shot of a gorgeous twentysomething woman named Camilla Garcia, arrested for running an illegal gambling ring. Ayse shrugged. "Besides being brunette, I don't see the connection."

Bard smiled. "Well, that's what is so interesting. Seems clear it was really her boyfriend's gambling ring, but Cami here took the fall. She even rejected two deals from the DA. I want to know why."

Ayse mustered as much strength as she could without going into full *fuck you* territory, "Great. Then ask her."

"No, no. *You* ask her. Or I make a call to the police about your dear sweet dad."

Ayse had bitten down on her own tongue to keep herself from jamming that damn pencil into his ear and giving it a twist. She stood up, about to walk out of the door, when Bard said something that felt like the only honest moment she had with him in three years.

"You know, it's funny. I don't trust altruism because it's always in service of ego even when people say it's not. And I have no respect for self-sacrifice for the same reason. It's sacrificing someone else for your own personal benefit, and living with that choice, that I find compelling."

Ayse had spent the last several weeks chewing on this demand from Bard to spy on the new inmate, unsure how to move the boulder up the hill without losing herself in the process. She found Cami to be mildly ridiculous but harmless, and it made Ayse's stomach twist at the thought of hurting her for Bard's pleasure. But if it was a choice between Cami and her dad, Ayse knew what she would do, and she'd planned to do it this very week.

Instead, Ayse had carried Bard's corpse, and she felt freer than she had since his surprise visit.

Bard's death ensured her father's safety, and she was elated every time she remembered his cold skin on her hands.

Several hours of quiet gardening passed. Each thing that Ayse saw, she found the equivalent word in Turkish, pushing her memory to list each noun.

Soil. *Toprak.*

Leaf. *Yaprak.*

Bush. *Çalı.*

Brick. *Tuğla.*

Fence. *Çit.*

Every word she could conjure felt like another point of connection with her father, until they weren't so far apart and these walls melted away.

A week before his stroke, Ayse felt like she could at last see the weight of this unlawful arrangement on her father. He had become physically smaller, his movements all either frantic or unsure. She asked, "Do you wish you had never started this?" He didn't answer her, and she wasn't surprised. He never talked about the past. So she rephrased: "*Baba*, do you want to go home?"

"We are home," he said, looking around their little apartment.

"Not our apartment. I mean your home. I mean Turkey. We could, you know."

He had sighed. "Perhaps, *balım.* One day." Ayse felt a lightness in her heart, until he added, "But it is too late to ask those questions now. What good will they do." He had said it in a way that made her know he had in fact spent many years wrestling with the question she had just asked.

As she weeded the last of the dandelions, Ayse made a private vow to get her father home to Istanbul. He deserved to hear the real trolley again while the red flags flapped overhead. He deserved to feel free from his choices. So did she.

Once the landscaping was done, it was time to clean the exterior walls with the power washer. Sister Bridget delighted in blasting debris out of the gutters, aiming the nozzle up the clogged drain pipes until there was a confetti of old leaves showering down around them.

"The Lord compels you!" Sister Bridget yelled, laughing.

Ayse had a turn as well, but with fewer invocations of Jesus.

Ayse somewhat envied the building, that it was so easy to restore to its original state. A few passes of pressurized water erased years of grime. Meanwhile, she would be chasing a clean record for the rest of her life. If only she could blast her past away. If only she could take her father home to Istanbul and leave this entire mess behind.

She was vaguely curious what the investigative faction was discovering inside, but she was happy to have a mental break from all the stress. Whatever exciting new clues those people found would be waiting for them at the end of the afternoon. There was no rush for her to return to the reality of murder.

In Ayse's entire life, there was no room for even the tiniest error. Pay to Stay had to go well so her business dealings could go well so her father could be well. Now she had to add a murder investigation to the top of that chain. In order for her father to be well, her business dealings had to go well. And in order for her business to go well, Pay to Stay had to go well. And in order for Pay to Stay to go well, she had to solve a murder. Her life was a house of cards in a windstorm. For now, she could focus on the manual tasks and let the ticker tape of worry have some time off.

Eventually, though, the sun started getting low, and the clouds were closing in again.

Sister Bridget came to Ayse's side, her hand on her lower back. "My back has officially seized up, and I'm not really interested in getting caught in the rain. Ready to be done for the day?"

Ayse said, "Yeah. You grab Janet, and let's head inside before the next wave of this storm breaks."

Sister Bridget was relieved. "I'll help Janet with the gardening tools and Nacho. God bless all of the Lord's creatures, but my goodness, that lizard." Bridget gave a little shiver of disgust, and Ayse laughed, agreeing that Nacho was at best unpopular and at worst kinda gross.

Ayse gathered up the gardening tools as Sister Bridget walked slowly around the corner of the building trying to take steps without tweaking whatever part of her back was in pain. Ayse was shoving a disobedient hose back into the shed when she heard Sister Bridget's voice with a note she didn't quite recognize. "Ayse! Can you come here?"

"Sure!" Ayse called out. With a final heave, she pushed the shed door closed and then walked over to join Janet and Sister Bridget at the end of the building. As Ayse came around the corner, she said, "Hey, Janet, this rain is about to—" but stopped short.

There was Sister Bridget.

There was Nacho the iguana, still tied to his fence post.

There was Janet's rake, discarded.

But nothing else.

No one else.

Janet was not there.

Ayse stood, dumbfounded, blinking like a cartoon, Sister Bridget's face a mirror of her own confusion. There had to be something she was missing, but there wasn't. Ayse spun around to see nothing but high fences, a folding chair, and a locked fire door. Long silent seconds passed, but Ayse couldn't shake the shock. The same surreal feeling from yesterday came back. She finally managed to stammer out, "M-maybe Janet went inside?"

Sister Bridget replied, "Perhaps. But how? I have the door pass." She pulled the small white security card from her pocket.

Ayse's mind was spinning, looking for logic. "Someone inside must have opened the door for her. That's all. Probably while you and I were using the power washer."

Sister Bridget nodded, dazed. "Yes. At the end of the building, we couldn't see the double doors. That must have been it."

Ayse and Sister Bridget went to the double doors at the center of the building, Ayse carrying Nacho on her shoulder like she had seen Janet do a hundred times.

Then an idea pinged in Ayse's mind. "Let's check the van!"

Relief lit up Sister Bridget's face. "Oh yes! She must be there!"

"Maybe taking a nap!" Ayse said with an enthusiasm she willed to be real.

Ayse and Sister Bridget looked in the windows of the van, but it was empty. Enthusiasm trounced.

At the double doors back inside, Ayse and Sister Bridget waited a tense beat. Ayse whispered, "She has to be in there, right?"

Sister Bridget responded with her God-sanctioned confidence. "Must be."

Ayse nodded. "Must be. But . . ." She paused, worry choking the word from her. "If for some reason Janet isn't there, you and I were together the whole time, right?"

Sister Bridget took Ayse's hand, holding it gently. "We were."

Sister Bridget swiped the security card. They heard the lock disengage, and Ayse opened the door.

The hallway was empty in a way that felt eerie. Perhaps even menacing.

As the door slammed behind them, both Ayse and Sister Bridget jumped.

Ayse said, "Let's check her cell."

They entered the rec room. Cami and Russell were still hard at work, sorting through the piles of paper.

Cami was her normal cheerful self. "Hiya. How was outside?"

Sister Bridget said, "Have you seen Janet?"

Cami exchanged a confused look with Russell and then said, "I thought she was with you."

Ayse was in Janet's empty cell, placing Nacho back in his terrarium. "She was. Did either of you open the door for her?"

Cami shook her head. "I got coffee for us a couple of hours ago, but since then we've both been in here the whole time."

"Perhaps she joined Didi and Maureen?" Sister Bridget wondered aloud.

The pit in Ayse's stomach was growing larger by the second. "I hope so."

As a group, the four of them went down the hallway, in silent agreement that "together was best."

Cami said, "Russell and I will check the bathroom and kitchen."

Ayse nodded. With Sister Bridget at her shoulder, Ayse knocked on the closed door to Bard's office, pushing it open only to find it was somehow blocked.

Didi's voice rang out from within the office. "Hold on!"

Maureen was laughing. "The whiteboard is in the way."

They could see now, through the crack in the door, that the whiteboard was in fact in the way, and they heard much shuffling as Maureen and Didi moved this and that, then rolled the whiteboard to the side. Maureen opened the door wide, rosy cheeks framed by her forensics jumpsuit. "Welcome to the highly organized crime scene!"

It was clear Maureen and Didi had been busy. There were stacks and stacks of little baggies with detailed labels. Didi had outlined the area under the desk chair with tape to protect the scuff marks. The deadly Saran Wrap and vest combo had been delicately separated, bagged, and tagged. Maureen's handwriting had filled every inch of the whiteboard cataloging the location of each bit of hair found. They were beaming with pride. Ayse almost didn't want to worry them, but she had to.

"Hey, have you two seen Janet?"

Maureen looked confused. "I thought she was with you."

"She was, but when we came inside she was gone."

Didi laughed. "She's probably meditating in her cell. *Ommmmmm, speak to me, Nacho. Ommmmm.*"

Maureen was laughing, too. "Didi! That is so offensive!"

Ayse said, a little more loudly than she intended, "She's not in her cell."

Maureen's laughter died quickly. "What? Okay, fine. Maybe she's in the bathroom."

But Cami and Russell had rejoined the group during this exchange. "No. We just looked there and the kitchen."

Didi rolled her eyes at what she was clearly chalking up to be some kind of inconvenience. "Well, she has to be somewhere."

Sister Bridget said, "I had the door pass on me the whole time. I didn't let her back into the building. None of you opened the door for her. But she is nowhere outside."

Maureen was serious now. "Nowhere? You checked the shed? You checked the van? Maybe she is in the van!"

Ayse shook her head. "She's not in the shed. She's not in the van. She's not in her cell."

Didi's familiar hysteria was rising again. "This is absurd. She has to be somewhere! You don't think she escaped, do you?"

Maureen's impatience surprised Ayse, even though it was deserved. "Of course she didn't escape, Didi. Don't be ridiculous."

Didi's feelings were clearly stung. "Well, then, where is she?"

Maureen regained her composure. "We'll find her. Let's start out front. Work our way back. Be *methodical*." She said this last word like it was a protection spell. As if Janet would be conjured back into their presence by the sheer power of organization.

As a group, they turned right and went down the hallway to the front doors. Sister Bridget swiped the door pass and said, "Saint Anthony, please come around. Help us find Janet, who cannot be found."

Maureen and Ayse crossed the parking lot while the rest of the group stood just inside the threshold, keeping the doors open.

Ayse reported as they walked. "Janet's car is still here, so unless she fled on foot . . ." She trailed off, with nothing to add to the bizarre sentence. Besides, the chain was still visibly looped and locked around the gate.

Maureen leaned against the passenger window of the Eco Volvo, her face cupped against the glass. "She's not in here."

The group then did a lap of the entire southside courtyard, Ayse and Sister Bridget trying not to be annoyed when they also found the shed and the van empty.

The group went back inside, sweeping every cell, the kitchen, and the bathroom once again. Everything came up empty.

Every single step increased the tension. Ayse felt the familiar knot in her chest tightening across her sternum, making it hard to get a full breath. *Where are you, Janet?*

It was Maureen and Didi's turn to be annoyed when everyone double-checked Bard's office and sleeping quarters.

Didi's arms were crossed. "We told you we haven't seen her, either. And don't touch anything!" she snapped when Cami's elbow got too close to a stack of bagged evidence.

The group reconvened in the hallway, tempers short and nowhere left to go.

Then Cami said, in a small voice full of dread, "What's that?"

Everyone looked in the direction her bejeweled nail was pointing. After the kitchen and the bathroom was a third door no one had thought to check—the supply closet. Seeping out from under the door was a dark liquid.

Blood.

Thick and viscous.

Ayse felt sick, the pit in her stomach now roiling. But she had to see it—to know for sure. Ayse took her first step forward and was relieved when she heard the group moving with her. She reached her hand out to the doorknob. She twisted, pulled, and held her breath.

The door opened slowly.

In the center of the closet, Janet was slumped over herself. Her curly hair obscured her face. They didn't need to see it, though. They knew.

Janet was dead.

She was held half up by a length of rope around her chest that had been tied high on the hooks out of her reach. Ayse could see a rag in her mouth, held in place by Janet's own head wrap.

But her sage-green linen pants were stained dark, from waist to ankle.

A single rip at the leg showed them the cause of death.

Her femoral artery had been cut.

# CHAPTER 9

## Cami Garcia: One of Us

Cami screamed.

She didn't even realize she was the one screaming until she felt Ayse holding her, soothing her.

Didi ran from the group, and Cami heard the vague echo of Didi being sick in the bathroom.

Sister Bridget stood in shock. Prayers abandoned.

Russell leaned against the wall, staring at Janet, two sets of eyes unblinking.

Maureen crumbled to the floor like a doll who had been forgotten mid-game.

Didi stumbled out of the bathroom, her face red from the exertion of vomiting, and limped next to Maureen.

One question swirled in Cami's mind, drowning out every other thought: Why? Why why why why? Why would someone kill Janet? Why would someone kill Bard *and* Janet?

Why?

"The blood is so thick. It doesn't even look liquid anymore," Ayse said in a hollow voice that almost sounded disembodied.

Maureen replied blankly, "Coagulation."

Didi dry heaved and then said, "That takes between two and eight minutes."

A sickening thought hit Cami. "Did she bleed out while we were looking for her?"

Sister Bridget crossed her hands over her heart. "We looked in the wrong places first."

Ayse shook her head. "She could have been dead longer than eight minutes."

"Does that help your alibi if it's longer?" Didi asked.

Ayse was shocked. Her mouth dropped open. "What do you mean? I didn't do this!"

Didi shrugged. "You were with her last."

Ayse yelled, "And I was outside of a locked door when it happened."

Didi shrugged again. "Says you."

Ayse's voice was so loud it ricocheted off the walls. "Says me? Says facts! You were *where* it happened, *when* it happened."

Maureen shook her head. "No, Didi was with me the entire time. You saw how the whiteboard was blocking the door. Neither of us could have snuck out."

Ayse replied quickly, "And I was with Sister Bridget."

And then, in a shocking moment, Sister Bridget said, "Well . . ."

Ayse's anger was instantaneous, ignited by the jet fuel of betrayal. Cami almost ducked as Ayse started yelling, "What do you mean, *well*?"

Sister Bridget looked like it pained her to continue, her mouth scrunched up, pushing words out. "When I had the power washer, I wasn't looking for you. It was extremely loud. You could have . . ." She had the decency to not finish the sentence.

Ayse was incensed. "This is ridiculous. So I, what, exactly? Lifted the security pass off you, lured Janet into a closet to truss her up like a pot roast, slashed her leg, and then bopped back out in seconds?"

Sister Bridget wouldn't backtrack, but she wasn't happy, either. "I just don't want to say I can swear to something when I can't."

"It would only take a second to . . ." Didi made a slicing gesture with her hand.

Ayse's arms were crossed in utter offense. "Well, you were a nurse. You would know where to find the artery."

Didi wasn't taking the bait, though. "True. But unlike you, I have an alibi for the whole time."

Sister Bridget tipped her head as if to say *Exactly*.

Ayse snapped, "Oh, can it, Sister. If you want to say I wasn't with you, then that means you also weren't with me. And you were the one with the door pass to get back in. Two of us can play this game."

Didi's bout of vomiting had seemed to crack something open in her, and her face was a strange leer as she said, "The reality is, we are a bunch of idiots locked together, and no CBS mastermind is coming to find the perfect exonerating fact. We are well and truly screwed even if we aren't the murderer. There's no going back now. Happy New Year!" She made a little fake horn sound like she was celebrating the ball drop in Times Square.

Maureen's face was serious when she started speaking. She took a moment to make eye contact with each of them. "There is something we need to talk about. As a group." She seemed to steady herself, putting her shoulders back, lifting her chest, bracing for what came next even if it was self-inflicted. "One of us here has a history of violence." There was a horrible pause. Then she turned to look at him at last as she said, "Russell, do you want to tell them, or should I?"

Cami felt a flash of panic and physically flung herself into the middle of the group in a desperate attempt to head this witch hunt off at the pass, "I was with Russell the entire time."

Didi gave Cami a look of pure pity. "Oh, sweetie, come on."

Cami's fury matched Ayse's. "I swear to God, if any of you try to pin this on him, I will call the cops myself."

Maureen stepped toward her in a move to both confront and quell. "That's all well and good, Cami, but our personal histories have to mean something here. Otherwise we've got nothing to go on."

Cami's tone was more vicious than she intended, but it felt so damn good. "Well, I don't know how to tell you this, but we already have nothing to go on. And now you're turning to rumors to support a sham!"

Cami was ready to boil over when she heard Russell's voice in her ear: "Cami. It's okay. It's inevitable."

Cami's eyes seared with tears. "No it's not. It's not inevitable."

"People like me don't get a happy ending," Russell said quietly.

Cami shook her head. "That's not true. It can't be."

Maureen was trying to find a way through that wouldn't tear the group apart, always the campaigner. "Russell, if you could just tell us what you're in for, what happened, why you ended up here, of all places, maybe that would help. So we can feel like we know you. Understand you."

But Russell wouldn't answer. This was a trap, and he wasn't dumb enough to walk into it.

Ayse held up her hands. "Wait, Maureen. I feel like we're skipping over something kind of crucial. How exactly do you know this about Russell?"

Cami relished yelling, "She has a secret phone."

This got a genuine rise out of Ayse. "Are you serious? You've had a phone this whole time?"

Maureen attempted to get this conversation back on track. "It's for emergencies."

Ayse was nearly screaming, her voice once again ricocheting off the walls. "And being trapped with a burgeoning serial killer does not qualify?"

Maureen's hands were balled into fists, but her voice was steady. "Can we please focus? Yes, I have a phone. I made a call the first day, *before* anything happened, and asked to get background on Russell. I just wanted to know who was here with us. *For all of our safety.*" She emphasized those last words.

"That's total bull," Cami yelled. "You don't know the first thing about him; you haven't even spoken to him since he got here! None of you have. You all think you're better than him."

Didi yelled back, "We are!"

Cami stepped up to her, ready to go. "You aren't! You're all felons, too. You're all in prison, too. You don't get to point the finger at him without pointing it at yourselves."

Maureen said, in a hushed tone reserved for breaking bad news, "Cami. He shot someone."

Russell sighed as if to say this was the moment he'd known would come.

Cami shook her head. "No." She turned to look at him, pleading with Russell to fight for himself, to join her in her anger. "No. Russell, say no. Say no!"

Russell finally said, "It's true."

Cami felt sick. It couldn't be true. She wouldn't accept it.

*Why was he lying?*

Then a worse thought came forward.

He wasn't lying.

Cami shook her head. "No. You wouldn't. You're a good person." But even as she said it, she could feel the logic dissolving. She just kept staring at him, and he kept not meeting her gaze, which felt as good as a confession.

Didi pushed through the group. "Well, if he's such a good guy, let's see then. Let's see what you all have been working on so diligently."

Didi stomped down the hallway toward the rec room with the group chaotically following behind.

Didi slammed open Cami's bars and ripped her printed woodland sheet down. "Hm! I see nothing! I see one single taped twenty-dollar bill. I see a bundle of yellow legal paper." As she spoke, she picked up each item and then tossed it out into the center of the rec room with the scorn of a betrayed lover tossing their beloved's wardrobe onto the lawn. "Oh, look, you've managed some photos! Look, it's me in my cell! Wow, that's gonna crack the case. And, uh, oooh, this one is Ayse putting a nickel in a parking meter. And this one is—" She looked down and then screamed. "Wait! What the hell is this?"

Didi dropped the photo like it had a venomous spider on it. It twisted through the air and came to land at Maureen's feet. Cami had an urge to dive to the floor, grab the photo, and eat it, destroying the evidence. But it was too late.

The LAPD photo of the bloody face, eye sockets hemorrhaged beyond recognition.

Ayse looked at it. "Whose file does that belong to?"

Cami said defensively, "We don't know. We were still figuring it out."

"Why didn't you show it to everyone?" Sister Bridget asked.

Cami bit her lip. She needed to lie or else Russell was going down for everything. "I thought we should wait. We didn't want to cause hysteria."

Ayse asked nicely but pointedly, "Are you sure that was your idea, Cami?"

It hadn't been. It had been Russell's. But Cami couldn't let them know that. She started to respond, but before she could, an alarm rang out and lights began to flash all over the building.

Maureen looked around. "What is that?"

Sister Bridget's nose went up to the air. "Do you smell smoke?"

There was a shared look between everyone, and they immediately ran back toward the rest of the building.

It was obvious where the fire was—Bard's office. Water from the sprinklers in his room poured out of the door and into the hallway.

Didi was in front, and when she tried to stop short in the puddle, she slipped, taking Sister Bridget and Maureen down into a pile of limbs. Didi scrambled out from the dogpile on all fours, shrieking, "The evidence!"

As she climbed back up onto her feet, using the wall to steady herself, Maureen yelled, "We have to shut off the water! I'll check the kitchen."

Ayse and Cami took the wide route around the gushing water on the ground as Ayse yelled, "I'll check the maintenance room."

Cami made a beeline for the bathroom, sure there would be some valve in there. But after checking high and low, she saw nothing that would connect to a sprinkler system, just basic shutoffs for the sinks and showers.

Then she heard Ayse call out, "I found it! But it's stuck!"

Cami ran from the bathroom and joined Ayse in the maintenance room at the end of the hall. There was a large lever marked *Los Angeles Fire Department*, and Ayse was pulling down on it with all her might, but it wasn't budging. Cami wrapped her hands around it, too, and soon they felt it give the smallest bit.

Ayse looked at Cami and said, "On the count of three. One, two, three."

Cami and Ayse both dropped their weight down at the same time. Finally, the lever released entirely and they heard the whooshing water stop.

Cami reentered Bard's office with Ayse right behind her. It wasn't a pretty sight.

Didi had been hunched over the desk, trying to protect as many baggies of evidence as she could. She stood up and made a childish blow of water out of her mouth, but it didn't matter. Her pile of hair extensions was its own weather system, dripping all over everything. When she saw that the whiteboard, once so detailed, was now 99 percent illegible, she let out a whimper.

Ayse looked around. "Where's Sister Bridget?"

The door to Bard's sleeping quarters opened, and Sister Bridget exited. She had a stack of baggies wrapped up in her habit in an effort to protect the precious collection from the deluge. Her nun's veil hung around her face like a basset hound's ears. She dropped her haul of baggies onto the desk alongside Didi's. Everything was now a drenched, soggy mess.

Cami asked, with more hope than she felt, "Do you think any of it is salvageable?"

"Who knows!" Didi replied in a tone that was coming close to unhinged. She pointed to the ruined whiteboard. "And even if it is, we don't know where we found it in the room."

Ayse turned around, and then found what she was looking for. "Well, we know how the fire started." She pointed to one of Janet's prayer candles, which had been lit to slowly ignite a braid of shredded records leading toward the smoke detector. "A homemade timer for a delayed inferno."

Cami couldn't help it—she looked to the craft queen, Didi, who had spent all her time in here. And so did everyone else.

Didi protested, "It wasn't me! *I* need to get out of here! *I* need to prove I didn't kill him! This ruins that!"

Ayse was clearly thrilled that Didi was in the hot seat now. "How do we know you weren't just *cleaning* the crime scene? Erasing anything that could connect you? And you lit the candle and led us away so the sprinkler would ruin any physical evidence that could exonerate the rest of us."

Didi turned it back on her. "Wow, what an amazingly detailed plan you *just happened to come up with out of nowhere*! That's sarcasm, by the way!"

The bickering started again, but with an edge that smelled like violence. Cami considered stepping in between them, but then she had another thought: Let them destroy each other. Why not? None of them had ever shown her kindness.

Just then, Maureen stumbled into the office. Her skin was white. Her eyes were unfocused, unseeing, as she groped for support. She tried to speak, but only a ghostly rasp came out. Then a thick rivulet of dark blood ran down her face, dripping into her eyes, around her nose, off her chin, and finally onto her stained crime scene overalls.

Ayse cried, "Oh my God, Maureen!" She reached out and took Maureen's arm just as Maureen's legs gave out. Ayse helped her to the poorly roped-off office chair, clumsy crime scene tape be damned.

And then Cami realized Maureen wasn't the only one gone. "Russell!" she yelled. She careened down to the kitchen and the bathroom—but thinking back, she hadn't seen him here at all. She ran back down to the rec room, and there was Russell, lying face down on the floor of his cell.

Cami screamed, "Russell!" She crossed the entire rec room in less than a second, running at top speed, her heart thundering, preparing herself to see a pool of blood beneath him. Except when she got closer, he rolled onto his side and sat up. His eyes stayed down.

Cami was still frantic. "Are you okay? Why are you laying on the floor?"

"When the alarm sounds, you get on the floor," he said blankly.

"What are you talking about? That was just a fire alarm," Cami said quickly. "Come to Bard's office; Maureen has been hurt."

But Russell didn't get up. He didn't even look at her. Instead, he turned his eyes to the window and said, "Cami. I can't do this anymore."

Cami was confused. "Do what?"

"I'm just gonna stay in here, Cami. I can't deal with this fantasy."

Cami was baffled. "What fantasy?"

"The fantasy that I can control what comes next."

"But you can," Cami said, reaching for him. That was a mistake.

Catching a glimpse of her hand coming toward him, Russell got to his feet quickly and moved out of her reach. His hands were balled into fists and primed for a fight. He yelled, "No, I can't! Okay? I! Can't! I'm going back inside no matter what happens." His breath was ragged, and his anger, while palpable, wasn't directed at Cami so much as it was directed at the world at large. Cami felt an icy shock. This was a whole new side of Russell, and it felt unpredictable in a way that made her hair stand up. She took her own step back. He took a second to collect himself, then said, without an ounce of emotion, "I haven't been in control of my own life for a long time. I can't forget that."

Cami wanted to push, but the rec room door slammed open, and Maureen was being helped to her cell by Didi and Bridget. Maureen was assuring them, "I'm fine. Really."

Sister Bridget wasn't hearing it, though. "Your eyes won't focus, and you can't take two steps in a straight line."

They gently lowered Maureen onto her cot, and she did seem grateful to be off her feet.

"You really can't remember what happened?" Didi pressed.

Maureen shook her head and then winced from the motion. "I was running around with everyone else to find the shutoff valve. I was in the kitchen, looking by the sink, and then I felt a blow to the back of my head. I don't think I passed out, but the pain made me—" She winced again. "I don't know."

Didi asked again, more pointedly, "So you didn't see who it was?" She was staring at Russell when she said it, and he shrank deeper into his cell, knowing exactly the inference being made at his expense. His face was clouded over, the warmth in his eyes a distant memory.

It was clear: Didi wasn't asking an open question. Didi was offering Maureen a scapegoat.

Nevertheless, Maureen shook her head.

Russell's face was a mask of fury, brow furrowed, chin jutting out in defiance, but his eyes betrayed years of stress finally bubbling over. His hands were tense claws, and his shoulders were perched an inch closer to his ears. He stepped toward Cami, herding her backward with each word he spoke. "I know you don't know this yet, Cami. I know this place has an illusion of an exit. But there is no happily ever after. *There isn't even an After*. It's just *this* for the rest of your life."

He slid his bars shut in her face with an authoritative clang, and turned his back on her.

# CHAPTER 10

## Ayse Demiri: Turf War

"I got you more ice," Ayse said quietly.

Maureen, who had been lying down in the twenty minutes since the attack, sat up gingerly. A sign for Ayse to come into her cell. Ayse sat down at the foot of Maureen's bed. The act felt oddly intimate. Like in another life they were just two friends, as opposed to two captives. Ayse gently pressed the plastic bag of ice to Maureen's head.

"Ow." Maureen winced.

"Sorry," Ayse said, carefully adjusting the pokier ice cubes away from the staggeringly large lump easily visible through Maureen's hair.

Maureen helped Ayse place the bag on a better spot; then she asked, "You got this from the freezer?"

"Yup."

"The freezer with a dead body in it?"

Ayse looked her in the eye. "Do you really want me to answer that?"

"No." Maureen sighed, closing her eyes. After a beat, she asked, more quietly this time, "That has to be it, right?"

Ayse twitched out a laugh. "You'll have to be more specific. The end of the bodies? Of the fires?"

Maureen frowned. "Jeezy creezy."

Ayse shrugged. "Sorry. I shouldn't make a joke."

Maureen wasn't upset, though. "Why not? Can't hurt. Unlike everything else," she added, once again trying to find the most comfortable way to ice her injury. "We should move Janet."

Ayse nodded. "Didi and I already did. She's in the walk-in with Bard now."

"That explains that." Maureen pointed to Didi, who had changed into fresh clothes and was also furiously dousing her body in hand sanitizer.

Carrying Janet under her arms while Didi took her feet was a sense memory Ayse was eager to forget. She had even mopped up the blood, watching her reflection swirl and distort as she swept it into the waiting bucket. Itching to move on to another topic Ayse pulled the ice to the side and took a look, "Okay, seems like you've stopped bleeding, so we can knock that off the list of things to worry about."

Maureen gave a mock-pout. "Hey, don't stop worrying about me too quickly. I'll think you don't care."

Ayse was about to volley a fun retort back when a sound pricked both their ears.

Ayse's eyes shot to Maureen's, who was staring right back, both of them as tense as prey animals.

The high siren was far away, but unmistakably getting closer.

Maureen's hand was shaking, making the ice she was clutching gently chatter like a chilled maraca. Ayse took Maureen's hand in her own, a gesture that they were in this together. Ayse offered, "They might not be coming here."

Maureen's face was pale, and Ayse couldn't tell if it was from fear, blood loss, or some combination of the two. She tried to give Ayse a small nod as response, but it came out as more of a twitch.

The siren cut off for a split second, barely a moment but enough to let Ayse's hope bloom. Instead, the siren was replaced with the targeted gravely honk, telling stubborn cars to pull to the side, and then the siren picked up right where it left off.

Ayse jumped to her feet. She moved quickly to the center of the rec room, listening intently to see if the siren was in fact getting closer still. Willing it to grow faint, to careen elsewhere. Perhaps that gravel honk was to clear the way for a harrowing left turn? Or to signal a stop in a yellow zone several blocks away?

But no. The siren was closer.

Closer.

And then closer still.

Ayse looked around. Cami, Sister Bridget, and Didi were on their feet, too, their worries matching hers.

"Is that the police?" Didi's voice was pinched with panic.

Ayse's words came out as tight as a knot. "I don't know."

The siren let out another wail, closer still.

Cami had wrapped her arms around herself in an effort to quell whatever distress was rapidly rising. "Maybe they'll pass us."

Sister Bridget twisted the rosary on her belt. "God willing."

Ayse whispered, "I thought you said God wasn't here."

"Might as well play the odds?" Sister Bridget said.

But the odds were not in their favor. The siren wailed, ringing around the Pay to Stay walls, making their heads spin. A banshee here to claim her victim. A turbine arriving to chop them to pieces. A buzz saw ruffling the tiny hairs in their ears right before the blade made contact. The siren, and whatever vehicle it was attached to, came right to the north side of the building.

Ayse looked and saw that Russell was still lying flat on his back. He hadn't shifted a muscle. He appeared frozen, but she couldn't tell if it was from fear or anger or institutional compliance.

Cami made a move to go to him, but Ayse held her back. "Let him be. We have a bigger problem."

Cami cast him one last glance, then nodded. Everyone besides Russell left the rec room, closed the double doors behind them on instinct, and went to the exterior doors facing their dedicated parking lot. They crammed their faces around the one caged window and saw a heavy-duty flat-bed truck outfitted with Los Angeles Fire Department equipment pull up the driveway. Ayse felt some relief that Maureen had shaken off whatever catatonia had been threatening a minute ago and was standing next to her. She needed someone who could be calm in a crisis, and the other inmates did not fit the bill.

Didi was practically bouncing with nerves. "Oh God, oh God, oh God."

Sister Bridget whispered, "What are they doing here?"

Ayse knew the answer from her dad's buildings. "The fire alarm. Fire departments can be automatically notified if a sprinkler goes off."

Didi let out an animalistic little shriek of frustration. "Oh, that's just great. Just peachy."

Sister Bridget shushed her as they continued to look out the tiny window. An extremely tall woman with shaved short blond hair got out of the driver's seat and pulled at the bolted fence.

Cami let out a squee of relief. "Okay, maybe they'll leave!"

They weren't that lucky. The woman returned to the rig, but instead of getting back in her seat, she opened a side compartment of the truck bed and got out a pair of bolt cutters. Within seconds, she had snapped the chain holding the fence shut like it was a limp noodle, slid the gate to the side, and pulled the rig into the parking lot.

Cami was back to chewing her glittered fingernails. "How does this nightmare keep getting worse?"

Didi crossed her arms. "I say we don't let them in. Pretend we're not here."

Sister Bridget looked at Didi with something between pity and sheer annoyance. "So they walk around the building and go ask the cops ten yards away to come open the door for them?"

Didi made a little harrumph. "Well, fine, if you want to be all doom and gloom about it."

Cami whispered to Ayse, "I thought the whole point of jail was no one came in or out."

Ayse whispered back, "And now it's Incarceration Penn Station." Ayse thought back to when the fire department had come to her dad's building on Fairfax Avenue after a copier had decided to ignite like a demon. "Okay, normally they come in, check that the water is off in the sprinkler system, reset the alarm, and sometimes write up some paperwork for insurance."

Maureen was trying to hold on to Ayse's words through the fog of a near concussion. "So we let them see whatever they came to see, and they'll leave quickly?"

Ayse nodded. "That's our best chance."

Sister Bridget was mapping it out as well. "So that's the office and the maintenance room. No need for them to see the cells, or the kitchen, or the freezer." She had the good sense not to finish the rest of the sentence: *the freezer where there are two dead bodies.*

Maureen was on board. "Okay, in politics, you can lie more easily if you actually stick to the truth."

Didi shook her head. "Is that a riddle?"

"Just whatever happens next, whatever they ask us, try to tell the truth as much as possible," Maureen clarified. "If you can't, adjust the subject to a topic you can be truthful about."

Didi shrugged. "We went from *Weekend at Bernie's* to 'I Didn't Inhale' as our strategy. Great. Feeling very confident."

They peeked through the window again. The driver was out of the vehicle, and her doting attention toward her passenger made the ranking between them clear even from a distance.

Ayse felt like there was something they were forgetting, but there was no time. "Shit, here they come." She turned to say something more to Maureen but only saw her back as she trotted away into the rec room. Ayse couldn't help but feel a little abandoned. "Okay. Do you, then."

As the two firefighters approached, Cami, Didi, Sister Bridget, and Ayse pressed themselves up against the wall.

Didi hissed, "I say Sister Bridget opens the door."

Sister Bridget hissed back, "That's the second time you've tried to make me take the lead. You take the lead."

Ayse couldn't think. She knew she needed to open the door, but she couldn't move off the wall. She saw the shadows coming through the window, and then they heard the authoritative knock.

No one moved.

Muffled voices made their way through the doors.

The woman who had snipped off the chain said, "Captain, seems like the building is vacant for the holiday."

A second woman's voice answered, "Lieutenant, are you saying vacant buildings can't burn down?"

The lieutenant was dutifully ashamed. "No, Captain."

The captain replied, "Good. Let's get the battering ram."

Cami, Ayse, Didi, and Sister Bridget stood frozen, unsure what to do, when Maureen came careening around the corner. She had changed out of her crime scene scrubs and back into the business suit she had arrived in.

She called out cheerfully, "Coming! Coming. I'm so sorry." She gestured to Sister Bridget, who instantly understood and handed her the key pass to the door. Maureen opened the door with the welcoming demeanor of a neighborhood granny hosting a tea party. "Come in, come in! Welcome!"

The captain was shorter than her (extremely tall) lieutenant. Her dark hair had wide streaks of gray at the temples, and it was all pulled back into a French braid so tight it also worked as a DIY facelift. Her double-breasted uniform coat was fastened to the top, the brass buttons gleaming, along with official commendation buttons on her lapels. "Hello, ma'am. LAFD got an alert that a sprinkler system went off in this building. We're here to ensure that there are no lingering fire risks."

Maureen was all *aw, shucks* guffaws. "Yes. That was me. But I can assure you it was just a tiny candle."

The captain stepped forward to cross the threshold and was surprised when Maureen moved with her, delicately blocking the way. The captain's voice betrayed a slight tone of annoyance. "We really should take a look. Make sure there's no possibility of an electrical fire."

Maureen knew a losing hand, and stepped aside. "Ah, yes. Anything for safety."

The captain entered with authority, but she was immediately thrown off her Boss Energy when she saw the other four women pressed to either side of the door. "Good God!" she called out in alarm.

The lieutenant leaped to put her body between her beloved captain and whatever threat had been identified, and seemed oddly disappointed when it was just four people waving sheepish hellos.

Cami smiled her big Bambi smile. "Sorry, we were waiting for the key."

The captain was trying to shake off that she had jumped like she had seen a Victorian ghost and said, "Of course." She looked around. "So what is this place?"

Ayse felt these words hit her in the chest like the aforementioned battering ram. She didn't know if she dared to hope, so she repeated, "What is this place?"

The lieutenant was looking around, too. "Yeah. This is listed as a city building. Is it an office?"

Clinging to Maureen's idea of lying through truth, Ayse said, "Something like that. Let's show you where the fire was." With Maureen at her shoulder, Ayse confidently led them toward Bard's office and, more importantly, away from the cells. Ayse noticed that as they turned, Cami, Didi, and Sister Bridget lingered in front of the doors to the rec room, acting as another barrier between their unexpected visitors and the dead giveaway at the end of the hall. They looked like three kids trying to hide that they'd broken a window, all cold sweat and awkward smiles.

Meanwhile, Maureen was really laying it on thick, and Ayse was here for it. "Captain, how long have you been in the LAFD?"

The captain sniffed with self-importance, "Thirty-two years."

The lieutenant added, "And I have been with the department for thirteen years."

The captain held up a hand in impatience. "No one asked, Chelsea."

"Yes, Captain. My apologies, Captain. It won't happen again, Captain," Chelsea the lieutenant said, but the smile on her face revealed her humiliation kink.

Ayse opened the door to Bard's office. "So the tiny fire was in here." She caught a glimpse of the piles of evidence bags and the crime scene tape behind the desk, and promptly slammed the door shut again. So *that* was what she had almost remembered.

The captain, who was mid-step, collided with Ayse. "Uh, you are gonna need to open the door for me."

Chelsea the Kink added, in a tone desperate for more praise, "Captain needs that door open now!"

Maureen laughed a tinkling giggle. "Oh, we just need to give you a little context."

Ayse met Maureen's eyes in panic, wondering/telegraphing if Maureen had forgotten what was on the other side of this metal door. "Is there context, Maureen?"

Didi, Cami, and Sister Bridget had joined them, their eyes darting around like dogs who had stolen the Christmas ham.

Maureen laughed again. "Well, let's see what you make of it, actually." And with that, Maureen swung the door open, not a care in the world. Ayse wondered if perhaps letting the person with the concussion lead this operation wasn't the savviest choice and, relatedly, if it was too late to make a run for it.

Captain and her lieutenant entered the office and took a slow turn around the desk. The captain looked at the puddles of water and the bags of evidence. The lieutenant gave the crime scene tape around the desk chair a little scrape with her heavy boot. Ayse's eyes lingered on the gouges Bard's nails had made on the desk as he died, then willed herself to look anywhere else.

The captain was a professional through and through, and immediately homed in on the scorch marks on the wall and the tiny pile of ash near the candle. "Ah. I see what's happening here."

Ayse heard a uniform sharp intake of breath from her fellow inmates, and even Maureen's can-do smile slipped a single notch. Ayse had to get in front of this. "We can explain."

The captain held up her hand, but it was the lieutenant who spoke. "Don't interrupt the captain!"

The captain hissed, "Jesus Christ, Chelsea, can you take it down?"

"Sorry, ma'am."

"No more double espresso for you. It makes you way too hyper."

"Yes, ma'am."

The captain turned back to the inmates. "So this is some kind of crime scene training program. Interesting."

Ayse's voice caught in her throat. "Training program?"

Maureen stepped forward. "Oh, Ayse, don't be so sensitive." Maureen turned to the captain. "It's technically a Crime Scene Readiness Exam. We've already completed the training."

Chelsea tried to regain some ground. "Oh yes. I've heard about this. Read a lot of articles. They're planning one for the fire department."

The captain was confused. "Really? I didn't hear about that. And I see the director, Jill, every first Monday for Stitch 'n Bitch."

Maureen was thrilled to follow the captain's line of (misguided) thought. "Oh, Jill. She's a hoot." Maureen tried to turn the captain toward the door, but the captain stayed put, much to everyone's chagrin.

The captain shrugged. "I think she's a real pain."

Maureen pivoted fast. "How did you know this was a Crime Scene Readiness Exam?"

The captain looked so pleased, with a sly grin and a puffed-out chest, that Ayse almost expected her to brush some imaginary dirt off her shoulder. "First off, this is a city-owned building, and I saw all the cops on the back side of the block. So whatever is happening in here has to do with law enforcement."

Maureen was nodding. "Absolutely. All true."

The captain smirked with satisfaction, and was about to speak when Chelsea jumped in, a little too confidently, "Secondly, this is clearly a fake crime scene."

Cami let out a nervous giggle, which Sister Bridget covered by patting her on the back the way a mother pats a baby who needs to burp.

"Lieutenant! I'm doing the list. I am *listing*. You are *listening*." The captain regained her composure and turned back to the (unbeknownst to her) inmates. "So, as I was saying, yes, this is fake crime scene, but what really gave it away were your costumes."

Ayse couldn't help herself. "Our . . . costumes?"

"Yeah, you're clearly all playing some kind of preassigned role in the examination scenario." The captain pointed to Cami. "You have the actress." Captain pointed to Didi. "There is the high-end sex worker." Didi let out a humph of offense, but luckily the captain had moved on. "I must admit, I think a nun is when the whole scenario falls apart. Kind of takes it to a wacky place." The captain looked to Maureen. "As the administrator of the exam, I think you should keep the narrative more realistic. It's not fair to the test-taker." The captain put her hand on Ayse's shoulder, designating her as the person being examined.

Ayse was more than happy to play her role. "Yes. The nun really threw me." And this was true, but Ayse was thinking about her first day at Pay to Stay when she had met her holy cellie.

The captain kept her hand on Ayse's shoulder for a bit too long, then gave it a series of squeezes like it was an avocado she was testing for readiness. "Impressive deltoid work . . ."

She left the sentence on a lingering note as a hint.

"My name is Ayse," Ayse offered, catching said hint while also trying to figure out how to remove her arm from the captain's assessing grip.

The captain was looking Ayse over. "Great height, too. Ever thought about becoming a firefighter?"

Ayse smiled, hunt-and-pecking her way through her truthful reply. "I don't know if it's a career path that's available to me."

"Why? You got a criminal record or something?" Chelsea snarked.

Didi let out a weird shriek of a laugh, and everyone else's eyes went wide.

Ayse chose total truth dressed up as a joke. "Yup. Big-time felon. Serving time right now."

The captain cackled. "Strong physicality and a sense of humor? You would make a great member of any firehouse. Have your training officer call me. I can help you out." She winked, giving Ayse's shoulder a last squeeze.

Ayse returned the captain's smile, until she saw Lieutenant Chelsea's envy flash. Ayse's pulse was already racing, and a jealous underling was not helping her keep her nerve.

Maureen had taken a clipboard off the shelf and was taking notes. "Well, thank you for your support, Captain. I guess we got a little carried away with the scenario. Should not have lit a real candle. Note for next time."

Lieutenant Chelsea added, "And ditch the nun."

Maureen wrote that down, too, nodding. "The good news is, the candidate passed the test, so we are all done here."

The captain clapped her hands. "Fantastic." Then, to Ayse, she said in a softer tone, "You have plans to celebrate? I know a great place not too far from here, opens in an hour. We could talk about your future."

Ayse's eyes went wide, and she felt her throat go dry. "Wow, that is an incredible offer, Captain."

The captain demurred, "Please. Call me Lilah."

Lieutenant Chelsea let out a gasp that said she had never been allowed first-name privileges.

Ayse nodded. "Lilah. I appreciate your generosity. My schedule is, um, really locked down for the next few days." She was scrambling with what to say next. Rejecting this offer seemed only slightly dumber than accepting it.

Luckily for Ayse, Chelsea's envy was untethered. "Captain, we also need to check the sprinkler system. Reset the alarm."

Cami raised her hand. "I can show you where those are."

The captain said, "Great. You can handle that, Chelsea."

Chelsea was clearly miffed to be separated from her fearless leader, and stomped off like a disgruntled child.

The captain pulled her card from her coat pocket and pressed it into Ayse's hand. "You let me know if you want to come tour the firehouse. No pressure."

Ayse took the card and placed it in her own pocket. "Thank you so much."

"Any other sections of plumbing we should check? Bathrooms? A kitchen?" the captain asked.

Maureen said through tight lips, "Nope! No sprinklers were set off there. You have seen all there is for you to see!"

The captain sucked on her teeth. "Better take a spin to be sure."

Just then, Chelsea returned with Cami right behind her. "Sprinkler and alarms are charged and reset." Then, to Ayse: "Do you know how to repressurize a pipe for future emergency activation? No? I didn't think so." If Chelsea had hair, she would have flipped it over her shoulder in triumph. Instead, she flicked the bangs on her butch fade.

The captain sighed, mortified. "Chelsea! Honest to God!" She looked around. "Overall, your water damage doesn't seem too bad, but sometimes a full building inspection is necessary."

Maureen agreed while disagreeing, "If more water had come out, definitely. But this was quite minor."

The captain's professionalism was becoming a problem. "Eh, you'd be surprised. These older systems can still shoot about eight gallons of water per minute."

Maureen gasped. "Incredible! How much water do you think we had?" She looked to the other inmates, her face a plastered smile, pleading for anyone to guess. "Cami, what do you think?"

Cami said, "Water was on for five minutes, max, so forty gallons. But this eight-by-eight room is 512 cubic feet, and one cubic foot of water is only seven-ish gallons. So forty gallons is not going to make a huge impact, considering the drain."

Ayse looked where Cami was pointing. There was, in fact, a drain in the floor that she had not noticed until this moment.

The captain begrudgingly agreed, "Yeah, I don't see any real water damage. You're lucky you have cinder block and not dry wall."

Didi's eyes were rolling. "Yeah. Gotta love cinder blocks." Ayse shot her a *What the hell are you doing?* look that Didi knew she deserved.

Luckily, the captain didn't catch her snark. "Okay. Lieutenant, let's help these ladies clean up."

Didi coughed. "What?"

Chelsea reached into her utility belt and pulled out a tiny black square, which she shook with a flourish into a ballooned trash bag. "Absolutely." Without a single second of pause, Chelsea the Lieutenant swept the entire desk of collected evidence into her waiting garbage bag.

Didi let out a tiny gulp of horror as her precious work disappeared. Cami put an arm around her, partially in support and partially to keep her from grabbing baggies off the table before they were binned.

Sister Bridget stepped forward. "You all must be very busy. We can finish the cleanup."

Maureen added, "And we could reuse some of the evidence for another scenario."

Ayse put her hand out for the garbage bag, slowly, gently, palm open, in the same way she would offer an apple to an angry horse. Chelsea yanked the bag away, miffed yet again to have her captain-given task threatened. "Hands off."

The captain's mood darkened. "Reuse the evidence? But that could compromise the integrity of the exam. Is your superior telling you to reuse exams? Because if so, I can file a formal complaint. Where is the exam scenario? I'll reach out to the supervising examiner personally. Is it Jill? I knew she was shifty."

This turn made everyone's pulse jump up in speed. Losing the evidence was going to be a catastrophe, but Ayse had to wonder if getting these two out of Pay to Stay was actually more important. She decided it was. "Of course, we weren't thinking. Thank you, Chelsea."

Chelsea flashed Ayse a smile with all teeth and no warmth.

Ayse started to gently turn the captain out of the office and into the hallway. "I don't want to cut this short—"

"Me neither," the captain said in a low voice. "You know, I have a lot of really interesting stories from my time. I would be happy to share my experience with you. It could streamline your application. It would be no trouble."

Ayse willed herself to relax. "Oh my goodness. Wow. That is an incredible offer."

"Are you free next weekend?" the captain asked.

Ayse replied, "Weekends are hard for me. Let's keep in touch."

Didi, Cami, and Sister Bridget had lined up in front of the rec room doors again, a bizarre tableau of casual *who, me?* poses that conveyed more stress than someone catching a bullet in their teeth.

Ayse had gotten the captain and her lieutenant all the way to the end of the hallway. She was turning them to the right. The doors to the parking lot were just a few feet away. They were minutes—no, seconds—from being free of them.

Then, behind them, there was a knock on the south door.

A knock that said through sheer force *Open up or else.* No words required.

Everyone froze.

The only people who had access to the south side of the building were cops.

Ayse tried to pick up the pace, get the captain out, but the captain stayed put. "Are you going to answer that?"

Maureen smiled her big smile, but it was less convincing than before. "Oh, sure. Probably just someone wanting updated test results."

Another chest-crushing knock banged on the door.

The captain turned on her heel and walked right up to the back door. She held her hand out. "Who has the key card for this?"

Ayse tried to signal to Maureen to play dumb, to do anything besides hand the key card over. Instead, Maureen did exactly that, her face telegraphing how trapped she felt. How trapped they all were.

The captain swiped the key card and opened the door. On the other side was a young police officer. He was short in stature, but muscular to the point of comedy, with traps so pronounced they were threatening to become earmuffs. Instead of reading as intimidating, his muscles communicated his insecurity around his diminutive height. Even so, the fire department captain was shorter. She sniped, "Who the hell are you?"

Not the opening Ayse would have chosen.

The officer was clearly shocked to see another person in uniform. "I saw your rig in the parking lot, and I wanted to see what was up."

The captain gathered herself up to her full height. "Nothing is up, Boot."

Cami mouthed, "Boot?" to Ayse, who mouthed back, unsure, "A rookie?"

The cop did not like his authority being challenged from the jump. "I don't think your tone is necessary, ma'am."

"It's *Captain*, actually. And her tone is fine," Chelsea said over her beloved captain's head.

"Thank you, Lieutenant," the captain said, at last reveling in her overcaffeinated underling.

The cop was clearly not ready for a captain rank, but somewhere between his youth and his ego, he wasn't deterred. "I need to come in, take a look around."

The captain blocked him to the left, then to the right. It was a game of human pong, each trying to outmaneuver the other. Ayse's head was melting from the tension. How on God's green earth had they ended up in a turf war between the LAFD and the LAPD? She suddenly wondered if there had been innocent bystanders during the shoot-out at the O.K. Corral.

Lieutenant Chelsea snapped back, "You don't *need* anything, Boot. We have already secured this location."

Baby Boot couldn't back down, though. "I think it needs to be *properly* secured."

The word *properly* was received as intended: an insult.

The captain was really on a roll now. "You cowboys just want to stomp all over everything. I'm in emergency services, too, and I outrank you. If I tell you this area is secure, then it is secure. And you can take my word for it, or you can shove it. But you aren't disturbing these women because you're in need of an activity." The captain put her arm around Ayse, and Ayse struggled to know how to arrange her face. Match the captain's smug pout? Give the cop sympathetic eyes so he doesn't tally her up as an adversary? Shrink into a small puddle of fear on the ground and try to disappear? All bad options. The chances of this going right were getting slimmer by the second.

"I am going to enter these premises," the cop said in his best Cop Voice as his hand drifted toward his service weapon.

Ayse's body was drenched in sweaty fear. The chances of this going right had just dropped from slim to near zero.

The captain was raging now. "The hell you are!"

The police officer drew his weapon. "I have reason to believe this is a jail facility, and you are in extreme danger."

Chelsea laughed. "Are you serious?"

Ayse felt her stomach drop, and the sweat on her back quadrupled in less than a second. But the captain let out a bark of a laugh. "Ayse, tell the truth. Is this a jail?"

Ayse said, "Absolutely."

Then, like the damn angel she was, Sister Bridget put her hand on the captain's shoulder. Ayse noticed Sister Bridget had wrapped her rosary through her fingers for extra oomph. The Sister's face was as serene as her voice. "Oh, Captain, my Captain. Do not throw stones at he who has misstepped. And, Officer"—she read his name tag—"Kemper. You are only doing your job. May I share what I see?" There were reluctant nods from everyone in uniform. Apparently, Officer Kemper agreed God outranked them all. "I see three exemplary public servants whose goals for safety are in perfect alignment."

Ayse felt a light open up. Sister Bridget had found a way out for everyone, with their egos intact.

The cop sniffed. "That's true. That's all I cared about."

Sister Bridget put her hand on her heart. "Of course, Officer. Captain here has properly secured the premises for fire damage, water damage, and reset all systems. Now she needs to be on her way."

The captain liked this framing, as she was very important. "That's true. I don't even normally respond to field calls like this. I just happened to be in the area because we are on our way to City Hall." She said the last two words with all the inference of a threat.

The cop took a long breath, weighing his options. Unknowingly he was weighing all their fates, too.

At long last, Officer Kemper put his service weapon back in his holster and said, "Well, I need to get back to work, too. The mountain lion P-22 ate another celebrity dog, so the paperwork is going to take all night."

The captain gave him a nod of understanding, "Gotta keep your head on a swivel when you're walking those little dogs."

Officer Kemper agreed, "Ain't that the truth. The City of Angels, where lions live in our backyard."

The captain offered, as a joke and a truce, "Only outnumbered by the human cougars."

Kemper was pleasantly surprised by this genuinely funny quip, and laughed. "Oh God, yes."

The captain shook the officer's hand. "Take care, Boot."

Officer Kemper walked away, still smiling. He was halfway back to the maintenance lot when he called back, "Hey, I didn't mean to be insubordinate. The guys told me this was a jail, so that's why I was checking."

The captain laughed again, with Chelsea joining in much too loudly, which luckily covered the nauseating forced giggles from Cami and Didi. "They're just hazing you, Kemper. Don't take it personally."

As he waved and turned away, Maureen shut the back door, and the *ca-thunk* of the lock engaging was music to Ayse's distressed ears.

One down, two to go. Ayse wanted this "exiting" momentum to continue. "Well, we won't keep you any longer. Thank you so much for coming." Ayse attempted to find a pace that was authoritatively *leave now* but not tipping into *suspicious rushing*. Luckily, Cami had chosen to channel her anxiousness into some kind of zippy bouncing, which put her ahead of everyone else, and continued to draw their eyes toward the exit/away from the rec room doors. Without conversation, Maureen swiped the key card, and they opened the doors together.

Maureen trilled, "Take care. And thank you so much for your feedback on the exam."

The captain turned as if she had more to say, but in the face of five women waving goodbye, she waved, too. Chelsea only seemed too happy to get her captain back to herself, and was practically galloping to the truck as Maureen closed the door.

*Ca-thunk* went the lock.

# CHAPTER 11

## Cami Garcia: Information Drip

After the near miss of the fire department and the police knocking on the back door, everyone retreated to their cells in the kind of shared exhaustion that can only come after a fierce adrenaline spike. However, what began as rest turned into a fog of silence that smelled of fear, defeat, and simmering panic. The quiet was suffocating, but even the smallest exchange of words felt dangerous, as if the most innocuous sentence could morph into, at best, an accusation or, at worst, another attack. And through everything, Russell had not moved. His presence hung heavy, immovable and intimidating. Cami was worried about him, but her mind had not been idle. She had been brewing on an idea, and knew it was the only way forward.

First she went to Maureen. "Hey. How's your head?"

Maureen shrugged. "Fine enough. Just a big lump now."

"I have ibuprofen if you need it."

Maureen reached over to her side table and shook a tiny plastic bottle. "Thank you, but I'm a woman in my fifties. I don't go anywhere without ibuprofen. Besides, I have Mother Teresa over here."

It was true. Sister Bridget was sitting on the floor by Maureen's bed. "Hardly," she said. "But we don't know if you are concussed, and I don't want you falling asleep."

Cami nodded. "Good point. You did great with the captain and the cop."

Sister Bridget seemed genuinely flattered. "Thank you. I figured if we could keep everyone calm, we had a chance."

"Did you learn that at the convent?" Cami asked, curious.

The Sister smiled. "I worked at the nonprofit salsa company for former gang members. De-escalation on the kitchen line was a daily occurrence."

"I didn't know you worked there!" Maureen was bemused.

Sister Bridget nodded. "Oh yeah. Unfortunately, I was a little too trusting and unknowingly transported some drugs across state lines along with the pico de gallo. Now I'm here." She shrugged as if to say that was the cost of doing business. "Cami, if you could stay with Maureen for a second, I am going to get another book."

Once Sister Bridget left, Cami turned toward her goal. "Thank you for not saying it was Russell who attacked you."

"I wouldn't do that unless I was sure," Maureen responded in kind. "But you have to understand, it still could have been him."

Cami nodded. "That's why I need a favor."

A few minutes later, Ayse said from the center of the room, "It's dinnertime."

They moved as a group to the kitchen, nary a chat between them. In a single-file line, each heated their food and then went back to their cells. When Cami reentered the rec room, she walked past her own cell and instead gave a gentle knock at Russell's cell. He hadn't moved or talked to her since he had retreated there, and Cami had given him his space. But that was going to end now. "Hey. Join me for dinner?"

She could see in his eyes that Russell wanted to refuse, but then, at the last second, he softened. "Sure."

Cami had reheated several dishes, and after they had sat down, she set them up on her little side table into the tiniest picnic. As was her habit, she saved her favorite meals for her lowest moods, and she felt sure today definitely qualified for both of them. Cami set down two bowls of white rice topped with her mother's chicken adobo. She felt some tension release with every bite they shared, the scent of garlic and peppercorns filling the cell quickly. They ate for a while, passing food back and forth. The slight pucker on the inside of her cheeks from the rice vinegar, followed by the lingering sweetness, felt like her mother's love, whispering from outside the walls.

After the adobo, Cami gave Russell her absolute favorite thing: sticky rice cakes. "My Lola makes these *biko* every Christmas. They are like gold. So if you don't like it, give it back." She gently handed him the square, sweet with coconut milk and glistening with a caramelized-sugar exterior.

Russell took a small bite and closed his eyes. He said quietly, "I see what you mean. Definitely gold."

Cami leaned back and ate her *biko*, imagining her Lola seated at the kitchen table, the marigold-yellow oilcloth creating a glow, her wrinkled hands expertly forming the little squares of love while tiny grandchildren ran around the house, squealing with anticipation.

The quiet camaraderie nourished them as much as the sugar.

Once dinner was done, Cami reached into her pocket. She pulled out Maureen's second cell phone. This was the favor she had asked for. She handed it to Russell, and he took it like it was a deadly jack-in-the-box ready to pop.

"Your arrest file is on there."

Russell nodded. "Did you read it?"

Cami nodded. "Yes."

"It was all true, what she said. I shot someone."

"I know."

"I could spend a lot of time telling you why I did it or making it sound not as bad. That he made a full recovery. That I was young. That I would never do it again. And that's all true. But it doesn't change what I did. I can't have you turning me into some kind of prop."

Cami simply said again, "I know."

There was a beat; then he asked, "So what now? What do you want me to do with this?" He sounded a bit annoyed, but there was something else, something vulnerable in his posture. His shoulders were curled over as if to protect his soft emotional underbelly.

"Nothing. I guess I wanted you to know that I know what you did and I still want to be your friend."

Russell looked at Cami with amusement. "You're a trip."

Cami smiled, feeling the tension crack between them. "I thought I was living in a fantasy."

He laughed. "Oh, trust me. You are. This Pay to Stay shit is wild. People inside aren't going to believe me when I tell them about this place."

Cami took on a faux-serious tone. "All right, then, Washington. Tell me what it's really like. Tell me what I'm missing."

Russell thought for a second, then said, "Where I grew up, opioids hit hard. Gangs at the fringes of the neighborhood supplying when pharmacies closed up. I saw boys go into prison and come out men. My parents would make us go to their welcome-home parties when they were released. I hated those parties." He whispered the last sentence, a tinge of shame in his voice.

"Why?" Cami asked.

"Something always felt off to me. Whoever the center of attention was, they were so happy to be out. But even though they were physically there with us in the room, I felt like there was some part of them that hadn't really come back. Especially the ones who had been inside for a while. I saw their eyes casting about rooms they used to know, tallying up all the changes. Neighborhoods that were no longer familiar. Strangers in their own lives. The silent mourning for all the time they had lost that they would never get back. I think about that now. I think about every day that I've missed . . . that I'm still missing. It's a lot of days, Cami."

Cami struggled with what to say. Everything that came to her felt either trite or dismissive. She hadn't known the people Russell had grown up with. How was she supposed to counter a narrative that he had so much experience with, both first- and secondhand? "That doesn't have to be you, though," she said finally.

"Maybe. But it was weird—when I was in the convenience store, holding the gun at the clerk, I saw all those men from my neighborhood in my mind. They were warning me to stop, to throw the gun down a gutter and never stop running. Instead, I pulled the trigger. I was a bad little kid who was becoming a bad man, and I needed to end the suspense. I wanted to rush towards what felt inevitable, because the tension in waiting was so painful and I couldn't stand it anymore."

Cami didn't say anything this time. She just waited.

After a few minutes, Russell said, in a voice so quiet she had to lean forward to hear him, "A few years into my sentence, I got to take a writing class. That was dope. We read about Persephone. You know who that is?"

Cami smiled. "Yes, I know who that is."

"Persephone. The goddess of spring, born in the light, always on her way back to the underworld. Barely able to enjoy life with the living when she knew every day brought her closer to the River Styx. *I felt that.* I had been feeling like that my whole life. And this"—he looked around Pay to Stay—"has brought that feeling back. I'm not in max right now, and that's nice. But I am always on my way back to hell. So what's the use in trying to stay out."

Cami took the phone back and opened a search window for *San Quentin News*, the newspaper written by and for incarcerated people. She held it out to him. "This is why. And I want you to read it to me."

Russell was confused. He looked at the phone screen. Then his frown was replaced with an expression of recognition.

"I want you to read it," Cami said again.

Russell cleared his throat and settled in:

> INMATE 431130 Russell Washington (Huntsville—Texas) entered via mail the following essay for San Quentin News. Reprinted with permission:
>
> For most people once upon a time means fairy tales of sweeping love, and justice restored. For them, once upon a time always ended with happily ever after. But *we* know the truth: Happily Ever After is sanitized cartoon garbage for children. Happily Ever After is only for people who never read the originals where Once Upon A Time is closer to a warning than an invitation to dream.

The real fairy tales are stories of patterned cruelty, unanswered injustices, and a whole lot of death.

Fairy tales are still being written today, and they go something like this: Once upon a time there was a large system of the government that ensnared thousands of people per day, entrapping them for the rest of their lives in an endless maze. It stole children like the Pied Piper. It cursed people to endless labor like Sisyphus. It tore families into little pieces based on nothing but rumor.

There were many people who all were part of this system, and who revered the system as if it were real. As if the system was a sorceress on a mountain peak raining down hell. As if the system was an ogre, terrorizing a small town in the countryside. As if the system was a hungry wolf, and they absolutely must feed him. Feed him feed him feed him.

The people all threw up their hands, claiming that the system insisted it be this way, and they begged for mercy. Except they themselves were the system. Behind their desks, pushing piles of paper, they were the ogres, the sorcerers, and the insatiable wolves scratching at the door. The system was a broken puppet screaming orders, and the people whose hands were making the puppet move were playing the biggest game of all—pretending to be powerless.

I wonder what life will be like when I get released. I wonder what happens after the story is over, or at least this part.

We have all seen people leave prison only to return. To recidivate on purpose because life outside was too hard, too complicated to navigate. Imagine a world where the ogre makes you feel lost without his foot on your neck. I know life outside has changed since I left it. I know it will feel impossible to rejoin a world that doesn't want me. Felon is a permanent status that if you let it will chew away at your identity until only that word is left.

Not me.

Never me.

Once I get out, I will not let the wolf at my door drag me back here no matter how many nights he howls.

When I get my chance, I will be free—in every sense of the word.

Editor's note: Inmate 431130's essay caused significant disruption to his overall prison environment. He is being transferred from his current residence to resolve the unrest.

Russell put the phone down and rubbed his eyes. He took several deep, shuddering breaths. When he finally looked up, his gaze settled somewhere in the middle distance. "So that *is* why I'm being transferred."

"You didn't know that was why? They didn't tell you?" Cami asked.

Russell shook his head. "Nope. I wrote that essay. Mailed it off. Really didn't think anything of it. Suddenly, I was in SHU—solitary," he clarified off Cami's look, "and then I was being transferred."

Cami felt naive but still couldn't contain her shock. "How can they do that to you?"

Russell, for his part, appeared to cherish the naivete; his smile was soft when he said, "Cami, that's what I keep trying to tell you. Once you're inside, they can do whatever they want."

As soon as he said it, something in Cami clicked. "Wait. Wait, wait, wait." She stood up, pacing a bit. "What's happening to you now—this transfer—is about what happened when you were already in prison. It's not about your original arrest."

Russell nodded. At this point, he seemed willing to follow Cami anywhere her mind took them. "Yes, agreed."

"That has to apply to us, too. Right? Most of these printed files, they're all old. Arrest records. Minute orders from the court. District attorney recommendations. This is all public knowledge. What got Bard killed has to be related to *now*, to something that happened *here* after our arrests. Even Janet's motive was related to Bard stalking her at the fundraiser."

Russell was with her. "Right. Okay. So you think whoever killed Bard, it was because of something that happened with him since they were locked up."

Cami nodded. "And that narrows down how much of this"—she gestured to the pile of shredded paper—"we need to focus on. The printed stuff isn't from now. It's from before. We need to find anything that has Bard's writing on it."

"Absolutely."

As they started working through the piles of paper, looking for any scribble, Cami felt Russell's eyes on her, nervous and unsure. "What is it?" she asked.

Russell looked over his shoulder, clocking that no one else was within earshot. "I know you're new here in Pay to Stay, but do you have an idea? Of who the killer could be?"

Cami shook her head. "At first I thought Janet. But . . ." She didn't have to finish the sentence. He understood.

Russell lowered his voice even more. "What do you think about Sister Bridget?"

Cami was shocked. "Seriously?"

Russell nodded.

"Why?"

Russell waited, and Cami realized he didn't want to tell her. His eyes were darting around, and he seemed to regret bringing this up.

"Russell, why?" she pushed.

Finally, he said, "I don't think she's a real nun."

Cami was bewildered. Her brain felt like it had slid out of her ears. "What are you talking about?"

Russell grimaced, clearly wishing Cami had bought into his theory more quickly. "She doesn't say grace. She didn't flinch when I took the Lord's name in vain. And that is not the prayer to Saint Anthony." Cami was struggling to see it, but he pushed on, "She just . . . she feels off. I can't totally explain it."

Cami turned this over in her mind. She wondered, aside from the habit, what had made her believe Sister Bridget was a nun. She was surprised to realize she couldn't come up with anything. "You think she's faking it?"

Russell shrugged. "I don't know. I do know that people in prison adopt all kinds of identities if they think it will keep them safe, if they think it will give them power. Something about her reminds me of that."

Cami didn't want to lie to Russell. "Okay, I hear that. But I don't know if that makes her capable of two murders."

Russell nodded, agreeing. "Fair. I just think we need to be a little wary."

They turned back to the piles of paper, searching for handwritten notes. Even with this narrowed focus, progress was slow. Several hours passed by, and they had little to show for it.

Cami felt nothing but relief when Didi announced to the group, "Lights will shut off in fifteen minutes." No one had figured out how to turn off the timer, and Cami wondered if any of them had tried that hard. Having the day definitively end for all of them felt like their closest version of safety.

Once Cami was in bed, she said, "Hey, Russell."

"Yeah?" he answered, his mattress back on her floor, his hands petting the faux-fur area rug.

"That essay you wrote—it was good. Really good."

Russell was grateful for the praise, but couldn't help rolling his eyes a bit. "Maybe. But I also fucked myself in the process. Just like Persephone. Always on my way back to hell."

Cami held his gaze, dead serious. "Always on your way back to life."

# CHAPTER 12

## Ayse Demiri: Persona

Before she fell asleep, Ayse lay in her cot and plotted which version of herself she would be tomorrow. Not that long ago, she didn't have to do this planning. She used to feel agile in her various roles, able to shift at will depending on who she was with. The Russians saw nothing of her except a stern exterior of efficiency. The doctors caring for her father met a woman who took copious notes in every appointment, with follow-up emails typed in succinct bullet points. That version of Ayse was also charming, all in service of endearing herself and her father to the people in charge of his health. The tenderness Ayse embodied while caring for her dad felt like the truest version of herself, which she fastidiously guarded from the prying eyes of the world, saving it only for him. At first, Pay to Stay seemed like nothing more than a new role she would have to don at will. Every Friday through Monday, Ayse had projected a frosty detachment to the others that offered no opening for closeness or questions.

However, in the weeks since Bard's ambush at the doctor's office, this never-ending carousel of roles had become more taxing. Her emotional reflexes weren't as speedy. She was showing up to illegal cash drops all accommodating smiles. Once, when she was in a physical therapy appointment for her dad, she realized she was reacting as if she were in a hostile police interrogation instead of just a clinical welfare check on her dad's mobility level. Worst of all, there were exactly three moments when Ayse hadn't been able to access the kindness her father deserved, instead meeting him with shrewd efficiency and zero care in her eyes.

Ayse had to meld these personas now to get through this weekend. She couldn't totally become the doting daughter—that was too vulnerable. But she needed others to trust her, and no one felt trust with the emotional equivalent of granite. She chose her doctor's office identity—careful, caring, and focused on the details.

But what were the details? Besides the dead bodies and the possible crack in Maureen's skull?

Ayse could hear whispering. She had to assume it was coming from Russell and Cami, who had been bunking together.

She heard Didi tossing and turning in her cell, like a piece of chicken in Shake 'n Bake.

Sister Bridget was still, but there was a quiet murmur. A prayer?

Lastly, there was Maureen's cell, from which Ayse heard no noise at all.

Ayse knew who she thought was behind it all, but her theories wouldn't mean anything if no one was on her side. She needed to look for a moment to tell the others, to create a majority so that when the weekend ended, they would have a united front and one mutually agreed upon suspect.

At last, Ayse fell into an uneasy sleep.

# DAY 4

## DECEMBER 30

# CHAPTER 13

## Ayse Demiri: Teamwork Makes the Dream Work

The previous evening had ended with each inmate retreating to the relative safety of their cells and using some amount of homespun security measures to fasten their bars shut. The morning began with people regretting the furious knots they had tied the night before. What had seemed shrewd then now looked paranoid in the daylight.

"I haven't had enough coffee for this," Maureen whined as she struggled with a series of knotted dress shirt sleeves.

Didi quickly snipped her heavy-duty zip ties with craft scissors and slipped her bars open. "And you all said my zip ties were flex-cuff coded. Well, look who's free now."

Ayse yanked the last of her own knot apart. "Free at last!" She stepped out of her cell and into the rec room's center. "Okay, well . . . relatively free. Do you need help, Maureen?"

"Please, thank you so much," Maureen replied.

Meanwhile, Russell was wrestling with the extra pillowcase Sister Bridget had knotted. "Good Lord, Sister. How did you do this?"

Sister Bridget looked sheepish. "I don't really know. The lights were already out."

"Sorry about taking the Lord's name in vain," Russell said with remorse.

Sister Bridget missed his apology entirely and instead clapped happily when she saw the knot finally come loose.

Ayse was changing shoes when she saw Maureen waiting for her in the center of the rec room, everyone else having left for breakfast. "What's up? You feeling okay?" Ayse asked.

Maureen smiled. "Yeah, much better. Thank you." She looked over her shoulder to make sure they were alone; then she asked quietly, "What do you know about Cami?"

Ayse shrugged. "Not much, honestly."

"Did you know she has this terrible boyfriend on the outside?" Maureen said, her voice even lower. "He controls her whole life."

Ayse wished she was more surprised. "That's terrible."

"You don't think it could be happening again?" Maureen gave a subtle flick of her eyes toward Russell's empty cell, her meaning clear.

Ayse wanted to push back immediately, but tried to play it cooler than that. "They just met."

Maureen sucked her teeth. "Did they? And I just don't totally trust the nicest-felon routine. Seems like an act."

Ayse didn't like where this was going. "There is literally no way you can know that."

Maureen lowered her voice even more. "I think mostly I'm mad at myself."

"For what?"

Maureen was clearly battling some shame, her eyes to the floor. "I think we should have called the cops the second we found Bard. I shouldn't have let him convince us to stay inside, or for us to immediately rule out someone else coming in to kill Bard. That was a huge mistake."

Ayse felt a little sick at this framing; it had traction. "Hey, if it was a mistake, it was a mistake we all made. Together. And for what it's worth,

I think he was right: No one would have bothered to investigate this properly with seven perfect suspects already on hand."

Maureen grimaced. "I know he seems nice, but from the second we found Bard, Russell set the stage for how this week would go. That was smart—maybe too smart. This whole murder has a ticking clock and limited suspects. No one can get through this without an ally, agreed?"

Ayse nodded, as much as she didn't want to.

Maureen continued, "Day one, Russell clocked the most easily manipulated person here the second he walked in. He has nothing to lose; he's going back to prison no matter what. So why not kill someone he hated?"

"But why did he hate Bard?"

Maureen had an answer for that: "Seemed like they maybe knew each other. Remember that private conversation they had the first night? Bard worked at other prisons before here. Maybe their paths crossed. Maybe Bard made him snap. I don't know. But I do know Russell is the only new factor, who manipulated us into staying here—and by staying inside we are all muddying the waters of what happened, making us all look guilty even though we aren't."

Ayse didn't like how much sense this was making. She couldn't tell if she was rejecting it for emotional reasons or logical ones. Regardless, she couldn't sign on just yet. "You're forgetting about the transfer letters, though. Those were new this weekend."

Maureen waved her words away like they were nothing more than a pesky fly at a DNC barbecue. "Those letters were shitty but nothing new. Bard was always pulling crap like that. We knew better than to react. My lawyer would have shredded the transfer in an afternoon."

Ayse could hear the chatter of everyone else in the kitchen. The microwave dinging. Cutlery scraping on plates. They needed to wrap this up before someone came out and discovered this little confab.

Maureen pressed, her voice getting even more urgent and hushed, "I don't care what Cami says. *We* are different. *We* all have a lot to lose. Janet understood that. She was suspicious of him, too. You know that.

And now she's dead." Maureen took a second, then added, seemingly against her better judgment, "Didi agrees that he's the one. If you do, too, that's three of us."

A majority.

Ayse could see the path ahead. If she went along with pinning it all on Russell, they could skate away. It was so tempting. Her life: restored. Her father: safe. All she had to do was sign on. She had chosen her father over Cami when Bard made her. What was so different about this?

The best Ayse could muster was, "I'll think about it."

"Thank you," Maureen said with a sigh of genuine gratitude.

They left the rec room and entered the kitchen. Ayse drank a large glass of water at the sink as a way to steady her nerves before sitting down, waiting until Maureen's words stopped rattling around her brain. When she felt like she could hear only her own thoughts again, she took a seat, happy to refocus her attention on the börek she had brought for breakfast.

Everyone was politely passing this and that along the long metal table. If Ayse squinted, she could imagine this was not prison at all, but instead just the worst bed-and-breakfast on the planet. The thought oddly cheered her as she imagined writing a review for a travel site. *Welcome to PTS B&B. No windows. Everything bolted to the floor. Two dead bodies. One lizard. Zero stars.*

Sister Bridget saw her smile and asked, "What are you thinking about, Ayse?"

"Nacho," Ayse said simply.

After her third cup of coffee, Maureen tentatively spoke up. "Maybe we see what evidence we can salvage?"

Ayse shrugged. "Can't hurt, I guess."

"What do you think, Didi?" Maureen asked.

Didi's eyes were wild. "Sure!" She gave an awkward double thumbs-up, and her normally perfectly beach-waved hair was a pile of frizz.

Sister Bridget was immediately concerned. "Didi, dear, are you feeling all right?"

Didi shot up. "Me? I'm great! I actually had an amazing idea last night. A real brainstorm of fun!"

Ayse tried to keep her face neutral, but despite her effort, a grimace itched at the edges. "What kind of idea?"

Didi put her arms up above her head in triumph. "A *surprise* idea."

"Why am I scared right now?" Ayse's deadpan delivery seemed to give voice to how everyone was clearly feeling.

Cami was also unsure. "Haven't we had enough surprises?"

Didi waved her away. "Oh, pish. Let's see what evidence we can salvage. Then this afternoon, while you all go outside for the second day of building maintenance, I will set up the fun!"

Maureen's smile was full, but her voice had a distinct note of trepidation. "I think that's a good plan." She added pointedly for the rest of the group, "And we can always reassess at lunch the best course of action for the afternoon."

Didi started bouncing around. "Who's ready to search for some evidence we may have missed? Come on, Sister, pray for a miracle! Your lot love a little Jesus in the everyday."

"If she's on something, I want some," Ayse said under her breath.

Maureen added, "And if she's not on something, we should all be scared."

As breakfast was finished, Ayse saw Russell pull Cami aside. He said quietly, "Cami, can you secure me back in my cell?"

Cami's head whipped around, her voice much louder than his. "What? Why?"

The strength and confidence Russell had had on day one was gone completely now as he said, "I feel safer in there."

Ayse wondered if this was the act that Maureen was suspicious of. He looked genuine—but what did that mean?

Cami was ready to argue with Russell, but Ayse stepped in, her doctor's office persona—charming, kind—at the ready. "Russell, are you saying you don't want to find some wisp of possibly bullshit evidence while Didi breathes stinky gold-leaf kale smoothie breath down your neck? Does that seriously not feel like a fun time? We can get her a mint."

Russell laughed, seeming grateful for the comical excuse. "Yeah, I am just super bad at looking for stuff. I never learned how. Hard to lose stuff in a cell."

Cami rolled her eyes and laughed along. "Wow, so you get to go nap, and meanwhile I am recreating a crime scene?"

Russell gave a quirky shrug. "What can I say? I'm a real grinch like that."

If Maureen was right and he was danger masquerading as harmless, Russell was really selling it. Ayse shook this thought away. She had to rely on what she saw with her own eyes; otherwise what was to keep her from suspecting everyone of being a sociopath? If Russell did something shady, she could decide then.

After returning to the rec room, Cami covered her shoes in little booties. "Good thing this is the last day. We're running out of foot booties."

Ayse had to help Sister Bridget into her forensic coveralls. "Reach your left arm a little lower; there ya go."

"My back has been spasming since yesterday," Sister Bridget said by way of an apology to Ayse.

Ayse didn't mind, though. "Of course." Helping Bridget made Ayse miss her father even more than she normally did. Letting her guard down even this tiny bit felt surprisingly welcome. Two parts of her psyche at last integrating into a harmonious whole, and she could finally take a full breath without policing her every move.

As Ayse zipped into her own suit, she saw Cami securing Russell into his cell by triple-knotting a spare sheet she had apparently packed. Cami was also giving him detailed instructions.

"So first you take the little yellow pouch. In there is a set of under-eye patches. Get them as close to your lash line as possible and tap tap tap them into place using your ring finger."

"My ring finger?" he asked, incredulous but clearly loving the attention.

"Yes," Cami answered firmly. "Your index finger can damage the delicate skin. Then lay over the eye patches this snail essence sheet mask. Those both need to be on for at least thirty minutes."

Russell's eyes popped. "Thirty minutes?"

"*At least.* Ideally, sixty minutes. When you take the masks off, do not rinse off the goo. You take the *gua sha*—yes, that little thingy—and sweep it up your face like this." Cami did some smooth motions from her chin toward her hairline with a tiny jade crescent. "I will know if you don't. Your skin is in desperate need of hydration, and don't even get me started on your lack of lymphatic drainage."

Laughing and utterly charmed, Russell was already opening his first tiny pouch and navigating the two under-eye patches that were consistently sticking to him and then to each other. "Are you sure these aren't the slugs?"

"Hush. Tonight, we will do some paraffin socks."

Russell saw Ayse watching this exchange and said to her, "If I die of poisoning, you know where it came from."

Cami waved him off and said, "See you in a couple hours. Holler if you need anything."

Ayse was surprised to see Cami's face go from a cheerful smile to a crumbled squish of distress as she turned away from Russell. "Are you okay?" she asked Cami quietly, as it was clear she was trying to hide whatever she was feeling from Russell.

Cami shook her head. "I don't know why—you'd think I would be used to it by now for myself and for him—but locking someone up makes me feel horrible. Really, truly rotten. I mean, I'm imprisoning him. Me. I'm doing it."

Ayse couldn't resist the simplicity of this and the lens it cast on their own incarceration. "Yeah. You have to wonder how this all helps."

Cami's voice was harsh in a way that surprised Ayse. "It doesn't help. It doesn't help anyone. And I am not saying that in a bratty woe-is-me way. Literally every prison policy report reflects that. Every iota of data shows that how we go about 'solving crime' in America actually makes crime rise, and prisons are a huge part of that. I mean, did you feel rehabilitated by Bard, the worst person in here by a mile? Did he ever help anyone? No. Prison doesn't work, but yet here we all are."

Ayse stopped in her tracks. "Did you just cite . . . prison policy?"

Cami looked up as if she was coming back to her senses. "What? Oh, don't listen to me. I saw a TikTok about it."

Ayse nodded along. Nevertheless, something about Cami's TikTok response didn't track, and Ayse couldn't quite place which part of it was sticking for her. Personal experience said that Cami's silly explanation of "reciting a TikTok" was the correct one. (And wasn't one of the Kardashians allegedly a criminal lawyer now?) Yes. Surely that was where Cami was getting this from. Ayse heard Maureen's voice in her head and had to use this second of privacy to ask, "Cami, why do you trust Russell?"

Cami looked genuinely surprised. "Why wouldn't I trust him?"

Ayse tried for a face that said *Come on, now* without tipping into condescension. "It's just . . . I know about your boyfriend."

Cami's mouth dropped open, but she tried to regain her (limited) composure. "Who have you been talking with?"

Ayse was regretting this. "Maureen and I are just worried that maybe you have been too trusting, that's all."

Cami's voice had an edge that Ayse had never heard before. "Wow. I thought you were different, Ayse. How do you not see that if you're more than your record, so is he?" And on that, Cami walked off.

Cami's social media sourced information aside, Ayse agreed. She thought back to her arrest and how, afterward, she had spent months volunteering at a shelter to prove remorse to the court ahead of her sentencing. How she had meticulously tracked every fine and fee, all of which she paid before their due dates and arrived at court with receipts printed in triplicate. What had struck her most of all was that she hadn't proved her goodness so much as she had proved that she had means to prove goodness. Everything she did cost money in some regard—via either time spent or funds committed. She had had the time and money to craft yet another persona—a *persona of remorse*—for the court, even as she continued to commit crime in her daily life. She had been able to afford the lawyer who could sell the narrative best suited to the judge whom he knew personally. When in reality, she felt no remorse at all. She felt only an unrelenting fear that her family would be torn apart by her absence.

Oddly, it was Bard's death that had allowed her the space to realize just how silly imprisonment was as a concept. Once he was dead, she could see that they were trapped in a bare stage play where they all acted their roles of reformed offender for a (now-murdered) audience of one who didn't care one way or another. That was the ideal scenario, as laid out by the American legal system. That was the best they could come up with. Without Bard here to play his role of antagonist, it all felt ridiculous.

Ayse entered Bard's office; Maureen, Sister Bridget, and Didi were already crawling all over the floor in their matching overalls. It was surreal and bizarre. Ayse was reminded of an ant farm after a new sprinkling of sugar, everyone so busy busy busy.

Cami joined Ayse and the rest of the group last. Ayse saw on her cheeks what looked like the remnants of tears that had been hastily wiped away. Still, Cami smiled at Ayse, and Ayse felt the weight in her chest soften, relieved to be forgiven for her assumptions.

Maureen took stock of the scene. "Why did the sprinklers only go off in here? Why didn't they go off in the rest of the building?"

"Most commercial sprinklers are designed to go off room by room instead of system wide, in order to reduce water damage to the rest of the structure," Ayse replied.

Maureen traced the water pipes with her eyes. "Makes sense."

Sister Bridget was running her rosary through her fingers. "And good thing, too. Water damage could have ruined all the files."

Cami nodded. "Oh, wow, I hadn't thought of that. Do you think whoever lit the candle wanted the files ruined?"

Ayse shrugged. "Who can say?"

Maureen took charge. "Okay, let me tell you what we had collected before Chelsea swiped it away."

"I still think there was a way we could have kept the evidence with us," Didi declared for the record.

Maureen said, not unkindly, "Perhaps, but the risk of them figuring out everything else was too great. I'll give up some random fibers if it means two bodies stay in the freezer."

Didi sighed, all petulance and annoyance. "Maureen had made this awesome tracking grid on the whiteboard, with ID numbers on the side."

Even though a lot of the writing had washed away, there was just enough that they were able to recreate a fair amount of what Didi and Maureen had accomplished previously. Maureen and Didi filled in the parts of the tracking grid through context clues.

"We had collected a variety of hairs from around the room," Didi recalled.

Maureen added, "There was that thread that could have been extremely important!" Then, biting her lip: "Or maybe it was just a thread."

Meanwhile, Ayse, Sister Bridget, and Cami sat to the side, like three JV players hoping to get subbed in to the varsity game. Nothing to do and nowhere to go.

Once again, Ayse stared for too long at the plastic scrapings from the desk mat, ripped off by Bard's fingernails during the attack. She wondered why her eyes kept being pulled back to that spot. Did she care whether Bard had suffered? No. She cared that a human suffered in the way that any suffering felt wrong. But him? Specifically? That added no extra level. Maybe the nail scrapings were one of the few signs that he was in fact human, and not what he had appeared to be: a bottomless pit of cruelty.

At one point, when Didi and Maureen were deeply ensconced in a tête-à-tête regarding a place where they thought they had found a scuff mark, Sister Bridget whispered to Ayse and Cami, "Do we really think any of this is going to make a difference? We don't even have this evidence that we are clinging so hard to."

Ayse whispered back, "Maybe it won't be helpful in proving anyone's innocence, but it's giving Cocaine Karen over there something to focus on."

It was true. Didi was spinning like a top and talking a mile a minute. "We are making tremendous progress! Excellent! Astounding!"

"*Nurse Jackie* meets Tony Montana at the end of *Scarface*," Ayse whispered.

Sister Bridget snorted a laugh. "Say hello to my little baggie."

Now it was Ayse's turn to snort.

Didi paid them zero attention, though. "So there are eight types of evidence. One: biological evidence. So blood, body fluids, hair, tissue. Had tons of that. Oh well. Next is what's called *latent prints*: fingerprints, palm prints, footprints. We got a lot of those yesterday, thank God! And I actually had stuck those in this file cabinet." She slid the drawer open and fanned out the print cards. "Next category is trace evidence, like fibers, soil, glass fragments. *Nada mucho*."

Maureen nodded. "We didn't find any of that." She seemed to say that more to assure the rest of the group that Didi was recalling things correctly, even if she seemed insane.

Didi was still talking, oblivious to her waning audience. "Digital evidence, tool marks—oh, and drug evidence. None of that was present. Finally, there's firearm evidence." Didi slid the desk drawer open, and all her momentum slammed into a brick wall. "Where's the gun?"

Maureen nearly leaped over to her. "What?"

Didi started laughing hysterically. "Oh my God. The gun is missing!" She was wheezing with laughter. "Of course it is! It's gone!" She grabbed her sides, wheezing with high-pitched giggles. "Where is it? Who took it? Who will die by it? Oh my God, have you ever heard anything so funny?!"

The old well of irritation at Didi flared up in Ayse again. "Hey! This is serious!"

Didi was bent in half, her laughter so intense she couldn't catch her breath. "It's so serious! Someone else is going to die! Is it you? Is it me? Maybe we can pull Bard out of the freezer and shoot him, too! Why not! Each take a turn like this is the Orient Express!"

Ayse looked to Maureen. "When did you last see it?"

Maureen thought hard. "We actually hadn't opened the desk once. We were just doing the areas around the desk."

"Do we make everyone turn out their cells?" Cami asked.

"I'm game if you are," Ayse said.

Maureen nodded. "Let's do it."

With that, Didi skipped down the hallway, the rest of the group following in her wake.

Maureen said, "I am officially worried about Didi."

Ayse reverted to her deadpan delivery. "Oh, really? Why now?"

Maureen entered the rec room and immediately went into campaign manager role. "Everyone sit here at the center tables. If your cell is getting searched, you stay put on the table. Let the rest of us do it. Fair?"

Ayse nodded. "I like that plan."

Sister Bridget raised her hand. "I volunteer my cell first. Mostly because I can't stand up again."

Cami met Russell's questioning eyes. "Bard's gun is missing."

The shock on his face and the flash of fear felt real to Ayse. They would search his cell regardless, though.

Sister Bridget's search took less than two minutes, considering her cell was the definition of *sparse*.

Ayse's cell was equally quick. Hard to hide a gun in a book, but they opened each one all the same. As they touched her belongings, she cycled through her rusty Turkish vocabulary: Book. *Kitap.* Blanket. *Battaniye.* Pillow. *Yastik.* Coat hanger. *Elbise askısı.*

Ayse hadn't spent any extended time in Istanbul since she was thirteen, when she was there for a distant relative's wedding. Because of this, her Turkish seemed to be frozen in time. It didn't matter that she was an adult woman now. When she spoke in her family tongue, she sounded like a petulant child, whining for more freedom, using slang that was woefully out of date. No wonder her father didn't know what year it was. The gray hair at Ayse's temples couldn't compete with someone who spoke in the lingua franca of *Tiger Beat.* (*Tiger Beat*: *Kaplan Vurmak.*)

At long last, they were done, and Maureen announced, "Okay, Cami, your turn."

Cami chewed on one of her colorful fake nails. "If you could keep my face masks in alphabetical order, I would really appreciate it."

As they rifled through Cami's cell, Ayse was surprised to see yet another shade of blurry-pinky-beige, yet another skin care routine, and yet another pair of fuzzy socks. Cami liked what she liked.

Maureen's cell was easily tossed, as it mostly contained stacks of paperwork, and cardboard Mayor Pete wasn't packing heat.

Didi's cell was the opposite extreme. Ayse dedicated herself to the craft boxes, and after the twenty-minute mark, she thought she had gone semi-blind from all the glitter refracting into her eyes. At last, they finished.

Everyone—even Russell, at Cami's prompting—reconvened in the center of the room.

Maureen looked over her shoulder. "We should toss Janet's cell."

"I already did," Cami answered.

Maureen was oddly miffed. "What? When?"

"While you were looking through mine, I went through Janet's," Cami said simply.

Maureen was surprised. "I saw you talking to Russell."

Cami smiled. "Yeah, after I tossed Janet's cell. Besides Nacho and the sound bowls, she didn't have much stuff."

Ayse was delighted they could end what was increasingly feeling like a fool's errand. "Nice. Very efficient."

"Did you find anything?" Maureen pressed.

Cami shook her head. "No gun. But a shocking amount of linen. Who has linen underwear?" She made a disgusted face. "So itchy."

Maureen crossed her arms. "Cami, we were supposed to do these things as a team. For accountability."

Cami's feelings appeared bruised. "I thought I was helping."

Ayse was annoyed that Maureen wanted to micromanage their every move. "Cami knows what a gun looks like, Maureen."

There was an awkward beat, tinged with disappointment and failure. The gun was still missing. No one wanted to say that, so Ayse said the only thing she could think of: "Lunch?"

The relief from having a benign reason to leave the room was visible on every face.

As the group made their way to the hallway, Maureen held Ayse back. Her voice was so low that Ayse had to lean in to hear her. "I don't like Cami going off on her own."

Ayse tried to find a balance between validating her feelings and checking her reality. "Cami thought she was helping."

"But what if she found the gun in Janet's cell and then gave it to Russell?"

"Maureen, you need to take a breath. This is Cami we're talking about."

"I heard them whispering last night after we all went to bed." Maureen sighed. "You think I'm being paranoid."

"I think we're all paranoid," Ayse replied.

"It's only paranoia if we're wrong."

# CHAPTER 14

## Ayse Demiri: A Majority

The mood at lunch was subdued among the sane. Meanwhile, Didi's unhinged energy continued to fizz like a two liter of Pepsi that had been tossed off a high building. "Ooooh, if someone else dies, this will be a murder-turducken! One, two, three birds; one, two, three bodies! That's fun! It's even kind of festive, when you think about it!"

Maureen gently held Didi's wrist, and Ayse saw that she was surreptitiously taking her pulse. "Didi, are you feeling all right?"

"Me?" Didi chirped. "I feel amazing! I am so excited for the big surprise!"

"Is it the gun?" Ayse asked sarcastically.

Didi pointed at her. "Oh my God. That would be so funny! Merry murder to all and to all a good fright!" She made a series of finger guns to the ceiling. "But no. Boo, hiss!" Didi gave an exaggerated pout, then flipped to a grin. "Is everyone done with their food?"

Cami, still chewing, gestured to her half-full plate. "Um, not really."

Didi took zero notice and unceremoniously ushered them out of the kitchen and down the hall. "I will need maybe an hour to execute." She saw everyone's alarmed looks and laughed. "My plan! Execute *my plan*! You all just go outside and see if you can find some festive cheer while you are out there." Russell started toward the cells again, but Didi hopped in front of him. "You all. *All.* Meaning you, too, Mr. Man."

Russell's body tensed. "I would just really like to go back to a secure location. I won't ruin the surprise."

There was a note of pleading in his voice that wrenched at Ayse's heart. She caught his eye and said, in her most maternal tone, "I think we are the secure location, Russell."

Her meaning was clear: Whatever was happening with Didi was unpredictable, and he didn't want to be alone with her. He nodded, joining the group. Cami gave Ayse a grateful smile; clearly she had been thinking the same thing.

Didi was back to bouncing on her toes. "Shoo! Shoo! All of you, shoo! Oh, and, Maureen, can I borrow your phone, pretty please?" She cupped her hands under her chin and did exaggerated blinking with her eyes. The entire effect was off-putting, evoking psycho Baby Jane instead of cutie Shirley Temple.

Reluctantly, Maureen took her phone from her back pocket and handed it over. "What do you need it for?"

Didi gave an exaggerated eye roll. "That will ruin the surprise, silly!"

"We'll be keeping one of the door passes with us, though. Just in case," Ayse said.

"As long as you promise to not use it until I get you!" With that, Didi did several pirouettes and gave a froufrou bow, then closed the double doors behind her, leaving them all outside.

For a second, what struck Ayse most was the quiet. A city filled with young transplants, Los Angeles had emptied out over the holidays, as twentysomethings returned to whatever beige town their parents called home, and this year was no exception. With the added deterrent of recent torrential rain, it felt like perhaps they were the only ones around for several square miles. There wasn't even anyone visible at the car repair. Was this quiet afternoon welcome? Was it unnerving? Normally, Ayse craved silence during her incarceration. Sometimes she would lie awake all night just to enjoy the only moments of silence offered to her while being trapped in close quarters with people whose rhythms did not match her own. She had been desperate to get away from Didi's inane chatter, but now she wondered if its absence left an opportunity for something at best unpredictable, at worst sinister, to step in: Maureen's panicked accusations, Cami's blind optimism, Russell's simmering trauma.

Ayse shook her head and cracked her knuckles to pull her thinking out of her own paranoia and back into her body. They were just outside, in the courtyard, where they had been one hundred times before. Nothing to panic about right now.

Just like the day before, Ayse and Sister Bridget took a seat on the retaining wall. Cami and Russell leaned against the passenger van. Maureen chose the wild card option and lay down on the ground, her work-detail vest spread underneath her like a blanket.

Cami looked at Russell as he relaxed into the sunshine. "Ooooh, your skin is looking hydrated."

Russell gave a sheepish grin. "I'm still not totally into having snail goo on my face, but I gotta say: I'm glowing."

Cami laughed. "Absolutely. A real starlet over here."

There was a tittering in the trees, and Russell's eyes darted up. "You got parrots in LA?"

Cami shielded her eyes from the low winter sun with her hand. "My mom told me that the parrots used to live in one of those wildlife theme parks, and when the park closed, the staff just let all the birds go."

"When did the park close?" Russell asked.

"A long time ago. Almost fifty years."

Russell smiled. "Fifty years of thriving in the wild after living in captivity." Then he must have heard himself. "Wait, wait. Don't make this into some inspirational moment. They're just birds, okay!"

Ayse put her hands up playfully. "I wasn't going to say it."

Cami smiled. "Sometimes the metaphor finds you, Russell."

"Yeah, yeah, yeah," Russell said in good humor.

Ayse felt like a voyeur watching these two young people dance around whatever they may be feeling, and so instead she busied herself with looking at the parrots, as did everyone else. Their vibrant-green feathers blended beautifully with the palm trees still shimmering with rainwater.

From the ground, Maureen said, "I can't tell if I want tomorrow to come as soon as possible so we can get out of here or if I want to stay inside as long as possible until we figure this whole mess out. Prolong it to resolve it, if that makes sense."

Ayse nodded. "I've been thinking the same thing. It feels like we have the murderer here with us, and that is bad." (Everyone agreed: Murderer is bad.) "But time is our nemesis, too. Even if we aren't killed, time is slowly crushing us."

Sister Bridget's eyes were still closed, but she said, "The Lord works in his mysterious ways."

Russell said to Sister Bridget, "Making the best use of the hour, because the days are evil." It seemed Russell had expected some kind of a reaction from Bridget, but he didn't get one.

Ayse saw her opening. "Russell makes a good point. We need to forget about Bard."

Maureen scoffed. "Gladly!"

Ayse continued, "I'm serious. We spent all morning processing evidence for only *one* of the murders that have happened. We all hated Bard. We all had motive." This was met with reluctant nods from everyone else. Murder: Bad. Bard: Worse. "So in order to actually find the killer, we should be focusing on the narrower pool of suspects. Namely, who had a reason to kill Janet."

Sister Bridget nodded. "Okay, that makes sense. Do you have a suspect in mind, Ayse?"

Ayse bit her lip. This was the moment to perfectly perform Doctor's Office Ayse: calm, factual, charismatic. If she failed the performance, her theory would fail with it. "You aren't gonna trust that this is coming from a logical place, but . . . I think it was Didi."

Maureen's mouth dropped open, clearly disappointed in Ayse's change of heart from their previous discussion. "I'm hoping you have a reason beyond the fact that you two are like chalk and cheese."

Ayse nodded. "That's fair, but please hear me out. Yesterday, when we were outside, Janet told me Bard made her spy on Didi so he could blackmail her. What if Didi found out and wanted to kill Janet for whatever she discovered about Didi's life?"

Maureen was following but wasn't on board. "But Bard was dead. Whatever Janet *maybe* had on Didi didn't matter anymore without Bard alive to weaponize it."

Ayse shrugged. "Maybe? Or maybe Janet found out something so damaging that even with Bard dead, Didi had to silence her."

Cami asked with genuine curiosity, "What would that even be, though? Do any of us know why Didi is in here?"

Sister Bridget thought back. "One time we both got to the parking lot early, and I heard Didi on the phone. You know how she sometimes pulls up mid-conversation? Bluetooth positively blaring?"

Ayse chuckled. "Oh my goodness, yes."

Sister Bridget continued, "She was talking to her lawyer. I thought she was just in here for DUIs, but apparently she was using her husband's script pad to get high. He was lucky not to lose his medical license."

Ayse was nodding along. "Okay, so maybe stuff with his licensing board wasn't all done and dusted. Maybe she was still using, and Janet saw. If so, Janet could get his medical license revoked, blow up their whole life. Right before Janet was killed, she said to me that she had a plan to get us out of here. I am wondering if those were more than empty words. Maybe she knew it was Didi and was going to confront her."

Maureen still wasn't totally convinced, though. "*If, maybe, perhaps.* This feels like total conjecture. Plus, Bard drug-tested Didi every week. She was clean." When she said this, Ayse gave Maureen a pointed looked. "Or at least she was clean until this morning."

Sister Bridget gasped. "You really think she's abusing drugs again? I thought we were just joking before."

Ayse gave Sister Bridget a look of near pity. "Sister, look at her. It's a short walk from Christmas spirits to drinking spirits."

Sister Bridget sighed deeply. "Right. Of course. I guess I hoped she had truly found repentance."

Ayse added a detail that just came to her: "I saw Didi stash some extra drug-testing kits while we were at the morgue, and she didn't put them in the pile for our evidence collection. Likely, she got them for herself. I can only assume maybe she failed her most recent test and she wanted a second chance at a clean sample."

Cami scowled. "If she failed recently, it would explain why he made her submit her sample in full view of everyone this week."

Ayse pointed at Cami, grateful for the backup. "Excellent point. That was new."

Sister Bridget let out a long slow breath. "Didi, the murderer. May God have mercy."

Ayse felt the tide turning and willed herself to stay quiet, not to solidify her advantage into a formal alliance just yet.

Maureen still wasn't buying this new idea, though. "Stop. We are all forgetting something. How did Didi kill Janet when I was with her?"

Ayse was gentle, but really wanted to get her point across. Her voice was relentlessness wrapped in velvet. "Were you, though, Maureen? Were there ever a few minutes when you were going over Bard's sleeping quarters and Didi was in the front office, out of sight?"

Maureen thought back. "Technically, yes."

Cami's frustration was visible. "Seriously? And you're only telling us this now?"

Maureen was flustered. "She was moving a cabinet or something! It blocked the door to the back, and I was stuck in his bedroom. But it was so fast!"

"So she could have slipped out," Ayse said. "She said herself it would only take a second to slice the artery. She knew where it was more than any of us."

Sister Bridget was nodding. "That was a deep cut, made perfectly on the first try. A steady hand did that."

Ayse nodded, too. "Plus, she has all those little crafting tools in her art kit. It would be easy to slip an X-Acto knife up her sleeve and then put it right back."

Maureen's brow was beyond knit—it was a brow knot. "Yes, all true. But I still don't think she had the time."

"You don't think. But you aren't sure," Ayse replied. "In every theory, the murderer only had minutes to kill Janet, so that can't be what rules her out unless it also rules everyone else out." Ayse took a deep breath. She didn't feel great about how this theory had gone over with Maureen, and she was starting to worry Maureen would suspect her of deflection. Or at least, not agree because she felt betrayed by Ayse's apparent change of heart. "I will totally own that Didi and I have never gotten along. I mean, honestly, the woman's entire life is a lie. The endless bragging about her status. And the pushing out of the stepkids, trashing the first wife whose husband she stole—*blech*. But I would never accuse someone of murder just because I didn't like them."

Sister Bridget connected some additional dots. "When the sprinklers went off, she told me to go into Bard's bedroom. I was laying on the bed, trying to cover evidence with my habit. She could have been the one who attacked Maureen."

Cami added, "And then she immediately tried to blame it on Russell. How did she know he wasn't with us in the little maintenance closet unless she was out in the hallway, too?"

Sister Bridget nodded. "That's true. I didn't think about that."

Ayse felt nothing but relief, like she had successfully built a parachute after she had jumped out of the plane. "So we all agree: Didi is the most likely one of all of us. She is clearly not well mentally. She had opportunity with both victims. She has a clear motive to kill Janet, which is more than I can say for any of us. And she had the skill to slice Janet's femoral artery with a tool she brought into the prison. Plus, she had the time to hurt Maureen unseen."

Sister Bridget made the sign of the cross. "Heaven help us if we are wrong."

Maureen was chewing on the inside of her mouth, weighing the evidence that was laid out before her. She was clearly at a loss. Little Miss Plan for Everything did not have a plan for this. "So what do we do? Go in there and interrogate her?"

Cami shook her hands in distress. "Oh, no. No, I really don't want to do that."

Ayse thought for a moment. She also didn't have a plan. She hadn't really expected them to go along with her theory, and hadn't gone beyond *Step 1: Convince others* in her mind. "No, I don't think confronting Didi is the right move. She's too unpredictable, and clearly becoming more unhinged by the hour. We just need to live through the night. Then, first thing in the morning, Maureen, you call those police contacts you said you have, and we let the police take over. Sound good?" This was met with unenthusiastic nods. "Whatever cuckoo nonsense she has cooked up in there, I just want us all to be safe and keep our wits about us, okay?"

Cami was still shaking out her hands in distress. "I hate all of this so much."

"Which part? It's a real buffet of bad options," Maureen asked gently.

Cami said quietly, "I don't want it to be any of us. I know that sounds silly."

Ayse realized, with a tangible amount of surprise, that she felt the same. She didn't know when she had started caring about her fellow inmates, but it had happened at the exact same moment she needed to accuse one of them of two murders. Highly inconvenient timing, to say the very least. There was a weird sound, and it took a moment for Ayse to even realize where it was coming from. Maureen was crying.

Ayse was shocked. "Maureen, what happened?" She had to restrain her impulse to check to see if Maureen was surprise-bleeding again like when she'd stumbled in after being attacked.

Maureen shook her head. "I don't even know. I guess it's all really getting to me, you know? Like, *what* are we even *doing*? Ayse, it took you maybe two minutes of laying out your theory and I just decided to agree that the person I am closest to here is a killer. It wasn't even hard for me to change my mind! That's insane! An hour ago I would have bet my life on Didi's innocence, and now I'm shoving her out of the lifeboat." She made her voice a mockery of casual: "Didi? Didi, who? Oh, that serial killer? Sure, yeah, whatever." She gulped down some tears. "I am someone who sets a course and sticks it out no matter what. I stay until the bitter end. I have worked on campaigns when we knew four months before Election Day that we would lose. But I would stay on the trail, hitting up undecideds, fundraising for every last leaflet. I am an idealist. I know that's hokey to say. But I am. I believe in things, and I don't give up. Ever. But something about all of this has shattered me." There was a long pause. "I hate myself. I hate what this has made me."

Ayse sat down next to Maureen. She didn't take her hand or rub her shoulder. She just sat close, her voice low. "I feel insane, too. I feel like even saying what I think—that Didi could be guilty—is a betrayal. Why do we have to hurt one of us to get justice for Bard? He was a horrible person. I'm glad he's dead; we all are. But Janet does need justice."

Cami wondered aloud, to no one, "Okay, but even if Didi killed Janet, I still say the blame for that lands on Bard. He pushed us to places we would never have gone otherwise. Janet didn't volunteer to spy on Didi. It was all him. It was always him." Everyone nodded at this logic. "I wish justice could just exist here, within us. I wish we could avoid putting someone in jail for longer."

Russell asked with some trepidation, "Do you mean, take care of it like a vigilante?"

Cami smiled at the idea even as big tears leaked down her face. "Ha! No. I guess I want to know who did it and why, but I don't want to punish them. We've all been punished enough."

"That's exactly it, Cami." Maureen sighed like the world rested on her shoulders. "I thought I could come out of this the same person I was. That was my goal. But I feel like my sense of self has just been washed away. And it's not just in Pay to Stay; it's the whole entire mess that got me here." For a long minute, no one spoke. It was clear Maureen wanted to share, and they wanted to listen. "I was working for a candidate. He was a good person. An actual good person is rare. A good person in politics? Forget about it. Normally, you're picking between the hornet and the wasp. Henry Carlson was a one-in-a-million candidate. He held strong values around the safety net for the vulnerable and was interested in the policy nitty-gritty to make it happen. He could work a room of big-time donors like it was his own wedding. And then he would walk into a community center of people who had never had a day of luck in their life, and he would connect. People cried, talking to him. They shared worries, fears, hopes—and he met every single person with such kindness. I swear to God, I saw people get taller after talking to him, their dignity restored. I realized I would do anything to get him elected. He had a tough race against a rich and embedded incumbent. It was going to take more money than we could ever raise in small amounts. So I cut some corners. I connected some people who technically, legally, never should have met. I may have even sold a few favors. But I could see that it was all in service of the greater good."

Ayse knew where this story ended. "And you were the one who got caught?"

Maureen's face was puzzled. "Of course I was the one who got caught. I did it. Henry didn't have anything to do with it; he didn't even know." Her gaze shifted to the middle distance, a beautiful, serene smile on her face. "He won the election. He's doing so much good. I hope when the big tally machine of life gives me my score, the good he did will be worth my sacrifice."

"Do you still talk to him?" Cami asked.

"Not now. It could be messy—make it seem like he was involved. I have to protect him. But he promised me a place on his team when I get out."

"Why haven't you ever run for office yourself?" Cami asked.

Maureen said, "It was a dream I had for maybe one day in the future, but that's over now."

Ayse smiled. "Hey, I think catching a double murderer could be super good for poll numbers, you know?"

Maureen laughed in spite of herself. "I can't believe I never thought of that."

Russell added, "A lot of incarcerated people and their families might like that you've been inside. If you talk about reform, they'll know you know what that means. Just maybe don't tell them you only went to jail on the weekend."

Ayse laughed. "Yeah, that does kind of undercut the whole narrative."

Maureen gasped in realization. "But I won't even be able to vote for myself!"

"Why?" Sister Bridget asked.

"Because felons can't vote!"

At this, they all started really laughing. The tension flowed out of them as they wheezed and wiped tears from their eyes. Even Russell was in on the joke, his head tossed back at the comedy of it all.

There was a strange zapping sound, and everyone ducked before looking around—a testament to their frayed nerves. Once they realized there were no projectiles coming at them, Cami found the source of the noise.

"The floodlights are going in and out again." She pointed.

Sister Bridget rolled her eyes. "Have those ever worked properly?"

Maureen added, "I keep wondering if they are going to electrocute us if we touch them."

Meanwhile, Russell had stood up and was digging in the shed. He emerged with a ladder and set it up under the light closest to the door. He climbed the ladder, and in a few short movements, the main light had stopped making its hideous zipping sound, and the flickering ceased. When he turned back to the group, he was surprised to see their marvel.

"I had grounds for work duty one year. I can do basic electrical stuff like this," he explained. "It's supposed to be job training. Not that I can be an electrician with a record."

Ayse's wheels were turning. "Maybe not an electrician, but definitely a building manager for a property company."

Russell snorted. "Oh yeah? You know someone who owns a property company?"

Ayse smiled, loving the reveal. "Actually, yes. Me."

Russell was taken aback, a mix of hope and nerves. "Wait. For real?"

Ayse was serious. "Absolutely. Normally, I'm the one googling how to fix stuff. When you get out, do you want to come work for me?"

Russell looked like he was going to pass out. "Y-yes," he finally managed to stammer. "Yeah, that would be amazing."

Ayse was just as thrilled. "Okay, then. It's settled." She shook his hand, his face beaming.

At that exact second, the back door opened, and Didi stood there, her entire torso wound up in tinsel. "Surprise is ready!"

The promise of a surprise dampened the joyful mood.

# CHAPTER 15

## Cami Garcia: Mandatory Fun

As they reentered the building, Cami wanted to take Russell's hand to steady her nerves, but she realized, with a start, that they had never actually made any physical contact. Cami was so accustomed to men always trying to paw at her that she felt awkward at her desire for closeness she couldn't initiate. Not that she could actually explore this thought all the way to its conclusion, because Didi was buzzing around them like a Christmas elf who had been huffing glue.

"Come in! Come in!" Didi put on Judy Garland's singsong voice. "Tinsel and presents and Santa—oh my!" She laughed. She twirled. She did not notice everyone else taking a step back. "Okay, clap if you've been good girls and boys!"

No one clapped.

Didi unrolled a scroll she had clearly made herself. In wild calligraphy, Ayse, Cami, Maureen, Sister Bridget, Maureen, and Russell were all listed as *Good Girls & Boys*. Janet was listed as a *Bad Girl*. There was a third category, *Demon Seed*. That was where Bard's name was.

If they had worries about her body being encased in tinsel, the rec room showed Didi had gone entirely around the twist. She had managed to create one hundred snowflakes, which Cami recognized from Instagram patterns she had never once been able to follow. Garlands of wrapping-paper chains looped through every bar. She had dragged her artificial tree into the center of the room and painted a dozen presents on the floor. The last empty cell was totally obscured, as Didi had wrapped the bars with a plain sheet in place of wrapping paper and added a bow made of twenty yards of ribbon, making it look like a giant gift. Overall, the effect was nice, although bizarre when taken in conjunction with the space, akin to a sumptuous Thanksgiving feast in an active operating theater or a masquerade ball in a dodgy CVS.

There was a loud pop that made Cami jump.

Didi was holding two sides of an oddly shaped tubular gift. "It's not Christmas without Christmas crackers!" Didi produced a box from under the bolted table. "Everyone take one!"

As they each took a cracker, they pulled it apart, causing the loud pop and revealing a tiny toy and a paper crown inside.

Didi announced with glee, "That sound is made with a tiiiiiiiny bit of gunpowder."

Russell saw his Christmas cracker gift was a miniature deck of cards. "You know, these are actually going to be useful."

Sister Bridget was turning her gift over and over. "What is this?"

Ayse looked at it. "I think it's a child's magic trick?"

Didi stumbled over like only someone feigning sobriety can. "Ooooh, magic!"

Ayse sniffed the air. "Do I smell alcohol?"

Didi looked sheepish but also a little proud, "I may have smuggled in some vodka. Do you want some?"

Ayse answered honestly: "Actually, yes. Please." Didi skipped to her cell, thrilled to have a drinking buddy, and brought one of her water bottles to Ayse. Ayse was confused. "The cap is still sealed."

Didi waved her off. "No, no. I fill them with vodka and then gently melt the cap back together with a lighter."

Maureen was putting things together. "So you would arrive to Pay to Stay sober, take your drug test, then get sloshed the rest of the weekend."

"Ding ding ding!" Didi chimed. "Maureen, do you want some vodka? Cami? You're twenty-one, right?" She started back toward her cell for more vodka.

Ayse called out, "They can have some of my vodka, Didi."

Didi was surprised. "I have plenty! It's top shelf!"

Ayse offered her bottle to Cami and Maureen. "Anyone need twelve ounces of room-temp hooch?"

Didi came out of her cell, wheeling her craft tackle box. "I have other goodies in here." She opened and closed several drawers containing glitter. She found one and shook some into her hand, then looked around for her vodka to wash it down.

"Are you eating plastic?" Maureen asked.

Didi laughed. "Of course not! This is beta-blockers, which you can eat like Skittles. That's oxy, that's Ambien. Then all the benzo besties: Valium, Xanax, Halcion, Ativan, and Klonopin."

Sister Bridget was looking over her shoulder. "You smuggled drugs in via confetti?"

Didi nodded. "It was so easy. Men never look at glitter or confetti or sprinkles. Not even you noticed, Ayse."

This was true.

"So all those weekends you were making centerpieces for fundraisers . . . ?" Cami asked.

Didi smiled. "Honey, those galas raise millions. You really think I am going to cheap out on some shit centerpieces made by me? I hire people to do that."

Cami was a little impressed, but also considered how much this added to Didi's presumed guilt among the group. The clouded looks on everyone else's faces and furtive glances told Cami they were thinking the same.

Maureen was pacing round the room, restless, and then noticed the food spread on the center tables. "Where did this come from?"

Didi said simply, "Well I noticed Chelsea didn't relock the gate out front, so I called in for delivery. I mean, it's New Year's Eve—well almost New Year's Eve. New Year's Eve Eve. We gotta celebrate! Finally, some spicy tuna on crispy rice." Didi gobbled several of the little squares and sighed in a state of deep contentment. "So glad that vegan drip isn't here to complain."

Cami needed the clarity, but didn't want it. "Vegan drip? Do you mean Janet?"

"Shhhh. Don't say her name. Her ghost will make the tempura go soggy." Didi passed the platter to Ayse and said, "Come on, have some."

Ayse said through a tight-lipped smile, "No thanks."

Didi was annoyed. "Come on. I know it's not your favorite oysters on the pier, but it's still very good—"

Before Didi had even finished, Ayse was on her feet, screaming, "How did you know that?"

Didi was startled and lost her balance, tipping over into the table. Tempura flew through the air and landed with a wet squelch in the dipping sauces. "What? Oh my God."

Ayse's fury was searing, though. "Look at me, Didi. Look at me! How did you know I get oysters on the pier?! *How?*"

The color had drained from Didi's face. "What? I just, I mean . . ."

Maureen had joined them and was trying to get between Didi and Ayse. "Ayse, stop it!"

Ayse turned her fury toward Maureen. "No! I need to know and I need to know now!"

Didi was scared, her breath shallow as she cowered. Finally, she blurted out, "Because I followed you."

The room went silent.

Then Ayse shoved Didi hard into the wall. "I am going to fucking kill you."

Didi was hysterical. "He made me! Bard made me! He told me if I didn't follow you, he would submit my drug test. Which I had failed. Obviously." Didi slid down the wall into a pathetic heap. "And then my husband would definitely leave me. He made me swear to get clean. He made me sign a post-nup! If I fail a drug test, he doesn't have to give me a penny. I would be broke. No job. No house. No . . . oh God, whatever their names are."

Maureen let a slip of frustration come out when she offered, "Your stepkids."

Didi nodded bleakly. "I would be all alone. And poor! Alone and rich, I can deal with. But alone and poor? So Bard told me if I followed you, he would trash the results."

Ayse thought back to the morgue. "Is that why you stole a new drug test?"

Didi nodded again. "I was going to make what's-her-name take it for me."

"Your stepdaughter," Maureen offered again.

Didi sniffed. "Yeah. Her." She tried to meet Ayse's gaze but immediately lowered her eyes. "Bard gave me your home address, and I waited outside for you to leave. I followed you to that little doctor in San Clemente. I watched you walk down to the pier with your dad, and saw that the hostess knew you. Clearly you went there a lot. So I called the office pretending to be part of your dad's extended care team, and got more information, how often you went, why, who was the primary patient. I am so sorry, Ayse. I told him as little as I could. I swear. I am so sorry. I am so so so so sorry. I will be sorry for the rest of my life."

Ayse softened, but her rage still burned. "I know Janet was spying on you. What did she find out? Did you kill her?"

Didi was shaking her head. "No. No no no. I would never do that. Never."

Maureen met Ayse's eyes. "Ayse, take a breath. Please."

Ayse was still furious, and for a tense second, Cami braced for some kind of punch to connect to Didi's face. Instead, Ayse took a huge step back, and though her entire body was like a coiled spring of anger, it seemed the moment had passed. Didi relaxed a little, which made Ayse coil up again. "Don't feel good about this. I still might kill you, Didi."

Everyone who had been outside exchanged more quiet looks between them. The case against Didi was only getting stronger. It felt like a noxious gas that was slowly poisoning them all.

Cami put her head in her hands. "I hate this. I hate all this suspicion. It's exhausting. Actually, it's worse than exhausting. This is exactly what Bard wanted. He wanted us to hate each other. He wanted to toy with us. He had our files. He could have called the DA. He didn't need us spying on each other. Instead, this was his joy—fucking with us. Every second we turn on each other, the happier he would be."

This hit the group heavily.

"I've been here the longest. Before any of you. I would watch each new inmate come, and all I could do was wait for him to strike. To pull them into his games and watch them desperately look for a way out," Sister Bridget said quietly.

Ayse sighed. "She's right. That is exactly what happened." Ayse to Didi: "I knew he got you after Memorial Day."

"You knew?" Didi asked, her voice like a child's who was begging for forgiveness. "That was when I failed my drug test. Which I honestly can't understand. I was so careful. I had never tested positive before. He wrote on my transfer letter 'you failed again.' So I was screwed in every way."

Ayse nodded, the catharsis in full swing now. "And I know Bard *made* you spy on me, Didi." She emphasized the word *made*. "I know because I was supposed to get info on Cami."

"Did you?" Cami asked, terrified, thinking of the photo of her outside the credit union.

"No," Ayse said.

Maureen whispered, "I told Bard about Janet's fundraiser for Marcello. I was the reason he was there." And with those words, the last vestige of her can-do-attitude mask slipped. Cami felt like Maureen looked weak for the first time since she had known her. All gumption replaced with defeat, her steel spine now only limp tissue paper.

It was a testament to how depressed they felt that no one blinked when Didi left the rec room. She returned a minute later, her arms full of the mugs that lived in the kitchen. She poured a measure of vodka into each one and handed everyone a drink. "To Bard. A son of a bitch so terrible he made us friends."

Everyone raised their mugs and took a sip, even Russell.

"I can't believe we've almost made it to New Year's Eve," Maureen said blankly. "I used to love New Year's Eve."

Ayse smiled. "It's actually my favorite holiday. My family is Muslim, so after being excluded from Christmas stuff, New Year's Eve always feels like a holiday for everyone on the whole planet. I like that."

Sister Bridget smiled. "I love New Year's Day. I love the feeling of being washed clean."

Cami said quietly, "Have you guys ever heard of *hatsuyume*?" No one had, as evidenced by the silence. "In Japan, that's what they call the first dream you have in the New Year. I always have had a lot of nightmares—my whole life—so I like reading about dreams, what they mean, how to control them. For *hatsuyume*, some dreams are supposed to be lucky. Like Mount Fuji. Or a hawk. Every year I try to dream I'm a hawk."

"Has it worked?" Russell asked.

Cami smiled. "Not yet. Maybe this year." Then she asked in a small voice, "After we leave here, will you all tell me what you dream on New Year's Day?"

Sister Bridget smiled. "Absolutely."

Maureen lifted her cup. "I would love to."

Russell took another sip of warm vodka from his mug, then said, "Maybe I'll dream of those parrots. They feel lucky to me."

There was a moment of quiet, and then Didi started humming "Auld Lang Syne," and soon everyone was humming along.

Then Didi started singing, but with her own awkward spin on the lyrics:

Should all dead bodies be forgot,
the murderer never come to light,
should we all be killed tonight,
and auld lang syne.

Cami looked to Ayse, expecting to see irritation, but instead Ayse was smiling serenely.

Clearly also feeling festive, Maureen asked hopefully, "Does anyone have any resolutions?"

Ayse thought for a second. "I'm going to finally take the Turkish classes I've been putting off. And not like an app. I am going to take an actual class, commit it to my memory, build my conversation skills. I don't want to lose the language of my father."

Maureen smiled. "That's a really good one. I was supposed to run a campaign for a real dirtbag next year. I hated him, but the pay is great and I don't have any other prospects for that cycle. I'm going to back out. I need to work for people that are going to do good. I might even look into running for something myself. You've inspired me."

"My resolution is to stop living in other people's version of me," Cami said truthfully.

Didi's eyes watered at this. "That's beautiful, Cami." Then she said, "My resolution is to be honest with myself. I deserved to be arrested. I broke the law a lot—like, *a lot* a lot. I'm not a victim."

Maureen lifted her mug. "That's a great resolution. I notice you didn't say *get sober*. These vodka water bottles coming back to Pay to Stay next year?" she added with a wink.

Didi smiled slyly. "Now, now, Maureen. We all still get to have our secrets, don't we? I mean, this place is nothing but secrets, and we can keep them for each other. Right?" There was a pause; then she turned. "Russell, what about you?"

He took a second. "I'm going to hope again."

Cami had to bite back tears. "Really?"

He looked at her. "Really. Like you said: I'm on my way back to life."

Sister Bridget thought deeply. "My resolution is to recommit to my Savior. Bard's note on my transfer was 'Repent.' He was right. I lost my focus this week. Now that I think of it, you've all backslid, too. It's almost funny. Ayse, you're offering a job to Russell, so you're working with even more criminals than before. Didi, back to taking drugs openly, not a care in sight and no intention to stop anytime soon. Cami is in yet another dead-end romance with a bad boy. Maureen's back-slide is her stage-managing selfish people for her own personal gain." Everyone was giggling, knowing that Sister Bridget was being mean but also fair. A huge grin spread across Sister Bridget's face. "You can make all the resolutions you want, but you are never going to change." She let out a wild laugh that Didi immcdiatcly cchocd.

Cami started to laugh, too, and nudged Russell in a playful way. But instead of feeling his arm give, she immediately realized he had gone rigid. Cami looked to his face, and his eyes met hers, wild with worry. He was desperately trying to convey something without words, afraid to speak. Cami didn't understand. She couldn't see what he saw.

Sister Bridget was still laughing, her voice getting higher with each screechy word. "None of you can change! You are all too broken! Unless I take it upon myself to change you."

In a motion so quiet and meditative, Sister Bridget unhooked the long rosary from her habit, then wound her hands through it so that it was wrapped tightly around her palms. With the same steadiness, but with increasing speed, Sister Bridget draped the rosary over Ayse's neck and then pulled it tight.

Ayse made a disgusting croaking sound as the wooden beads pressed against her throat.

Sister Bridget yelled, "You will all repent! Or you will all die!"

Didi screamed unhelpfully.

Maureen grabbed at Sister Bridget's arms, trying to get her to release.

Russell and Cami stood up in unison and ran toward the fray.

Sister Bridget was seconds away from completing her third murder.

# CHAPTER 16

## Cami Garcia: Nowhere Is Safe

As she pulled on Sister Bridget's arms, Maureen shrieked, "Stop stop stop!" But instead of helping, it only seemed to add pressure to Ayse's throat, which was bleeding from her nails scraping into the skin.

Didi continued to scream, "No! Sister Bridget! Someone do something!"

Cami started rifling through Didi's crafting cart, which was still in the middle of the room. "Where are your scissors?"

Didi was spinning in circles like a dog trying to catch its own tail. "What?"

Cami yelled, "You used giant craft scissors to cut the zip ties. Where are they?"

Didi stopped spinning on a dime and pointed to the lowest drawer of the rolling craft center, and Cami quickly found the scissors. She saw, with horror, that the fight was going out in Ayse even as Maureen desperately tried to help.

Cami ran right up to Sister Bridget and stabbed the open blades into her back shoulder, spreading them farther to maximize the pain and impact.

Sister Bridget screamed and dropped her death grip on the rosary.

The beads loosened, and Ayse collapsed to the ground, clutching at her throat, taking in giant gasps of raspy breath. Maureen ran toward her and dragged her away from Sister Bridget, who frantically grabbed for but narrowly missed the scissors.

Russell grabbed Cami, who reached out a hand to Didi. "Didi, get over here!"

Didi's alcohol-benzo haze was a real liability now as she clumsily joined Cami and Russell.

Maureen pulled Ayse to her feet. "Come on, we have to go!"

The non-murderous five met at the rec center doors and turned just in time to see Sister Bridget get hold of the scissors. With an unholy scream, she eased the blades from her flesh. She held them out, blood dripping to the floor and the back of her habit stained with crimson. "You all must *repent*!" she shrieked, and she ran toward them.

Russell yelled, "Go go go!"

Maureen, Didi, Cami, and Ayse ran farther down the hallway as Russell closed the double doors to the rec room. There was a single quiet second before there was a huge angry thud from the other side. Sister Bridget was clearly throwing her body against the doors repeatedly.

Didi's face was streaked with tears. "I thought she had sciatica!"

"I'm guessing that was a lie," Ayse rasped.

Maureen was baffled. "She's a nun, though! Aren't nuns supposed to be nonviolent?!"

Russell was still holding the door shut as he gritted out, "She's not a real nun."

Ayse joined Russell at the doors, helping him brace them shut. "How do you know she's not a nun?"

"She didn't say grace. She didn't care that I took the Lord's name in vain. I quoted a Bible verse and she didn't recognize it."

Didi was stunned. "Well, that was sneaky."

Ayse's old frustration with Didi was back. "How are you always so focused on the exact wrong thing?!"

Russel continued, "Plus, you know, the whole trying-to-murder-someone-with-a-rosary thing is kind of a dead giveaway."

Didi frowned. "Good point."

Cami added to Maureen, "Guessing her story about working at the charity salsa company was also fake."

Didi was frantic. "What do we do? Do we run? Let's run!"

Maureen shook her head. "I say we get her outside, lock her out. Then call the police."

"We can push her out of the back double doors," Cami agreed. "Maureen, Didi, come with me. Ayse, open the back doors. Russell, hold her in there until we say." Cami, Maureen, and Didi stood by the front doors of the building, braced. Ayse went to the back door and opened it wide so that she was hidden from view, ready to shut it. Once Ayse was in position, Cami yelled, "Russell, on three. One, two, three!"

Russell let the doors swing open on Sister Bridget's next giant heave, pressing himself against the wall behind the left door.

Sister Bridget ran headlong into the hallway, and as she passed the cross hall, Cami, Maureen, and Didi ran toward her, screaming like a fleet of incarcerated wraiths let free. They made impact with Sister Bridget, and between the three of them they each took some blows, but Bridget couldn't get a direct hit on any of them enough to slow their progress. Within seconds, and with an almighty shove, Sister Bridget was outside, and Ayse slammed the back door closed on her.

Through the metal, they heard Sister Bridget scream in frustration, and then silence.

They stood there, every one of them leaning against the double doors, gasping for breath. Ayse's throat was still the quality of an old zipper, all friction and tension.

Cami felt a rush of relief. They had done it. Safe inside. She laughed. "Never thought I would be so happy to be in jail."

Maureen laughed, too. "Love a locked door."

Ayse joined in. "No windows, no problem."

Even Russell looked relieved. "Y'all finally coming around to my lifestyle."

Then something perked Cami's ears. "Wait. Shhh. What is that?" In a split second, it all came together for her. *"Run!"*

Without hesitation, everyone ran away from the door, and not a moment too soon, as the prisoner passenger van rammed through the doors at full speed.

The mix of exhaust, steam, and crooked metal rained down on them all. Cami saw, with a flicker of fear, Russell flat on his stomach, a piece of the doorframe over his neck.

"Russell!" Cami screamed as she crawled toward him. "Russell, I got you." Cami gingerly pulled the metal off him, and he slowly turned over. "Are you okay? Are you hurt?"

Russell groaned in pain, barely able to move. "Well, I'm not dead."

Cami nodded, moving more of the crumbled door away so he could move safely. "I'll take that. Let's get you up, slowly." As she pulled Russell up, his leg was bleeding profusely, leaving a trail of red with every movement.

The front half of the van was inside the building now, the windshield smashed to opacity.

Ayse cradled her left arm across her chest; her shoulder was six inches lower than the other, clearly dislocated, as she had been pushed into the wall by the fender. She whispered, "Do we think Bridget's in there?"

Cami said, in a tone that was braver than she felt, "Only one way to find out."

Russell dragged one leg delicately toward her. "I'm coming with you."

Maureen was holding up Didi, who was bleeding from her temple. "Be careful!" she called out.

Ayse and Cami helped Russell as they all three wound themselves through the passenger side of the wreckage. In silence, they gathered at the front passenger door and wrenched it open. They expected to see a bloody pile of nun slumped over the steering wheel.

Instead, they saw nothing.

Only an empty seat, the open driver's door, and the stunning awareness that this was far from over.

Maureen yelled from inside, "Is she dead?!"

Cami stood on tiptoes to see over the crumpled hood. "She's not here! She's not here! She's gone!"

Didi's hysteria was instantaneous. "What the hell do you mean?! She has to be dead!"

Maureen, ever the planner, said, "Get back inside; you're safer in here!"

There was a familiar CLUNK, and the power in the entire building shut off, plunging them all into an eerie darkness, the one functional van headlight the only thing illuminating the inside.

And then, like a specter from hell, Cami saw Sister Bridget slowly appear behind Maureen and Didi. Her face looked like a twisted mask of her normal benevolence. Her grin widened as she lifted a fire extinguisher, which Cami recognized as the one from down the hall, above her head.

Cami screamed, "Look out!!! BEHIND YOU!"

Bridget brought the metal canister down hard on Didi, however Cami's warning had given just enough notice that Didi was only hit in the shoulder, as she had moved her head at the last possible second.

Still, she crumpled to the floor in pain, screaming uncontrollably. She neither ran nor fought. She just lay there, the willing victim. Sister Bridget turned her attention toward Maureen. She grabbed her shirt collar and yanked her half up off the ground. Maureen was yelling something Cami couldn't hear. Sister Bridget pulled from her pocket one of the Christmas crackers and shoved it into Maureen's open mouth, then slammed her head down on her knee. There was a sickening pop muffled by Maureen's own flesh.

Maureen let out a wild scream, clutching her face.

Cami winced, remembering the tiny pocket of gunpowder that was concealed in those wrapped tubes.

With Maureen occupied with her pain, Sister Bridget grabbed the fire extinguisher again, then returned to Didi, who was still paralyzed with fear on the floor. Bridget cocked her weapon of choice back over her shoulder like it was a Louisville Slugger, and readied to end Didi's life without hesitation. Cami braced herself to see it, but instead Bridget slipped out of view at the last second.

Maureen cried, her voice warped from whatever injury she had sustained in her mouth. "Run, Didi!"

Cami realized Maureen had pulled Bridget down onto the floor to save Didi. Maureen awkwardly wrangled herself in a position to get one good kick in on the impostor. Her foot connected with Bridget's ear, blood spraying up. This blow bought Maureen precious seconds to grab Didi and scramble away from the dazed nun on her back.

Ayse, Cami, and Russell regrouped behind the van.

"Do we go back in?" Ayse asked.

Russell was unsure. "It's more secure in there than out here."

Cami measured. "On the other hand, inside is also where the psycho killer is."

Ayse was considering. "How did she get back inside after crashing the van?!"

Cami shrugged. "I don't know, but I don't want her popping up behind me from the dark."

They looked out at the diminutive and sparse yard, which now looked like a minefield of murderer hidey-holes.

Cami was trying to be strategic even as her head swam with images of Bridget's terrifying leer. "We can't run in circles while she murders us one by one."

"The gate is open. Maybe we run. Find help," Ayse suggested.

Cami wouldn't hear of it, though. "Russell can't leave the property without being tagged as an escapee, and I'm not leaving him here on his own."

Russell looked Cami dead in the eyes. "No. You need to go. You need to run."

The steel in Cami's eyes made it clear she wasn't having a discussion about it. "No. Never. Maureen has a phone. Let's get to her, barricade ourselves in whatever spot we can, and then we call for help. Together."

Russell and Ayse nodded in agreement, and started their way back toward the front of the van, inching along as quietly as they could through the wreckage. Once they had all clambered back inside the twisted metal door, they stood still as stone, listening. However, the slow hissing from the van acted like a postapocalyptic-sound machine, and they couldn't hear much beyond their own racing heartbeats.

Russell whispered, "Maybe we check the rec room first since it's the easiest to see from one vantage point."

Ayse nodded. "Yeah, I'm not keen to go knocking on mystery doors."

Cami was in agreement. "Definitely. I don't think it's a washer-dryer prize behind Door Number Three."

Ayse leaned forward and looked down the hallway. "No one in the hallway. But . . . Oh."

Cami leaned forward, too. "What?"

Russell, the tallest of them by several inches, looked as well. "Guess that's how she could get back inside."

At the end of the hall, the fire door stood wide open. No alarm sounded.

Cami vaguely wondered, "How long has the alarm been disconnected?"

"Something tells me Bard did it a long time ago," Ayse said. "One of his little power trips."

Cami said through a scowl, "Oh, man, Chelsea noticed this when she was resetting the sprinkler system—said the code was wrong."

"Okay, let's go check the cells," Ayse whispered.

Ayse pushed the rec room door open slowly, not making a single sound.

The eerie effect of seeing the cells in the dark, each one empty, was unnerving, like ghosts were just out of her periphery at all times. There was a scraping sound, and Cami looked to Nacho the iguana, stretching his neck high, oblivious to the chaos.

Then she saw a figure and jumped back, clutching Ayse. "There!"

Ayse and Russell turned, ready to fight. Then Ayse relaxed. "That's just Maureen's Mayor Pete."

Cami could see his boyish grin and sensible suit now, and felt foolish. "I'm sorry."

Ayse shook her head. "Don't be. I'd rather you see more than less."

Russell completed a slow loop around the room. "No one is hiding in here."

Cami thought this would make her feel better, but it felt more like Russian roulette. Perhaps this round wasn't deadly, but each step they took got them closer to a murderer.

They quietly went back to the rec room door, unsure if they wanted to keep going. Cami reached for the flashlight that was next to the manual lock panel. Russell and Ayse nodded, glad to have some light as they opened the door to the darkened hallway.

"Did she cut the lights herself?" Cami asked.

Ayse pointed to the maintenance room door at the end of the hall, which was ajar. "Seems so."

As they passed the hissing car, they heard it—the distinct and undeniable sound of a physical altercation.

Didi's voice rang out, "No! No! What are you doing?! I won't tell anyone!"

Then they heard a heavy bang.

"The gun!" Ayse yelled.

They ran toward the sound as Didi stumbled out of Bard's office, clutching the space just below her clavicle, which was pouring blood.

Cami was able to catch Didi as her legs went out. "Didi! Didi! Listen to me! Stay with me! We will get you some help!"

She pressed her hands to Didi's chest, trying to apply pressure, but blood pooled relentlessly and poured down the sides of Didi's torso.

Didi's gurgling ended. Her eyes went dim.

Cami screamed, "Oh God! No! No no no no no!"

But before anyone could mourn, Cami felt the weight of Russell's body collide into her. Sister Bridget had barreled out of the office, knocking Russell off his feet, with Ayse, also losing her footing, ending up on the floor in a discombobulated sprawl next to Cami.

Then Cami felt, with horror, two strong hands grab her ankles and start dragging her toward the office. She reached for something to hold on to, at first taking a handful of Didi's clothing, but her grip slipped. She struggled to look over her shoulder and saw Sister Bridget's bloody, sweaty face smiling back at her. Her habit was askew, and tufts of her gray hair were pressed against her skin. She was elated, dragging Cami to her death.

At the last possible moment, a hand clasped around Cami's wrist. Russell! He pulled, trying to keep her from going into the office. But he was on the floor, and due to the puddle of Didi's blood, he was unable to get enough traction. Even as he slipped, spreading the blood across the floor with his body, Russell held his grip tight and Cami desperately clung to him, but Bridget was easily pulling them both now.

"Help me! Help!" Cami screamed.

"We got you! We won't let go!" Ayse yelled.

Ayse wrapped her one functioning arm around Russell's waist and pulled back, but Cami was already in Bard's office. Bridget whirled around her and slammed the door over and over on Russell's wrist until he let go.

Russell let out a tortured "CAMI!"

But Sister Bridget slammed the door closed and locked it.

Cami scrambled away as best she could, but she was slower than Bridget, who towered over her, enjoying Cami's panic.

"It's just the three of us now," Bridget said. Her voice was different. Gone was the calm benevolence Cami knew. A high-pitched squeeze with a hint of drip was apparently Bridget's true voice, and it made Cami's ears sting like someone scraping a chalkboard.

"Bridget, please. Don't do this. Please, please." The words tumbled out of Cami's mouth, and she could taste her tears. She was too stunned to move. Her thoughts were sluggish, unable to comprehend what was happening and how to make it stop.

Bridget replied, her voice eerily calm, as she slowly sat down on Cami's chest, "Shhh, shhh. It will all be over soon. I will make your sins go away. Just like he wanted me to. He will see that I was the best all along. The truest."

Bridget had pinned Cami's arms down with her knees and then put her hands on the sides of Cami's face in a way that felt comforting. Cami wondered if maybe this was it. Maybe Bridget just needed to do some awkward blessing, and Cami could claim being reborn.

Instead, Cami felt Bridget's thumbs sliding across her cheeks toward their destination: her eyes.

A surge of fear rocked Cami from within her bones. The police photo of the person with no eyes! The mystery photo! Cami realized in seconds, her mind riffling through facts, through images, through clues, until it was a perfect narrative: Bridget was going to crush her eyes.

Cami screamed and shook her head back and forth to try to delay the horror. As she did, she realized she wasn't lying flat on her back—her feet were planted squarely on the floor, her knees up. Bridget leaned forward to try to grasp Cami's face harder, and in that second of lift, Cami whipped her knees forward as hard as she could in a swift one-two into Bridget's back. Bridget toppled forward. She was lying with her stomach over Cami's face, which seemed like a step back, until Cami realized her arms were free.

First Cami bit down hard on whatever part of Bridget's abdomen was currently pressed against her mouth. She bit down harder than she ever had in her life. With satisfaction, she heard Bridget screaming like hell, and the hot wetness Cami felt on her lips meant she had drawn blood. The faux nun instinctually scrambled off Cami and toward the door, meaning the safe direction for Cami to move was toward Bard's bedroom.

Cami lunged for the awkwardly small door, slamming it shut behind her. The only lock was on the knob, and that wouldn't buy her much time. She had to secure the door. First she tried to slide one of the file cabinets in front of the door, but it was bolted to the wall and wouldn't budge. As she looked around for another idea, the terrifying sound of Bridget throwing her body against the door began.

*Slam.*

*Slam.*

*Slam.*

Vaguely, Cami could hear slamming farther away, and Russell's voice, echoed by Ayse, asking if she was okay.

Cami ran around Bard's bed and pushed it with all her might. It slid more easily than she anticipated, and blocked the door well enough to give her three seconds to think.

The single window was too high and lined with wire, so that was not an escape. She looked around all the Christmas crap to see if perhaps there was another phone. There was not. She looked for a weapon, and while there were some sensible make-shift options, she wanted to avoid another physical fight if possible.

Suddenly, something caught her eye: a source of light low to the floor. She realized there was an access panel behind the bed that she had exposed when she moved the bed toward the door. The wood that normally closed off the square had fallen over, and Cami could tell that she may just be able to fit. She got down on her hands and knees and started to crawl through the square, relieved to see that after three feet, the access panel ended in the maintenance room.

Cami pulled her feet through and stood up. She saw how the light from the open fire door had been perfectly angled into the little passage. She could have cheered, but she couldn't stay here. There was no time to rest.

Cami came down the hallway just as Russell and Ayse were both ramming Bard's office door with their remaining functioning shoulders. "Russell! Ayse!"

They turned, both in disbelief that she was no longer trapped with Bridget.

"How did you—" Ayse asked.

"There's an access panel to the electrical closet. Where's Maureen?"

"We haven't seen her," Russell said.

Cami looked around. "We need to find her and call for help before Bridget realizes I'm not in Bard's bedroom anymore."

Ayse nodded. "You two keep that door closed. I'll find her."

After Ayse sprinted away on her search, Cami looked at Russell. He was bleeding, his leg was clearly damaged from the van, and his shoulder looked ready to pop out of his shoulder from ramming it into the door. None of that compared to the relief in his eyes. "Cami, I thought you were gone. I thought—" His voice caught.

Cami smiled. "I'm here. And we are going to get out of this." Then she put her finger to her lips. "Shhhh." They listened at the door and could still hear Bridget slamming as she tried to get into Bard's bedroom. But that lock wasn't going to last much longer.

Just then, Maureen and Ayse came back to the group. "I found her in the walk-in freezer," Ayse said.

Maureen's teeth were chattering, and her skin was like ice. "I didn't know where else to go. And then I was too scared to leave." Her voice was garbled, and Cami could see that her mouth was severely burned from the Christmas cracker.

Cami heard Bard's bed being moved again, its legs scraping across the floor as Bridget was forcing the door open to his sleeping quarters. Cami whispered urgently, "Go go go!" She didn't know if Bridget was about to crawl out of the access panel or bash her way out the door. Either way, the only way forward was through the cells.

Then she had an idea.

Cami spoke quickly, unsure if anyone was following. "Ayse and Russell, you need to go to the van. Lock the doors. You are too injured to help."

Ayse and Russell both protested, but Cami held up her hand. "We don't have time to argue. Maureen, you need to wait behind the check-in kiosk until you see Bridget pass. When I say *now*, press number four."

Maureen asked, "What does—"

But Cami was already running into the rec room.

"Where are you going?" Maureen asked in a panicked whisper.

"To lure her out," Cami said, a lump in her throat the size of a melon.

A minute later, her meager plan in place, Cami was alone, holding her breath. The cell floor was cold and rough under her hands.

There was a moment of silence, and then she heard, from all the way down the hall, Bridget screaming in fury: "Where are you, Cami! Where the fuck did you go?" Her voice was high and reedy. Cami heard the door to Bard's office slam open, bashing into the wall. The sound clanged around the building like lightning. Then the clomping of Bridget's shoes down the hall. Cami heard the bathroom door slamming open. Then the kitchen door. Bridget was looking for them, and she wouldn't stop until she found another victim.

Then the rec room door opened. The creak of the hinges made Cami feel like vomiting.

If Cami moved any part of her body one inch forward, if she moved a second too early, Bridget would see her. And Cami would be dead in seconds. She had to stay still. She had to wait.

Cami heard footsteps crossing the room. Getting closer.

Closer.

And then closer still.

For good measure, Cami put her hand over her mouth.

Bridget's footsteps were slow at first, deciding.

Then a hard sprint.

Cami listened, not moving, knowing her life was on the line.

But she had to wait. For as long as her body would allow.

Then she heard the sound she had been waiting for.

A distinct crunch.

From the floor of Russell's cell, hidden under his bed and behind his rolled-up mattress, Cami yanked on the Christmas ribbon she had tied to the bottom of the empty cell's bars, sliding them shut.

"MAUREEN, NOW!" Cami screamed.

Maureen ran out from her hiding spot and pressed the manual door-lock button for cell 4 on the far wall.

There was an unholy scream from behind the cell bars. Bridget ripped the sheet down and yanked on the lock, but it was no use. Screaming. Hissing. Spitting. But all from behind locked bars they controlled.

Russell limped back into the rec room, Ayse holding him up while he helped keep her dislocated shoulder stable.

Cami collapsed in relief, then explained, "I put cardboard Mayor Pete in the empty cell behind the sheet. I hoped she would see the figure backlit by the window and run headlong into the cell thinking it was one of us."

Ayse nodded. "Just like we did."

"Exactly."

Maureen looked at Cami, amazed. "Leaving Didi's glitter on the ground so you knew she was all the way in the cell was inspired. You're brilliant, Cami."

Cami smiled. "Thank you." There was a strange cold burst of air, and Cami had the vague awareness that the breeze was inside her own body. Then she passed out.

# DAY 5

DECEMBER 31

# CHAPTER 17

## Ayse Demiri: New Year's Eve

Ayse, Maureen, and Russell sat at the collection of tables in the center of the rec room, looking at their prisoner. Cami was lying down still, wrapped in a blanket. Her fainting spell was over, but the chill remained.

Bridget had railed against the bars for a while. Then, out of energy, she'd resorted to screaming about repentance. At last, she was now in a quiet, never-wavering stream of biblical quotes that had been put through the blender of her broken brain. All under the serene, watchful eye of 2D Pete Buttigieg.

Cami looked up at the ceiling. "We have a problem."

"Besides the three bodies and the fake nun with a thirst for blood?" Russell asked genuinely.

Cami nodded. "Yup. We can't prove Bridget killed Bard, or Janet, or Didi. We have no evidence, no confession, and everything that implicates Bridget—"

"Means," Ayse offered.

"Motive," Maureen said, picking up the thread.

Russell rounded it out. "Opportunity."

Cami kept it going. "All of those apply to us as well."

Maureen put her head in her hands. "Well, that's nifty."

Ayse rolled that information over in her mind and was struck with something she could only identify as mental claustrophobia. Another locked room they couldn't find their way out of. "The reality is, we only have six hours left until it's time to leave Pay to Stay. We have to start making decisions while we still have that luxury. Let's start with the bad ideas first. So we don't want to call the police, agreed?"

Everyone nodded. When had cops ever made their lives better? Never. Not once.

Ayse continued, "But we need to call someone."

Everyone nodded again.

"Lawyers?" Cami offered without conviction.

Maureen nodded. "Eventually, yes. But my worry is, they will divide us up and pit us against each other."

Russell replied, "Most definitely."

Ayse summarized: "So no cops. No lawyers yet. And we need to be united."

Maureen suddenly seemed inspired. "What we need is a narrative."

Ayse's interest was piqued. "Go on."

Maureen was rolling with it now. "We need a concrete narrative from all of us in one voice, in one go. We need to set that in stone. So no matter what happens next, we are already all on the record. A public record."

Ayse wasn't following. "So like a notary public? What are we talking about?"

"Social media?" Cami once again offered without conviction.

Ayse snorted. "Those billionaire babies will scrub us from any platform so fast."

Maureen was really thrilled now. "No. We need traditional channels. We need to talk to the press."

Ayse was surprised but could see the idea forming. "Seriously?"

Maureen's energy was up. "Yes. One hundred percent. We get the entire story out into the open—before lawyers divvy us up, before cops make a mess. We publicly set the record straight."

Russell looked skeptical. "Do you really think that would work?"

Maureen was emphatic. "Absolutely. We create a media circus. We set this in motion our way, and the legal system will have to follow." There was a beat while everyone considered this. Maureen said, in her most assuring tone, "Guys, I got you. I got this. But I will only do it if we are all in."

With clarity, Ayse saw that Maureen was absolutely right. "I'm in."

"I'm in," Russell responded.

They all turned to Cami, who was back to biting her nails. "I will agree on one condition. If there is even a hint that Russell is going to get pinned for this, we close ranks. We don't say a word until we get assurances that he is protected."

Ayse and Maureen shared a look and nodded. Ayse spoke for both of them. "Russell, we will protect you."

Russell's head dipped to his chest. When he lifted his chin again, his eyes were bright with tears. "Thank you," he whispered.

Maureen got her phone from her cell and made a call on speaker. The call connected.

A groggy voice said, "Maureen? What the hell—it's one a.m."

Maureen said briskly, "Hi, Claire. You're gonna want to get up for this."

Claire said, "I'm staying in bed until I hear something good enough to get up for."

Maureen took a deep breath. "I'm in prison."

Claire yawned. "Uh-huh. Okay. That can wait until tomorrow. Bye."

Maureen added quickly, "We have a triple homicide."

"Still no," Claire said.

Maureen pushed, "Homicidal woman posing as a nun murdered a correctional officer and held five of us captive. We are all still here in the jail, and you get the exclusive sit-down if you come here in the next hour with a camera crew."

There was a beat.

Finally, Claire said, "I'm getting up."

Maureen pumped her fist in triumph but managed to keep her voice steady. "I'll text you the address."

They didn't have to wait long.

Apparently, Maureen's pitch was good enough that they saw the turn of headlights through the double doors in less than forty minutes.

Maureen pulled the gate to the side as a news van turned into the parking lot, the chain cut by firefighter Chelsea pointlessly dangling from the end. Once stopped, the side door slid open, and there was Claire. Her hair looked permanently coiffed into a giant helmet that was off-putting in person, but Ayse could tell would read great on camera. Her face was already primed, powdered, and contoured. Even her eyeliner was tattooed on.

"Maureen, if you lied to me, we are done," Claire said by way of a greeting.

Maureen gave a wolfish grin that made Ayse uneasy. "It's even better than you can imagine."

A cameraman got out of the front seat and joined them at the side of the van.

Claire pointed. "This is Doug."

Doug surveyed his truck of gadgets, then said, "I can have three cameras set, a boom mic hot, and a balloon light up in maybe half an hour."

Ayse felt compelled to add, "The power is on now, but we can't be sure it won't fail again."

"Good to know," Doug replied. "I'll use the van as a power source."

With the efficiency of a seasoned pro, the cameraman began to unspool a huge loop of power cords in the direction of the door while also pushing a camera cart that had a mini control room. Meanwhile, Claire had changed into a power blazer (complete with tasteful broach) and was sipping on a thermos of tea while doing vocal warm-ups. Ayse couldn't help but be impressed. Maureen clearly hadn't called the B team.

This cool professionalism seemed unbreakable until Claire entered the rec room. She took one look at Sister Bridget (who had moved on to catatonia with a side of religious muttering), and her jaw dropped. "Is that Kelly McPatrick?"

Ayse was about to answer no but then realized she had no way of knowing. "Well, we know she's not a nun, but that's as far as we got."

Claire turned to Doug with the same energy as a child on Christmas morning who'd gotten everything on her list. "Doug. Doug. DOUG."

Doug was also agog. "Holy hell. Claire. This is it. This is the Pulitzer."

Maureen was trying to be in this energy with them but was clearly as confused as everyone else. "So happy you're happy, but who is Kelly McPatrick?"

Claire, practically giddy, said, "Dougie, my ace, tell me you have access to that piece we did."

Doug, who was furiously typing on his laptop, said, "You know I do."

He turned the camera cart around so the inmates could see the screen on his monitor; then he pressed play.

On the screen was Claire with the same hair and in a similar power suit. There was a Channel 3 news logo across the lower third, marking that this had been broadcast nearly four years ago. Claire spoke directly to camera, a microphone in her hand. "What started out as a regular bus ride became a harrowing fight for life for one Angeleno." The footage cut to one of Los Angeles's orange buses, which was surrounded by crime scene tape and a collection of various legal professionals. Claire's voice-over continued, "At approximately eleven thirty a.m., on the Metro 2 westbound bus line, an argument broke out among the passengers as they crossed into Hollywood on a popular section of the Sunset Strip."

A bus driver, who was identified by the chyron as Chris Zedan, was visibly shaken as he spoke. "I have been driving this line for three years, and I have been a driver with the Los Angeles bus system longer than that. I have never, ever seen anything like this."

Claire was back on-screen now. "According to eyewitnesses who chose not to be identified on camera"—cue blurry footage with no sound of people's heads—"two passengers got into an altercation. The victim was said to have come onto the bus in a state of distress, with most people assuming they were intoxicated in some way. A nun who was known on the bus route, as she rode it most days, offered to help the victim to their seat. This is when things took a violent turn. We have exclusive footage from a passenger. A warning: This video is deeply disturbing and should be viewed with extreme caution."

An awkward angle from the front of the bus showed Sister Bridget approach someone who was clearly not in their right mind. The sound was muffled, but the inmates all shared a look, bracing themselves for what they were about to see.

On the bus, Sister Bridget reached out a hand, but the man slapped it away. "Don't touch me! Don't you dare lay a hand on me!" he screamed, his words slurring.

Sister Bridget remained calm. "The Lord sends his blessings to you."

That sent the man over the edge. "Who the hell is that to me? And who are you? You are no one! You are not a woman of God! No one is!" He looked like he was about to swing, but instead of punching her, the man ripped Bridget's habit off her head. He held it up like a carcass. "Look at this! No God under here! Just a person! Just a walking flaw!"

So far, people on the bus had been mostly calm, probably hoping whatever this outburst was, it would end as quickly as possible.

It did not.

Sister Bridget screamed, "I am a child of God, and I am here to punish you!" She tackled the man to the floor with an abandon that said she didn't care who lived or died, including herself. The man toppled backward, his head dangling down the stairs toward the back exit of the bus. She straddled his chest and moved her hands on top of his face.

At this point, everyone on the bus had started screaming or climbing over seats to get away. Bridget had gotten her thumbs over the man's eyes, and she was pushing down on his sockets with all her might. The man screamed out in pain, and everyone else on the bus screamed in terror.

Ayse winced and noticed that Cami's face was whiter than a sheet, possibly even green with nausea. "Are you okay?"

Cami raised a shaking finger to the screen. "She did that to me." Her body was rigid with fear. She mumbled to Russell, "It was her. From the photo. She tried to crush my eyes."

Russell looked shocked, then said, "She's not going to hurt you again."

"Stop! No! Stop! HELP ME!" the man on-screen screamed over and over.

But Sister Bridget only pushed down harder.

The footage went back to Claire with her perfect helmet hair. "While the exact motive of the attack is still unknown, our investigative team did uncover some distressing details."

A photo of Bridget came up on-screen, and Claire's voice-over continued, "The woman on the bus claims to be Sister Bridget Moran. Unfortunately, this woman"—another photo came onto the screen—"is the real Sister Bridget Moran, and she has been dead for three years. And this woman is actually Kelly McPatrick."

Claire paused the video, satisfied with her own work. "The piece goes on, but I can give you the gist. A whole lot more came out. Kelly apparently found Sister Bridget's habit in a room she rented and decided to pose as a nun for the attention, I guess. Seems it started as a con, but before too long, she got high on her own God supply."

Ayse felt ill. "The man on the bus—is he okay?"

Claire shook her head. "He lost his right eye. Left eye is severely damaged."

Cami asked, "How did Bridget—" She caught herself. "I mean, how did Kelly end up here? Pay to Stay is supposed to be only for nonviolent crimes."

Russell said, with no joy, "The system failed to protect you. Happens every day."

Claire smiled so wide Ayse almost expected her to lick her lips in a sign of eagerness. "What I want to know is, why did your CO let her pose as her alter ego?"

Ayse felt the truth before her mind could even find the words. After a hard swallow, she whispered, "He let her be a nun here because it's what she wanted most."

Cami connected the dots. "And if he let her have that, then she would do anything for him."

Russell repeated the phrase the nun had said so often since they had locked her in the cell: "I'm his eyes and ears."

Ayse nodded. "We thought she just meant God. Turns out she meant Bard, too."

# CHAPTER 18

## Cami Garcia: Loose Ends

The mood in the rec room was a mix of success, apprehension, and mania. While others seemed to be feeling a combination of the above, Cami felt herself firmly trapped in the apprehension camp. Apprehension wasn't exactly a new feeling to her in these walls, but something about this exact moment made her experience an uneasiness she struggled to understand. What exactly was bothering her? Was she nervous about leaving Pay to Stay? (Inevitable.) Was she unsure about the plan to tell their story to the press? (No feasible alternative.) There seemed to be something else just outside her emotional grasp. She attempted to chat with Doug or pack up her cell, but the only thing that actually felt right was staring into the distance in silence, trying to resolve this dangling distress.

Meanwhile, Claire was whirling around, abuzz with ambition and skill. "So you're all due to leave here in three hours, correct? Hm. Not a lot of time for me to do my thing. I like to get deep. I like to get to the heart of the matter. That's my approach—as a journalist and as a human. Three hours. Hm. That means, realistically, we don't have time for one-on-one interviews."

Maureen said, "Actually, that works great for all of us because we are one hundred percent united. *We want* a group interview. *We want* to control the narrative from the jump. *We want* to own the story." She was emphasizing the words *we want* like she had just learned the conjugation in Duolingo.

Claire nodded along. "Absolutely. Brilliant strategy. This is our story, and we don't want anyone else to tell it."

Cami bristled at Claire's choice of words: *our story.*

Maureen didn't blink, though. "You get it. Once we get the facts down today, it will be impossible for someone to rewrite what happened here." Clearly, having Claire on their side was central to Maureen's plan.

Cami took a deep breath, willing herself to revert to her passive persona. *Let them make all the decisions. Play dumb, smile, disarm.*

Maureen had already given Claire a full tour of Pay to Stay, but now they stood in the center of the rec room, surveying. Claire was doing a kind of slow pivot, taking in every possible setup. At last, she declared, "Let's do the interview right here, with the cells in the background. Really telegraph the whole scene-of-the-crime angle. Doug?"

He appeared at her shoulder, taking in the backdrop. "What if the nun screams through the interview?"

Claire's eyes were greedy. "Even better."

Doug smiled. "Copy that. I can get that lighting set in no time." He looked to Ayse, Cami, and Russell, who had been more or less stationary since learning the truth about Bridget. "You can all take five."

*Our story. Angle. Take 5.*

These words pinged around Cami's head like a mosquito, adding to her disquiet.

Russell rubbed his eyes. "I'm going to wash my face. I feel wrecked. Be right back."

Cami gave him a weak smile, desperately trying to project a feeling of calm that she did not possess. She wanted to yell that it wasn't safe to be alone. Except it was. Bridget was in her cell, locked away.

Ayse sidled up next to her. "Are you okay?"

Cami dug deep and found one of her cutesy smiles. "Yeah, everything is great."

Ayse gave her an exasperated look and said, "Cami. We're past that." She asked again, pointedly, "Are you okay?"

Cami let the smile fade and answered honestly, "I don't know. Something is bothering me, but I don't know if it's something specific or if I just need a second to wrap my mind around everything that happened."

Ayse sighed. "Yeah, I get what you're saying. I feel like now that the danger has passed, we can actually realize how much danger we were in. A delayed response."

Cami nodded. "Yeah, maybe that's it."

Ayse gave Cami a little side hug and said, "I'm going to finish packing up my stuff."

What Cami wanted right now was a task. She cast her eyes about the room, looking for something she could do to busy her hands and mind. The perfect solution came in the form of a neglected emotional support iguana.

Cami entered Janet's cell. Even with the flurry of action a few feet away, this square felt quiet. A tomb longing for its designated occupant.

Cami lifted the lid off Nacho's terrarium while also flipping on his sunlamp. "Oh, Nacho, I'm so sorry. Janet is not coming back—" Her voice caught. "She really loved you. You meant so much to her." Cami felt tears on her face. She sniffed. "Do you want to come home with me, Nacho? I can take care of you." Cami pet the iguana on his nose like she had seen Janet do so many times. He lifted his head and scratched his long slender toes in appreciation.

Then Cami saw something in the sand of the terrarium. She gingerly picked Nacho up and placed him on his climbing apparatus so she could sweep the sand and wood chips to the side.

Buried in the terrarium was a flash drive. There, in Bard's handwriting, was a name.

Just reading that name, every sticking point that had been bothering Cami for days suddenly snapped into focus. Moments she hadn't even realized she was holding on to were contextualized. Comments connected to evidence, and evidence led to murders.

Cami's disquiet evaporated in an instant, replaced by total clarity.

She went to the bathroom to splash cold water on her face. She hadn't anticipated being pushed out of her mental hiding place so quickly, but she knew it was time. She had to leap. Everything was on the line. First she had to find Russell.

A few minutes later, the lights were set and three cameras had been organized. One got the wide angle of the inmates and Claire. One was focused solely on the inmates. The last one had a tight three-quarter shot of Claire only. As soon as Doug turned on the lights, Cami felt her temperature rise.

Doug reminded them as they chose their seats, "We only have the boom mic overhead for you all, so make sure you project, okay?"

Russell sat on Cami's right side at the end of the row. Ayse chose the seat on Cami's left. Maureen was on the other side of Ayse.

Cami whispered to Russell, "Did you have what I need?"

Russell nodded, albeit seeming confused. "All here under my seat."

Cami smiled, took a few deep breaths.

Ayse looked at Cami and asked, "Feeling better?"

Cami said, dead serious, "I'm about to."

Doug cut in, "All right, everyone. We are looking somber. We are victims. Sound is speeding. Starting camera three, two, one."

Claire didn't wait for an extra cue. She was ready, and spoke directly to the camera solely focused on her face. "Welcome to our exclusive with the victims of the New Year's Eve Nun Attack. I'm Claire Curtis, and I am honored to be getting this watershed sit-down." She turned to the inmates. "Maureen Weber, how about you start us off? What happened here in the last few days, and why did you call me, Claire Curtis, to be with you during this emotional time?"

Maureen was poised. "Claire, it's great to see you again. Although I wish it was under different circumstances." (Both Maureen and Claire gave identical sad nods.) "We four have been terrorized for several days by a woman we knew as Sister Bridget, but who you informed us is actually Kelly McPatrick. On our first night here, she brutally murdered our correctional officer, Steven Bard. Then, in a spree of violence, she also killed a pillar of the community, Janet Fox, to protect her secret, and when we found her out, she killed again. This time, loving mother, philanthropist, and health care worker Didi Sorel. We called you here today because we are united in our experience, and wanted to get our story into your safe and powerful hands before the levers of the justice system try to pry us apart."

Claire's voice was (fake) emotional, with the perfect measure of quavering. "This seems to me a story of survival. Triumph of the human spirit. You had to trust in each other to live. Were you always so united?"

Maureen nodded along, the picture of engagement. "Yes. Always. From the day we met, we were a team. You have to be, in a place like this."

Cami cleared her throat. "That's not true."

Claire was startled at this new version of the story, and her eyes twinkled with greed. Drama on camera? Her dream. "Say more about that, Cami."

"Before this week, we never spoke to each other. Ever. We didn't like each other. We were not close. They don't know anything about me."

Maureen was shocked, and clearly unhappy that Cami was diverting from the united-victimhood-message she had set the stage for. She attempted to smooth and pivot. "Well, that's what our CO wanted us to feel. But we overcame that."

"No. You don't know me at all, Maureen," Cami replied. "Until suddenly, you did."

Maureen was taken aback, her irritation rising. "What's that supposed to mean?"

"How did you know I'm good at math?" Cami asked simply.

"W-what?" Maureen sputtered.

Cami looked to Claire. "I almost didn't notice it. It was so small, especially compared to all the other secrets that have been forced into the light over the last few days."

Claire's eyes gleamed. "Other secrets?"

Cami obliged. "Like that our correctional officer was forcing us all to spy on each other so he could use information against us, to stalk us, to ruin our lives."

Claire was loving this Russian doll of betrayal. "Your CO was pitting you against each other?"

Ayse was tense, but her voice was strong when she said, "Yes. He was. He wanted me to spy on Cami. He made Maureen feed him information about Janet. It was horrible."

Claire turned to Maureen, performing curiosity while loving the budding division. "Maureen, I must confess, I am confused now. In your summary of these terrible events, you were so neutral about your correctional officer. Why?"

Before Maureen could answer, Cami cut in, "Because she wants to skip over that aspect of the story entirely. Much cleaner that way. *Homicidal Woman Poses as Nun, Kills Three People* is a simple story to tell. A perfectly contained narrative."

"Why is that important?" Claire asked.

Again, Cami replied before Maureen could get a word in, "That was exactly my question. Who benefits from protecting Bard? But that was just the most recent question I couldn't find a satisfactory answer to. So again, I go back to what I said a few minutes ago: Maureen, I can't understand how you knew I was good at math. No one knows that. I worked very hard to hide that. And yet, when the fire inspection happened, you asked me to estimate the water damage from the sprinklers."

Maureen was on the back foot. "I was scrambling, I was asking everyone, and my eyes just landed on you."

Cami put on a show of being somewhat convinced. "Okay. Maybe. Russell, did you bring the photos?"

Russell reached under his seat and handed Cami the four photos they had taped together earlier in the week. "Here they are."

Cami spread them out on the metal rec room table in front of them, angled toward Claire, who made a dramatic show of taking in each photo. "You'll recognize Bridget's handiwork from the bus. That photo is Ayse taking her dad to the doctor—that's her car under the office sign."

Ayse nodded to Claire to show that was true.

Cami pointed to the next photo. "That's me getting money from the bank, money that I skimmed from my boyfriend using my math skills. This photo really put me into a tailspin. My whole life on a knife's edge if Bard understood what this photo proved. I have to admit, though, it was this one that actually put it all together for me."

It was the photo of Didi in her cell, going through her craft supplies.

Claire was rapt. "What made this photo different to you, Cami?"

Cami smiled. "Great question. This." Cami pointed to the side of the photo, the very edge, which was somewhat blurred. "These other photos take place outside of Pay to Stay. A bank, a street corner. But this one was taken inside Pay to Stay, and this right here"—she pointed again to the blurred edge—"is a cell bar. This was taken from a cell. Your cell, Maureen."

Maureen was getting angry now. "So what? So Bard took a photo from my cell. What does that mean?"

Cami wasn't put off—not in the slightest. "I don't think it was Bard who took this photo. Besides, the only person who had a camera inside Pay to Stay was you. On your secret second phone."

Ayse took a sharp intake of breath. "Didi admitted she spied on me, but she never said she took photos."

"And remember what Maureen said at the morgue?" Cami added. "The B.E. F.A.S.T. stroke test?"

Ayse's eyes narrowed in fury. "That's a poster in the doctor's waiting room. Maureen, you went to my dad's doctor's office?"

Cami nodded. "I think so. We found out later that this craft-supply kit was how Didi was smuggling her drugs into jail. That's what you were documenting here, right, Maureen? And if Ayse was supposed to gather information on me but she hadn't started yet, why were there already photos of me outside of jail?"

Maureen was spinning. "This is insane."

Cami smiled. "But it's not. You've been stage-managing this the entire time. You convinced Didi that Russell was the prime suspect. Not that it was hard. She was a naturally prejudiced person—"

Ayse nodded. "No kidding."

Cami continued, "You even got Russell's record to help."

Ayse cut in, "Maureen tried to make me suspect him, too."

Cami smiled with satisfaction. "My friendship with Russell was slowing her progress, so Maureen had to make you doubt my judgment. And she did that by citing my controlling boyfriend, Thad—right, Ayse?"

Ayse nodded. "Yes."

"Even Janet made a comment about Thad, that I 'really know how to pick 'em,' and asked Maureen to back her up. How did Maureen know about Thad at all? I never talked about him here. He never dropped me off or picked me up. So, stands to reason Maureen knew about Thad from following me. This became handy when she was setting up Russell as the perfect suspect that we could all get behind. But when the tide turned against Didi, Maureen was all in. Sure, she made a big show, lots of tears—but really she couldn't throw her friend under the bus fast enough. Until Sister Bridget surprised us all, Maureen included. Then Maureen saw the perfect opportunity to tie up every loose end that proved her involvement in the entire thing, starting from the lies and ending with the murders."

Maureen was shaking her head, but her words were soft. "I didn't kill anyone! I wouldn't! I couldn't!"

Cami took a deep breath. "Claire, I must ask for your patience. I don't have everything all sorted out perfectly, but I think if I lay it out we will see."

Claire was thrilled. "Please. The floor is yours."

"It does unfortunately all go back to Bard. Besides Bridget, Maureen, you had been here the longest. You knew from your political career how to align yourself with power, and I am sure those skills came in handy here. I don't know what he got on you, but it must have been good. And I think it's all on here." Cami pulled the flash drive out of her pocket, Bard's label *Maureen* visible to everyone. "So he gets you under his thumb, and you decide to go above and beyond to get in his favor. Maybe he promised you a recommendation for early release? Perks? Whatever it was, you went to work. You followed each of us, giving him information he could use in whatever way he saw fit."

"When he told me to spy on you, Cami, he definitely hinted in what direction I should go," Ayse offered. "He wanted to know why you took an early plea."

Cami nodded. "He wanted results quickly, and so, using the information Maureen had observed, told you where to look. Sure, Maureen had often already told him everything there was to know, but the bonus to him assigning each of us a target was that we were all so busy distrusting each other we missed the snake in the grass right next to us. So he documents all the ways Maureen has been especially helpful. Puts it on this lovely little drive. Then he gives us all our transfer letters. Every single one of us was going to be off to state prison before New Year's Day, tying up all of *his* loose ends. Maureen most of all." Cami tossed the flash drive to Doug. "I bet there are answers on this, Doug, if you want to copy the files."

Maureen made a move to snatch the drive in midair but then thought better of it. Doug quickly inserted the USB into his laptop.

Cami winced. "Maureen, I don't know what happened that night. Maybe you just went to talk to him, to ask him if this was real, and things got out of hand." She was genuinely sad at this next part. "Bard was a cruel son of a bitch. You thought after all you had done for him, you would be safe. Instead, all you had done for him was exactly why you had to go. I bet that made you so angry. Angry enough to kill him."

Maureen's chin was set, her mouth was tight as a fist.

"Now you have a dead CO, and it's time for damage control. You need to distance yourself from Bard as much as possible. You can't find Bard's personal records of your bad behavior, which would give you the most motive, so you decide to shred everything just to be safe. You didn't realize that it wasn't in your paper file. Somehow Janet found this flash drive and decided to hold on to it."

Ayse's eyes were closed in frustrated recollection. "I saw her. When we first found Bard, Janet took something from the body and put it in her pocket."

"Sounds right," Cami replied. "Janet was willing to screw over anyone to save herself, and this looked like a nice insurance policy. She hid it in Nacho's terrarium, by the way. At some point, she tells you she has it. Now you've gotten rid of Bard only to find yourself under Janet's thumb. And that was not an acceptable position for you. You align yourself with power. Janet did not fit the bill. She wasn't power; she was an opportunist. So she had to go."

Maureen snorted. "Well, this is where this whole fantasy falls apart. I was in a locked room with a witness when Janet was killed in the hallway."

Cami nodded. "That's true. That was very smart. How could you be in Bard's bedroom and the hallway at the same time, with Didi between you and the murder victim? Impossible. Except this is where things actually start to tie together for me." Cami turned her attention back to Claire. "When Bridget dragged me into Bard's locked office to murder me, she said 'It's just the three of us now.' I was too focused on her desire to gouge out my eyes to think about it much. When I moved the bed to bar the door, I found an access panel in the wall. I wonder, Maureen, did you find that panel as well when you were looking for this flash drive? Or did you know about it before that? Either way, when Bridget dragged me into the office, she thought you were still there, but you had escaped by the access panel. So I think that is that how you got out of Bard's sleeping quarters without Didi seeing you. It makes sense. You tell Janet to be alone by the fire door during the building-maintenance shift. You slip out of the office by the access panel and open the fire door for her. Perhaps Bard had even shown you the alarm wasn't working. He loved his little tricks. Janet comes in, you ask her for the drive, she won't give it to you without extracting her price, and so you do the next best thing. You kill her."

Ayse was on the trail now. "Is this why you were annoyed Cami searched Janet's cell for the gun without you? You wanted to search it for the drive."

"That's exactly what I think, Ayse," Cami agreed. "Maureen hid the gun, let Didi 'discover' it was missing with us all there so she could have an excuse to turn everyone's cells."

Maureen cackled, "I can't even follow this anymore. You said yourself you don't know what's on that alleged secret drive, but now it's so important that I'm killing Janet by walking through walls."

Russell spoke for the first time, also pulling threads together. "I think Didi noticed you were missing that day when Janet was killed. She made a comment last night about keeping secrets for each other. She made it to you."

Cami said, with genuine sadness, "I think you were gonna find a way forward with Didi until that comment. Instead, Didi had to go, too."

Maureen stood up, her hands balled into fists. "None of this is true. None of it. I mean, for God's sake, I was attacked!"

"Were you, though?" Russell wondered. "Or did you slam your own head against the wall to avoid suspicion?"

Maureen was flabbergasted. "I get that you're all desperate, but what are any of you talking about? I'm murdering people left and right. I'm in multiple rooms at once. I'm giving myself concussions. Let me know when the facts start."

Cami nodded. "I admit, I am making a lot of leaps. Luckily, there is one piece of hard evidence we can check."

In a swift motion, Cami grabbed Maureen's hand and wiped it with a swab she had at the ready. She passed the swab back to Russell, who had an evidence bag open.

"What are you doing?" Maureen shrieked.

Cami asked, "Ayse, do you still have the gunshot residue–test kit from the morgue?"

Ayse's eyes lit up. "Yes."

"Go grab it, please."

They waited in silence until Ayse returned. She dipped the swab from the evidence bag into the test solution and waited. Ayse watched as the color on the test swatch changed. "Her hands are positive for gunshot residue."

Cami was matter-of-fact now. "It occurred to me that if Bridget had shot Didi, she could have just shot me once she got me into the office. But she didn't. Because she never had the gun. You did. And you used the cover of Bridget's attack to tie up your one last loose end. You shot Didi. You were probably going to kill Bridget, too, and then pin Didi on her. But unfortunately, we three got to you too quickly. So you had to improvise. You ran into Bard's office and left by the access panel. Hey, it had worked once, why not use it again? In fact, I'm betting, if we go into the walk-in freezer, where we found you hiding, you stashed the gun somewhere in there."

Maureen's breathing was rapid, and her neck was flushed a deep red. At long last, her anger forced her true self to emerge. She hissed, "I did everything Bard wanted. I was perfect. I made his dream of manipulating you all into a reality. I spent three years being his flawless little partner. He promised to release me early. He promised he would write recommendations for my felony to be expunged. Instead, he betrayed me. Just like Henry Carlson."

Claire asked in a hushed tone, "Carlson knew about the bribes?"

Maureen cackled. "That saint? No. Of course not. I had a lot I could have traded for a shorter sentence, but I kept my mouth shut. I took the fall to protect him because I am an idealist! Because he said he would protect me! He said he would save me. He promised me a position in his cabinet from here to the governor's mansion. And I trusted him. Instead, after I got arrested, I never heard from him again. Blocked my number. Blocked my email. Disavowed me publicly. Political scorched earth. Well, he didn't know who he was messing with. I had to get out to teach him a lesson, and Bard held the ticket to my revenge. His price was, I had to destroy all of you first. And who are any of you? You're all nobodies. You don't matter to me in the slightest. So I made all of Bard's dreams come true so my dream could come true. It was very simple. Transactional."

Ayse was seething. "Transactional? My father could have died alone in a cell, confused and scared, because of what you did. And you are making it sound like nothing."

"It was nothing," Maureen said without an iota of emotion.

Cami held up a hand to keep Ayse from losing her shit, and instead continued calmly, "If you were so perfect, why did Bard go back on your arrangement?"

Maureen's nose flared and her throat was tight. "He wrote me a little note on my transfer letter, too. He wrote I had gotten *too friendly*. He wrote that I was no longer trustworthy. Nothing had changed. I hadn't done anything differently. He was just done with me. And so he was going to throw me away. But he messed with the wrong woman. It was more than my freedom he took from me. He took away my opportunity to right a wrong. He took away my hope of restoring balance. He used me, and thought because of his position, there would be no repercussions. I have been used enough! I will not be used anymore!"

"And yet, you wanted to use all of us," Cami replied. "You exploited us. You hunted us. And then you were going to use us to support your cover story. You were going to tie all of our freedom to yours. So even if we started to suspect you later, we wouldn't be able to implicate you without jeopardizing ourselves. You were so close. Two minutes from the end."

"I can still go," Maureen spat out. "I can still make it." She stood up.

Cami shook her head. "No. You can't."

Five police officers arrived through the rec room doors, guns drawn. Cami's lawyer was right behind them.

# CHAPTER 19

## Cami Garcia: The After Begins

An hour later, it was departure time.

Except this was a departure like no other. Instead of six women quietly slinking off back into their lives, it was an absolute circus of activity.

As expected, once the police were on the scene (called by Cami right before the interview), they demanded that everyone be separated and remanded into custody. Bridget and Maureen had been loaded into separate police cars, and were headed to secure units for their continued incarceration. Meanwhile, Ayse and Cami had waited in their cars while their legal representation were running a furious screen between their clients and the LAPD. Cami took some pleasure in seeing that her previous lawyer had been kicked to second position and a partner at the firm, Stassi Rivera, had taken hold of her fate.

An officer exited Pay to Stay with the gun in an evidence bag, and yelled at the top of his lungs, "It was in the freezer, just like she said it would be."

Cami blithely said, "Called it."

Ayse called out to Cami, "Hey, Cami."

"Yeah," Cami replied.

"When you were asking Leclair about the murder in the movie?"

Cami smiled. "Yeah."

Ayse asked, "None of that was an accident was it?"

Cami, reveling in the fact that someone had noticed, grinned. "I planned every word."

Doug and Claire came between their cars as casually as possible, but their smiles betrayed less than model citizen motives.

Claire's voice was positively chipper. "We posted the interview online. It has gone more than viral. It has been banned!"

Ayse was confused. "And we are happy about that?"

Claire nodded emphatically. "Absolutely! Every time the social media CEOs take it down, fifty more people post it. Getting your story out has become a de facto sticking it to the man. #FreeAyse and #FreeCami are both trending."

"What about #FreeRussell?" Cami asked.

Claire gave an eager clap. "Someone is already selling T-shirts with his face!"

Ayse asked again, "And we are happy about that?"

Claire pounded her fist on Ayse's car and squealed, "You guys are going to be memes!"

Ayse shrugged. "I guess I will focus on the fact that we aren't being pinned for it."

Doug said in a low voice, "Just so you know, I had to turn Bard's flash drive over to the cops."

"Yeah, we figured," Ayse replied.

Doug smiled. "But I also forwarded copies to your lawyers."

Cami smiled back. "Yeah, we figured." Cami pointed to their two slicker-than-slick lawyers, hunched over their laptops and furiously making calls.

Stassi saw Cami and Ayse looking her way and came over to them. "Holy hell, this is a gold mine. Maureen did even more than you said."

Ayse had to laugh a little. "More than the murders?"

"Absolutely. For example, she suggested that Bard use the twelve-panel drug test on Didi instead of the standard five. That's why she popped positive all of the sudden. Maureen used contacts from her work with the police union to find out how Janet had gotten out of hard time. Apparently, that little kiss ass even came to PTS during the week sometimes to help him decorate his office."

Ayse started putting it together. "So that's how she knew about the fire door and the access panel."

Stassi pointed at her. "Bingo."

Cami had to ask, even though she didn't want to know the answer: "How much did she know about me? Is my money safe?"

Stassi smirked. "She had a lot, but nothing I can't argue away. Your money is safe."

Cami felt some tightness in her chest release.

Stassi shot a look at the junior associate holding her coffee and said, "I can't say the same for your job, Adam. This is some seriously shoddy work." Adam had the good sense to look embarrassed, and Cami had to admit she liked it.

Ayse had another question, though. "What did Bard have on Maureen to make her do all of this?"

Stassi answered without pleasure, "As far as we can see in these documents? Nothing. Nothing beyond what was in the original file."

Ayse's anger was visible. "She really did all this harm voluntarily."

Cami wanted to be surprised, but this was what she had expected. "Maureen had a goal and was willing to do anything to achieve it."

Ayse reverted to her regular deadpan delivery. "See, this is why I don't trust motivated people. They have a dark side."

Stassi laughed. "And on that note, you all are free to go."

Ayse leaned back, the relief on her face at the fact that she would be home in a matter of minutes washing over her. She gave Cami a wave. "I'll call you this week, Cami."

Cami waved back. "Can't wait."

Ayse asked, "If we have lunch, can I bring my dad?"

Cami said with her whole heart, "I would love to meet him. *Merhaba . . . ?* Is that right?" Cami said, checking her Turkish.

Ayse laughed. "When did you learn that? Never mind. Tell me over lunch." And with that, Ayse drove out of the parking lot.

Cami couldn't leave just yet, though. She had her own loose ends she needed to tie up.

Getting out of her car, Cami asked Stassi, "Is the other firm partner here yet?"

Stassi looked around. "Oh, he's here somewhere. I'll send him over to you." She turned and went on the hunt for her colleague.

Cami surveyed the scene, her eyes scanning for one face in particular. At last, Cami found Russell in the crowd. She hadn't seen or talked to him since the police arrived, as he had been whisked away immediately as some misguided show of strength. Whatever threat they had perceived had apparently passed, because finally Russell was sitting quietly on the bench by the front door, enjoying the sunshine, his attending officer several feet away, flirting with Claire Curtis, who was covertly recording him.

Cami locked eyes with Stassi, who pointed Cami out to the man next to her. Cami then crossed over to Russell, the other man joining her as she made her way through the melee. "Russell, I want you to meet Mr. Cole."

The man reached his hand out. "Mr. Washington, it's a pleasure to meet you. I'm Daniel Cole." His closely cropped silver hair, expensive knit tie, and bounce in his step made him seem easily fifteen years younger than he was. He was a man easy in his extraordinary professional talents, and was ready to make this entire parking lot of law enforcement bend to his will by choice.

Russell extended a hand, but was wary. "Hello."

Mr. Cole opened his brief case and handed Russell a contract. "If you can sign here, this will make me your official legal representative."

Russell looked at the form, which was printed on heavy cream card stock, a gold letterhead glinting in the sun. "That's very nice of you, but I can tell by this nice paper that I can't afford you."

Mr. Cole smiled gently. "Ms. Garcia has paid my retainer. Now, if you will excuse me, I am going to start getting some background for your dismissal." At this, Mr. Cole departed to discuss his client's legal rights with the prisoner-transport van that had just pulled into the lot.

Russell looked at Cami in bewilderment. "Cami, what? How?"

Cami smiled slyly. "I have my own money, and this is what I want to spend it on."

Russell was overwhelmed. "Cami, you can't."

Cami was resolute. "I already have. I saved that money for my freedom. I don't see why your freedom can't be a part of that."

The correctional officer in charge of transport crossed over to them. "Washington, it's time to go."

Russell stood up and offered his wrists for cuffs.

Hovering behind the officer, Mr. Cole said, in a tone that was a gentle request with a dare at the center, "I don't think restraints are necessary for my client. Not after the extreme emotional distress he suffered during this transport, with an unsanctioned incarceration during which he sustained multiple injuries, putting him at risk of death. Which we will be filing a civil suit over. If you would like your name added to the suit, please, by all means, cuff my client."

The correctional officer sighed and put the cuffs back on his belt.

Russell looked to Cami before going to the van. He seemed nervous, and he gripped and then shook out his hands several times before finally saying, "So, can I see you after I get released?"

"You told me you don't believe in the After?" Cami asked with a smile.

Russell smiled in spite of himself. "I guess I do now."

Cami took his hands in hers and said, "Eighteen months left on your sentence, right?"

Mr. Cole chimed in, "I think I can get him released in six."

Cami smiled at Russell. "Six months sounds good. How about I come pick you up?"

Russell held her hands so gently, and looked at her with so much care. "Cami Garcia, you are one in a million."

"You don't even know the half of it." Cami kissed Russell, and it felt like the very first kiss of her life. The first kiss from someone who knew all of her. She felt alive and free and grounded all at once.

With that, Russell was gently guided to the transport van.

Cami watched the van leave the parking lot until she lost sight of it, her heart still a swirl of emotion.

And now, at long last, it was time to go.

Cami heard a familiar voice from the perimeter: "Cami! Camilla!"

There, pressed to the fence, was her mother. The surprise of seeing Lourdes there was only second to the shock that her mother was standing in front of the family car, which she had parked at such an angle that one and a half tires were on the curb, and the hazard lights were flashing.

Cami walked over, smiling ear to ear. "Mom, did you drive here?" She directed her mom toward the entrance.

Lourdes yelled, "Of course I did! I had to get to you!" She pressed her way through the police officers. "Are you okay? Are you all right?" She pressed her hands to Cami's cheeks, looking into her eyes until satisfied; then she pulled Cami into a hug that conveyed immeasurable love.

Cami leaned in to the hug, waves of relief washing over her. "Let's go home, Mama."

---

Four months later, Cami was lying on her childhood bed, enjoying the view of the eight-foot bird-of-paradise that grew outside her window. Nacho was basking on his perch in the corner, utterly content under his sunlamp. Cami's ankle ached from the house arrest monitor strapped to her, but she had only a week left. She unclipped the (faulty) charger that she had to use for one hour twice per day. She felt like an outdated cell phone with a scorched battery. She didn't really care, though. Overall, life was good. Cami was finally, completely free of all the bounds she had created for herself. She felt like she was flying, her whole life open, no restrictions.

Long gone was the ice cube–tray apartment, and long gone was Thad. Cami had broken up with him, and all the gifts that had kept her tethered to him, within hours of leaving Pay to Stay on New Year's Eve. For a second, she had contemplated seeing the plan through, but it was intolerable. The idea of going back to her old passive, ditzy self being the most intolerable of all. She had started this new calendar year on the right (electronically monitored) foot, and she hadn't looked back once.

There was a soft knock on the door, and Lourdes came in with her one millionth tray of food for Cami. Lourdes looked around for a place to set it down, and saw a pile of drafts on the table. "What are you working on, Camilla?"

"My admission essay for UCLA," Cami said.

Her mother smiled. "What is it about?"

Cami said, "I think it might be easier if you just read it."

So while Cami ate, Lourdes sat and read her daughter's admission essay.

*"At this moment, as I write this, I am still incarcerated. Allegedly, I am a unique applicant because I have a criminal record. Except that in America the number of people with a felony record is estimated to be 100,000,000. And only 170,000 people apply to UCLA every year. That means that if you meet someone on the street, it is 588,235 times more likely that they have a record than they have applied to be a Bruin. The numbers grow even more stark if we only count people who are accepted into the freshman class. So if the numbers are on my side—the felon side—why should I feel shame? I don't.*

*"There is a crucial difference between guilt and shame. Guilt is when you regret doing a bad thing. Shame is when you think you are a bad person. I feel guilt for my actions. I feel remorse. I will never repeat them. But I do not feel shame about who I am. I do not feel ashamed of my record.*

*"The broken criminal system in America should feel shame, though. My brilliant, kind boyfriend Russell taught me that. The system uses tools of harm and cruelty to achieve this aim. I have been subjected to this cruelty and it nearly killed me. It killed people I know. It has tried to kill my boyfriend 100 times over. And it continues its reign of cruelty unchecked for the nearly 2 million people who are currently in the American prison system, with no signs of stopping.*

*"But I learned something else: Cruelty is at its core so very boring. Cruelty exists in service of nothing. No creativity. No end goal greater than the sum of its parts. Nothing built on its foundation. Cruelty is a song of only one note pounded over and over until someone has the good sense to turn the piano into firewood.*

*"I am applying to college with a record and I am not ashamed. I will not allow the cruelty to come with me, to harm me from within. I have paid more than my debt. I am free."*

At long last, Lourdes put the essay down, her eyes shiny with tears. "Oh, my Camilla, you are so smart."

# Author's Note

This book exists at a knotty intersection of truth and fiction.

The characters are all fictional, including any crimes they have committed.

Pay to Stay—a separate prison where people pay fees to only serve time on the weekend—is real.

My worry in writing this book would be that people may imagine my point was this separate jail was privilege to the point of immorality. My personal opinion could not be further from that position. While Pay to Stay is far from perfect, and inaccessible to most, alternatives to incarceration where people get to stay in their homes, with their families, and continue being members of their communities is a good first step to creating a more just world, where accountability and rehabilitation are the goals, instead of the punishment and painful cycles that impact so many.

Incarceration, as we have constructed it in America, is a harmful practice that does nothing to rehabilitate people, make victims whole, or prevent future crime. In fact, statistically it fails on all three of those goals. I wonder if part of the inertia in correcting the problem is that we cannot repair a system that is so deeply broken by design. We must start over from scratch. We must imagine a world beyond prisons. By studying the work of brilliant prison abolitionists who have long advocated for change, I am hopeful that a different world is not only possible, but inevitable.

I want to credit Prison Policy Initiative for their exhaustive research and data gathering on the fractured and harmful incarceration practices in the United States. I also want to highlight the incredible work being achieved at the time of printing by the Pollen Initiative, led by Jesse Vasquez. This nonprofit is focused on cultivating media centers inside prisons across the country in an effort to train system-impacted individuals to become journalists and effect change. The Initiative has a 0 percent recidivism rate among its graduates, and it also just launched the first newspaper produced by incarcerated women at Central California Women's Facility in Chowchilla.

Currently and formerly incarcerated people deserve to tell their own stories, to build better futures for themselves and their communities, and to lead the movement toward abolition. My dearest hope is we listen.

Thank you for reading this book.

# Acknowledgments

While it may be my words on the page, there are so many people who must be thanked for their efforts in bringing this book to fruition. Writing a novel is a team sport.

Ryan, my success is always shared with you, but this book in particular was carried by you. I write this long before the manuscript is due because the circumstances are so bonkers. Christmas morning at 7:00 a.m., I managed to break my ankle in spectacular fashion while merely walking down my own stairs. This is important because I am currently in a giant cast, unable to walk for over three months, awkwardly getting about on a knee scooter. On the one hand, being homebound has given me a lot of time to write this book. (I made many, many jokes related to Stephen King's *Misery*, and that I had somehow cast myself as both Paul Sheldon and Annie Wilkes.) On the other, much less fortunate hand, this means my lovely husband has had to do almost everything. As ever and even more than normal, I am so grateful to you, Ryan, for your dedication to our family. Thank you for supporting my work in both word and, crucially, deed. Thank for you for making time, space, and quiet for me to write. (No small feat with small children.) Thank you for supporting my writing for all those years, even when there was no money, just my own dream.

I also must express my deep gratitude to Sue Shore, who did so many school runs, and child minding, and general child entertaining during this injury. I struggle to think how we would have managed without you.

My book certainly would not have been finished on deadline, and there would have been many more tears of frustration from my children (and me). Your endless cheer is so wonderful to have in our lives.

Thank you to my incredible siblings, my siblings-in-law, and my fleet of nieces and nephews. (And I am sorry to every restaurant we try to patron as a group.) We only have one mode: joyful chaos. My dearest hope is even as we grow, we never lose that. I love you all so much.

My books have been shepherded from beginning to end by an incredible team of people. Megha Parekh, Liz Parker, David Boxerbaum, Selina McLemore, and Megan Beatie, thank you for your tireless efforts. The staff at Verve, MBC, and Thomas & Mercer are truly spectacular.

Thank you to William Luther for answering my 8:00 a.m. text of "Do you have time to talk about crime?" (His response: "Why? You looking to get into the scene?" Perfect.)

The real Ayse, and Burcu, thank you for checking all my Turkish, but also sharing so many beautiful details about your lovely Istanbul. I hope I made you proud.

Loren Chase, you are an excellent firefighter and friend. Your texts solved three story problems for me! Possibly a record.

Thank you, Dana Cole, for your guidance and your knit ties.

I can write each day because of the incredible teachers and staff at my children's schools. You are truly doing the most important work there is, and I am forever in your debts.

My New Mexico friends who have welcomed us all, making the Land of Enchantment live up to its name.

Thank you to Alyona & David, Isabelle & Nick, Sean & Anna, Amy & Jim, Sam & Pete, Dani & Matt, Brandon & Michelle, Chris & Aimee, Jenny & Nash, Adam & Karina, and all of your beautiful children who I am privileged to know. This book is my tiny love letter to Los Angeles, and you are the heart of that city to me.

To the real Lourdes, *Lola* to my nephews, Ms. Josephine Amador Courtney. I feel so fortunate that I knew you. Your children and grandchildren live in your spirit of fearless perseverance, and endless generosity.

Thank you to my mother, Barney Jean. Most parents would be relieved if their struggling writer child said, "I am going to grad school for a real job." Not you. You were worried a steady career would derail my writing. You helped me stay the course. You saw my destiny before I did. I love you.

And finally, my children. You are the greatest dream of my life.

# About the Author

Elizabeth Rose Quinn is a novelist and screenwriter. She graduated with a BA in English from UC Berkeley and a master's degree in marriage and family therapy. Born and raised in Berkeley, California, Elizabeth lived in Los Angeles for fifteen years while working in production and writing for television. Her novel *Follow Me* was optioned by Amazon MGM Studios and is currently in production as a feature film. She is married with two children and currently lives in New Mexico. In addition to traveling and exploring nature with her family, Elizabeth loves rolling fresh pasta, swimming in the Pacific Ocean, and looking for rainbows in the desert sunsets. For more information, visit www.elizabethrosequinn.com.